# TYRE T...
# CONSTANTI...

## 5th Century A.D.
by land ..... by sea .....

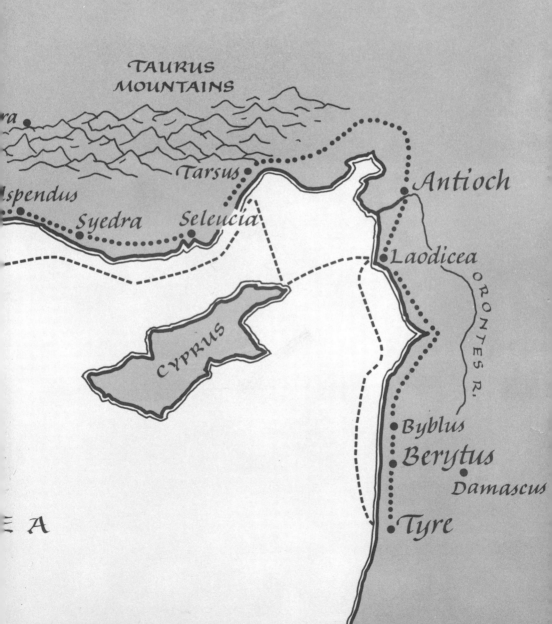

TAURUS
MOUNTAINS

...ra

Tarsus

...spendus

Syedra

Seleucia

Antioch

Laodicea

ORONTES R.

CYPRUS

Byblus

Berytus

Damascus

...E A

Tyre

# IMPERIAL
# PURPLE

BOOKS BY GILLIAN BRADSHAW

Hawk of May
Kingdom of Summer
In Winter's Shadow
The Beacon at Alexandria
The Bearkeeper's Daughter
Imperial Purple

# GILLIAN BRADSHAW

# IMPERIAL PURPLE

HOUGHTON MIFFLIN COMPANY   BOSTON   1988

Copyright © 1988 by Gillian Bradshaw.
ALL RIGHTS RESERVED.

For information about permission to reproduce selections from
this book, write to Permissions, Houghton Mifflin Company,
2 Park Street, Boston, Massachusetts 02108.

Library of Congress Cataloging-in-Publication Data

Bradshaw, Gillian, date.
Imperial purple / Gillian Bradshaw.
p.     cm.
ISBN 0-395-43635-4
1. Byzantine Empire — History — Theodosius II, 408–450 — Fiction.
PS3552.R235I48    1988    88-11923
813'.54 — dc19    CIP

Printed in the United States of America


P  10 9 8 7 6 5 4 3 2 1


The display type is sixth-century Roman Calligraphy from
*Arthur Baker's Historic Calligraphic Alphabets*
(New York: Dover Publications, 1980).


Endpaper map by Jacqueline Sakwa.

FOR NANCY

*a design with some movement*

# IMPERIAL
# PURPLE

SHE WAS WEAVING a picture of Christ giving sight to the blind when the supervisor came to fetch her.

The picture was one of six commissioned from the imperial silk manufactory of Tyre, destined to adorn the curtains ordered for the private chambers of the emperor himself. The designs had been specified in the commission: six scenes from the Gospels, to be made in silk tapestry by the factory's finest weavers, on curtains of purple silk shot with gold. Philotimos, supervisor of His Sacred Majesty's silk factory, who had come to fetch the weaver Demetrias to his superior, hesitated behind her to study the work. The tapestry was a rondel of fabric about eighteen inches in diameter, suspended on the purple silk warp that dressed the tall upright loom, and woven seamlessly into the substance of the curtain itself. It covered about three quarters of the design cartoon behind it, which Philotimos himself had drawn. Demetrias had been working on this picture for nearly two months, and had now reached the level of the figures' eyes. The Christ's hand hovered in the blue air, just lifted from the beggar's face; the newly opened eyes would fix on it in wonder.

Demetrias tied back the light saffron silk of the flesh and reached, carefully, for a filament of gold from the low table beside her. Smiling, she threaded a tapestry needle, then carefully wove a strand of pure gold into the center of the beggar's eye, crossing a mere three of the thousands of warp threads before tying it off and reaching for the needle already threaded with black. On the finished picture the gold would be almost invisible — but the pictured eyes would glitter as though they were alive. The supervisor let out his breath in a soundless sigh. He had grown old in the factory, and nothing on earth gave him so much pleasure as a good piece of weaving. *Another weaver would have made the whole eye gold*, he thought, *and strung pearls in. But Demetrias achieves more with far less show. God knows who'll finish the picture if the procurator gives her this other "urgent commission." Perhaps we can leave it until the other work's done.*

Demetrias again took up the needle with the saffron thread. If she sensed her supervisor behind her, she gave no sign of it, and he remained standing, reluctant to disturb such fine work. At the next loom, Demetrias' mother, Laodiki, was singing as she finished off the plain-weave part of the previous curtain section, bringing down the mallet on the weaver's comb with a musical chink in unison with two of the other women in the room. Demetrias did not sing: tapestry work required too much concentration. She was a small, neat woman, just beginning to grow plump; her light blue tunic pulled tight across her breasts as she leaned forward, frowning slightly, and the tapestry needle glinted in her swift deft hand. It was a hot day, and the tunic was patchily damp with sweat; the dim sunlight that filtered through the factory's high windows brought out the gold in the thick brown hair piled behind her head, and showed her green eyes vivid in her pale face. *A very pretty woman*, the supervisor thought, unhappily. *I hope that's not what the procurator really wants her for; everyone knows she's married, as much as a slave of the state can be. Well, I was sent to fetch her; fetch her I must.*

"Demetrias," he said, aloud. She hesitated, then set the tapestry needle carefully into the fabric of the rondel before she turned to look up at him inquiringly, folding her hands in her lap. Philotimos approved the attentive respect, and his approval made him feel still more unhappy. "His Eminence the procurator wishes to see you at once," he said, hurrying to get it over with.

Her eyes widened, and the folded hands suddenly gripped each other hard. At the next loom, Laodiki stopped both her singing and her weaving and looked over anxiously. As she stopped, so did the others; the chink of mallet on comb ceased, and the whole roomful of women and girls turned from their work to stare. Philotimos winced. Most of the weavers had grown up in the factory, as he had himself. They had no difficulty in remembering Demetrias, at sixteen, receiving a similar summons from another procurator. There hadn't been any pretense then that it was concerned with her weaving —

but then she hadn't been married. Married women, the weavers thought, so clearly that they might have been shouting at him, ought to be safe, even from procurators. Summoning a married woman is wantonly cruel. It can do nothing but cause trouble for her.

"He says he's received an urgent commission," Philotimos said, trying to reassure them and himself. It was, he knew and they all knew, unusual for a procurator to summon a particular weaver, even for an urgent commission — but it was not impossible. Patrons did, after all, often request a specific design for a piece of tapestry work, and if the patron were sufficiently important, the procurator himself might well want to explain to one of his most skilled workers precisely what was required.

Demetrias' clenched hands relaxed a little. She glanced back at the three-quarters-finished picture on the loom, touched it gently, then sighed, and stood up.

"He said, 'at once'?" she asked him, in the low, even voice he had always found so attractive. It gave a truer impression of her, he thought, than the soft, fair prettiness of her face. It was the voice of someone who watched words: guarded, choosing when to speak and when not to speak, and saying only what was necessary. And in fact she was a woman who always thought before she acted — *a great advantage in a weaver*, Philotimos thought, still with the anxious warmth of his approval, *where a moment's careless mistake may need a month's work pulled out before it's set right*.

The supervisor nodded, and Demetrias again glanced at her work, and this time stood staring at it a moment before picking up her light cloak of rose-colored wool, which she had put aside when she sat down to work. It was an hour before noon and outside the sun struck against the stone streets so that they glared heat like an oven, but Demetrias wrapped herself in the cloak carefully, pulling it well over her head and tossing one end over her shoulder so that she was hidden from chin to toe. Philotimos suppressed a smile: she'd be careful not to give the procurator ideas — if he didn't have them already. Demetrias nodded to the other workers, waved to her mother, and walked quickly from the room, Philotimos following. As the door at the far end closed behind them, the chink of the little mallets began again — but not the singing.

The street outside reeked indescribably of rotten shellfish, wood ash, sulfur, and stale urine — the stink of the adjacent dyeworks that brewed the famous Tyrian purple dye. Neither Demetrias nor Philotimos flinched at it. The natives of Tyre accepted the smell without question; for them, smell even more than color was purple, and purple was the source of wealth and fame, the dye of emperors, the color of power. It was sacred, distinct, above the level of common humanity; an ordinary man who dared to wear it would be condemned to death. Senators were allowed a narrow vertical stripe of it to adorn their cloaks; the highest ministers of state a wider horizontal one. Only God's church and the emperor could use it freely. Even the imitations of true purple, quick-fading vegetable dyes, widespread and immensely popular, were regarded by the law with suspicion. To work with the real purple, stinking though it was, could be a cause for nothing but pride.

Demetrias stopped at the corner of the works, in the full blast of the stench, and looked toward the Egyptian harbor, where the factory fishing fleet brought the shellfish from which the dye was made. The water was brilliantly blue, glittering under the heavy weight of the August sun. A merchant ship was lashed to the pier, unmoving in the heat; a few boats were pulled up onto the gravel beach. Demetrias looked at these carefully a moment, then swept the glittering water with her eyes before walking on. Philotimos followed, like her, relieved. Demetrias' husband was a purple-fisher, and his blue-and-white boat was not among those drawn up on the beach. *Just as well for him,* thought Philotimos, *if the procurator does have something improper in mind. Purple-fishers may be the best off of all state slaves, better off than most free men, but a state slave is no match for an imperial procurator, and the best thing a husband can hope for in such cases is to know nothing about it.*

Natives of Tyre and purple-workers might not object to the smell of purple, but the procurators, appointed by the emperor to oversee factories, fleet, and dyeworks, were rarely natives of the city, and the procurator's office was well away from the harbor and safely upwind. Philotimos and Demetrias turned left onto the great Eurychoros street that led to the city's praetorian prefecture on the southwestern extremity of the rocky promontory. The street was almost empty, and the shopkeepers were beginning to take their merchandise in out of the noonday heat, piling the baskets of peaches and figs, the white rounds

4

of cheese or basins of fish, in the dark caverns of the stores. By the public fountains the camels knelt in the dust, chewing their cuds; a few donkeys and beggars rested motionless in the shade.

Demetrias and Philotimos walked quickly, despite the beating of the sun, and the imposing front of the prefecture reared up before them unexpectedly soon, rising sheer out of a tiny public square at the street's end. Demetrias stopped short, and stood a moment fingering the edge of her cloak. The woolen border was decorated with a silk pattern of woven flowers — gentian violets, twining dark blue and green, the center of each blossom delicately touched with gold. It was her own work, and the twisting curls of the silk were cool and familiar under her hot, tense fingers. After a moment, she shrugged, smiled apologetically at her supervisor, and allowed him to precede her into the shade behind the columns of red-veined Carian marble that lined the porch.

Just before the main doorway Philotimos paused, staring at a new statue that had been placed on the left side of the entrance.

For almost as long as he could remember, the statues of the emperor, Theodosius II, and of his sister, the reigning Augusta, Pulcheria, had stood to the right and to the left of the entrance to the prefecture, both made of painted marble and set on columns of porphyry. Until six years before, the statue of Theodosius' wife, Eudokia, had stood beside that of her husband, but Eudokia was out of favor now, stripped of her honors, and exiled in Jerusalem, and people were openly saying that it was only a matter of time before Pulcheria's statue went, too. The new statue was standing so close beside Pulcheria's that it seemed as though it meant to edge her out any minute: a man, carved in marble, his stone cloak painted with the wide purple stripe of the patrician order, booted and helmeted like a general, and holding in his hand a model of a castle. Philotimos hesitated, then crossed over to read the inscription on the pedestal: "The Council and People of the most illustrious city of the Tyrians honor the most noble Nomos, twice consul, master of the offices of His Sacred Majesty." He frowned. Nomos was supposed by some to be out of favor.

Demetrias, too, had stopped to read the inscription — unlike many of the weavers, she could read, though slowly — and she, too, frowned, tilting her head back to look at the carved face. It was not

5

a good portrait: the childishly painted eyes stared blandly into nothing; no trace of the subject's personality was impressed upon the stone. "Why Nomos?" she asked.

"Why indeed?" returned Philotimos, and sighed. *I wish the emperor would sort out his government,* he thought — but did not quite dare to say. Tyre was remote from the imperial court at Constantinople, but the factories, together with their staff, were owned and controlled by the offices of the empire. The workers seized greedily on gossip about events in the capital, but to have opinions about those events could be dangerous. Even Philotimos was a slave, owned by the state, and the state could punish disloyalty. Everyone knew, though, that the emperor would not sort out his government; that, indeed, the emperor was incapable of sorting out anything. He was a mild, gentle man, so merciful that he had never in his life passed the death sentence; he was a devout Christian who was generous to the poor, who hated war and violence and loved peace; he was a thoughtful, artistic man, the founder of a university, and a generous patron; he was a man admired for the chastity and virtue of his private life. He had everything an emperor should have — except the least vestige of the ability to rule. He couldn't follow state business or begin to understand public crises, and he would blindly sign any document his advisers set before him. Since his accession, the empire had been run by whoever could control him. For a time "the most noble Nomos" had been particularly prominent, but Nomos was currently a private citizen — though one rumor had it he was not really out, but merely bargaining with the emperor's chamberlain for a higher rank. *Is that why he has a new statue?* wondered Philotimos. *An impending promotion? But why "most noble"? Usually the emperor's kin are the only ones with that title.*

Philotimos shook his head, looked at Demetrias, and shrugged.

Demetrias smiled, then nodded at the statue of Nomos. "Perhaps we're to weave him the short purple tunic?" she suggested. This garment was traditionally allotted to the chief imperial minister, the praetorian prefect.

"Perhaps," said Philotimos slowly, considering it. It would fit. The procurator would be anxious to have a good tunic for Nomos. If the rumors were true, he owed the man his appointment. The procurator was ostentatiously a pagan, a stance that gained him considerable

6

respect among other upper-class young men, who still admired the traditional religion that almost no one seriously believed. Paganism, however, was a great obstacle to advancement; indeed, an insurmountable obstacle unless it was coupled with the support of a powerful, preferably Christian, patron — which Nomos was. "We'll find out," said Philotimos, adding, as they entered the prefecture, "They say Nomos is a traditionalist — he's supposed to prefer mythological scenes to scriptural ones."

"That would make a change," Demetrias observed, following him. Her sense of dread — the dry, sick tension that had gripped her with the announcement of the summons — was easing. The procurator might well have a good and proper reason to send for her. "I haven't done a mythological scene for six years."

"His Sacred Majesty is very pious," agreed Philotimos, and sighed. He, too, was growing a little tired of piety. *Under Eudokia,* he remembered, regretfully, *we got to do a bit of everything.*

The procurator's office was in the south wing of the prefecture on the second floor. The secretary admitted them at once. The procurator, Marcus Acilius Heraklas, was sitting slouched at his desk, reading a book in an undertone. The window behind him was open for the sea breeze, giving a view eastward toward the Egyptian harbor; the walls were decorated with frescoes of boats and sea animals, the purple-giving murex prominent. Heraklas was a young man in his early twenties, brown haired, dark eyed, clean shaven, and dressed in the most exquisite silken tunic and cloak, the edges and decorative medallions lavishly worked with gold. He was, he liked to boast, one of the Acilii Glabrones, one of the most distinguished senatorial families in the entire empire. He had been in Tyre for precisely ten months and was expected to remain another eight at the most. The position of procurator of the imperial factories of Tyre was a useful step in a senatorial career: good administrative experience, good salary, good contacts to be made, good perquisites. And, like all imperial appointments, it was strictly temporary. The actual running of the state factories was left to the state slaves.

Philotimos stood beside Demetrias, waiting for the procurator to look up from his book. Relations between procurator and factory supervisor were usually formal, gracious condescension on the one side matched by obedience and deference — but not servility — on

7

the other. Heraklas, however, was casual and arrogant. He had scarcely been twice to the factories and left all the paperwork to the factory supervisors and his secretary — *as though*, thought Philotimos irritably, when the bored young face looked up at last from its volume, *I were his own slave, not the emperor's*. He bowed deeply on the thought. "The weaver Demetrias, Your Eminence, as you requested," he announced.

Demetrias held her cloak up to hide her face and bowed.

"Ah," said Heraklas, and put his book down. He sat up, leaning over the desk. "Very well, Philotimos, you may go."

Philotimos felt a tremor of alarm: he had expected to remain in the office and escort Demetrias back to the factory. "Go, Your Eminence?" he asked, uncertainly.

Heraklas waved him away with a casual hand. "Back to your work. See that those women get their jobs done, go on! I'm sure, um, Demetrias, can find her own way back."

Philotimos hesitated, aware that behind him Demetrias had gone rigid. *Bastard*, he thought, surprising himself with his own vehemence. "I had hoped, sir," he said, cautiously, "that you could first provide me with the authorization for the supplies she will need for this commission."

"She can tell you what she needs, can't she? I don't know how you people set up looms or what you need for them. Go on, old man, leave. The commission is secret as well as urgent, and you're in the way."

Philotimos stood rigid for a moment. Demetrias said nothing, and did not look at him. Slowly, stiffly, he bowed and left the room.

*Lord of All, I hope he leaves her alone*, he thought, as he walked slowly back through the prefecture. *My best weaver — quick, cunning, subtle, faultless color sense, faultlessly neat — never leaves one mistake in the weave, never a badly knotted edge or a miscast thread — never loses her temper, and, on top of that, as pretty a girl as you could find in the whole city. And I have to leave her with that young idiot of a procurator, who can't even be bothered to learn enough about weaving to do his job. Lord of All!*

He tried not to remember Demetrias at sixteen, clinging to her mother and sobbing frantically when the other summons had come.

*But the procurator represents the state*, he told himself, miserably, *and we are slaves of the state, she and I both. There's no way out: we simply have to accept and make the best of it. And perhaps he does just want to commission the short purple tunic, but doesn't want any gossip about it. That could well be. I hope so, for her sake.*

Alone with the procurator, Demetrias stood with her head bowed, still holding the rose-colored cloak up to veil her face, remembering the other procurator. Flavius Pamphilos, his name had been. Her cheek felt hot against the back of her fingers, and her throat was tight. Beneath the cloak, her tunic was damp with sweat, sticking to her back; her knees ached with the effort of keeping still. Pamphilos had been older than this man, though not by much. Paler, too — white, soft, damp hands feeling her, a hot, wet mouth, eyes that, for all they had followed her, studied her, savored her, never really saw her. *Eight years since he left Tyre,* she told herself angrily, *eight years ago; you're married, you've a child: forget it. Oh dear Lord Jesus Christ, St. Tyrannion of Tyre, Mary Mother of God, don't let him want me.*

"Yes . . . ," said the procurator, flicking his eyes over the short, shapeless figure in rose-colored wool before him. "Demetrias, wasn't it?"

The figure nodded its head slightly and he peered at it, irritated, trying to meet the eyes. "You're the best weaver here, aren't you?" he asked.

"Some people say that, Your Reverence," she replied cautiously. *I'll give him no excuse for singling me out.* "Others prefer Red Maria, or Theoktiste, or Porphyria. We are all skilled workers, sir, but in different styles. It's a question of taste, Your Beneficence." She kept her eyes firmly on the floor.

He snorted, further irritated. "But you wove the cloak that His Sacred Majesty sent as a gift to the king of the Huns last year, didn't you? And the altarcloth for the Blessed Virgin's church in Ephesus?"

"Part of the altarcloth, Your Excellency," she corrected, humbly. "There were six of us who worked on that."

"Well, but you are one of the finest weavers in the city?" Irritation was joined by impatience. *These factory women are all half witted, away from their looms,* he thought. *Why won't the creature look up?*

"They say so, Your Reverence," Demetrias admitted reluctantly. "In silk, anyway. I can't speak for the woolen weavers."

"What I want must be woven in silk," Heraklas stated. "And it must

9

be done by the finest weaver in the city. Very well, by *one* of the finest weavers. But I liked the style of the cloak that was sent to the king of the Huns, so I asked for the worker who had done that."

Demetrias risked a glance up. There did not seem to be any double meaning implied in the statement. "Your Nobility wants a special commission?" she asked, fighting back the gasp of relief.

"What else would I have you called here for?" snapped Heraklas. "I want a cloak made, a purple cloak, a *paludamentum*, to go to Constantinople. Five feet three inches long, with a seven-inch band around the hem to be decorated with tapestry pictures of the Choice of Herakles and a Victory Crowning Alexander, and the shoulders to be worked with gold."

Demetrias bowed her head. *What else would he have me called for?* she asked herself, intense relief yielding to an urge to laugh. *Why on earth would he want me? If he fancies a woman, he can have his pick of golden courtesans: he doesn't need to summon tired young mothers from his factory. Holy Mary, blessed St. Tyrannion, thank you. A paludamentum, an emperor's cloak. A seven-inch tapestry band around the hem — that will take time. The Choice of Herakles.*

Only in envisaging this did the realization hit her with a jolt. The pious emperor Theodosius commissioned only scriptural scenes — and his cloaks were generally four inches shorter. It was not for him.

And for anyone who was not an Augustus to own such a cloak was treason. To make a cloak using the sacred purple for a usurper, even to make it innocently at the procurator's orders, was sacrilege and treason.

"And it's to be kept secret," Heraklas was continuing. "It's . . . a surprise gift. I don't want every visitor to Tyre coming in and gaping at it, and I don't want you to discuss it with your friends and spread the description over the marketplace. You can do it at a private room in the factory. If news of it gets out, you'll be punished, but if you tell no one about it, I'll reward you well."

Demetrias swallowed, the dread back, doubly strong. "Your Eminence, excuse me, but the factory has no private rooms," she said hurriedly, desperately trying to think of some good reasons not to touch the commission.

"Then have someone take one of the looms to your home. You have a home near the factory, I presume?"

"Yes, Your Eminence, but . . ."

"But?"

"But a loom that big . . . it's a small place, Your Distinction. One room, Your Eminence, and I have a child — it would get dirtied, Your Honor, or broken; I couldn't possibly do it there."

"Then tell Philotimos to see that you get a private room somewhere else! He can surely do that. How long will it take you?"

Demetrias licked her lips. *Perhaps Nomos, or whoever it's for, is to be given the title of Augustus openly,* she thought. *His Sacred Majesty has no heir; he'll have to choose someone for his colleague, to share the purple with him now and inherit his authority when he is dead. Nomos would be an obvious person to pick — noble birth, senatorial rank, experience in the army and the sacred offices alike. No one would object to him. And they might want to keep it all secret until they were ready to announce it to the whole empire.*

*Or perhaps Nomos thinks he might legitimately wear the purple, and wants this held ready to support his hopes.*

*But suppose it's not legitimate; suppose that Nomos, or whoever it is, intends to usurp? And suppose someone suspects, investigates, and I'm discovered secretly weaving the cloak?*

She closed her eyes, trying to shut out the vision of torture and death.

*If it is legitimate he will tell me so, if I press him. I am to weave in secret; I may as well be told the reason for secrecy.* "Your Eminence," she whispered, afraid of asking but more afraid of what might happen if she didn't, "who is the cloak to be for?"

He stared at the faceless rose-wrapped bundle in astonishment, and, just for a moment, in fear. Then he snapped, "For the emperor, of course! Would I be guilty of treason? Treat your betters with more respect, woman!"

Respect, or be punished for disrespect. The procurator had the authority to order a state slave whipped for insolence or branded for disobedience. Sick with fear, she fumbled at the edge of her cloak; the flowers were smooth and cool under her fingers. She twisted the edge between her hands, trying to clutch some of the coolness for herself; the hot weight of the hood slipped from her hair, and the breeze from the window dried the sweat on her neck. "Please, Your Honor, I don't mean any disrespect," she said, somehow keeping her voice even and calm. "But it's the wrong size for His Sacred Majesty, and the wrong kind of pattern, too. I just . . ." She saw the fear flicker back over his face, briefly, before his expression settled into outrage, and she stopped, blinking miserably.

The procurator stared back angrily. The creature met his eyes now, and plainly she was not half-witted, despite her performance earlier. A sharp thing, he admitted sourly, younger than he'd thought, and no doubt expecting him to have mercy on her pretty green eyes. He had expected the weaver to agree without question; he had never considered that she would know the emperor's cloak size. But of course, the cloaks had always been made in Tyre. Probably everyone in the factory knew. *And yet*, he thought, *this is barefaced insolence, this questioning me: her task is to do what the state, which I represent, commands her. If she were mine I'd have her whipped. Perhaps I should have her whipped anyway. No, that would draw too much attention to the matter, and we still need the utmost secrecy.* "I say it is for the emperor," he stated flatly, seeing the way out. "Do you wish to accuse me of lying?"

Demetrias looked down. Her mouth was dry, and her legs felt unsteady again. *It's treason*, she thought numbly. *If he hadn't been afraid, if he had admitted who it was for, it might have been legal. But to deny outright . . . it must be treason. Oh God, if I'm caught doing it they will destroy me.*

"Well?" demanded Heraklas. "Speak up! I will permit you to speak; I will even permit you to repeat your accusation to the prefect, which is more than I'm bound to do. But I would think twice before I accused my superiors, girl, and reverence the immortal gods. I am entitled to your obedience and your respect, and if you brazenly defy me and offend me with your trivial and frivolous accusations, I am also entitled to enforce that obedience by having you flogged within an inch of your life."

She looked up again and met his eyes; they glared back at her across the desk and she dropped her own eyes hurriedly, afraid of offending him with the insolence of an open stare. His official signet rings gleamed on his hand; the silk of his cloak rustled, the heavy brocade of the border shining. On the inside of the brocade was the narrow purple stripe, the badge of his wealth and nobility. Her gaze rested on it a moment, then dropped tamely to the desk top. *I cannot accuse him,* she realized, despairingly. *The prefect must be a part of it, or he wouldn't have offered to let me speak to him. I have no one to appeal to; I would simply be punished, and still end up weaving the cloak. And if I said anything in return, no one would believe me. A slave may not accuse her master. I must obey him, despite the risk, or suffer at once whatever punishment he wishes.*

She bowed, slowly. "It would not be proper for your slave to accuse you of anything," she whispered, "I will obey Your Excellency."

Heraklas' eyelids drooped over the dark eyes. "Good," he said, and leaned back in his seat again. *The creature knows her place after all,* he thought — *though I don't like it at all, the way she understood what we're doing, and so quickly. I'll mention it in my letter to him.* "Speak to Philotimos at once and have him get you a private place to work and the supplies you'll need for it, and start as soon as you can."

She stood a moment, her head still bowed, her fingers motionless on the curve of the silk flowers. The risk was accepted, and already the fear was less, dwarfed by some other feeling, a hard, swollen, bitter feeling she knew and refused to recognize and name. "Shall I write Your Excellency a list of what I'll need, sir?" she asked quietly. "Then you could authorize . . ."

"Speak to Philotimos about it," he replied airily, "and tell him to come talk to me if he has any questions. How long will it take you?"

*There will be nothing in writing,* she thought, unsurprised. *If it comes to light, he will deny that he knew anything about it. But I won't be able to deny. Oh God. Adultery would have been preferable.*

*Almost. Adultery would have been certain humiliation, here and now. But if I do as he wants, and finish it quickly and secretly, I'm out of danger. Either the treason will succeed, in which case I don't have to worry; or it will fail, in which case they won't bother with the slave who wove the cloak because they'll have the traitor himself. And they're trying to keep it secret; if they're caught, surely they'll be caught later in their plans?*

"Five or six months, sir," she told him.

"That long? Can't it be speeded up?"

"Tapestry is slow work, Your Wisdom, and silk is a fine weave. We could do it on the draw loom, with a repeat pattern instead of tapestries. We might finish it in three months that way."

He considered it. "The draw loom needs two to work it, doesn't it? And there's something already set up on it, isn't there, which you'd need my authorization to remove? No, not that. But six months . . ."

"It could be speeded up a little, sir, if you had two tapestry panels instead of a band. Four and a half to five months that way, sir."

"Two panels? Very well — but not small ones, mind you. The cloak must be as good as anything the emperor owns — already owns, I mean. Five months, then, at the most. Go, start on it immediately."

"Yes, Your Eminence." Helplessly, she bowed to him and slipped from the room.

She stopped in the porch of the prefecture, looking up again at the statue of Nomos. It still smiled blandly into nothing, staring with bright blue eyes. *Is it for him,* she wondered, *or for someone else?*

*It doesn't matter. If he fails he'll never think of any slave who was killed because of it, so why should I bother to know more of him than he does of me? Oh God.*

The other emotion swelled into her throat and she bit her tongue to hold it back. A compound of humiliation, shame, and rage, familiar for eight years now, and good for nothing but inflicting more pain on herself. There was no possibility of escaping the order; there was no safety in anything but swift obedience and silence. Defiance was senseless and, worse, dangerous. And yet, she found that she was shaking with anger; she wanted to scream; she wanted to burst into tears. She felt suffocated with a violent hatred, for Nomos, for Heraklas, and most of all, for herself, for consenting to be used.

*I must do it quickly,* she told herself, *as quickly as possible, and be free again.* She pulled her cloak over her head again and took a deep breath, trembling, then set off with a quick angry stride back to the factory.

Philotimos was sitting at his own desk in the back of the factory when she returned. She told him that the procurator wanted her to weave a cloak as a surprise gift for the emperor, and that it was to be seen by no one until it was finished. "He wants me to have somewhere private to work on it," she said.

He looked at her a moment uncertainly. Her voice, as always, was calm and even, but the face gave more away, tense, set, and very pale. He scowled savagely. *Bastard,* he thought again, *son of the*

*Devil.* "If it's a private gift, he'll be paying for it, will he?" he said. "It won't come out of state funds?"

"He didn't say. He didn't want to sign any authorization for it."

"He can hardly give the emperor a gift and expect the emperor to pay for it. I'll issue you the silk — and gold as well? — and give him the bill for it tomorrow." Philotimos pulled out his accounts ledger and wrote out debits for silk and gold, half again as much as would be needed; it gave him considerable pleasure to see how much the bill amounted to. Anything left over when a commission was finished by tradition belonged to the weaver, though she usually tipped her supervisor for the favor. All the women at the factory earned some money out of such leftovers, weaving clothing or small items either for themselves or for sale. Even purple, which could not be sold in a market, could be traded to the woolen factory supervisor, who resold it to the silk works at a profit. With this amount of silk Demetrias could earn a great deal. *Let Heraklas pay for his indulgence,* thought Philotimos, *and let Demetrias be the one to profit by it.*

*Though I doubt she'd think it worth it for ten times the amount. What happened after I left? He'd hardly leap on her in the office — perhaps she'll manage to put him off, even in this convenient "private working place," where no doubt he means to visit her. I'll make it uncomfortable for him, anyway.* "As to a private place, there's a shed behind the dyeworks," he suggested, smiling maliciously. "It stinks, of course, but it gets good shade and is fairly roomy; shall I have it cleaned up for you?"

Demetrias glanced at him in surprise, and only then realized what he was thinking. *But why not?* she thought. *If I'm forced in on the secret, I must at least try to keep it. Let them think Heraklas is pursuing me, and that, when he doesn't come, the stink of the dyeworks is what keeps him away.* "Yes," she said, smiling back, "thank you."

Philotimos wrote out a note to his colleague in the dyeworks asking him to clean out the shelling shed for an extra loom that was temporarily required; Demetrias took the note over to the works, then went to see the shed. It was a small building, built of uncured cedar with a rough straw thatch. It had two shuttered windows of horn, a door with a massive padlock, and it was full of barrels of buccina shells. In the close heat inside, the stink of purple was almost thick enough to be visible, and the air stuck flat and gluey to the tongue.

Demetrias tried to imagine Heraklas visiting it, pictured the procurator undressing amid the barrels and glaring fastidiously down his nose as he tried to find somewhere to hang his clothes, and she laughed. Feeling somewhat happier, she began to plan how to dress the loom, marking out lengths on the wooden wall with a lump of fuller's chalk. Two dyeworkers came to clear the shed for her, and joked cheerfully about the smell. She laughed and joked back. They were rough men, but safe. They knew her; her long-dead father had been one of their own, and her husband was known and respected by them. They could be relied upon to help, not to interfere, and not to pry. By the time she finished calculating the shape of the warp the shed was cleared, swept clean, and washed with brine, and the dyeworkers were going to fetch the loom.

It was evening, and the dyeworks were locking up, when her mother came to fetch her. By then, Demetrias was in the works office, drawing the designs for the tapestry panels: the Choice of Herakles and Victory Crowning Alexander. She turned the sketches over quickly as Laodiki entered the room.

"Here you are!" said Laodiki, standing in the door and smiling at her. Laodiki was a plump, fair, tidy woman, and so amiable that even her daughter could scarcely remember her ever being angry. "Dear, you'll have to come home; why, Symeon and the boy must have been back hours ago!"

Demetrias nodded, carefully rolled the sketches up, tied them with the strands of silk she had been choosing colors from, and thrust them through her belt. If she confided in anyone it would not be her mother; Laodiki was the last person in the world to entrust with a secret. She could neither lie nor keep silence. Demetrias gave her an affectionate smile, and the two women set off for home.

Like many others of the factory workers, Demetrias and Laodiki lived in a large apartment block at the far end of the Egyptian harbor, and they walked slowly along the seafront from the dyeworks. The city was alive again, now that the murderous sun had withdrawn, and the harbor was crowded. Fishwives hawked mussels or mullet beside the boats; octopus and squid hung roasting over charcoal fires; sellers of water and wine wandered in the crowd, rattling their drinking cups. The western sky was still crimson, limning the rock of the citadel black behind them, but the soft summer stars had already risen in the east, and the half moon was high, beginning to gather light. "Dear," said Laodiki, very hesitantly, when they were nearing home, "the procurator . . . he doesn't want . . . ?"

"He wants me to weave a cloak," said Demetrias. "If he wants more than that, it's not my business to take any notice of it."

"There's a good girl," said Laodiki, but without sounding very reassured. "Do you think . . . that is, can you . . . ?"

Demetrias said nothing for a moment. "I don't have to sleep with him, no," she replied, at last.

Laodiki gave a sigh of relief. "Thank God for that! Well, just work on his cloak, then, and hope the dyeworks keep him away. What will you say to Symeon?"

Demetrias looked away, glancing back along the gravel beach at the boats drawn up there. It was there, now: a sixteen-foot, lateen-rigged craft, its cedar hull painted blue and white, and its high stern post carved with the figure of a woman holding a bird, flying against the crimson sunset. Symeon's boat was in; Symeon would be at home, waiting. "I don't know," she said. "Perhaps I'll wait till he asks me."

They walked on slowly to the apartment block.

It was a large one, three stories tall, and fairly comfortable. A public fountain on the landward side provided clean water, and the sewage ran into the harbor and was swept out to sea. Demetrias' room was on the ground floor, the favored position; Laodiki's was two flights up. They stopped at the foot of the stairs and looked at each other. "Well," said Laodiki, "he's a good husband; he won't beat you for something that's not your fault. Good night, my dear."

Demetrias kissed her and waited a moment while her mother puffed up the steep steps, then turned and went into her home.

As she had told the procurator, it was only one room, but that one was large, and could be divided with screens; it already contained a loom, which she used to weave clothing for the family. The window was of glass — poor quality glass, perhaps, but better than horn — and the area beneath it was tiled, with a brick fireplace set out of the main living area to reduce the heat. Symeon had already lit a charcoal fire and was sitting on the couch that doubled as their bed, mending a murex trap by the light of a double-wicked oil lamp. Their son, Meletios — nicknamed Meli, "honey," by his parents — sat on the floor, trying to whittle a piece of driftwood with his new horn-handled knife, which his father had given him a month before, and which he prized above all earthly possessions. Meletios had been going out in the boat with his father since he was four. Now, at five, he knew how to swim, bait a murex trap, cast out a fishing line, brail up or let down the sails, and he could steer the boat in open water if the wind wasn't too strong and a straight course too essential. He was very much his father's child, to the extent that his mother often felt irrelevant.

"You're late," said Symeon, looking up from his work as the door opened. He was a lean, sinewy man, tanned very dark. His hair was black, even in bright sunlight, and curled tightly; even his short beard curled. His brown eyes looked oddly light in his dark face.

"I've been given an urgent commission by the procurator," Demetrias replied. "I'll probably be late most of the time until it's finished."

"The son of a whore!" Symeon tossed his murex trap into the corner and stood. "If he managed the factory properly, the commission wouldn't be so urgent." He crossed to his wife, put his arms about her, and kissed her firmly. "Well, I suppose there's no help for it. I caught a mullet this afternoon, if you want to cook it." It was beneath his dignity to do the cooking himself, however hungry he was.

"We saw the dolphin again!" announced Meletios, coming over and putting an arm round his mother's hips, which was as high as he could reach. He wrinkled his nose. "You smell purple," he accused.

Demetrias stooped to kiss his head. Meletios was almost as brown as his father, but his hair was lighter, bronze colored in the sun, though dark now in the lamplight, and it, too, curled tightly. "You saw the dolphin!" she exclaimed, not answering the accusation. She dropped her cloak on the couch and went over to the fire, the boy trailing her. Symeon had gutted the mullet on catching it and it lay ready in the cooking pot. Beside the fire stood a bucket of water that Meletios had fetched from the public fountain. "And did you go swimming with him? You taste of salt."

"I tried to swim over to him," said Meletios, "but he wouldn't let me get too close. I want to tame him and ride on his back, like Arion in the story."

"You'll have to feed him, then." Demetrias poured some oil into the bronze saucepan and set it on the gridiron. "Perhaps your father could give you some of the bait for him?"

Symeon laughed. "The beast ate half the bait today. Don't encourage the boy, or we'll have no bait left to fish with and no fish to feed us or the dolphin."

Demetrias smiled, shifted the fish, which now sizzled in the pan, and turned it. She sprinkled it with pepper and oregano, checked the wicker food chest and found dried dates, filberts, and a little wilted mint. She threw these into a mortar and began to crush them. "But you caught more than the mullet," she said, "with what bait the dolphin left."

She did not have to look at Symeon to see how he stretched and shrugged, slouching comfortably on the couch. "I caught five mullet and some cuttlefish. I gave them to Daniel to sell in the harbor. God is good."

Just as a weaver could earn money by selling the leftovers of her commission, so a purple-fisher was allowed to sell any fish he caught, once he had given the dye-producing shellfish to the state. The factory provided a generous food ration to all its slaves and let them live rent-free in the apartments that it owned. Compared to a free fisherman, a purple-fisher was wealthy, with no need to worry about the present or to fear the future. If the fishing was good, he had money to spend on whatever he pleased; if it was bad, he still didn't go hungry. God was good.

*But a free weaver*, thought Demetrias, crushing the dates and nuts violently in the mortar, *a free weaver wouldn't have to make treasonous cloaks against her wishes. And if I'd been free, perhaps I wouldn't have had to sleep with Flavius Pamphilos.*

She added some honey and some vinegar to the mortar, with a pinch of rue, then tipped the sticky mixture onto the fish. Perhaps. But she had always suspected that such things happened to the free as well as to the slave; that poor freeborn weavers sometimes found themselves wretchedly bedded by wealthy employers, and equally bore the humiliation in silent helplessness. She picked up the sizzling pan and carried it over to the small table beside the couch, then fetched the wine, a jug of water from the bucket, and the cups. The evening's loaf of bread was already on the table and, in fact, partly eaten — the other two had found it hard to wait. Symeon broke off the largest part of what remained as she seated herself beside him on the couch and handed it to her, grinning, his white teeth flashing in the lamp-

19

light. She took it and heaped some of the fish onto it, turning the bread to catch all the drippings. Meletios climbed onto the couch between his parents and helped himself.

"We don't have any vegetables," complained Symeon, pouring wine for himself and his family.

"I didn't have time to buy any," returned Demetrias, through a full mouth. "I came straight home, and I had no time for lunch today."

Meletios sniffed at his mother's tunic and wrinkled his nose again. "You really do smell purple."

She smiled and rumpled his hair. "I was working at the dyeworks. You and your father catch the creatures, Meli love. You can hardly complain at the smell of them."

"They don't smell that bad when we catch them," protested Meli.

"At the dyeworks?" Symeon's hand hesitated on the water jug. "Why there?"

"I'll be weaving this new commission there. The procurator doesn't want anyone to see it till it's finished, and you know how people are always in and out of the factory." Demetrias did not look at her husband.

Symeon grunted and added water to the wine. "What is this new commission?"

Demetrias took her cup and nodded thanks without looking from the food. "A cloak. The procurator wants it as a surprise gift for someone and is trying to keep it a secret."

Symeon grunted again. "And you'll have to work late for how long?"

"Till it's done. I'll try to have it finished by Christmas."

"Phew! Couldn't Philotimos assign this job to someone else? Someone without a family?"

Demetrias was silent for a minute. She had hoped that her husband would not ask awkward questions — at least, not yet, not tonight, while she was tired and angry about it herself. He would certainly learn, however, that it was not Philotimos who had assigned her the job, and that she had been taken to the prefecture and left alone with the procurator. The workers would be full of this bit of gossip by the morning, and if Demetrias tried to conceal it from her husband, he would suspect her. Her throat felt suddenly so tight with anger that she could barely swallow, and she sat glaring at the chip in the rim of her wine cup. *I'm twice a slave*, she thought bitterly, *being a slave and a wife. I was born a slave, but why should Symeon have such rights over me? If he believes that the procurator wants to sleep with me, he will think it more an insult to himself than an injury to me.*

"The procurator specifically asked that I do it," she said, grimly. "He wanted it done by the weaver who'd made that cloak that went to the king of the Huns last year. He had me summoned and told me so himself."

Symeon looked at her a moment, then scowled. He said nothing more, but ate his fish in silence. Meletios looked uncertainly at his parents, not sure what the matter was but sensitive to the anger in both.

"Go to bed now, Meli," Demetrias said, when the meal was finished. "Tomorrow you can hunt for your dolphin."

Meletios made none of his usual objections but went at once to the trundle bed in the corner, stripped, and lay down on the straw mattress. Just before putting his head down, he remembered his knife, jumped up, found it, sheathed it, and put it under the pillow before climbing back into the bed.

Demetrias smiled and knelt beside the bed. "Mind you don't cut yourself on it!" she warned. She draped the boy's light linen cloak over him.

He nodded, looking up at her unsmilingly. "Is the procurator a bad man?" he asked.

"Why do you say that?" she replied, after an awkward moment of silence.

"Daddy's angry that he talked to you."

"Yes, he is. Your father doesn't want me to work late. But don't worry, my love, it won't be for so very long."

"Will you still have time to weave me that cloak with the dolphins on it?"

"I don't know. If I don't have time, I'll buy you a little boat, shall I?"

"A trireme!" he agreed — this was much better than a cloak. "Like the one we saw at the market on St. Tyrannion's day."

"We'll see," she told him. "Now go to sleep, Meli love." She kissed the child, then rose and went to do the washing up.

Symeon watched her, still scowling. He would speak, she knew, when they were in bed together and Meli was asleep. He would want to talk about the procurator, and he would want to make love. She tightened her shoulders against his eyes. She felt, suddenly, violently, the solidness of her own body, the intense privacy of it that Symeon would invade. Pamphilos had left her with a loathing for men and their heavy hands; in the six years of her marriage, that had largely worn away — but it was back now. She dragged out the washing up as long as she could. Turning from it at last, she saw Symeon still watching her, no longer scowling but bewildered and anxious. She looked away from him quickly and picked up the bucket of dirty water. "I'll fetch some water for tomorrow," she announced, and walked out the door.

It was cooler now outside and the crowds had gone. The gold stars glowed over the black water of the harbor, the moonlight shimmered on the waves, and the windows of Tyre gleamed with lamps. The waves hissed loudly in the gravel of the beach, and a gust of wind rustled the date palms by the fountain. From inside the building came a muffled sound of voices, laughing; down the road someone was playing a lute and singing mournfully.

She tipped the dirty water over the grapevine by the door, then walked along the front of the building to the fountain. The water gurgled quietly into the bucket; she held her hot wrists under the cold, feeling the ache stretch along the tensed muscles. The water pooled in her palms, clear and gleaming in the moonlight, trickled through her fingers in round heavy rivulets.

*My hands,* she thought, staring at them. *And yet the state — Heraklas — can direct them as he pleases.* She flexed the fingers, watching how the flow of the water shifted. Silk, too, could flow, shifting at the twist of a finger, falling into any pattern she wished. She had been born in the shadow of a loom, and her first toys had been spindles; she could not remember learning to weave. She had been permitted to help with the factory's draw-loom when she was eleven; allowed to do plain-weave when she was twelve; patterns when she was sixteen; and tapestry, the most sensitive and delicate of the weaver's arts, when she was seventeen. The woven stuffs of Tyre were the envy of the world, and she was one of the finest weavers in the city: she had never felt anything but pride in her skill. She had often regretted her looks, her face, which attracted so much unwanted attention, but she had never regretted her skilled hands. And she could not regret them now, even though they had brought her whole life into danger.

*And yet*, she thought, staring at them, *how can anyone own my hands but me?* For a moment the whole structure of the world — the factory, the laws, the hierarchies of the imperial administration — seemed fabulous and unreal. The hands were hers: she alone could feel the cold of the water or the ache in her wrists; how could anyone else claim them? Then, just as suddenly, the pattern shifted back, the structure was real, and it was her own questioning astonishment that seemed fabulous. Of course the state could own her; everyone was controlled, one way or another, woven into the fabric of the world, one thread entwined among myriads. The state had raised and trained her — and she had, anyway, no choice but obedience.

The bucket was overflowing. She stopped the tap and carried the water back. In the door of the apartment block she stopped. She stood still a moment, looking at the harbor, then set down the bucket and leaned her head against the cool stone of the doorpost. She felt hot inside her tunic, sticky with stale sweat and the smell of purple. She remembered Flavius Pamphilos with the old sick shame; remembered Heraklas' dark eyes drooping away from her, satisfied.

Behind her, she heard a door open inside the apartment block. Symeon came quietly up behind her and put one hand, gently, hesitantly, on her shoulder. She did not turn.

"It isn't your fault if he wants to sleep with you," said Symeon quietly. "I know that. It's not you I'm angry with."

She shook her head, pressed closer to the doorpost.

"Please," he said. "Tell me what happened."

"He doesn't want to sleep with me," she said wearily. "You can rest easy."

He brushed her hair from the back of her neck; under his hand, her muscles were tense and hard — like halyards, he thought, on a boat under full sail. The mixture of tenderness and regret that choked him now was familiar, tinged with resignation. He knew that her head would not turn toward him at his touch, nor her eyes meet his and soften. She was a dutiful and obedient wife, at times even an affectionate one; he had no right to ask for love as well. "I know it's not your fault," he repeated. "Mother of God, it took me long enough to persuade you that it was no shame for *me* to touch you; I know you'd never want this man, however much he offers you. Tell me. I'll go see him, if you like."

Her head did turn, at that, but the look was scornful. "What would

23

you do?" she asked sharply. "Hit him? The procurator, His Eminence Marcus Acilius Heraklas? Do you think you'd be allowed anywhere near him? And if you were, what do you think would happen to you afterward? I don't want a husband flogged half to death for me."

"He wouldn't dare," said Symeon, just as sharply. "I'm not *his* slave, and my supervisor still has some influence in this city, thank God. But I wouldn't hit him. I'd simply talk to him — I'd find some excuse to make an appointment. I'd just show him that you have a husband who thinks you're worth defending. That alone should put him off."

She shook her head violently, turning away again. "Why should a procurator worry about a factory slave? And anyway, I told you, he doesn't want to sleep with me. That's what everyone will think, of course; that's what I was afraid of when I was summoned. I admit, it upset me, it reminded me of . . . of Pamphilos. But it wasn't what he wanted, that, not at all."

He stood behind her, his hand still on her shoulder. "What did he want then?" he asked, uncertainly.

"I told you. He wanted me to weave a cloak."

He moved to stand beside her, ran the side of one finger down her face and took her chin, turning it to face him. "There's something wrong," he said, flatly, reading her face. "My life, tell me what it is."

She pulled away. "I told you, he reminded me of Pamphilos, and he made me think . . ." She stopped. Symeon had taken both shoulders. He did not shake her or offer to kiss her, merely stood looking down at her face. The half moon lit his own face, chiseling out the set of his lips, clear and precise, black and white; glinting on the eyes under the tangle of black hair.

"Very well," she said bitterly, after a moment of silence. "The cloak is a *paludamentum*, an emperor's cloak. Imperial purple with two tapestry panels to show the Choice of Herakles and Victory Crowning Alexander. And His Sacred Majesty has never, so far as anyone at the factory can remember, commissioned any tapestry scenes but scriptural ones. What's more, this cloak is four inches too long. But the procurator insists that it's for the emperor, and when I dared to question that, he was angry and afraid, and silenced me at once. Do you see?"

The fingers tightened on her shoulders. "We must report him," he said after a long silence.

"Don't be absurd! Report him to whom?"

"To the prefect. Charge him with treason."

"The prefect's a part of it. He offered to let me talk to the prefect. And they say that he and the prefect are friends, and indebted to the same patron for their jobs. And even if he isn't, if I reported it, if they believed me they'd probably torture me to be sure I was telling everything I know, and if they didn't believe me, the procurator would have me flogged for betraying him — and I'd still have to weave the cloak, because he wouldn't risk someone else's making the same accusation. No, I have no choice but to do as I was told."

He shook his head. "You can't . . . if it comes out . . ."

"If it comes out, if they catch me making it, they'll put me on the rack until they've pulled every bone in me from its socket and flog me until I haven't an inch of skin, and then, if they're merciful and sure I know nothing more than what I've said, they'll kill me. So it mustn't come out! It must be kept secret, utterly and absolutely. And I must do it quickly and get it over with." She pushed herself impatiently away from the doorpost and picked up the bucket of water.

"You can't do it! The risk is too great — he has no right to inflict it on you for his miserable little scheme. You must refuse!"

"We don't have any choice!" she said vehemently, facing him. "He is stronger than we are! And he is the master, with every right in law to order slaves as he pleases!" She turned and walked rapidly back into the apartment.

Symeon stood looking after her for a moment, then turned and looked down the harbor. He could make out the outline of his boat, a dark shape on the dark gravel at the edge of the shimmering, moon-drunk sea. He had a sudden violent urge to go to it, take it out into that field of light, away from the heavy, treacherous earth. But every boat that puts out must put in again, unless it sinks, and the urge went as quickly as it came. He sat down in the doorway, resting his hot face in his purple-stained hands, and tried to think. It was difficult because his mind was confused with fury.

*They think they rule the world, these procurators,* he told himself hotly. *They think that they can do as they please, and order the rest of us as they wish. That other one, that Pamphilos, took her virginity as though he had a right to it, as though any pretty young worker in the factory was for his personal use. And so I'm left with a beautiful wife who hates it if any man, even me, touches her. And now this*

*Heraklas wants to risk her life in his own treachery. I won't have it; I'll stop him somehow if I have to risk my own life to do it.*

"He is the master," Demetrias had said. *But not my master,* thought Symeon angrily, *nor my wife's, either. Our owner is the emperor, who owns the whole world; and the moment this procurator, this Acilius Heraklas, rebels against his master, he falls below us. God in Heaven, he has no right at all, none! I'll make him regret it!*

"Why should a procurator worry about a factory slave?" Demetrias had asked bitterly. *She is a woman, and yields. Just as she yielded to that other. Not willingly, hating it, but accepting servility as her lot. God destroy me if I do, if I bow my head and say, "Sir, I am your slave." If he schemes to give his patron a purple cloak, there must be other men, other patrons, who are scheming too, and one of them might be happy to strike a bargain with me. All I need to know is who the cloak is for — if I know that, I'll know who to oppose to him. And she must have some idea who wants it. Once I know, I can go to one of his enemies, I can get a promise of protection for her, for us, and Heraklas will . . .*

He smiled, picturing Heraklas bound and paraded through the streets as a traitor. He rose, shook himself, and went back into the apartment.

The moonlight fractured in the window, casting a faint light over the whole of the room, enough for him to make out the shape of Demetrias already lying motionless on the couch with her back to him. He came a few steps closer and looked down at her; her eyes were closed and she did not stir, though he was sure she was not asleep. Her hair was black in the dimness, and fell in masses over her neck and bare shoulder; one clenched hand lay on the pillow by her face, as though trying to fend off the weight of the night. His anger suddenly vanished, and he stood motionless, looking at her, his throat aching. *They are so powerful,* he thought. *Of course she is afraid. So am I.*

He sat down on the couch; she still did not move. He would not disturb her; he did not want the forced resignation of her acceptance. *If only you trusted me,* he thought longingly. *If only we could fight them together; we'd win then, I know it. If only, if only . . .*

He sighed, then took off his sandals and lay down beside her in silence.

26

# ≈ II ≈

SYMEON SLEPT BADLY that night. For long hours his mind restlessly
sought pretenders and protectors amid fragments of half-heard, disregarded political gossip, uselessly and in ignorance. When sleep
came, it came unperceived into the restless drowsing. He lay awake;
painfully aware of Demetrias' back turned toward him on the couch,
staring at the pattern the moonlight made through the window and
listening to the whisper of the waves on the beach outside; he slept,
and dreamed that he was in his fishing boat, *Prokne*, sailing through
the night. The steering oar jerked unsteadily against his hand, as
though caught by currents of rough sea; it was so dark he could not
see the boat's side, but the sails flapped in gusts of a strong wind, and
from all about him came the sound of waves breaking. He realized
that he was guiding the craft through a narrow channel bounded by
sheer rock. He went cold with terror and stared open-eyed into the
blackness ahead; the salt spray froze against his face. The noise of the
waves slackened suddenly, and in the lull he heard Demetrias crying
in agony. He jumped up, shouting, and the steering oar broke; the
boat lurched, rolled over splintering, and he fell into the bitter sea,
and woke.

He pulled himself up onto his elbows, trembling. The moon was
down now, and the room was black. He felt on the couch beside him
and found no one there; Demetrias was gone. He jerked back as
though he had indeed rolled into the sea, then forced himself to lie
still. From the streets outside came the first sounds of the new day: a
cock crowed; some children ran past the window to fetch water from
the fountain; a dog barked, and somewhere a vendor, hoarse with
sleep, was beginning to hawk fresh bread. Symeon let out a long,

unsteady breath: it was almost day, and she must have got up to light the fire or fetch the day's ration of bread.

"Demetrias?" he called softly into the darkness.

But it was Meletios who replied, sleepily, "I think she went out a couple of minutes ago. I woke up when the door closed."

Symeon put his head down against his arm. Disaster, if it meant to strike, was still far away. *And I'll get us protection*, he told himself, determinedly; *I won't let it happen.*

The door opened, there was a smell of fresh bread, and Demetrias came in, carrying a lantern. The soft light turned her fair skin to gold and made her rose-colored cloak glow warm; the loaves of bread in the crook of her arm steamed fragrantly. Symeon felt his heart stop for a moment: after the dream and the darkness, she seemed as necessary as the day, as the bread she carried. But her face was set and unsmiling, and she moved quickly and abruptly, setting down the bread, lighting the lamp and extinguishing her lantern, armoring herself against him in brisk efficiency. Symeon sighed, stretched wearily, and got up.

When they had breakfasted, Symeon handed Meletios a few bronze coins. "Take these and go buy some lamp oil and incense from John the Deacon," he ordered. "I had a bad dream last night about shipwreck. I'll meet you at Saint Peter's shrine once I've seen to *Prokne*."

Wide-eyed, Meletios took the money. While, as everyone knew, there were true dreams and false, any sensible person took all dreams seriously, and nothing could be a worse omen for a fisherman than a dream of shipwreck. It was obviously necessary to pray and make sure of the protection of the saints before taking the boat out that morning. Saint Peter had a shrine on the harbor front so that the fishers of Tyre could do just that. Meletios bobbed his head and obediently ran off to buy the incense.

Symeon watched him go. While he fully intended to invoke divine aid, he was sure that his dream had not been an omen of literal shipwreck: Saint Peter might not be the best saint to call on. But he'd wanted to keep Meletios innocent of the trouble. He looked back at Demetrias. She was already tossing her cloak over her shoulder, preparing to set off to work. "Come with me to the boat?" he asked quietly.

She hesitated, the corners of her mouth drawing down. *What's the use of going over it again?* she wondered, bitterly. *I wish I'd told him nothing last night.*

But there was no use in defiance, either, and obedience was a wife's duty. She nodded, picked up the basket that held Symeon and Meletios' lunch, as well as the one that held her own, blew out the lamp, and set off with her husband out the door.

On the eastern horizon a faint smear of salmon-pink showed above the mountains, though the stars still shone over the citadel in the west. The harbor front was bustling again and they walked through the busy throng in silence. Opposite the boat, Symeon jumped from the sea wall down onto the beach with a crunch of gravel, and Demetrias followed reluctantly. Once away from the crowds it was quiet; the sea was almost calm, breaking in tiny translucent ripples that hissed in the small stones. *Prokne* lay half in, half out of the water, her carved sternpost rising from the sea, shaped like a woman who held a swallow in one upraised hand. Like many of the other purple-fishers' boats her name was connected with the cloth trade: Prokne, who according to legend had been transformed into a swallow, had been a famous weaver. In daylight the figure on the sternpost looked stiff, her colors garish, but in the pale dawn she seemed half alive. Symeon patted her wooden shoulder affectionately when he stowed his lunch under the stern bench, then came forward and jumped back onto the beach beside his wife.

"About that cloak," he said, quietly, in a tone that was almost casual, though she knew that the whole trip to the boat was to avoid the danger of anyone else catching even a whisper. "Who is it for?"

She turned away, gripping the gunwale of the boat. "How should I know?" she demanded bitterly. "I told you, he claims it's for the emperor. He's hardly going to spill out his secrets to me!"

"But you must have some idea."

She looked back at him, angrily. He stood quite still beside the boat; the dawn behind her showed his face clearly. It held the same quiet, unsmiling regard that it had held the night before. She bit her lip. *Why must he know?* she asked herself. *What good will it do? And why did I tell him anything? Because it's my duty as his wife to obey, and I hate to be at fault? But it's dangerous to talk about this, dangerous even to think about it! It would have been much better to have pretended I believed what I was told, and said that it was for the emperor.*

29

"I can guess," she said, evenly, "but I can't know. What do you hope to gain by worrying at it?"

"We have to take steps to guard ourselves," he replied earnestly. "We must have someone to turn to if something goes wrong. If we know who it's for, we'll know where to go."

She stared at him for a moment incredulously, then pulled her hand from the boat. "We can turn to no one!" she exclaimed fiercely. "*Anyone* who knows of this is dangerous to us, anyone! It *must not come out!*"

"But suppose it does come out?" he insisted impatiently. "These would-be traitors always have enemies; there are always spies and false friends. Do you think the chamberlain Chrysaphios is likely to miss a conspiracy against his master?"

Demetrias winced and looked away. If Nomos had been a leading power in the state, the chamberlain Chrysaphios was the greatest power. It was whispered that he controlled his master, the emperor, absolutely; that he had contrived the disgrace of the emperor's wife and the retirement of his sister; that he had destroyed a hundred others, bishops and noblemen, out of greed or for fear of a rival, by a thousand arts of deceit and corruption; that he ruled alone through an army of spies. Like all imperial chamberlains he was a eunuch, originally a slave imported from Persia, and he was profoundly hated. But he was also profoundly feared, and no whisperer ever dared to raise his voice.

"We need protection," Symeon said harshly into the silence. "We can't just wait and hope that no one finds out; we must get ourselves clear of the whole thing, as quickly as possible!"

"Lord of All!" She glared at him, her teeth set. "Do you think I don't *want* to get clear of it? I can't! If you go running to some powerful man hoping for protection, he'll betray us both as soon as it's convenient. We'd be nothing to him; why should he keep his word to us? And even if he did, if he tried to protect us, the very fact that he knew, that he tried to act against the treason, would treble the risk of discovery! For God's sake, please, put the idea out of your head!"

"I don't want you killed! Do you expect me to stand here humbly and watch while you're destroyed? We've got to guard ourselves. And we're not as insignificant as you pretend; we're not helpless. My supervisor was on the city council . . ."

"He was thrown off it last year on the grounds that he was a slave!"

"He's still respected in the city! The council could give us some protection, and would, if he asked it. And we could ask sanctuary from the bishop . . ."

"The new bishop doesn't even know who we are; he doesn't know anything, doesn't want to know anything, that would offend his friends at court. The council can't protect us against the prefect, and the procurator could have any of us, even your supervisor, flogged for disobedience. Please believe me! We have no choice!"

He stared at her, his jaw set and his eyes bright with anger. "You've been forced into danger whether we act or not," he said, biting each word off. "We have a choice: we can accept it slavishly — or we can fight it."

She dropped her eyes. *But we can't fight it*, she thought, hot with the old mixture of shame and rage. *We must accept it as what we are — slaves. The powers that ordered this, like the powers that would stop it, rule the world, and either of them could crush us without noticing. And it is idiocy to deny that, Symeon: sheer, perverse, self-willed, blind idiocy.*

But she did not say this. "If it is Nomos who wants the cloak," she replied instead, deliberately, lifting her eyes again, "I think the danger won't be too great, if the secret is kept. He was master of the offices until last year. He was head of the chamberlain's spies, and he knows them all, the men and the methods."

There was a moment of silence. The waves hissed in the gravel, and the first small breeze caught at Demetrias' hair. Behind her, the dawn was brightening. "So you think it's Nomos," Symeon said at last.

She shrugged. "That's what I guess. I'd heard that he'd quarreled with the chamberlain. They say he likes mythological scenes — though the choice of subjects may have been Heraklas'. But they say he was responsible for appointing both the procurator and the prefect. And there's a new statue of him at the prefecture, which calls him 'most noble.' If it's *him*, I don't think he'll be caught until later, if at all. But of course I don't know. I can't know. Only I am certain" — she fixed him with a bitter intensity — "*certain*, that my best hope of safety is to do the thing secretly and do it fast."

Symeon bowed his head, biting his tongue to stop the words. The best hope of safety lay in slavish obedience to the procurator? The prospect sickened him. And did it really offer any greater hope of safety? Even if it were Nomos who had ordered the cloak, could they trust that it wouldn't be discovered? The man had been master of the offices — but a person who merely "had been" powerful, and wasn't, might as well be dead. The empresses had been powerful, too, and where were they now? No, he was as convinced as ever that the only thing to do was seek protection from some powerful enemy of Nomos, expose the plot, and make sure they stood well clear of the ruins.

But he had not convinced her of this, and looking back at her set, bitter face, he knew that he could not convince her. More words would only lead to more anger, a slow poison between them. After a long silence, he shrugged and said, slowly, "Very well."

She dropped her eyes and stood still, her cheeks flushed. For a moment he thought she would say something more, an apology or word of thanks, but in the end she only murmured, defensively, "It is best," nodded, tossed her cloak over her shoulder, and strode back off toward the harbor wall. Symeon sat down on the side of the boat, staring bleakly after her. If it were done, if he could find someone to enlist as an ally, he would have to do it without telling his wife.

When Demetrias climbed back up the sea wall onto Harbor street, she heard a shout of her name and paused, glancing back toward the apartment. The short round figure of her mother was ambling toward her through the crowd, smiling cheerfully. Demetrias made herself smile in return and waited for Laodiki to join her.

"Much joy, darling," Laodiki declared as she trotted the last few feet to join her daughter. "Isn't it a fine morning? Why, child, you're in a temper! What's the matter?"

Demetrias bit her lip, angry that her anger was apparent. She straightened her cloak and began walking on toward the factory — slowly, because Laodiki always went slowly and could not be hurried. "Symeon is angry because the procurator gave me this private commission," she said bitterly, "and he wants to go directly to His Eminence Acilius Heraklas and complain."

Laodiki laughed. "Mother of God! But he always believes he's a match for any man in the empire, doesn't he? You've told him that he doesn't need to worry, you can get out of sleeping with the man without that?"

Demetrias nodded sharply. "He's agreed not to."

"I don't know why you're angry, then," said Laodiki comfortably.

"He was a fool to think of it! What good did he suppose it would do? Why should he think that the procurator would pay any attention to one of his workers, a slave?"

"Oh well . . . we're not real slaves, are we?"

"That's not what Granny used to say."

Demetrias' grandmother, dead now for nine years, had been a Goth, freeborn, captured in the wars of the emperor Theodosius the Great, and bought for the factory by a forgotten procurator, ostensibly for her spinning and actually out of lust. Beautiful, savage, and domineering, she had treated her daughter and granddaughter with contempt. "Slaves born and bred," she called them, and had insisted that they wait on her as though she were still the barbarian noblewoman she had been among her own people. Demetrias had been glad of her death, though bitterly ashamed of her own gladness.

Laodiki crossed herself, as she always did at the mention of the dead. "Oh well, you know your grandmother . . . she never did settle down in Tyre, and she never did understand how things really are, among the Romans. There's a world of difference between us and common slaves, and you know it as well as I do, but she, poor creature, never would believe it. The shock of being bought and sold, I've always thought; it must have been dreadful for her; she never got over it. But really, we're only slaves in name. There's not much difference between us and the military, really: the soldiers get rations same as us, and not much more, either. And they can't earn anything much on the side, poor things. Why, Symeon wasn't even all that foolish to think of complaining to the procurator. His father was on the city council the year he died, and his supervisor . . ."

"Was thrown off last year. He reminded me. But Barak *was* thrown off, as a slave — and even if he hadn't been, what difference would it make? A person like Acilius Heraklas would take no more notice of him than he would of Symeon."

"Another procurator, a more cautious procurator, would back away from insulting an important purple-fisher, city councilor or not. This one . . . well, I agree, it wouldn't do any good if Symeon talked to him, it would just offend him. But that's not because we're slaves; he'd be just as offended if it were some petty merchant or banker in the same circumstances. There's no use asking for respect from the powerful!"

Demetrias walked a few steps in silence. "A merchant or banker would be legally married," she said at last. "The circumstances wouldn't be the same at all. He could prosecute for adultery."

"You and Symeon are married. Everyone knows you are, and the bishop blessed it."

"That counts for nothing in the law. Slaves cannot marry and cannot commit adultery. It's not the same. We are . . . less . . . than freeborn people."

Laodiki shook her head. "Darling, you should never pay any attention to what your grandmother said; I told you so at the time."

"We are less able to defend ourselves," Demetrias told her evenly. "You know that. We have no rights, and nowhere to turn if we are wronged. And in our hearts we never forget it. Granny slept with her procurator, and two or three others after him; I promised myself I wouldn't sleep with Pamphilos — and when the moment came, I yielded without a struggle."

Laodiki touched her arm, and Demetrias looked up to see the deep fear in her mother's eyes. "You said you could get out of it this time," Laodiki whispered.

Demetrias sighed. "I can. I can worm my way out of going to bed with Heraklas. But I wish" — her anger suddenly flooded her voice — "I wish I could tell him honestly to take himself off to Hell."

"Child!" exclaimed Laodiki, relieved and amused again. "You're the same fool as Symeon!"

"I've got the sense not to actually do it!" Demetrias replied. "He hasn't."

They had reached the gates of the dyeworks, and Demetrias stopped. She managed to smile at her mother, though a bit sourly. "Don't wait for me tonight," she told her. "I'm dressing the loom today, and I'll have to work late; you go on home when the factory closes."

Laodiki nodded. "Shall I do your shopping for you on the way home?"

"Oh! Yes, please. We had no greens last night, and Symeon wasn't happy. I'll pay you back when I get home. Much joy!" She kissed her mother's cheek and went into the dyeworks, nerving herself to dress the loom with the web of treachery and death.

It took all that day and part of the next to suspend the warp on the loom; when it was done Demetrias again went to the prefecture and asked to see the procurator.

She was admitted at once. This time Heraklas was writing a letter. He glanced up when Demetrias entered with his secretary, nodded slightly when she bowed very low, but continued to write. The secretary left the room, and Demetrias stood by the door, holding the scrolled designs for the tapestry before her in both hands.

Heraklas was finding the letter a difficult one. His patron had openly commissioned a woolen carpet from his factories, and privately instructed the procurator to discuss this when he reported on the secret commission. Heraklas appreciated the need for the precaution — but he found it difficult to keep his sense of the importance of what he did from getting into his pen. The brief acknowledgment required — "I have placed Your Eminence's commission with a skilled weaver and the work is under way" — seemed altogether too bald, too trivial, for the bold and dangerous scheme to which he had pledged his own illustrious name. He had drafted several graceful and ambiguous missives, full of pointed literary allusions — then, on rereading them, had felt a shock of cold fear and destroyed them hastily. *Spies*, he had reminded himself; and remembered with the vividness of nightmare the maze of corridors in the Great Palace in Constantinople and the whispering silks of the officials who peopled them, all of them eager to please the chamberlain Chrysaphios — his patron's enemy. Now he bit the end of his pen and stared at the new draft of the letter. Formal salutations — good, good — wishes for his patron's health, good — "As regards the carpet Your Eminence was pleased to request, I am delighted to say that the work has been entrusted to a skilled worker and is already under way. I hope to send it to Your Distinction before Christmas."

A very bare assessment. And it said nothing of his doubts about the weaver. He glanced up at her again, standing there wrapped in her cloak as before, shapeless and humble. Did he really need to say anything? After all, she had agreed to obey — and it reflected badly on him if he couldn't manage the slaves in his own factory. Very well, leave that out. What could he safely add?

35

*Nothing*. Reluctantly, still dissatisfied with the plain and unexciting tone of the communication, he wrote in another line of formal greeting, then leaned back in his chair and wiped his pen. He nodded to the weaver to show her that she could now approach. "So," he said, "have you started?"

She bowed again. "I am ready to start, Your Eminence. I wanted to be certain that Your Discernment approved the designs."

"Very good!" He dropped the pen and smiled, leaning across his desk. "Are those them? Let's have a look!"

She slipped the twist of silk off the end of the scroll and extended it toward him at arm's length. He snatched it impatiently and unrolled it.

Demetrias stood back, folding her hands. Despite everything, she had enjoyed designing the cloak. Ordinarily the task was left to Philotimos or one of the other supervisors, and her job was merely to weave according to their plans, permitted at most to choose the colors. This time the patterns were entirely her own — drawn after some of Philotimos' designs, yes, but drawn principally to give her pleasure in making them. Alexander would be shown in full armor, standing, sword in hand, above the prostrate figure of the king he had defeated; Victory, robed and winged, stooped to set the crown of laurel upon his head. The hero Herakles, club on shoulder and lion skin thrown back from his massive head, ignoring the smiling blandishments and easy lowland road of Vice, was about to take the hand of Virtue and follow the steep mountain path she indicated.

Heraklas smiled, smoothing the parchment. "Yes . . . and these will face each other? One in each corner of the front of the cloak?"

"Not quite in the corner, sir. I thought you would approve of a line of bees around the bottom edge, sir, to be done in gold, and a gold scroll pattern, a thin one, up the side. I've drawn it in, sir, underneath the pictures."

"Yes, I see. And the gold on the shoulders?"

"I thought for that, sir, a simple circular pattern would do, with a scrolled frame, repeated. I've drawn it on the back of the picture of Herakles, sir."

"Yes . . . yes, that will do very well." He glanced at it briefly, then again turned the parchment to examine the tapestry designs. "And this is the size the finished pictures will be?" Each picture was about a foot high.

36

"Yes, sir. If you approve them, these are the pictures I will use as a base for the tapestry. As for the colors, sir, I have the silks here . . ." Demetrias took the last step toward the desk, and held out the skein of threads. "The gold, of course, you know; this will be the purple for the cloak itself . . ." She dropped a strand of silk onto the picture, where it lay gleaming against the yellow parchment: the double-dyed Tyrian purple, weight for weight more precious than gold. "Alexander's armor will be the gold again, but for his cloak this scarlet, and this saffron for his hair . . ." She dropped thread after thread shining onto the parchment: black of oak gall, red of kermes, and rose of madder, bright and dark saffron, dyer's broom and indigo, the double-dyed greens and walnut browns. The picture was already woven in her mind, and she smiled at it, seeing how the flanks of the mountain stood mottled green and brown before Herakles, and how the white robe of Victory flashed blue, rippled by the beat of her black-tipped wings.

Heraklas looked at the silk and the drawings and smiled again, complacently this time. *The cloak will be magnificent*, he thought happily; *he will be pleased. And the Alexander, standing triumphant over a purple-cloaked king — how appropriate!*

It was the Herakles, however, that he commented on. "I thought this scene a suitable gift from myself," he remarked, indicating it. "A Herakles from Heraklas!" He gave a snort of amusement.

"It will certainly recall to his mind the giver of such a princely gift," Demetrias agreed smoothly. *He's very pleased*, she thought, pleased herself for her design's sake.

Heraklas nodded graciously. "A princely gift," he repeated. *At a princely cost*, he thought to himself, with less pleasure: Philotimos had sent him the bill. *Still, worth the expense. He will remember me now, when he's in power. I was wrong to worry about the weaver, she'll do very well. Pretty thing she is, too. Wonder where she gets that coloring from — it's rare, here in Tyre. Probably part Gothic.*

He gave her a condescending smile. "And you have a private place to work on it?"

"Yes, Excellency." She began to gather up the silk. The light from the window snared in her hair, and her eyes, fixed on the threads, were half-masked by the long lashes. Her expression was gentle, contented: she had work before her. "A shed at the dyeworks. The

37

door can be locked, sir, or bolted on the inside: there's no danger of strangers coming in and seeing the work before it's completed. Philotimos has had the loom set up there and I've dressed it; I was only waiting for Your Eminence's approval to begin weaving."

"Excellent!" He caught her wrist and held it to his desk. She looked up quickly, not moving her hand, but her eyes became bright and hard. He smiled again, lazily. The prospect of the completed cloak, delivered to his patron, filled him with delighted excitement, but the necessity of waiting five months for its completion was tedious. *But you, my dear, could help amuse me for a few hours, I think.* "Then you can begin at once," he told her. "I hope you've told no one what you're doing?"

"No one, sir," she said at once. *And I wish,* she thought, *that it was true, and that I had kept quiet about it with Symeon as well. Still, he seems resigned now. Why is this man holding me? Just to frighten me into silence, or does he . . . ?*

"There's a good girl," said Heraklas, and ran his hand up her arm; it made her flesh crawl. She edged back, pulling away as much as she dared. He allowed it but kept hold of her hand, amused already.

"My husband, sir, is suspicious about it," she told him, hoping this would indeed be enough. "He tends to be a jealous man, sir: he doesn't like it that I've been singled out."

He raised his eyebrows and let out a long breath through his nose, half snort and half sigh. "Your husband?" he said. "Come, girl, slaves don't have husbands."

"Perhaps not in law, sir, but custom has some weight, too, and my husband is as able to be jealous as any freeborn person."

He laughed and let go of her hand. "If your jealous husband beats you, come to me. I'll sort him out, eh? Here, pick up your silks."

She hesitated, then quickly picked up the threads and twisted them together. Heraklas sat in his seat watching her, still smiling with amusement. She paused again, then began to pick up the designs; he once more caught her wrist, and this time pulled her forward and kissed her, sliding a hand up her side.

She didn't move for a moment, frozen with the old shame. Then she jerked back. *No,* she thought, *I'm weaving the cloak; I don't have to do this, too.*

Heraklas laughed again and caught her other wrist. "By Apollo, girl, don't get into a panic! I won't hurt you." He pulled her forward again, so that she had to sit on the desk before him, and let go one of her hands to take hold of her chin. "You're a pretty thing, did you know that? Don't worry about your jealous husband. I can deal with slaves. Where did you get such green eyes?"

She said nothing for a moment, choked by anger and humiliation. *No*, she told herself again, *this I can get out of.* "Your Excellency," she whispered, "please let me go."

He chucked her under the chin, "Now, my dear, I said I wouldn't hurt you. Don't be afraid. It's the dyeworks you're working in, is it? Not a pleasant place for such a sweet thing. Let's have the loom moved to somewhere more comfortable for you . . . I could get you a room in town where . . ."

"I told Your Excellency that custom has some weight here," she said, still whispering but with a hard edge to her voice; the word for *custom* was the usual Greek one, *nomos.* "You know the saying, 'Custom is king.' And you think that he should be, don't you? Do you think that Nomos will like the cloak?"

He let her go as though she had burned him. She slipped off the desk, hurriedly grabbed the designs, and backed off to a safe distance.

"Who told you?" Heraklas demanded, getting to his feet. "Who's been talking?" He felt quite sick with terror. If a factory slave knew, everyone must know: they would catch him; he would die. It had never crossed his mind that his political history and allegiances were the common gossip of the factory floor, and that even slaves can reason.

Demetrias bowed her head demurely, though her heart was pounding and, at the same time, she wanted to laugh. "Since the cloak is clearly not meant for His Sacred Majesty, sir, I assumed that it must be for your own patron," she said quietly. "We do know in the factory, sir, to whom we owe your presence here. I am sorry if I have said something I shouldn't."

"I told you the cloak was for the emperor!" Heraklas whispered. "Nomos . . . he commissioned a carpet. Not a cloak, a carpet."

She looked up and met his eyes; his bored complacent expression was gone altogether, and he looked young and terrified. She felt her own face flush with the heat of triumph. *Good*, she thought. *He realizes that he can't involve me in high treason and then push me into bed for a game. Tool I may be, but tools used for dangerous work must be treated with respect; if they turn, they can cut the hand that used them.* "If you say so, sir," she replied quietly. "As I said before, it would not be proper for your slave to accuse you of anything. I understand my position, sir — as I hope you understand yours."

He swallowed loudly, then sat down at his desk again, staring at her uncertainly. "So you have said . . ."

"Nothing about this to anyone, sir."

He rubbed a damp palm nervously against his thigh. "The cloak is for the emperor. I told you that before."

She smiled. "How foolish of me to forget, sir. I will start on the emperor's cloak at once."

She bowed low and left the room.

Heraklas sat motionless at his desk for several minutes, cold despite the warmth of the morning. Distant through the open window came the sorrowful calls of a street vender; the sea breeze fluttered the papers on his desk. Even at this distance from the harbor it smelled faintly of purple. *I hate this stinking city,* he thought vehemently. *I'll be glad when it's time to leave it.*

*But will there be any life for me afterward?*

He shivered, remembering his one meeting with the chamberlain Chrysaphios. It had been immediately before his audience with the emperor and his official appointment as procurator. The eunuch had received him in a luxurious office at the very heart of the emperor's palace and instructed him on the correct protocol. Chrysaphios had been unexpectedly young and handsome — smooth, slightly effeminate, in the manner of eunuchs, but unquestionably elegant. From the golden toes of his sandals to his neatly trimmed dark gold hair he was the picture of grace, poise, and good taste. He had sat at his desk, smiling disdainfully, when Heraklas was admitted and had bowed to the ground before him. Heraklas had made a few remarks about "wishing to live up to my illustrious ancestors," at which Chrysaphios had hidden a smile behind a long, manicured hand. After the audience, asking for his tip for arranging it (a pound of gold! Heraklas remembered indignantly), he had casually referred to the numerous indiscretions of Heraklas' father, and implied, ever so delicately, that he could easily lay his hands on several young men who shared the same "illustrious ancestors."

*The miserable slave!* thought Heraklas. *His ancestors scrubbed latrines for the Persians, and he himself was sold to the highest bidder in Constantine's market, but there he is, running the state, and making me, an Acilius, a descendant of a hundred consuls, bow down to him!*

He did not like to admit, even to himself, that he was afraid of the eunuch, that the extent of the chamberlain's knowledge about him had shocked him, and that the thought of those arrogant and disdainful eyes scanning reports on the factories of Tyre terrified him. Particularly when a weaver, a mere slave, was so easily able to guess not just the fact of a planned treachery but its leader.

He clapped his hands to fetch in his secretary. "Send a runner over to the prefect's office," he ordered. "Tell him something's come up, and ask him if I could see him this morning."

Half an hour later the prefect Marcellus Philippos, governor of Syria Phoenice, himself appeared at the procurator's office.

He did not need to come when summoned. He outranked Heraklas, and could have summoned the procurator instead — but that would have taken more of his time than this informal visit, and time was precious. Philippos was older than Heraklas, a stout man in his early thirties with a permanently shadowed jaw and coarse black hair; his family, though less ancient than the Acilii, was even more powerful — and had never stood on ceremony. "So, what is it?" he asked briskly, as soon as the door had closed behind him.

Heraklas, who had risen to shake hands, sat down again and looked nervously at the paper on the desk. "It's . . . it's this . . . business," he said uncertainly. "I've got it under way, but . . ."

"But?" demanded Philippos impatiently. He disliked Heraklas. *A weak, unreliable man,* he reckoned bitterly, assessing the nervous look with a cynical eye. *He's having second thoughts now that he's committed. He only joined us because he knows he'll never get anywhere in government without His Excellency's support, and because the chamberlain offends his vanity. He never will be more than a dabbler in affairs of state. Vanity isn't enough for a political career: you need a stomach for it, you need hard work. Even if he were an orthodox believer in the true faith, instead of an adherent of that ridiculous paganism, he'd still never govern any place that matters. Well, I have to put up with him for the sake of the cause: I'll say what's required to reassure him.*

"I think the weaver's guessed something," Heraklas admitted unhappily, lowering his voice. "Do you think it's safe to go on just now?"

Philippos stared at him in disbelief. "The weaver's guessed something? Guessed what? How?" *Ten to one she's young and pretty,* he thought bitterly, *and he's blabbed everything to her to show her how important he is. The idiot!*

Heraklas made a helpless little gesture with his hands. "She knew the emperor's cloak size, and she knew who my patron is, and she asked me if I thought he'd like the cloak. I didn't know what to say."

"Didn't you tell her to keep it secret?"

"Of course I did! And I threatened her, and let her understand that it was no good complaining to you. And of course I haven't *admitted* it; I told her it was for the emperor. But I never thought she'd guess."

Philippos shrugged. For a moment he had been alarmed, but it seemed that alarm was unnecessary. "Well, provided that she understands the situation, it makes no difference if she knows. She'll be punished by us and tortured by the authorities if she's found out, and if she's clever enough to guess at our business from a cloak size and a piece of factory gossip, she's clever enough to understand that. If she hadn't guessed who the cloak was for, anyone who put her to the question would have; we're in no additional danger because of her."

"But . . . but how did she know it was His Excellency?"

"You can't really be surprised that your factory workers know who appointed you, can you? My dear fellow, you expect your domestic slaves to know all about your business at home; you must expect state slaves to know all about the factory. They gossip with each other — they'll find out anything, discover any secret that isn't coded and locked up in a box. That's why you should follow the precautions His Excellency recommended. You have followed them, haven't you?"

Heraklas glanced again at the innocuous letter on his desk. "Oh, yes. But . . . but it's dangerous, isn't it? I thought . . ."

*You thought you could keep your hands clean and that no one could pin anything on you even if the rest of us were caught,* Philippos thought contemptuously. *And now, lo and behold, it seems that even a slave can see when an Acilius is guilty.* "There is some danger," he said quietly. "But if we're careful, and particularly if we move quickly, the risk is minimal. The important thing is to remain calm and to remember what we're working for." Heraklas still looked uncertain, and the prefect went on, in a whisper but urgently. "You know as well as I that neither of us has anything to hope for without His Excellency. That golden snake Chrysaphios has a stranglehold on the palace, and that useless nonentity who wears the purple will never get rid of him; no one can even get near him to complain. Chrysaphios has quarreled with His Excellency now, and you know what that means, for him and for all of us who rose through him. Where we had help and preferment before, we'll face malice and neglect; sudden unheard-of taxes, demands for bribe upon bribe, trouble in the courts, unjust requisitions — everything that the chamberlain visits on his enemies.

"And" — Philippos grew even more vehement, though he still did not raise his voice above a whisper — "think what that Persian slave has done with our noble and ancient empire! He can't trust the generals, and dares not give power and men to them. Therefore, we must sit here, extorting tax upon tax from our wretched provinces to pay for another shameful peace with the Huns! We've given the whole diocese of Thrace to them, handed it over on a platter! And those Vandal pirates are swarming out of Africa as far as Greece, and we do nothing about it! No, the chamberlain can't trust a man of quality, and he's turned against the best man in his government, the only man who might have stemmed the tide! So why shouldn't our patron — a man who ought to have been born in a Golden Age, when Rome was great, a man of true culture and nobility — take away from the nonentity and his slave the power they have abused? And why shouldn't he succeed in doing so? He knows better even than Chrysaphios how the sacred offices are run, how to manage an affair like this safely. And once he wears the purple, what can't we, his friends and supporters, hope for? He is a great man, and loyal to those who are loyal to him."

Heraklas had expressed the same sentiments himself on previous occasions, and his doubts were washed away by their repetition. He nodded vigorously. "You're right!" he exclaimed. "We have everything to hope for, and every reason to expect success."

Demetrias returned from the dyeworks after dark, exhausted, her back and arms aching from the hundreds of small adjustments she had made to the heddles, leashes, and tension sticks of the loom, but smiling contentedly. She arrived at the apartment to find that her mother had cooked a fish soup for the family and that she had nothing to do but sit down and join the others at the table.

"You looked pleased," said Laodiki, moving over from her place on the couch and handing her daughter a bowl of the soup.

Demetrias nodded. "I had another meeting with the procurator, to get his approval of the designs. He offered to find me a private room in town to work in."

Laodiki looked alarmed, then, quickly reassessing Demetrias' smile, expectant. "But you managed to refuse the offer."

Demetrias laughed. "I convinced him that I couldn't possibly work anywhere but the dyeworks. He is most dissatisfied."

Laodiki chortled delightedly. "That's my love." She beamed at Symeon, who merely scowled and ate his soup in silence.

"What did he really want?" Symeon demanded when he and Demetrias were in bed together, Meletios asleep, and Laodiki long departed to her room upstairs.

Demetrias propped herself up on her elbows and looked at him. He was no more than a shadow and a gleam of eyes in the dimness. *This will satisfy him*, she thought happily. *Not only have I made it clear to Heraklas that he can't sleep with me, I now know that the whole scheme is as secure as it can be.* "He offered exactly what I told my mother," she replied in a whisper. "A private room in the town. And yes, it was for the obvious reason. When he refused to be put off I asked him if he thought Nomos would like the cloak. He was terrified. It is Nomos. He as good as admitted it." She smiled again to herself, remembering his terror. It seemed to cancel, somehow, her own humiliation. The work remained dangerous, and would require great effort to complete in time, but danger and hard work she could come to terms with. Particularly when the final result would be beautiful. *And it will be*, she thought, picturing it again. *It will be the best thing I've ever done.*

"He admitted it?" Symeon repeated, hesitantly.

"He demanded to know who had told me. So you see, the plan really does involve the man who has most chance of success. The risk shouldn't be too great — if I can only get the thing finished quickly!"

Symeon grunted and rested his chin on his hands, thinking hard.

"What will they do?" he asked, after a silence. "Will they . . . kill the emperor?" The question frightened him even as he asked it. It made real a possibility that before had been only a vague nightmare, remote as an earthquake rumored in another city.

Demetrias turned on her side and glared at him, her moment of happiness vanished. "How should I know?" she demanded in an angry whisper. "If he was idiot enough to tell *me* anything, I really would have cause to worry."

"But . . ." Symeon began, then stopped, still frightened and confused by his own question. Would they — Nomos, Heraklas, the prefect, and their friends — kill the emperor? The *emperor*, who had worn the sacred purple from his birth, been acclaimed Augustus at his christening, in whose name the world had been ruled for as long as Symeon could remember; the son of Arcadius, the grandson of Theodosius the Great, the heir of Constantine — and, beyond all else, the chosen vice-regent of Christ upon earth! No emperor in living memory had died by violence. Symeon had no personal feeling toward Theodosius II, who was to him merely a statue in the prefecture and a name prefacing official communications, and he was vaguely aware that Theodosius did not rule well — but it seemed a violation almost of nature itself that the sacred Augustus should be butchered for the advancement of a few ambitious men. And this woman beside him, whose warmth he could feel in the darkness, whom he loved: she had been seized by this monstrous thing, this plot against all order, and forced to serve its own purposes. For an instant he was afraid to touch her.

Demetrias put her head down on the couch. She had managed during the day to forget the immensity of what she was involved in; now Symeon had reminded her. "I don't think they'll kill him," she whispered uncertainly, as much to herself as to her husband. "I would have thought they'd just force him to get rid of his chamberlain and adopt Nomos as his colleague. Killing . . . that's too big. Nobody would want to kill him; nobody would follow a usurper who'd destroyed the Theodosian house."

*But nobody could trust the Theodosian house at liberty and opposed,* Symeon thought grimly. *It would be too powerful and too dangerous an enemy. And surely even an emperor as mild as Theodosius wouldn't forgive Nomos for usurping the purple: Nomos would have to kill him for his own security. But if the emperor were murdered, it's perfectly true that his murderer would face opposition when he tried to claim the purple. There would probably be other pretenders and a civil war.* He forced himself to lie still, but the fear grew: his mind threw up a tormented image of the statue in the porch of the prefecture shattered and oozing blood, of the prefecture itself breaking open and collapsing into the street. What began so terribly could not end peacefully: murder must lead to civil war, to barbarian invasion, to plague, famine, and death. "Lord of All!" he whispered. "We can't just . . ." He stopped himself.

"Can't just what?" Demetrias demanded.

"Can't just sit here and watch while these people . . . murder . . . It must be prevented!"

"We can't do anything else!" she whispered back. "The powerful always arrange things among themselves, and ordinary people like us always accept the result; the only difference this time is that we happen to know a little bit, a fragment of their secrets, in advance. What they'll really do . . . I can't believe they'd murder . . . except the chamberlain, perhaps. And everyone hates him. And we have no choice, anyway."

She pressed her head against the couch, closing her eyes and trying to breathe evenly. In the dark behind the lids she saw the loom she had arranged that day, and behind it, massive and towering, a wall of water about to break upon her. She shut the image out. She could not afford to think of the risks. She had to rest; there was much work to be done next day. *And*, she consoled herself, *it will be beautiful*.

Symeon also lay still, gnawing on his knuckles and trying not to think of disaster. *I will stop it, somehow*, he promised himself. *I will discover who it's safe to turn to, and I will get a promise of protection from them and then expose the whole business. Otherwise we will certainly suffer whether the plot succeeds or not.*

A few weeks later, Symeon was discussing politics in a harbor tavern. It was a plain building with two floors, the upper one for serving food, and the lower one for drinks; it was located near the eastern end of the Egyptian harbor, and was called the Isis. It had a floor of bare concrete and plaster walls painted garishly with crocodiles and ibis, but it was clean, served good wine, and was much favored by the better-off of the factory workers — the factory supervisors, in particular, tended to stop there for a drink before returning home in the evening. It was early evening now, and the tavern was crowded.

"So," Symeon asked Philotimos cheerfully, "do you think Nomos is in line for the short purple tunic?"

Philotimos frowned into his cup of well-watered Egyptian white wine. Symeon had been in the tavern quite a lot of late, and was taking an uncharacteristic interest in politics. *Of course*, Philotimos admitted, *his wife has been working late, the man has every reason to spend a bit more time out drinking*. Nonetheless, it made him obscurely uneasy.

"What have you done with your son?" he asked, ignoring Symeon's question.

"At home with his grandmother," Symeon replied easily. "No, who do you think will be our next praetorian prefect? Nomos?"

Philotimos considered carefully, began to speak, then reconsidered. "God knows!" he exclaimed, and rolled his eyes piously heavenward.

"I bet Chrysaphios knows too," put in his colleague Daniel, supervisor of the woolen factory, catching the discussion and coming eagerly over to join it. He was a younger man than Philotimos and lacked the silk supervisor's excessive caution. He loved nothing better than political gossip, and he was notorious for not only having heard everything but for saying it as well. Philotimos scowled at his appearance, but Symeon welcomed him with a wide smile and made room for him on the bench. "Nomos is out of the running," Daniel announced, settling himself astraddle. "He had a quarrel with the emperor's most illustrious chamberlain Chrysaphios, and you know what that means. My money's on Anatolios."

"Everybody's been saying that Nomos quarreled with Chrysaphios," said Symeon irritably, "but nobody seems to know anything about it. It's not clear to me that it happened at all."

"Oh, it happened! I heard about it day before yesterday from my friend Agathon at the prefecture — he's a clerk in the assessor's office, and he heard about it from the prefect's secretary, who read it in a letter sent to his master from Nomos himself. The new prefect Philippos was appointed by Nomos, you know. That's why Nomos' statue has been put up in the prefecture — have you seen it? It's right beside Pulcheria's and it calls him 'most noble.' No, this letter said that

Nomos fell out with Chrysaphios after Chrysaphios quarreled with Nomos' friend Zeno."

"What did Zeno find to quarrel about?" asked Symeon, frowning. "He owes his whole career to Chrysaphios. If it weren't for Chrysaphios, he'd still be a robber in the Isaurian mountains!"

"Sst!" exclaimed Philotimos in horror. "That is no way to speak of the palace master of arms."

Symeon shrugged. Daniel grinned and began to relay his piece of gossip. It was a prize piece, and he was proud of it. "Zeno has a friend called Rufus, who was engaged to a noblewoman, a real plum of an heiress. Then the king of the Huns sent the emperor a message: it seemed that his Latin secretary wanted to marry a rich wife, and the emperor was to provide one. Well, King Attila's wish is Chrysaphios' command" — "Sst!" exclaimed Philotimos again — "and Chrysaphios looked about and found the same heiress that Zeno's friend was engaged to, and promised Attila to send her off as soon as he could. The woman didn't like the idea of being the wife of a Hun's secretary, and she tore off to her estate in Phrygia, went to her strongest castle, and locked herself in. 'Well, Zeno, my dear friend,' said Chrysaphios, 'go fetch her back.' Zeno went to her estate with a troop of the imperial guards, carried her off — and married her to his friend Rufus. Chrysaphios was furious. There was nothing he could do about the wedding, but he had all the woman's estates confiscated to the crown, and Rufus discovered that instead of a rich wife he had a poor one. Zeno was furious and went to Chrysaphios to complain; Chrysaphios had him thrown out of the house and ordered him to respect his master in the future. Zeno swore he'd have nothing more to do with 'eunuchs who do nothing but lick the boots of stinking fur-clad barbarians.' Nomos tried to soothe him, pointed out to him that he'd upset one of Chrysaphios' plans, and eventually got him into a state where he'd apologize to Chrysaphios if Chrysaphios sent for him civilly. Then, feeling very pleased with his intervention, Nomos went off to Chrysaphios and told him how things stood with Zeno. Instead of being grateful, Chrysaphios turned on Nomos, called him 'masterless dog' and warned him not to support 'that Isaurian brigand' if he ever wanted to hold office again. Nomos was most offended, and left in a huff, saying he'd support whomever he pleased."

"Sst!" said Philotimos again, shocked even by the report of such language. "I am sure, Daniel, that there's nothing to such a . . . an improper story."

Daniel grinned, took a swallow of wine, and winked at Symeon. "Well, that's what it said in the letter the prefect's secretary saw."

"Are Nomos and Zeno good friends?" asked Symeon with interest. "I would have thought that together they'd be too powerful for even Chrysaphios to offend. After all, Zeno controls the army, and Nomos can rely on the sacred offices."

"But Chrysaphios controls the emperor," said Daniel, "and whoever controls the emperor can raise up new office holders and new masters of arms as quickly as he pleases. Though good generals are in short supply these days, and Chrysaphios is leaving Zeno be, for the time being anyway."

*So the obvious solution for Nomos,* thought Symeon, with satisfaction, *is to get rid of the emperor.*

He sighed. It was more difficult than he had expected to find an enemy of Nomos to ally himself to. There was certainly no one in Tyre who could be trusted to provide protection, and how could he commit such a dangerous plea to a letter to some man a thousand miles away in Constantinople? And Demetrias made it still more difficult. She was working hard on the cloak now and seemed not just resigned, but happy. *The work seduces her,* he thought. *God knows, she loves it far more than she's ever loved me.*

"What other generals are there?" Symeon asked Daniel. "What about Aspar, for instance? Couldn't Chrysaphios appoint him in Zeno's place?"

The supervisor shrugged. "Chrysaphios trusts him least of any general living. Do you think a man like Aspar would be willing to take his orders from Chrysaphios? He's still loyal to the Augusta Pulcheria, and he's been kicking his heels since she was forced out of power eight years ago."

Philotimos nodded at this, forgetting caution. "If we had Aspar as master of arms," he said wistfully, "we wouldn't have to ransack the country to find bribes for the Huns. He'd lead our armies out and defeat the savages. And if Kyros of Panopolis were praetorian prefect again — ah, then!" He sipped his wine, holding it in his mouth for a moment and savoring both it and the memory of Kyros of Panopolis. "He ordered a carpet once — twenty feet by fifteen, pure silk, showing the Loves of Zeus; he had chosen the designs for it himself, and it was exquisite — I simply can't describe how magnificent it looked when it was finished. He gave it as a present to the empress Eudokia. There was a woman who knew how to be an Augusta! I am sure she never did anything unworthy of her position, that the suspicion against her virtue was . . . umm . . ." He stopped himself before saying "a fabrication" and gazed down sadly into his wine. It was Chrysaphios who had contrived Eudokia's disgrace under suspicion of adultery, and it would be rash to accuse Chrysaphios of fabrication.

Symeon was not interested in the ex-praetorian prefect, now bishop, Kyros of Panopolis, nor in the ex-empress Eudokia: both were too far from power now to offer any hope against Nomos and Zeno. General Aspar, however, was another matter. It was true that he had not held any office since his patroness, Pulcheria, was forced into retirement eight years before, but he was still a force to be reckoned with. Although he was related to the royal clans of the barbarian Goths and Halani, he had been born in Constantinople. He owned vast estates in Asia and others in the East — some in the vicinity of Tyre. He had been commander-in-chief in Italy, Africa, Thrace, and in the East; and, if he had not been invariably successful, he had at least earned the respect of the enemies of the Romans. Besides the loyalty of many of the regular troops, he had a small private army of retainers whom he still maintained at his own expense. And he had every reason to want to ruin his successor Zeno, if only to get his own job back.

"If Chrysaphios has quarreled with Zeno," Symeon suggested tentatively, "perhaps he might reappoint Aspar after all. He could probably negotiate something with the man!"

Daniel looked doubtful. "Even if Chrysaphios were willing to negotiate, I don't think Aspar would. They say he's a proud man."

"But loyal to the house of Theodosius," said Symeon. "He'd be willing to serve the emperor, if not to serve Chrysaphios."

"That's true," said Daniel. "I don't know . . . perhaps you're right." He paused, swallowed some wine, and added, "His deputy will be visiting Tyre in a couple of months; perhaps we'll hear something then."

Symeon caught his breath. "Aspar's deputy? Where did you hear this?"

"Agathon again. There's a question about taxes on the general's estates up in the mountains, and the deputy and the estate manager have been writing to Agathon's assessor. The deputy said he'd be here at the end of October and would straighten it out with the prefect then. Why are you so pleased about that?"

"I'd just be pleased if Aspar were reappointed." Symeon finished his wine with a gulp. "Much health! I think my wife will be home now; I'm off to get my supper."

"Has your wife managed to get rid of the procurator?" asked Daniel, before Symeon could rise.

Symeon shrugged. "I think so."

Philotimos gave a snort of laughter. "She told me that he suggested moving the loom into a room in the town, but she managed to convince him it would spoil the weave to do it now. He came to visit her once last week, to check on how the work was proceeding — he said. I asked the fellows at the dyeworks to clean out one of the boiling vats during the visit, and procurator Heraklas came out in about a minute, perfumed oil flask to his nose, looking green." He grinned maliciously.

Symeon grinned back and said, "Thanks."

Philotimos smiled and spread his hands.

"She's a fine woman, your wife," Daniel said, with a trace of regret in his voice. He had once wanted to marry her himself. "There are plenty of women who'd come to an arrangement with a procurator and say nothing about it. Demetrias is both pretty and chaste — you're a lucky man."

"Yes," agreed Symeon, after a moment of silence. "Well, much health!"

A *lucky man*, Symeon thought, walking the short block home. *Yes — I must be. Oh, Demetrias!*

He remembered, with the familiar stab of pain, the day he had fallen in love with her. It had been a few weeks after his father and younger brother had taken their boat out along the coast southward, been caught in a gale, and never come back: he had gone for a long walk inland, wanting to be alone and away from the sea. He was seventeen, then. It had taken more time than he expected to pass the suburbs of Tyre, and by the time he reached the unpeopled fields he was tired; he turned back, angry and discouraged, kicking at loose

51

stones in the rough paving of the road. He was walking back along the causeway that led from the "Old City" of Tyre on the mainland out to the citadel and harbors when he saw a girl sitting on the sea wall and staring into the water below. He recognized her as one of the factory weavers, the daughter of Demetrios the dyeworker: his first instinct was to avoid her as he would have avoided anyone he knew. But the way she sat, staring so intently into the water, caught his attention. Instead of crossing the street to go past her, he stopped beside her and curiously matched her stare into the sea. The waves were gentle that day. They lapped quietly against the heaped stones of the causeway, blue-green and clear. A few small fish glinted silver through the water, and an octopus, red-brown and mottled, clung to a rock green with weed.

"What are you looking at?" he asked; and the girl, half smiling, silently indicated the octopus. He stared at it again: it seemed thoroughly unremarkable.

"What color is it?" the girl asked him, and he looked away from it and at her. Her eyes remained fixed on the creature; her honey-colored hair was fastened in a thick braid at the back of her neck and the water cast a wavering reflection on her still face. She was fifteen, and he suddenly noticed that she was beautiful.

"I don't know. Red," he said awkwardly, feeling a sudden agonizing spasm of loneliness. A month before he would have discussed such a pretty girl with his brother.

She nodded impatiently. "But what color? Kermes? Buccina? Madder? Alum? Henna? I'm supposed to do a pattern of them on a carpet, and I'm trying to decide on the dye." She picked up a loose pebble from the wall and tossed it at the octopus; the pebble sank through the deep water and slid aside.

"Oh." Symeon stared again at the octopus. "I don't know."

"None of the dyes is right." She turned away from the octopus and stood up, brushing off her cloak, then paused and looked again into the water. "They're never the same color as the world. You can never find a silk the color of the sea."

He looked at the sea, seeing how the light went into the clear waves and became blue, then green, then dark, losing itself in the limitless mass of water. "There's no end to it," he said, grimly. His father's body was never found: it disappeared into that vastness without trace.

She made no comment about his father; no sympathy, no painful reminders. Perhaps she'd forgotten whose son he was, or perhaps she was simply engrossed by the problem of the dye. But her silence was comforting. "No," she agreed quietly, "it goes on forever, like the sky. And carpets are flat. Well, I'll try to get the effect of the contrast instead." And she remained staring into the sea for a moment, absorbing the image of the red-brown octopus on the green stone. The shape she made against the field of the water suddenly seemed to him perfect, as precise in its concentrated stillness as a bird balancing itself against the wind. She stood there, human and graceful, and the treacherous color of the sea resolved into a contrast of silks.

"What's your name?" he blurted out.

Demetrias, she told him, absently; and he walked back with her to the Egyptian harbor, telling her about his boat and the colors of the fish he caught. She seemed to be listening attentively, though much later he'd decided that she was probably thinking about dyestuffs the whole time. He found that evening that he could remember exactly how she had stood, what she had said and the tone she had said it in, and above all the stillness of her face. He had fallen in love with pretty girls before; he fell in love with one or two afterward — but the memory of that stillness persisted to haunt him. He had thought, after that first meeting and on many, many later occasions, that the man who had that stillness focused on himself would have all that could be offered by any woman's love.

He thought of her now as she had been recently: going about the apartment dreamily, her eyes softened by contentment, absorbed by the absent, unseen cloak at the dyeworks. When he first married her and found that his passion was met only by dutiful acceptance, he had thought that perhaps that stillness had been destroyed by Pamphilos, or perhaps had never existed at all. But then he had seen it again, seen it many different times now, always for one or another of her projects at work. Never for him.

She had told him once, shortly after Meletios' birth, that she had married him because she was tired of the attentions of procurators and supervisors. "And you were the man I disliked least," she had told me. She had said it in a joking tone and thought she was giving him a compliment. *Perhaps she was,* he thought now. *She could have married Daniel, or half a dozen others — she had suitors enough. But she chose me, let me know that if I spoke, she would listen. So I lost no time in speaking, and now I'm a "lucky man." And I don't regret it; God forbid that I should ever have any wife but her. But simply to be the least disliked, when I . . .*

*I have nothing to complain of. Oh, I want another child and she doesn't, yet; she uses sponges and medicines and whatnot to prevent it — but she tells me what she's doing. I could even forbid it if I was willing to force her; I have no cause for complaint. The Scriptures command me to love her, but only tell her to obey. And obey she does. No one could say that she's undutiful, that she fails in any of her obligations. And she's under no obligation to love me, simply because I love her.*

He shook his head and went into the apartment building. Through the closed door of their room he could hear his wife's voice, asking Meletios about the day's encounter with the dolphin, and he could smell the charcoal of the fire, and octopus stew cooking there.

*But isn't she happy with me?* he asked himself, pausing with one hand on the door. *As happy as she'd be with any man? She doesn't dislike me, and she's fond of the child. Perhaps, in time . . . if we have time, if she's not caught in this business, and tortured, and destroyed. Oh God, what would I do if . . .*

*Aspar's deputy will be here in October. It's a long time to wait, but worth waiting for: the most dangerous time for her would be the last two months anyway, when the cloak and the plot are nearer completion, when the design of it is obviously wrong for the emperor, and more conspirators are involved. October. I'll go see the man as soon as he arrives — and Acilius Heraklas will learn that, slave or not, I won't let him make a tool of my wife.*

# ~III~

IT WAS THE TWENTY-THIRD of October when Flavius Marcianus, the trusted deputy of General Aspar, arrived in Tyre. He had ridden with Aspar's steward and his own escort from the estates in the Syrian mountains that he had come to discuss, doing the long journey in two days. It was late in the afternoon by the time he entered the city, so he went directly to the house in Tyre that Aspar had purchased along with the mountain vineyards. This house was in the "Old City," the sprawling town on the mainland facing the rocky promontory of the citadel. It was a fine building, but grown ramshackle: the plaster of its walls was crumbled in places, and the tiles on fountain and floor were cracked; some of the windows were broken, the paint was fading, and the rooms had a musty, disused smell. The butler who had been in charge of it writhed with anxiety as he showed Marcianus and the steward into the dining room.

The steward, who was a slave and had been sold, like the house, with the estates, glared angrily at the nervous butler, then looked unhappily at Marcianus. "I apologize, sir; on behalf of all the staff I apologize," he said. "No one has been to stay here since the old master died, God rest him. I did send ahead to tell this oaf to have the place cleaned up for Your Honor . . ."

"Oh sir!" cried the butler, wringing his hands. "Your messenger only arrived yesterday. I've done what I can, sir, but there are only three of us here . . ."

"It will do very well," declared Marcianus firmly. "I understand that there's been no money in the house and that it hasn't been worth keeping the place up for a master who lives in Constantinople: rest easy. My men are accustomed to far worse. Is there room enough for all the horses?"

The steward and the butler looked at each other accusingly. "How many horses?" ventured the butler at last.

"A hundred and twenty-five horses and twenty mules," Marcianus told him, smiling. "And a hundred men."

The butler looked dismayed. The steward glared at him as if to say, "I warned you there were horses!"

"If they can't all be put up here, make arrangements for them to stay somewhere else," suggested Marcianus. "A nearby inn, or as paying guests of other gentlemen sympathetic to His Excellency the general."

"Yes, sir . . . . I'll see what can be done, sir," said the butler, and bowed himself out. At the door, he hesitated and asked, "Would Your Eminence like some wine to wash the dust of the journey from your throat?"

"Thank you," Marcianus said, with a nod. "And see that you get some for my men as well." He sat down on the couch and began unfastening his sword belt.

"I don't see why you needed a hundred cavalrymen for a visit to Tyre," said the steward plaintively, sitting down on the opposite couch and holding on his lap the pack of documents he had nursed all the way from the estate. Ordinarily, he would have proudly refused to sit in the presence of his master's representative, but he was not used to long rides on horseback, and every bone in his body ached.

Marcianus waved off the objection, setting his sword on the dining table before him. He took off the leather cap he had worn during the ride and rubbed his temples. He was sixty, but the journey seemed not to weigh on him at all. He was a square, solid, muscular man; his straight gray hair fell in tangles over his forehead, damp with sweat, but his strong authoritative face was as alert as ever. "Bandits," he said laconically. "I feared we might meet some Isaurians on the way through the Taurus."

"The Isaurians never come this far south," said the steward. "You could have left your men at the estate."

Marcianus chuckled. "My friend, it's better to bring troops when they're not needed, than not bring them and find that you want them. Besides, what would they do on the estate?"

The steward bowed his head humbly, admitting to himself that he was glad that the soldiers were not running about *his* estates unsupervised. (He always thought of the estates as his own; the previous owner had spent most of his time in Tyre, and Aspar had never visited at all.) He did not much like soldiers, and Marcianus' men, though admittedly well disciplined, seemed to him a fearful pack of savages. They were enormous men, fair-haired, shaggily bearded, armored, and armed to the teeth; all the way from the mountains they had been either singing loud songs in Gothic and Thracian or laughing uproariously over unintelligible jokes and terrorizing the country people by their very appearance. What was worse, most were quite plainly Arian heretics. If they passed a church they didn't cross themselves, and they galloped past priests and even monks without a nod, leaving the holy men coughing in the dust. The steward was appalled by them. Marcianus himself, though, the steward admitted silently, was an acceptable master. A Thracian foreigner, unfortunately, and a military man, but a gentleman, a senator, and an orthodox Christian. Though he had a disconcerting habit of guessing what a man was thinking.

The butler reappeared with a flask of watered wine and two silver goblets. He bowed and poured the wine for Marcianus, then filled the steward's cup, giving his superior a beseeching look. The steward took a mouthful of wine. It was a red wine from his own estates, and he recognized the vintage; it swept, fruity and biting, down his throat, washing away the taste of dust. He relented and smiled at the butler. The butler, relieved, went back out to see about the arrangements for the men.

*How on earth will we manage to look after them all?* wondered the steward. *A hundred cavalrymen! Even if they sleep in the hayloft, we'll still have to pay for at least twenty of them to stay elsewhere. And the horses, dear God, where will we put all those horses?*

"Cheer up!" said Marcianus, smiling shrewdly at his companion. "We can probably finish our business with the prefect tomorrow. Leave one extra day to rest the horses and for any additional business that crops up, and then we'll be gone. We can afford the tavern bills for the men for that length of time." He drained his cup of wine and poured himself another. "And while we're here," he added, "the men can do some repairs on the house. I'll give the orders for it in a moment. Yes, Paulus, what is it?" — this last was addressed to his secretary, who had just come into the room.

"If Your Eminence pleases, there's a fellow here who wants to make an appointment to speak with you," said the secretary, in an apologetic tone. "How long are we staying, sir, and when could I tell him to come?"

Marcianus yawned and rubbed his face. "A fellow?" he asked. "What sort of fellow? Is he from the prefect?"

Paulus shrugged. "No. I asked. No, sir, I would say he was a tradesman of some sort, a well-off one. He didn't want to state his name or business, except that he thought it would be of interest to you. Shall I tell him you're too busy to see anyone?"

Marcianus shook his head. "No, tell him I'll see him now, and send him in. And if anyone else comes, Paulus, I plan to stay only a day or two, so tell them to come tomorrow evening or the following day."

Paulus bowed and left, and Marcianus added, with a smile at the steward, "If he wants to supply us with new windows or pavements, he's welcome!"

After a couple of minutes, the secretary reappeared, leading Symeon. Paulus bowed and went back to talk to the butler about arrangements for the men.

Symeon had not expected to be admitted to Aspar's deputy that evening. He had put on his best clothes to impress the underlings and obtain an early appointment with the great man, but still he felt unprepared for the meeting. The mob of soldiers drinking in the courtyard had only encouraged him, but the short walk through the dim corridors of the great, creaking, dusty house had been long enough to fill him with terror. He looked about the dining room, frantically concentrating on his surroundings to keep the fear at bay. A worn carpet of local weave in dark red and dirty gold; a crack across the plaster on one wall; a dusty, dark painting of a hunting scene; the cedarwood table with the sword and goblets resting on it; the two men. He bowed deeply to both.

Marcianus in turn was studying Symeon with the quick intelligence with which he observed all who had dealings with him. The impression he received was of a vigorous young man of some substance. Symeon had trimmed his beard on hearing that Aspar's deputy had arrived, and had combed his hair and scrubbed the purple stains off his fingers. He wore the cloak Demetrias had given him as a wedding present: wool dyed scarlet, with a pattern of blue swallows spiraling up the edges; two silk tapestry rondels on the shoulders showed, blue and white on a green sea, a boat. His bow was one of respect that stopped well short of abasement, and he hesitated a moment, wondering which of the two confronting him he should address.

*A well-off tradesman?* Marcianus thought. *Perhaps. One with a shop and a few men under him. He regards me as his superior, but he expects to be received. Dark as an Egyptian — does some work out of doors. I'll be bound — master mason, perhaps, or horsebreeder. Sturdy-looking fellow — would make a good soldier. By his clothes, though, he has money. That cloak would cost a soldier three years' wages at the least. But he's frightened — resolute, carrying it well, but afraid. Why?*

"Your Eminence?" asked Symeon, addressing Marcianus.

Marcianus smiled and leaned forward slightly. "I am Flavius Marcianus, *domesticus* of the most distinguished Aspar. What is your business, friend?"

Symeon stared at Marcianus, realized that this would be considered rude, and stared at the table. "Your Eminence," he said, slowly, "I . . . there is a very serious matter which I thought you should know about. I didn't mean to disturb you on your arrival when you'd be tired after your journey, I only meant to make an appointment . . ."

"If I felt too tired to receive you now, I'd have told my secretary to make you an appointment for some other time," said Marcianus patiently. "Come, fellow, what is it?" *And it's something unusual for the man to be so afraid. Not just a mason or maker of windows, then. What?*

Symeon looked uneasily at the steward. "Your Distinction, I have some information," he said, "some — political information worth lives. Is this gentleman . . . ?"

Marcianus looked at him evenly for a moment, one finger tapping slowly on the table. *An informer,* he thought, with a shade of disappointment. *Well, well, I wouldn't have thought it of him. Still, with things as they are, I must take information wherever I can get it. Particularly if it's "worth lives."* "What sort of information?" he asked.

Symeon flushed slightly and swallowed. He felt suddenly that he had been an idiot to come. But it was already too late to back out.

"A secret the conspirators would kill to protect," he said quietly, "which might be of great importance to the state, and of great use to your patron, the most distinguished Aspar. And I would prefer to speak to Your Excellency in private."

Marcianus stared at him for another moment, then looked over at the steward. "Sir," he said politely, "please leave us a moment — and advise Paulus that I do not wish to be disturbed."

The steward rose to his aching legs, bowed unsteadily, and, with a disapproving look at Symeon, left the room.

Marcianus rose, picked up his sword belt from the table, and drew the sword from its sheath. Symeon stepped back, but Marcianus merely laid the sword back on the table, though he kept one hand on its hilt. "Now," he said, in a mild tone, "we are private. It is only fair to warn you, though, that I am the loyal servant of His Sacred Majesty, the emperor Theodosius, and I will hear no suggestions of treason."

Symeon caught his breath. "I want to prevent treason to the emperor," he said bluntly. "That's one of the reasons I've come."

Marcianus' eyes narrowed slightly and he sat down, leaving the drawn sword on the table. He held his face calm, but he could feel the cool jolt of excitement. Treason against the emperor, by an enemy of Aspar!

*It may not be true*, he warned himself. *Yet it feels —* "Speak, then," he told Symeon, quietly. "What is your name?"

Symeon hesitated again. Though he was afraid of the possible consequences of Nomos' treason, his first concern was still the safety of his own family. He was determined to reveal nothing, not so much as his name, without a guarantee that Demetrias would be unharmed — preferably an oath to that effect, and preferably expressed in writing so that he would have some recourse if his ally betrayed him. "Before I speak, sir, I need assurances from you," he said evenly.

"Protection?" asked Marcianus. "Or money?" Even as he asked, he answered himself silently: *Protection. The man's afraid — and he doesn't look like a man about to ask for money.*

"Protection," answered Symeon, and then, in a rush, "but not for myself — that is, not just for myself. There is another person involved, sir, unwillingly involved in the conspiracy itself. I must have your promise that you will protect that person."

"Tell me what the matter is, and I will see if it is possible to protect him."

Symeon shook his head. "I can't risk betraying this person into danger by what I have to say: I'm above all bound to protect . . . them. First swear to me that no harm will come to us."

Marcianus leaned back in his seat. "I do not swear oaths lightly," he said sharply. "How can I promise anything when I don't know who this friend of yours is or what he's done?"

*So he doesn't swear lightly,* thought Symeon, watching the strong suspicious face. *Good.* "The person involved has done nothing but obey those sh . . . those in authority. And that obedience was enforced by threat of punishment. I can swear to that by the Holy Spirit."

"And can you swear that it would be within my power to protect you?"

"You have troops," Symeon said flatly. "You could do it."

Marcianus sighed, studying Symeon. *I have troops — but using them against people "in authority" would be very complicated. If the fellow's honest, however, and if there really is a conspiracy against the emperor, it would be worth it. The man seems honest; I like the way he states his demands straight out — and yet it's a heavy demand, that I commit myself to buy before I know the cost.*

"If your patron knows what I have to tell you," Symeon said slowly, when the silence was drawn out, "he can prevent treason to the emperor. Sir, I don't want this plot to succeed, I want you to stop it. But I can't speak unless I know I'm not betraying anyone I'm obliged to guard."

Marcianus regarded Symeon for another moment: then he nodded. *Reasonable enough.* "I swear by the Holy Spirit," he said, slowly and solemnly, "and by the head of the emperor Theodosius Augustus, that, if what you say is true, and insofar as it lies within my power or influence, I will protect you and your friend. Does that content you, or shall I put it in writing?"

Symeon let out his breath unsteadily: he had been given more than he'd hoped for. The terms of the oath had been the strongest possible. To break an oath by the Holy Spirit and the emperor's head was both blasphemy and treason. But he merely said quietly, "I would prefer it in writing, sir."

Marcianus nodded, rose, glanced about, and rummaged in the

pack of documents the steward had left by the couch until he found parchment and pens. He wrote a few lines and extended the parchment to Symeon with a quizzical look.

Symeon took it and read it laboriously: "I, Flavius Marcianus of Thrace, did swear the strongest oaths to protect" — a blank space — "and" — another blank — "against the revenge or malice of their enemies, to the limits of my means."

"We will fill in the names when you think it appropriate," said Marcianus dryly. "And, obviously, if what you say is false, my oath does not hold. If it is true — well, you may ask my men, and they will tell you that I am a man of my word. Are you contented?"

"I am, sir," replied Symeon. He could ask for no more.

"Then proceed."

Symeon still hesitated, staring at the worn carpet and gathering his thoughts. "Sir," he said at last, "my wife is a weaver at the imperial silk manufactory. She is very skilled and is often given important commissions for the court." (Marcianus glanced again at Symeon's cloak, then smiled to himself, revising the estimate of wealth.) "In August she was summoned by the procurator, Marcus Acilius Heraklas. He ordered her to weave a cloak, a purple cloak, which he said was for the emperor. My wife recognized at once from her experience that it was not." Symeon hesitated, licking his lips, wondering if this official would blame Demetrias for yielding to treason.

"But the procurator, Heraklas, insisted that she weave it nonetheless," said Marcianus.

"Sir, she had to agree to weave the thing. She's a state slave and a woman, and the prefect is friendly with the procurator: there was no one to appeal to. What could she do? He made it clear he'd have her flogged for insolence if she disobeyed."

Marcianus nodded slightly. "I can see that she had no choice then but to agree; have no fear. Why didn't she believe it was for the emperor?"

"She says it's the wrong size," Symeon answered immediately, "and the wrong kind of pattern. And the procurator insisted that she weave in strict secrecy, and refused even to sign the authorization for the silk; she knew at once that he was demanding something criminal. But when she questioned it he threatened her."

"So, who does she believe the cloak is really for?"

Symeon snorted. "It's not just a question of 'believe': she *knows* who it's for. After she'd begun work, she challenged the procurator on it, and he admitted that it was for Nomos." He took a deep breath and tried to think how to continue, but couldn't. What he had said, now that he had finally said it, seemed almost nothing. He felt baffled and ridiculous and stood staring angrily at the carpet.

"And you want protection for your wife," said Marcianus after a minute.

Symeon looked up and saw that, though the officer's face was frozen in its stern expression, it still somehow burned with an excitement so intense that it showed in every hair. He felt weak with relief: what he had said, slight though it was, was evidently enough. "Yes, sir," he whispered. "If she were caught with the damned thing they'd torture her to death."

"Possibly," said Marcianus. "Yes." He paused, staring at Symeon without seeing him, his face set and bright. He had heard that Nomos and Zeno had quarreled with their former patron, but the news had seemed useless to his patron and to himself. Chrysaphios' friends were now his enemies, but Chrysaphios himself remained, left in his stranglehold on the emperor, and whoever was appointed master of arms and whoever master of the offices would necessarily pose no danger to the chamberlain. Aspar and the army would remain powerless and idle, and the empire's gold would continue to buy from the Huns a peace that should have been enforced by the sword. But now, perhaps there was hope after all. "Heraklas — he's from Bithynia, isn't he?" Marcianus asked, testing the pattern of the conspiracy. "A branch of the Acilii own land there. I believe I had heard that one of them was an adherent of Nomos, and was given some position in the East through his intercession. And Philippos the prefect is a Constantinopolitan and another friend of Nomos, one of his wife's relations. Yes. Well, fellow, I think my oath will have to be kept. Give me the paper and I'll put your wife's name in."

Symeon handed him the parchment, and Marcianus took his pen out and dipped it in the ink. "Your wife's name?" he asked expectantly.

"Demetrias, sir."

"Demetrias. And yours?"

"Symeon, sir. A purple-fisher. We have a little son, too, sir."

"I will take the son as included in the oath." Marcianus handed the parchment back to Symeon. He sat calmly, but still the great excitement burned, and it was only with the greatest difficulty that he held himself still. *Nomos plotting treason!* he thought, joyfully. *And I'd stake my sword on it that Zeno's in it too — and if we can catch him, we're back in power, back in command — and back in Thrace fighting those thrice-damned Huns who slaughtered my own people. Please God, let us catch them!*

He grinned at Symeon wolfishly. "Sit down, man," he ordered. "Have some wine, and we can discuss what to do."

Symeon sat down on the couch the steward had vacated. Marcianus gave him another fierce grin and handed him the steward's goblet, which was still half full of wine. "You did very well to come to me," he said. "You're a slave of the state? The emperor is fortunate in your loyalty."

Symeon's answering smile was wary. He took a sip of the wine, studying his new ally. *I think I can trust him,* he decided. *He's a straightforward man; he wouldn't swear lightly, but he'll keep his oath.* He felt a sudden wave of relief, still wavering after the long tension, but real. The danger was over; disaster could be averted after all. "What will you do?" he asked.

"I will write to His Distinction General Aspar tonight, and send the letter by my fastest courier. But I think, beyond that, we can do nothing — yet." Marcianus smiled again. "The cloak on a loom in Tyre, with a weaver's word that the procurator admitted it was for Nomos, is one thing. The cloak dispatched to Nomos by the procurator of Tyre, with letters from himself and the prefect, is another thing altogether. It would be enough to have Nomos arrested, and probably his friends with him. Your wife must finish it."

Symeon jumped up, the faint trust and uncertain relief turning to anger. "She risks everything every moment she works at the damned thing!" he exclaimed. "We need to get out of it now!"

Marcianus held up his hand restrainingly. "I will find some excuse to stay in the region, with my men, until it is finished. If your wife is threatened I will intervene at once. And I will try to make certain that she is not threatened. Don't you see, if we move while the cloak is still in her hands, it will be difficult to keep her out of it?"

Symeon hesitated, then, reluctantly, nodded. He sat down again, heavily. It was not over, after all.

"Good," said Marcianus, and gave a short, barking laugh. "When will it be finished?"

"About Christmas time, sir. Possibly a bit before. She's been working very hard."

"Christmas — well, I can stay here until then." He grinned again. "Raise problems with the prefect, and then negotiate to buy or sell house or lands in the province — yes, it won't be hard to delay here for two months. Does your wife know you came here?"

"No, sir," replied Symeon. "I didn't want to alarm her. She is very much afraid of the procurator, and only wants to finish the cloak and escape from him."

"Well, then, change nothing, tell no one. You have my promise of protection; keep the paper safe, and don't come back here unless you are threatened. If the prefect is cautious this house may be watched. My employer is not much trusted by those presently in authority."

Symeon nodded, stood, and drank off the wine. He set the goblet down.

"You can take that with you," said Marcianus, indicating the cup. "A pledge of my good will."

Symeon looked at it, then shook his head. "I don't want to explain how I got it, sir. I hope that . . . "

"You can trust me," replied Marcianus, smiling, when Symeon broke off. "Good luck — and remember, tell no one."

When Symeon had gone, Marcianus sat for a while longer in the empty room, considering him. *Honest and straightforward,* he decided, *loyal to the emperor and to his own family, with the sense to see how best to serve both and the initiative to act on it. He must have considered carefully before coming to me. He was impatient enough to see action, but he'd already made himself wait some months for a suitable ally. And he's not interested in money or he would have taken the goblet. Well, he may not be rich, but purple-fishers aren't poor, either, that I've heard: he's unlikely to accept a bribe to betray me. And he's not overly susceptible to threats or he wouldn't have come at all. Yes, a good man, and one I can safely rely on. Though he made it plain enough that his first loyalty is to his own, his wife and his family. And can I blame him?*

Marcianus sighed and turned the silver goblet between his hands;

his eyes, fixed on the gleaming metal, did not see it. He had had a wife and son of his own once. He remembered when he had been Symeon's age, recently married with a baby son, a young officer newly attached to the staff of Aspar's father, Ardaburius. Yes, he would then have preferred his wife and child to any emperor; probably he would still, if they were alive. But they were gone, and that ardent, arrogantly happy young officer with them: the daughter who remained to him could never weigh so heavily. Aspar's quiet gray deputy had to content himself with other loyalites. He had his oaths of allegiance to guard, to Aspar, and to the imperial house, and he had his private loyalty to his homeland, to Thrace — a province battered by invasion even when he was growing up in it, but then still strong, still fortified, still Roman. Now the Huns held half of it and half lay deserted and in ruins. Only the embassies crossed it, bringing gold to King Attila of the Huns, who had destroyed it. What did Marcianus' family — the son dead fighting the Huns, the mother dead grieving for him and her own slaughtered kindred — what did any private loyalties matter in that great devastation?

*Lord God, Master of the Universe,* he prayed silently, closing his eyes and setting down the goblet, *grant that this matter turns out fortunately: that the conspirators are brought down, the emperor guarded, and that my general is placed again in charge of armies. Bring us back to Thrace, and this time, Lord, give us the victory; we have suffered long enough in bitter defeat and worse peace.*

He sighed again, then rose and went to arrange with his secretary the lengthened stay in Tyre.

In the third week of November, the procurator Heraklas received a letter from Constantinople. As soon as he saw the seal he sent for the prefect, who, in turn, excused himself from the session of the city council he had been observing and came at once.

When Philippos entered the office Heraklas was sitting at his desk reading the letter, a worried frown on his face. He looked up quickly. "Oh, there you are!" he exclaimed, setting the letter down; then, to his secretary, "Go out and make absolutely certain that we're not disturbed."

When the door had closed, Philippos walked quickly round the desk and looked over Heraklas' shoulder at the letter. "It's from *him?*" he demanded sharply.

"Of course," said Heraklas, testily. "Would I have asked you to come if it was some stupid order for purple? It had the private seal on it — but it's not good news. Go ahead."

Philippos picked up the letter and read it. It was meant for him jointly with Heraklas — Nomos never sent any treasonous correspondence directly to Philippos, who was aware that his secretary gossiped. It was also written in oblique terms, was unsigned, mentioned no names, and was sealed with a special, private seal that could, if necessary, be destroyed: Nomos understood thoroughly how to conduct an intrigue.

To my esteemed friends in Tyre, very many greetings. The business we have discussed is in a delicate position. Our extravagant friend, having concluded the first part of a new investment in the north, began to look about at home for new means to finance himself, and, for one reason or another, has been looking into some of my affairs. I can assure you, my friends, that I and mine know how to conduct ourselves, but our business has naturally involved a number of dealers by now, and I fear that they are not all as discreet as I could wish. I am very concerned that our extravagant friend may soon be in a position to interfere. I have been investigating the possibility of distracting him with a crisis in his northern interests, but I can place no reliance on my contacts there, who eat money and do nothing in exchange. It is a very precarious position for us, and it is desirable that our deal be concluded as quickly as possible. Moreover, I have heard that an associate of an old Gothic acquaintance has unexpectedly decided to remain for a time in Tyre. His residence there may be unconnected with our concerns, but he is a man noted for his shrewdness and I distrust him. If we are not to lose all our profits we must act soon. Therefore, please send the consignment I requested with all convenient haste.

Philippos in turn frowned at the letter. "The business" was treachery; "our extravagant friend" was the chamberlain Chrysaphios; and his "investments in the north" referred to his treaties with the Huns. "The consignment" was the purple cloak, in which Nomos expected to appear before army and Senate when the emperor was overthrown.

"Who does he mean by this 'associate of a Gothic acquaintance'?" asked Heraklas, still frowning.

"Flavius Marcianus," Philippos said sourly, "Aspar's *domesticus*.

67

You should have understood that — I've complained about the man often enough this past month. But I think His Excellency is on a false track there — Marcianus has been trying to buy some crown lands on behalf of his patron, the legal position is fiendishly complicated, and the man's determined to have the best of the bargain. He's shrewd, I'll give him that, but I don't think he knows anything about our business. Still, I don't like the sound of this at all."

"Nor do I," agreed Heraklas, vehemently. "Why would Chrysaphios start investigating His Eminence? Has someone informed already?" He tried not to remember the chamberlain's disdainful, knowing eyes; tried not to picture them scanning reports on Nomos and his "consignment" in Tyre.

"The letter doesn't imply that," returned Philippos. "It sounds more like the creature was just looking around for estates to confiscate to pay for a new treaty with the Huns. He's quarreled with His Excellency; His Excellency is rich; he can afford to rob His Excellency. It's happened to plenty of others." He folded the letter and set it down. "How soon can we send him the cloak?"

Heraklas lifted his hands helplessly. "The last time I asked, the weaver said she'd have it the week before Christmas. We could try to speed it up — but last time I looked there seemed a lot left to do."

"Well, have your weaver summoned and tell her to get on with it!" said Philippos. "These people can always speed things up if they want to."

Heraklas still looked doubtful. "She's an obstinate thing. And don't forget, she knows who it's for. I'm afraid that if I threatened her she'd talk."

"Then don't threaten her! Bribe her! Try to get the cloak to Constantinople by the end of December. If it's finished in two weeks we could send it off by courier and he'd have it at the beginning of January."

"I'll have her summoned," Heraklas said, "but two weeks — I don't think it's possible."

Philippos looked at him with undisguised contempt. *Dabbler,* he thought again. *If we're caught, his first thought will be to save his own neck: he'll inform on all the rest of us. He has no discretion; even some silly factory weaver managed to get the truth from him. And I'd stake my fortune on it that she is young and pretty, and he let out all our secrets trying to get her into bed.* "You'd think you could manage some female slave better than that," he observed bitingly.

Heraklas' dark eyes glittered, but he said only, "If you're so good with slaves, you can talk to her yourself."

*Does he think that will silence me?* wondered Philippos. *That I'll be afraid to appear in my true colors before some factory slave who could already inform on my patron?* "I'll be delighted to talk to her," he told Heraklas. "Tell your secretary to send for her at once."

For the secretary to send a runner to the factory, the runner to reach Philotimos, Philotimos to tell Demetrias, and Demetrias to reach the prefecture, took more than half an hour. Heraklas, after a few lame attempts at conversation, worked ostentatiously at his desk; Philippos stared moodily out of the window, worrying about his patron. *The best man of our age,* he thought: *nobly born, bred to virtue and prudence, wise, brave, ten thousand times more suited to empire than that useless nonentity who wears the purple now. He'll need the cloak. He'll have to appear before the senate and the people just after they've heard that Theodosius is dead.*

Philippos had been told the whole of Nomos' plan. He remembered vividly how his patron had explained it to him, taking him privately to a concealed room in his Constantinopolitan mansion, showing him the secret letters and plans. "I haven't told this to anyone else," he had said, smiling with that particular, gracious warmth that Philippos had always loved in him, "but you, my dear Marcellus, you I can trust. And I want you to be certain in your mind that the business is well conceived and will succeed." And he had detailed it. There were two young men who had been unfairly dismissed by the chamberlain from the imperial guard and then ruined by the chamberlain's creatures: they had agreed to murder the emperor as he went riding in the grounds of the palace in return for a sum of money and a promise that they would be allowed to escape. Nomos' friend Zeno was commander of the palace guard. He was slowly, cautiously, to select men who could be trusted as part of the plan, then arrange for them all to be on guard on the same day. The assassins would be permitted to disappear in the confusion surrounding the murder, and nobody would ever catch them or connect them with Nomos.

When the city heard that the emperor was dead there would undoubtedly be a panic — and in the middle of that panic Nomos would

69

appear, wearing the purple cloak and claiming that the dying Theodosius had ordered it sent to him. Zeno's men would confirm this, and Nomos would be acclaimed Augustus; his first act would be to have the chamberlain Chrysaphios put to death. *Oh, if only I could be there!* Philippos thought ardently. *I can see it: the people crowding the hippodrome and the Augusteion market; the senators packed in the senate house; the consistory panicked in the palace; the palace guards angry and mutinous — and then* he *appears, dressed in the purple. All eyes are on him as he enters the senate house; they whisper to each other, seeing, beyond all expectation, an emperor, and one worthy of the Roman state. He takes his place at the tribunal — he speaks. They listen in silence. Then — "Long live Nomos Augustus! Reign forever!" They would acclaim him; they would have to acclaim him, if he appeared before them dressed as an emperor.*

*But if he appeared dressed like any other gentleman, or in a cloak stolen from Theodosius' body, the idiots might give the diadem to anyone. He must have the cloak. And this imbecile Heraklas has bungled even that.*

The secretary admitted Demetrias and bowed himself out again.

Demetrias stood motionless, her back to the closed door, tightly wrapped in her cloak. She held the rose-colored wool tightly against her, not so much for protection now as simply for warmth. She was chilled and exhausted. The shed at the dyeworks was unheated, and the November days were cold: despite wearing three tunics the damp chill soaked into her bones. She had asked the dyeworks supervisor for a brazier to provide some warmth, but he had put off the request, claiming that the smoke might discolor the new dyes on the silk. She had been working long hours since she was first given the commission and was sleeping badly, tormented by anxious nightmares of discovery and loss. The urgency, the need to finish the thing and get rid of it, seemed to grow with each day; she was reluctant to take time to eat, to visit the public baths, to rest. The cloak's tapestry panels were finished now and the glowing mass of purple and gold was mounting quickly up the loom — but, by that same token, the excitement of creation was over. The cold, the strain, the exhaustion all meant that she constantly made mistakes in the weave, so that she was continually unraveling a section already completed and doing it over. She looked pale, unwashed, and her eyes were shadowed.

*Young*, thought Philippos, with bitter triumph, *and yes, she's pretty, though a bit faded and unwell*. He glanced at Heraklas. The procurator nodded back and waved his hand in a "be my guest" gesture.

"Well, woman," said Philippos gruffly, "do you know who I am?"

She blinked. "No, sir," she replied, in a low, humble voice. "Excuse me my ignorance."

"I am Marcellus Philippos, prefect of Syria Phoenice. I understand that you have been entrusted with a special commission by my colleague Heraklas. I am concerned that the work is not yet finished."

Demetrias looked at the floor. *God rot them*, she thought, wearily. *Perish them and the miserable cloak. What am I to say to that? Don't the lunatics have any idea how long it takes to do a tapestry in a fine silk weave?* "Your Honor," she said, evenly, "I have been working on this commission from dawn to dusk since I was first appointed to it. I have taken only the briefest time off to eat or rest. If I work longer hours, I promise Your Wisdom that I will only make more mistakes, and the result will be that the cloak will take still more time to complete."

Philippos stared at her in open disbelief. "When were you given this commission?"

"The tenth of August, Your Excellency."

"You have been working for three and a half months. That seems a long time for a skilled weaver to work from dawn to dusk on one cloak."

She sighed. "Your Excellency, when His Eminence the procurator first gave me this commission, I told him it would take six months. By modifying the design I managed to reduce the time to four and a half or five months. I say now that I could finish it in four weeks, which is under the minimum time I allowed myself. Your Excellency, tapestry is slow work; God himself can't hasten it."

"Tapestry?" asked Philippos, with a startled glance at Heraklas.

Demetrias stared at the floor and repeated the specifications that had run steadily as water through her dreams: "Two tapestry panels representing Victory Crowning Alexander and the Choice of Herakles; a gold border and scroll design on the edges, and the shoulders to be worked in a circular pattern with gold; the whole to be five feet three inches long."

"Well, how was I to know it would become so urgent?" said Heraklas defensively. "We wanted it to look splendid and it will."

"You should have thought!" exclaimed Philippos. "You should have realized that we had to get this out of our hands as quickly as possible, and any fool knows that tapestry takes months; you could have ordered a simple patterned weave and had the cloak in a few weeks!" He turned back to Demetrias. "Cancel the tapestry."

She looked up and flushed red. *God rot it*, she had thought only a moment before — but the thought of the lovely thing destroyed now was unendurable. Her Victory was alive, gull-winged, hovering in the brilliant air; the mountain before Herakles shone with rain. Cancel the tapestry? It would die, and scream to her in dying. "But I've finished the tapestry, sir," she cried, stammering a little with urgency. "You can't cancel it! Sir, there's only the plain-weave left to do. It will be far quicker to finish what I've begun than to go back and start again from nothing!"

He looked at her in surprise. "Finished it? How much do you have left to do?"

"About half the body of the cloak, sir. If Your Excellency is in a great hurry now, I could leave out the pattern on the shoulders. It could always be embroidered in afterward. The scroll pattern on the front border has to be woven now; I've already put it in alongside the tapestry — but it isn't too much trouble, I have it down to a few heddles at either end, and it goes quickly. If we leave out the pattern on the shoulders, it will cut ten days off the time to complete the cloak."

*My God, the woman's as professional as they come,* Philippos thought angrily. *You couldn't ask for more efficiency or skill. And that imbecile Heraklas still couldn't manage to get a proper cloak commissioned! He should never have been brought into this plan at all; we should have arranged to buy some illegal purple elsewhere, and had the cloak made privately.* "So you could finish it in . . . two and a half weeks if you leave off this pattern?" he asked the weaver sharply.

"Yes, Your Eminence. Unless . . . I am very tired, sir: I've been working as hard as I can, and it's told on me. I make more mistakes than I usually do. But even so, not more than three weeks."

"If you finish it in two and a half weeks," said Philippos, "you will have a piece of gold for each day's weaving. If you exceed the time,

72

I will take away one piece of gold for each day, but if you better it, I will double the sum. Go back and try to finish it now — and tell your supervisor to send you some warmed wine; you look ill with fatigue."

Demetrias bowed and left. Philippos cast another contemptuous look at Heraklas. "Tapestry!" he exclaimed. "Mother of God!"

"I wanted it to look splendid," Heraklas repeated, guiltily.

Philippos snorted. "You wanted to make sure His Excellency remembered you — Choice of Herakles! That's what you wanted — that, and a good chance to bed that pretty little weaver."

"I haven't bedded her," Heraklas returned, affronted. "I simply had her work on the cloak."

"Well, she's worked better than you deserve; three and a half months to finish two tapestry panels and half a cloak is more than anyone can expect. Tapestry! My God!"

Demetrias left the prefecture feeling happier than she had for some time. She had thought for a few moments that the prefect's sharpness was directed at her, but had soon understood that its real object was Heraklas. And it had been clear from the manner of the two men that Heraklas was actually a very junior member of the conspiracy. *He won't get the reward he hoped for*, she thought, hugging the warm glow of vindication. *He hasn't managed his part of the plan as well as he should: he's shown himself a fool, and won't profit from what he's forced on me even if the plan succeeds.* She pictured again the prefect's anger, surely mirrored by some other anger far away in Constantinople; saw again the procurator's clumsily guilty response, and smiled.

But the warmth vanished. She had nothing to smile about. It was urgent that she finish the cloak. They were offering her large sums of money to speed up the work: the conspiracy must feel that the long wait had endangered it. And if the conspirators — powerful men, legally immune from the violence of the law — were anxious, how much more reason did she have to be afraid? *Oh God*, she prayed, silently, expecting no answer from heaven, *I'm so tired. How can I possibly get it done in time?*

It began to rain when she was halfway from the prefecture to the factory, a fine, cold rain blown in slanting from the sea. She pulled

73

her cloak farther over her face and plodded on. She had first to report back to Philotimos — but when she'd left the dyeworks, he'd been at the office there, ordering silks. There should be no need to go to the factory to find him, and she could start work again almost at once.

At the corner of the dyeworks she paused to glance at the sea: it was gray and white, choppy, dull with rain. Symeon's boat was drawn up on the beach and covered with tarpaulin — the sea had been too rough for him to go out that day. Probably he was in the boathouse with Meletios, working with the other fishers on repairs to boats or nets, talking and telling stories around a glowing brazier. Demetrias stood still for a moment, staring up the beach, then glanced back at the square, barnlike silk factory at the corner of the harbor. The building would be warm, she knew — Philotimos always had braziers set up in cold weather to keep the weavers' hands from becoming clumsy with the cold. The smoke from the charcoal could rise to the high roof without fear of its staining the silks. The weavers, too, would be warm, talking and telling stories, or singing together as they worked. Red Maria would have finished the tapestry panel of Christ giving sight to the blind — the curtains must have been sent off now. Demetrias found her eyes stinging, hot despite the icy rain on her face. *I'm like Eve, outcast from my own little paradise and alone. But I swear to God it wasn't for my own sin.*

*Don't be such an idiot,* she told herself, sternly. *It will be two or three more weeks, that's all. Yes, I hate that shed now, and the cold, and the silence, and being alone — but in two or three weeks it will all be over and things can be back as they were before.*

She turned and trudged into the dyeworks.

Philotimos was still in the office, arguing painedly with his colleague Eugenios about a batch of red silk. "But it's the wrong shade completely!" he was complaining as Demetrias came in. "It's the color of bloodstains, really! You left it to dry too long — yes, my dear! How was it?"

"He wants me to hurry it up," said Demetrias. "I'm to leave out the pattern on the shoulders and try to finish it in two and a half weeks."

"Two and a half weeks? Can you?"

"I think so." She had said all she needed to, but she remained a moment, staring bleakly at her supervisor. Desperate as she was to

74

finish the cloak, her flesh rebelled at returning to the cold shed, at being alone with the silence, the stink of purple, and the risks of treachery.

"You don't look well," said Philotimos, frowning at her.

"I'm cold," she replied. "Oh, the prefect was there. He said you should give me some warmed wine."

"The prefect?" asked Philotimos, frowning more. "Why was he there?"

"I don't know," she answered, wearily, "but I would like the wine."

"Of course . . ." Philotimos rose and touched her hand lightly. "My dear girl, you're frozen! Your fingers must be numb — you can't weave properly like that! Eugenios," to the dyeworks supervisor, "can we put a brazier in that shed?"

Eugenios looked doubtful. "In a small space like that?" he asked. "The purple's still new, and hasn't set firmly — the smoke might brown it."

"My dear friend, not in only two and a half weeks! It would simply help cure it. And Demetrias must keep her fingers supple if she's to weave properly, eh? Here, the cost of the charcoal will be borne by the silk factory."

"Very well, very well!" said Eugenios, with the air of a man making a great concession, though in fact his chief objection had been the cost of the charcoal.

"And you give your men warmed wine two or three times a day, don't you?" continued Philotimos. "Can you give Demetrias some when they get their ration?"

"She only needed to ask," Eugenios said, irritably, as though he had been reproached for not thinking of it.

"There's a good fellow!" Philotimos exclaimed with forced heartiness. "Come, Demetrias, I'll see where we can put your brazier." He led Demetrias back to the shed muttering, "Greedy fool — grudges a cup of wine and a little charcoal, as though he didn't have piles of the stuff! *And* adulterating the dyestuffs! God give me patience with the man!"

Demetrias made no comment on this monologue. Philotimos and Eugenios had been fighting for twenty years. At the shed, she unlocked the door and they went in. The loom now glowed in the far corner. Philotimos, with his usual enthusiasm for fine work, went first to examine it. Demetrias sat down on her bench and nursed her cold hands under her armpits, too weary to take any notice. After a moment, she glanced at Philotimos and saw that he was still staring at the half-finished cloak and was now frowning deeply. He knelt and, using his hand, began to measure the cloak. Demetrias watched, too tired to speak or feel alarmed. She had always kept the shed door bolted when she was working and locked it carefully when she left: until this moment, no one except Heraklas and herself had seen the cloak; no one had been able to suspect. *But does it matter if Philotimos knows?* she thought. *He had to see it sometime. And he won't betray me.*

Philotimos finished measuring the height of the cloak and stood for another moment, staring at the tapestry panels. He turned to Demetrias. His face was unfamiliar with shock and pity.

"My dear," he said, in a low voice, "you should have told me."

"I didn't want anyone to know," she replied quietly. "The fewer people who know, the better. I just want to finish it and send it away."

Philotimos shook his head. "You don't understand. There . . . there was a fellow here last week asking questions. I thought at first he was just some gentleman-visitor, come to stare at the factory; I gave him the tour. Were these all the weavers, he asked me, or were there others somewhere else? Usually, no, I told him; but I had one woman now at the dyeworks, doing a special commission for the procurator which was to be a surprise for the emperor. And he was so interested that I began to wish I hadn't said anything. I found out afterward that he asked the workers about you, wanted to know your name and what the commission was. My dear, somebody else has guessed what this is; somebody else will act on it."

Demetrias did not move or speak: she merely sat, wrapped in her cloak with her arms around herself for warmth, and stared at Philotimos with eyes huge in a white cold face. *No wonder they were in a hurry,* she thought. *They already knew that someone suspects us.*

"The prefect was there this morning?" asked Philotimos after a long silence. "He's part of it?"

She nodded. She felt as though she had turned to ice. The fear that had crouched beside her every moment she worked on the cloak had sprung now, but she could feel nothing but the cold.

"We have no one to appeal to."

"No."

"Then we must finish it at once." Philotimos glared at the loom and repeated vehemently, "At once. In a week, if we can."

Demetrias shook her head, tried to speak, and found she couldn't. She pulled her cloak before her face, shaking with suppressed tears.

"You can't, I know," Philotimos told her gently. "My dear girl, you must have half killed yourself to do this much in such a short time. But let me help. You go back to your home when the other workers do this evening and have a good rest. I'll bring some lamps and work on it till midnight — it's good plain-weave, and I can do that as well as anyone. Then we'll get someone else to work from midnight till dawn, and you can come in the morning and work the regular day. The man who asked about it must have been told it would take six weeks at the least. He hasn't acted yet. Perhaps he needs to report to someone, or get some authorization to move. Perhaps he wants to wait until it's finished. Either way, if it's finished four weeks before he expects it to be, you'll be safe. We'll say it wasn't purple — we'll say it was red, and a cloak for the procurator, or a friend of his. It never was in the books at the prefecture, and I'll change my accounts. Nobody will be able to prove anything and you'll be quite, quite safe."

Demetrias shook her head. "What if they torture you?"

"Why should they torture me? You wove a red cloak for the procurator — a minor misuse of state funds, but nothing very serious. The accounts will all be in order. I'm a slave of great experience and undoubted loyalty. No one has ever heard me say a word against my masters. And, my dear," Philotimos put his hand on Demetrias' shoulder, crouching before the bench to look at her earnestly, "we would both say the same if they did put us on the rack. If there's nothing to be proved they'll let us go quickly."

Demetrias abruptly put her hands to her face. The cold was gone now, and her face felt hot and swollen, as though in a fever. "I wish you weren't involved," she whispered. "Don't bring in anyone else. They'd only be caught too; I don't want anyone else suffering."

Philotimos hesitated, torn between fear for Demetrias and fear at involving another of his weavers, then nodded. "Very well. But since I know now, I will do my part, till midnight. I'll be fresh and can work quickly, and you'll do better for a good night's rest. We can get it done in ten days."

Demetrias gave a laugh; the sound threatened to get out of control and she clapped a hand over her own mouth to stop herself. "The prefect promised me a gold piece for each day, up to two and a half weeks, that I worked on it, and double if I finished it early," she told Philotimos. "Do you want the money?"

"I'll take a few pieces," he replied, smiling. "You keep the rest. I'll have them bring a brazier at once. Now, you had better get to work."

Philotimos returned in the late afternoon, carrying a lampstand and a basket that contained his supper, some wine, and three lamps. He set up the lampstand beside the loom and lit the lamps from the brazier, which had been brought in almost immediately after he first left. The heat and light transformed the shed. The brazier had dried out the damp walls, bringing a scent of cedar through the old stink of purple; the lamplight glowed warm and comfortable on the rich colors of the loom. Philotimos sat down on the bench and Demetrias showed him the heddling arrangements for the scrolled border. Male weavers were common in some parts of the empire — in the linen manufactories and in Egypt they were indeed the rule. In Tyre they were unheard-of for wool and unusual for silk — but supervisors were nearly all male and had to know how to use a loom. Philotimos had learned from his father, who had been his predecessor as supervisor, as well as from his mother, who had worked in the factory, and he regularly assisted in completing urgent commissions. Most of the women, however, still swore that men were no use at anything beyond the simplest of patterns.

"I shall manage," said Philotimos, with a smile at Demetrias. "You go home and rest."

It felt strange to Demetrias to return from work while it was still light. When she reached the apartment it was empty: Symeon and Meletios were still at the boathouse. Demetrias sat down on the couch. There was no food in the storechest, the room had not been cleaned for weeks, and the fire was unlit. Laodiki had been doing all the cooking and shopping for the family since the end of August. Demetrias knew she should make the fire, but she could not stir from the couch. She again pictured Symeon and Meletios at the boathouse, and this time felt the stab of longing not for the warmth and comfort, but for them. In the short evenings and mornings before work she had had scarcely a word to spare them. Meletios had grown aggressive and bad tempered with her, wanting attention he couldn't have; she had become bad tempered back, and remembering it now, seemed to herself to have been angry with him continuously for weeks. Symeon had become increasingly sullen, withdrawing from her own withdrawal. Now she wanted to cradle her child; wanted, even, to hold her husband tight against her body.

She leaned over on the couch and closed her eyes. Behind the lids she saw the loom, the half-finished cloak, suspended as before against a wave of angry, dull gray and white sea. She did not open her eyes: she was used to these nightmares now. Sometimes a lion crouched behind the loom; sometimes she worked balanced on a high wall, trying not to slip; once she had woven a cloth with living snakes that struck at her hands until they were bloodied and black. Now, already half asleep, she pictured Philotimos working on it by lamplight. How kind he is, she thought with a sense of wonder; how kind Mother has been, to do my work as well as her own. How kind . . .

She was deeply asleep when Symeon and Meletios returned half an hour later, lying wrapped in her cloak in the cold, dim, dirty room. Symeon stared at her for a moment, then went and heaped some kindling in the fireplace. Meletios sat on the couch beside his mother. He did not try to wake her. Whenever he had complained to his father that "Mama's cross with me and it wasn't my fault," he had been told that "Mama is tired from working so hard on that cloak." Mama resting could only mean that she would be less cross.

Symeon lit the fire, then used a stick of the kindling to light the lamps. The gold light washed over the room. Demetrias' face looked paler than ever, framed by hair darkened by dirt and the softness of the light. Her skin looked muddy, bruised about the eyes, and she was sleeping with the shallow, almost soundless breaths of profound exhaustion. Meletios sat watching her with the expression of anxious misery only seen on children who don't know why their parents are angry. Symeon rumpled his hair, and the boy looked up quickly.

"It's all right," whispered Symeon, vaguely. He shook Demetrias' shoulder lightly, and, after a moment, she stirred and opened her eyes. She saw Meletios and smiled, then sat up and put an arm around him. Meletios at once pushed his awkward, elbowy five-year-old body into his mother's lap, put his arms around her neck, and gave her a wet kiss smelling of tar and paint. She smiled again and looked up at Symeon; the smile softened, the look of tenderness embracing him, too. She stretched up her other arm. Symeon sat down beside her, astonished, and for a moment they sat locked together on the couch, three people in the cold, dirty room.

"You're back early," said Symeon after a moment.

She nodded. "Philotimos is helping me finish it. I was summoned to the prefecture today and told that it must be done in two and a half weeks; we agreed to simplify the design. Then when I got back to the dyeworks, Philotimos offered to help, and he's going to work on it till midnight till it's finished." She stopped, savoring it: the warmth, Symeon's arm against her back, Meletios' weight in her lap, and all this while the cloak was being woven for her. "We should have it done in ten days," she told them. "Just ten days!" She turned her mind quickly from the thought of the "gentleman" who had asked about it, who knew her name and was waiting for something, some unknown, unpredictable chance, before acting.

Symeon stared at her, then smiled hugely. "That soon?" He hugged her. "Thank God!"

"Will that be before Christmas?" asked Meletios hopefully.

"Well before Christmas," returned Demetrias. "We can spend the whole festival exactly as we please. We'll have money, too. The prefect promised me thirty-six *solidi* if I had it done before two and a half weeks. At least, I think he meant *solidi*. He said 'gold pieces.' Anyway, I'm giving some to Philotimos for helping, but we can spend all the rest."

"Probably he meant *tremisses*," said Symeon. A *tremissis* was a third of a *solidus*.

"People usually mean *solidi* when they say 'gold pieces,' " objected Demetrias. "But whatever it is, it's a lot of gold."

Meletios sat up and began bouncing up and down with delight. "Will you buy me that trireme?"

His mother laughed. "If you still want it. You almost look pleased that I had to work on that cloak!"

He shook his head violently. "I hate that cloak!" he exclaimed. "I don't want you to work on one ever again!"

"I don't, either," she told him, with some feeling.

"You'll have to have the day off after it's done," said Symeon.

"Philotimos is sure to give it to you. If it's fair weather, we can go out in *Prokne*, sail down the coast, maybe, as far as Ptolemais . . ."

"Why would I want to go to Ptolemais?" asked Demetrias, smiling. She was prone to seasickness and her reluctance to come on Symeon's sailing expeditions was a standing joke.

"It's a fine city," said Symeon. "It would be a day out."

She laughed. "I know what I want to do when I've finished," she told him. "I'm going to go to the Baths of Eudoxia. I'm going to have the steam bath, and the plunge bath, three hot baths, and a cold one, and then a massage, with oil of myrrh, and I'm going to rinse my hair with hyssop. Then, if you like, we can go to Ptolemais — but only if the weather's calm."

He pictured her, naked and glowing from the bath and smelling of myrrh and hyssop, and felt an awkward surge of heat to the groin. "Even with a calm sea you'd smell of seawater by the time we got there," he told her.

"So much the better. Then I can have another bath."

"We can go to the baths now," said Meletios, bouncing up and down again. "Daddy said we'd need to wash; we've been painting Barak's boat all day, in the boathouse. I helped too."

"I need to cook supper," said Demetrias. "Unless Mother has it ready."

"We can have supper at the Isis," returned Symeon, getting into the spirit of things. "Your mother too. Come on, let's tell her and go."

*Ten days!* he thought happily, as he went out the door with his wife and son. *Ten days, and we're safely beached. After that, the storm can rage as it likes.*

Marcianus was handed a note by his secretary when he sat down to breakfast next morning. In clumsy, unpracticed letters, it said:

> To Flavius Marcianus, from the purple-fisher Symeon, many greetings. Honred sir, the cloke we talked about will be dun in 10 days, all going well. My wyf says the prefect had her summuned Y'day and sayd she was to hury. He wanted the disign simplefyed, and offred her money to finish quickly. I thank Yr. Honor for yr protecshun, and hope the informashun will be usefull. I will tell Yr. Honor what hapens when it is dun.

Marcianus gave the secretary an inquiring look. "This came — when?" he asked.

"Before dawn this morning," replied the secretary Paulus. He had been admitted into the full details of the plan, though the rest of the party had merely been told that Marcianus had been offered an opportunity to buy land.

"Who brought it?"

"The fisherman himself, sir. Petrus and Plinta were on guard, and I sent a few of the other men out to check the streets: no one was watching when he came. I warned the man to be careful if he comes again, and told him that the prefect has been having the house watched."

"Why didn't you have me awakened?"

The secretary gave a deprecating smile. "It was very early, Your Excellency. I did not wish to disturb you. The fellow had no objection to writing his message — though I don't think his work accustoms him to writing. He broke two pens."

"Surprising he can write as well as he does," returned Marcianus sharply. He liked Symeon, and the secretary's veiled contempt grated. "If the man comes again, wake me, however early it is," he ordered. "He is taking risks, and we've done nothing for him so far: at the very least he should feel he can get me out of bed."

The secretary bobbed his head. "I will remember that, sir." And he would; he never had to be told anything twice. Though his opinion of informing fishermen was, Marcianus noted, unchanged. Well, Paulus had a noble family, a good education, and no money: a certain degree of contempt for uneducated but well-off state slaves was to be expected. It was not significant. Paulus was, like his employer, a Thracian, and, like his employer, he had hopes that this scheme would open a way to the reconquest of his home. If Symeon could give them that, Paulus was more than prepared to be civil to him. "Will you send a reply?" he asked.

"I think not. It might draw attention to the man and put him at risk. That creature of Chrysaphios' who left last week, that spy — he hasn't come back, has he?"

"I have a report that he took a post horse at Berytus and went north, sir."

"Good. Headed back to Constantinople, as we thought. Well, with this new date for the cloak's completion, our fisherman and his family should be safely out of the affair before Chrysaphios' friend gets back and the battle begins." Marcianus tapped the letter on the breakfast table, frowning thoughtfully, then said, "Paulus, make me an appointment with the prefect in the morning eleven days from now. And double the watch on the prefecture, if you can do it discreetly."

"As you say, sir," replied Paulus, and bowed himself off to work.

"Invaluable fellow!" exclaimed Marcianus, to no one in particular. He began to eat his porridge, rereading Symeon's letter as he ate.

The last bit of weaving on the cloak was finished on the first of December, in the middle of the afternoon. Demetrias eased the shuttle through the last shed, pushed the weft down with comb and mallet, tied the purple silk off neatly, then leaned back to study her work. Five feet three inches long, two tapestry panels, and worked with gold. She drew one hand gently over the silk, feeling the smoothness, her eyes looking for any defects in the weave. There were none. The two vertical edges tapered and were already smoothed off; there remained only the job of casting off from the loom, tying off, and trimming the top and bottom. She gave a long sigh, stretched muscles cramped from hours of sitting and reaching up the loom, then loosened the tension on the warp and knelt to begin casting off.

*Finished,* she thought, tying the first threads together. *Finished. And Heraklas will go away in the spring, and Philippos as well, and whatever becomes of them, it will be nothing more to do with me. Finished. I'll go down to Ptolemais with Symeon and Meli tomorrow, if it's fine. Finished, thank God and all the saints! Whatever will I do with all that time?*

She smiled to herself, her fingers quickly and invisibly knotting the threads. Philotimos arrived two hours later to find most of the bottom edge already done.

Demetrias climbed to her feet, a radiant smile on her face. Philotimos looked at her, at the cloak, then stepped forward and kissed her soundly. "There's my girl!" he exclaimed; then, looking a trifle embarrassed at his own enthusiasm, he added, "You can hand it to them tomorrow morning."

Demetrias nodded, still smiling a blissful, sleepwalking smile. "I'll finish the bottom edge if you don't mind," she told him.

"By all means! I'll begin on the top."

Demetrias finished casting off the bottom edge at half-past six and went home; Philotimos tied the last top thread at eight. He trimmed the edges with a pair of shears, then shook the cloak out: the purple billowed and glowed in the lamplight, rich as the sea. He folded it carefully, then glanced at the empty loom with its collection of limp purple threads drooping haphazardly from the gaping tension sticks and rollers. Slowly at first, then rapidly, grabbing handfuls at a time, he pulled every thread off the loom and dropped it into the brazier. The silk shriveled blackly, giving off an acrid stink, then vanished into a dust of gray ash upon the coal. Philotimos stirred the brazier, then heaped sand on it to extinguish it. He set the folded cloak in his basket on top of his uneaten supper and went home, locking the shed behind him. Tomorrow the cloak would be in the prefect's hands, and there would be nothing at his factory to show that it had ever existed.

# ~IV~

THE PROCURATOR Heraklas and the prefect Philippos were both in the office next morning when Demetrias was admitted. The two men were bent over a map on the desk, arguing in undertones; both looked up with stern, angry faces as the weaver came in. She bowed, saying nothing, advanced to set on Heraklas' desk a covered rush basket, and backed off again to the door. Heraklas looked at Philippos, then, incredulous, opened the basket. He stared into it in silence. He glanced at the window, glanced at the door, then, slowly, almost clumsily, drew the cloak shining from the basket and spread it over his desk. The two men stared at it wordlessly. After a moment, Heraklas touched it with a hesitant, disbelieving gentleness. After another moment, Philippos began to smile.

He turned to Demetrias. "You finished it early," he observed.

"My supervisor helped me, sir," she replied evenly.

He eyed her suspiciously for a moment. She no longer looked ill; her cheeks were flushed, her eyes brilliant, and the morning sun gleamed on her hair. She stood with her hands folded, but one foot was already turned toward the door. *I wouldn't have blamed Heraklas if he had bedded her,* thought Philippos. *But she's obviously delighted to be done with it and us, and can't wait to go.* "Your supervisor is discreet, I hope?" he asked.

She bowed her head. "There is no more discreet or trustworthy man in Tyre."

"Very good," he replied, approvingly: her tone carried conviction. He stared again at the cloak, fingered the tapestry panels with his thick hands.

"It's beautiful," said Heraklas, reverently.

85

Philippos nodded. "I can see him in it," he replied quietly. "It will suit him." He looked back at Demetrias, then reached in his purse and counted out thirty-six gold *solidi*. He paused a moment — then added another four. With a smile, he pushed the little pile toward her. "Our thanks for your industry and speed," he said. "You may go."

Demetrias took the gold, bowed swiftly, and fled.

In the porch of the prefecture she hesitated — then thumbed her nose and stuck out her tongue at the statue of Nomos, picked up her skirts, and ran laughing down the street.

Flavius Marcianus, who was standing at the far end of the porch, smiled as he watched her go. "There goes our fisherman's wife," he observed to Paulus. "And I think I can see why he's so eager to protect her."

"A fine young woman," agreed Paulus solemnly, "with admirable political sentiments."

Marcianus laughed. "She's got rid of her basket, though. Our men are watching all the exits?"

"I don't think they'd miss a clerk spitting date stones out a window," replied Paulus with satisfaction, "much less anyone carrying a cloak."

It was the answer Marcianus had expected, and he nodded complacently. "Well then . . . is it time for my appointment with the prefect?"

"Your Honor will be decently early."

"Good." Marcianus strolled up to the entrance of the prefecture. He, too, paused before the statue of Nomos. *Holding a fortress,* he observed, *to commemorate his refortification of the Danube frontier, no doubt. As though the walls had kept anyone out!*

The bubble of complacency burst, and Marcianus stood still for a moment, letting the sudden wave of bitterness and hatred sweep over him. The Danube frontier was long broken and abandoned, the north of Thrace part of the kingdom of the Huns, and the new border a no-man's-land five days' ride in width. The great cities of Thrace lay ruined, their shattered walls standing in a wilderness of weeds, inhabited only by those too weak to be worth enslaving and too sick to flee. Marcianus remembered a journey he had made, not so very long before, to Sardica, his home and once a great city. Sardica had resisted the Huns and been punished for it: most of the buildings in the city had been reduced to rubble, and Marcianus had had to ask the starving beggars to identify for him the street where he had grown up. The house — the big, rambling, comfortable house where his brother had lived with his large family — had only one wall left standing, and the sweet chestnut tree that had for so long adorned the courtyard had been chopped down. For fuel, probably. The beggars must have been cold in their roofless ruins.

He had come to Sardica to bury the bones of his dead. But the city was full of bones and they all lay unmarked: in the rubble; in the profaned, half-burned, and ruined church; scattered for miles before the walls. He searched for a day or so in the ruined house, hoping to discover some trinket on one of the skeletons by which he could identify it — but it was hopeless. And his brother had probably not been in the house at all, but had, most likely, died fighting by the walls. As for the women and children, no one knew whether they were even dead, or whether they still lived somewhere, slaves to the Huns who had conquered them. And Marcianus' adored and only son, who had been given Sardica's garrison for his first command — surely he, too, had fallen somewhere by the shattered walls? Near the gate, if he'd lived so long, defending his city to the end. And by the walls the bodies had all been stripped before they were left to rot: there was no hope of any ring or familiar piece of armor to mark out one of those broken skulls, buried under the sticky and entwining bindweed. Marcianus had paid for a mass in the ruined church, given money to the beggars, and ridden south again, empty-handed.

No, the walls, Nomos' walls, had kept no one out. Only men could have done that, and no troops had been sent to Sardica.

*But I'll see you ruined too, Nomos!* Marcianus thought, staring up at the statue's bland face. *You and your damned treaties with the Huns, you and your stone walls and your cuts in troop strength! You and Chrysaphios both, you'll pay!*

"Your Honor?" asked Paulus, waiting at his elbow.

Marcianus shook his head and looked away from the statue. Passion must be kept secret. It could not be permitted to interfere with action, with the business at hand. He looked up again, and this time noticed the other statue, the one Nomos seemed determined to edge out. The Augusta Pulcheria held a cross, not a fortress, but her square plain face bore an expression of practical shrewdness. She had opposed the treaty with the Huns, Marcianus remembered: she had wanted to fight. The granddaughter of Theodosius the Great, and the only member of that house where the blood ran true. He smiled at her and patted her foot; she seemed to stare back with an expression of irritated disapproval, warning him to get on with the job. "Nothing," Marcianus told Paulus. "Run ahead and announce me to the prefect."

The prefect Philippos received Marcianus soon after he was announced, and seemed only a little out of breath. But Marcianus noticed the covered rush basket beside the desk almost before glancing at the prefect's face, and had to fight to keep the heat of excitement from showing in his own face. It was too soon to act. The conspirators must be allowed to incriminate themselves deeply and irretrievably. As long as he knew precisely where the cloak was, Marcianus was content to wait.

"Greetings, Your Eminence," he said politely, taking a seat opposite Philippos. "I trust you are well?"

"Very well, very well — and Your Excellency?" said Philippos, then, without waiting for the reply, he asked, "And has your distinguished patron made up his mind? Will he buy those lands? — I presume that's what you wanted to talk about."

Marcianus smiled genially. "That's why I came. But I'm afraid that my patron has written to say he cannot afford the down payment just at the moment. If it could be spread out over a few months . . ."

Philippos spread his hands. "I can't adjust it, I'm afraid. They're not my lands. I would have thought that a man of his wealth . . ."

"He has other commitments," replied Marcianus. "He has other lands that must be kept up, and his retainers' salaries to pay. Well, if you can't adjust the down payment, I must reluctantly let the matter be — for now, anyway. Perhaps in a month the situation will have changed — can I contact you then?"

Philippos began a secretive, excited smile — and suppressed the expression almost before his lips had curled. "I fear not," he said quietly. "I am leaving for Constantinople in a few days."

"What? I thought your appointment lasted till the spring!" Marcianus carefully refrained from looking at the rush basket.

"It does — but I've had bad news from home. My mother has been taken ill, and I must hurry back at once."

"Your mother? Indeed you must hurry back. I hope you will find your journey wasted — that is, that your mother is recovered when you arrive."

"A kind wish, Your Distinction." Philippos got to his feet and held out his hand. "Well, if we cannot resolve the matter of the lands . . ."

"Then I must wish you much health and a safe journey." Marcianus smiled and shook the hand firmly. "Thank you for all your assistance; I am sure I have tried your patience sorely."

"Not at all," returned Philippos. "Much health!"

Marcianus and Paulus waited in front of the prefecture while one of their attendants fetched their horses. "He had it in the office," whispered Marcianus in joyful disbelief. "And he must have convinced himself that he couldn't trust it to a courier, because he's made up some excuse about his mother's falling ill: he means to take it to Constantinople himself!"

"Do I call off the watch on the prefecture?" asked Paulus, grinning.

"No. I might be mistaken. But move the watchers away from the silk factory, and make sure we keep our eyes on Philippos. Send riders up the road toward Constantinople, and I'll write a letter to Aspar and advise him to have watchers set at that end, too. We'll catch him when he hands the cloak to Nomos and get the lot of them."

"Do we follow him when he goes north?"

"Yes — at a safe distance. Half a day's ride behind. Or —" Marcianus hesitated, frowning, then said, "I think you had better stay here in Tyre a bit longer, with a few of the men. Just to make sure there are no reprisals against our fisherman and his family."

Paulus' face fell. "What could happen to them now?" he asked.

Marcianus shrugged. "Chrysaphios' creature isn't back yet. I don't believe that anything will come of it when he does arrive — but I swore by the Holy Spirit that I'd protect that fisherman and his wife. I'll write the fellow a letter when we get home, explaining what we're doing, and recommending you to him. I know, I'm sorry you'll miss the show — but I must keep my oaths."

Paulus sighed. "Yes, sir," he said, morosely, and glared at the grooms who appeared round the corner with the horses.

When Symeon left the boathouse with Meletios after work the next afternoon, a slight drab figure was waiting for him, huddled against the harbor wall. The weather had closed in the evening before, and the harbor front now was cold and windy, deserted apart from the watcher. Symeon noticed the figure and stopped, staring uncertainly. The man detached himself from the wall and hurried toward him. A short distance away he stopped. "Your name is Symeon?" he asked. His face was vaguely familiar.

Symeon straightened his shoulders. "Yes," he declared, simply, as though it were a casual matter, though his heart had begun pounding the moment he saw that someone was waiting for him. "What do you want?"

"From Flavius Marcianus," replied the other, showing Symeon a letter; and Symeon remembered where he had seen the watcher before: among Marcianus' servants in the house in the Old City. Not, as he had momentarily believed, at the prefecture.

He took the letter. At once the servant walked past him, going away without another glance, as though they had not spoken. Meletios stared after him in confusion.

"Who's that?" he asked.

Symeon shook his head. "Never mind, Meli. Just some business . . . some business you don't have to worry about, about *Prokne*'s refit. Here, you go home: I'll see what the matter is and then come join you. Shouldn't take long."

Meletios, though still slightly puzzled, shrugged the problem off and ran down the harbor front. The wind gusted and he jumped into the air, spreading his arms so that his cloak billowed like a sail, and he half ran, half flew on toward the apartment building.

Symeon smiled after him, then glanced around: the street was still deserted. To be certain, though, he jumped down from the harbor wall and seated himself out of sight on the gravel at its foot before opening the letter.

Muttering the words under his breath, he read:

Flavius Marcianus to the purple-fisher Symeon wishes much health. I am confident that the project your wife worked on is in the hands of the prefect, who intends to leave for Constantinople with it tomorrow. I will follow him to be certain that his prize reaches its destination safely before we act; I will take most of my men with me, but will leave behind my secretary, Paulus, whom you have met. An agent of the chamberlain has been seen visiting Tyre, and in fact left for Constantinople just under three weeks ago. I do not know what, if anything, he may have discovered, though I believe that he may intend to return. If the cloak is not listed in the prefecture's records and is not actually in Tyre, even if he does return neither you nor your wife will be in any danger: I would, however, check with your wife that there is no evidence of the prefect's burden about the factory. Should any trouble arise, Paulus will have enough troops to serve in an emergency, and you can rely on him as you would on me. I hope to meet with you again when this is over, to thank you as now I cannot. When you've read this letter, destroy it.

Symeon smiled and looked up at the gray, windswept sea. *A good ally, Marcianus. Though probably Demetrias was right: we would have been just as safe without him. There's been no trouble. Still, he'll make certain no harm comes to the state and that the conspirators get what they deserve.* He crumpled the letter, considered throwing it into the sea, then decided it would be safer to burn it than to risk its being washed up by the next storm. He shoved it into his belt purse, leaped back up the sea wall, and followed Meletios' steps home.

The apartment was warm and bright and smelled of lentils and onions. Demetrias was sitting with Meletios on the couch, showing him the letters of the alphabet; she smiled at Symeon when he came in. He grinned back and went to warm his hands at the fire. While Demetrias finished giving Meli his lesson, Symeon dropped the letter on the charcoal and watched contentedly as it shriveled to ash. The momentary blaze was hidden by his back, the burned-leather stink masked by the smell of cooking, and the two on the couch never noticed.

"There's nothing at the factory anyone could use to find out about that cloak, is there?" he whispered to his wife, later that night when Meletios was asleep and they lay together on the couch, huddled under the blankets.

She shook her head, then leaned her forehead against his shoulder. "Philotimos altered the accounts as soon as he realized what it really was," she told him happily. "We're saying that the cloak was red, a private commission for the procurator. Even if someone does suspect, it's too late for them to make trouble now. It's over, and we're safe."

He kissed her hair. "Thank God for that. What are you going to do with all that money?"

She propped herself up on an elbow. "Well, I gave ten *solidi* to

91

Philotimos for his part in the work. And today I made an anonymous donation at the cathedral as a thanks offering. Three *solidi*. We spent four in Ptolemais yesterday. Four months' earnings, in one day!"

"I thought you deserved those earrings!" he whispered back happily. He had seen them in a jeweler's shop in Ptolemais: gold and lapis lazuli. He'd pulled Demetrias inside and made her try them on: the gold gleamed against the soft whiteness of her neck, and the blue contrasted with her eyes. He'd made her buy them. That was after lunch at the city's grandest tavern, and Meletios had his model trireme out of the change. Walking back to the harbor afterward he had noticed how all the citizens of Ptolemais looked at them twice: the beautiful, elegantly dressed woman; the healthy, bright-eyed little boy fondling his new toy. He had felt a spring come into his step, and walked with his head up, like the ruler of a city. These are mine, he'd wanted to shout, my wife, my son; they're well worth defending, and I've defended them.

She shrugged, smiling. "I suppose we had the money . . . that leaves twenty-three *solidi* — plus another nine I got for the leftover silk I traded back to the woolen factory . . ."

"Wasn't that dangerous?" Symeon asked, alarmed again. "It was purple silk."

She shook her head, laughing. "I had all the purple silk from the last commission too, the curtains for the palace. And Philotimos had a batch of red silk from the dyeworks he wasn't satisfied with: he gave me some of that. He didn't want to use it anyway. So I destroyed some of the purple, and traded back the rest and a lot of red: Daniel's accounts will match with Philotimos'. Besides the nine *solidi* for the silk I got some wool — it's Phrygian and top quality, too. We have saffron, orseille-blue, and a green: I can make Meli some good dolphins with that."

"Profit all round." Symeon kissed her again, and she accepted the kiss almost warmly, without a hint of her usual withdrawn resignation. "So, we're safe and thirty-two *solidi* richer. What are we going to do with all that money? Would you like to buy a slave to do the housework for you?"

"Tch." Demetrias shook her head. "What do we want with a slave to keep one room? Where would she sleep? No, we don't need a slave. But" — she pulled herself up — "if we add all this money to what we had saved up already we might be able to get a bigger apartment. It would be useful to have more space."

Symeon looked at her happily. Her eyes gleamed in the dimness, and her skin showed pale; under the blanket her leg rested securely against his, soft and warm, curving deliciously against his thigh. *If we had more space we might well have another child to fill it,* he thought. "That's a good idea!" he said, aloud. "We'll have a look around." He put his arms around her and pulled her closer.

She came willingly. *He is a good husband,* she thought, affectionately. *I couldn't ask for better. He listens to what I say, and agrees to it most of the time; he's always kind and never beats me. I chose well, I'm lucky. A good husband, a healthy child, plenty of food, comfort, beautiful things to weave, money saved up, and every reason to have hope for the future. Life is, after all, very sweet.* Closing her eyes, her fingers tangled in Symeon's hair, she thought, *Very sweet.* Half surprised at it herself, she shifted into the caresses and kissed him in turn.

The prefect Philippos left the following morning. Marcianus' men watched his slaves load his private carriage and two carts with baggage; watched as the dozen armed retainers mounted their horses and arranged their weapons; watched as the prefect himself came out of the prefectural residence and climbed into the carriage. Philippos himself carried a rush basket that he refused to entrust to any of his slaves. The drivers shouted, the wheels creaked, the harness jingled, and the train of carriage, carts, and horsemen drove off through the streets of Tyre in the cold bright morning, heading north.

When this was reported to him, Marcianus smiled and ordered the final preparations for his own departure. At noon he, too, rode off, taking fifty of his men and twenty loaded mules. Thirty of the hundred men who had accompanied him to Tyre had already been sent north on various errands, and twenty were left at the big ramshackle house in the Old City, under the command of a dissatisfied Paulus, to keep up a cursory watch on the prefecture and guard against reprisals to Symeon and Demetrias.

Demetrias did not see him go; she was back in the factory, working on an altarcloth commissioned by the emperor as a present for the bishop of Antioch. Her section was to show Moses and the burning bush, and she chose the colors happily: scarlet kermes, orange saffron and yellow, crimson buccina, bright gold. Already the time spent working in the shed seemed a bad dream: only the money she had gained by it remained to remind her that it was real.

And then, ten days before the Christmas festival, she was once again summoned by the procurator.

It was early in the afternoon when the runner came from the prefecture and told Philotimos that he and the weaver Demetrias were required at once. Philotimos said only that, of course, he would come immediately, and trudged down the building to fetch Demetrias. She glanced up as his footsteps paused behind her, giving him the secretive smile with which they always greeted one another now. Her smile faded, however, at the anxious unhappiness on his face.

"His Eminence the procurator wishes to see us at once," said Philotimos.

Demetrias sat still for a moment. The other weavers again stopped their work and watched. To them, this could be nothing more than another unwanted advance from a procurator defeated once by the stink of purple. Demetrias could sense their anger behind her, their sympathy ready to urge her on in her chaste refusal. *Oh, the idiots!* she thought, irritated by this recurrence of a trouble she already regarded as done with. *They should have realized!*

*Better that they haven't.* She thrust her tapestry needle into the half-inch of fabric that decorated the loom and rose, pulling her cloak more tightly about her. Philotimos fell into step beside her, and they set off.

It was another gray, windy day. The waves crashed violently against the harbor wall, sending fountains of white spray stinging into the wind. Symeon's boat was not on the beach, but this was merely because it was being repainted in the boathouse: no one had been out fishing for a fortnight. Philotimos and Demetrias walked in silence until they were within sight of the prefecture, at which point Philotimos stopped.

"Remember, my dear," he said, quietly, "it was a red cloak."

He was saying it, she knew, not because he was afraid she'd forgotten, but simply to reassure himself. She smiled at him and nodded. "Dyed with kermes," she said, content to run over the whole account again, "with two tapestry panels — which we won't describe unless we have to."

"And if we have to?"

"Then they depict mythological scenes, erotic ones — and if we're asked specifically which scenes, we say Leda and the Swan and Europa and the Bull."

"But I should think we won't have to be that specific," Philotimos said. "I hope not. It would make it harder for the procurator to dig up a real cloak to show this gentleman. But even if he has no red cloaks with tapestry panels, even if he's made up a completely different story, we should be clear of trouble. We can say it's merely because he doesn't want to admit to having stolen state-supplied silk and labor for his private use." But he still looked miserable.

"It will turn out safely," she whispered, touching his hand.

He met her eyes, then nodded, smiling at last. "I really don't see how it could fail to."

The procurator's anteroom, an office usually occupied by Heraklas' irritable and overworked secretary, was full of soldiers when they entered it. For a moment there seemed dozens of them, tall men who wore mail coats over their military trousers, in the red-and-white uniform of one of the imperial offices. Spears and swords were everywhere, and angry, bearded faces turned toward them, the blue eyes questioning. Philotimos flinched and stopped short in the doorway. He had always been afraid of soldiers, and official guardsmen were the most dangerous, likely to beat civilians unless they were bribed not to, and sometimes, if drunk or bad tempered, even then.

"You are?" demanded one of the soldiers in a harsh voice. Demetrias, caught behind Philotimos in the doorway, recognized the accent instantly: Gothic. Barbarians were common in the army, of course; more common than Romans. She glanced quickly about the office and saw that there were, in fact, only four of the men and that Heraklas' secretary was standing against the far wall looking as nervous and frightened as Philotimos. She met his eyes and nodded slightly.

"That . . . that's the silk factory supervisor who was sent for," ventured the secretary. "And the weaver."

The soldier glanced at him, glared at Philotimos, who immediately bowed. Demetrias pulled her cloak up before her face and bowed as well. The soldier snorted. "He's waiting for you," he told them. "Go on in."

There were two more guardsmen in Heraklas' office. One was another chain-mailed Goth, even taller than his fellows; the other was a short, bow-legged man in a cloak of dirty furs, his head hideously misshapen and his face marked from cheek to chin with deep, even scars. Instead of a sword he carried a dagger and some loops of leather that might have been a rope or a whip, and he had a bow and quiver of arrows slung over his back. Demetrias stared at him for a moment in horrified fascination: a Hun. She had heard of the Huns all her life; her city, like all cities, had paid over and over again for peace with them; she had woven a cloak that had been sent as a gift to their king — but she had never seen one. They looked every bit as horrible as they were reported. The Hun noticed her stare and grinned at her: his scars twisted around the bared teeth, and she looked away quickly.

Heraklas was standing by the window, looking wretched, and a short, smooth, lean man was seated at the procurator's desk, flipping through some papers with sharp, angry movements. His fingers glittered with rings and his cloak and tunic were so thick with gold that he seemed a walking jeweler's shop. When the door closed behind them he looked up, studying them with small, savage, bloodshot eyes.

"Your name was Philotimos, wasn't it?" he asked, without introducing himself or giving Heraklas any chance to speak. "I remember you: you showed me the factory. And this is the woman who was working on the special commission?"

Demetrias bowed, holding her cloak up. "Umm," said Philotimos, "which special commission was that . . . um, sir?"

The man glared. "I toured your factory last month. You said you had one woman weaving a cloak specially commissioned by the procurator for the emperor, and that because it was to be a surprise, she was working in the dyeworks instead of the factory. Is this the woman?"

"Yes, sir," said Philotimos humbly. "I remember Your Honor, but I fear not Your Grace's name or dignity — sir," and turning to the procurator, he asked, "Is this gentleman to be Your Eminence's successor?"

Heraklas looked still more wretched and twisted a ring on his finger. He shook his head. "No . . . this is the most distinguished Eulogios, a . . . a *princeps* of the *agentes in rebus.*" The *agentes in rebus*, officially couriers, were often used as an imperial spy service, and *princeps* was their highest rank. "Just answer the man's questions," whispered Heraklas. "There's . . . there's been some . . . misunderstanding with the sacred offices."

Eulogios snorted. "Oh," said Philotimos, in a tone of surprise and concern so realistic that Demetrias held her cloak higher before her face to hide her smile. Though still nervous, she was beginning to find the situation funny.

The stranger squinted at Demetrias. "The procurator tells me that the cloak was finished at the beginning of the month," he said angrily.

She nodded. "Yes, Your Honor. I gave it to His Eminence Acilius Heraklas. I am working in the factory again now."

"What was the commission?" he demanded, his tone ugly.

Demetrias looked down and shuffled her feet. "Sir," she said to Heraklas, "am I to answer his questions?"

Heraklas bit his own finger. "I said you were! He has authority . . . he has full authority here, he's been given the rank of acting master of the offices." Demetrias looked back at the agent Eulogios, blinking rapidly. The master of the offices was head of all imperial ministries and factories, subject to the emperor alone; with an honorary rank equivalent to his, the agent's authority was greater than that of anyone else in Tyre. He could, if he pleased, shut down every factory in the city and have all the workers executed. *For an ordinary agent, even a* princeps *to be given a rank like that*, Demetrias realized, *someone in Constantinople must have been very alarmed indeed.* The situation no longer seemed funny.

Philotimos cleared his throat. "Your Honor," he said, "I think I know why you've come. Umm . . . it is difficult for us, for state slaves under the procurator's orders, to speak freely. May we have your protection if we do?"

Eulogios looked at him with narrowed eyes. "I offer no protection to criminals," he stated savagely. "You can choose to speak here — or on the prison rack."

There was a minute of silence. Philotimos swallowed loudly, his hands locking together. He glanced uncertainly at Demetrias; her face was very still, masked but calm. *She won't break*, he thought, reassuring himself again. *And why should I? This agent can't know anything.*

Philotimos swallowed again, then said, quietly, "Sir, His Honor Acilius Heraklas commissioned a cloak, privately and for his own use.

It was of silk, dyed with kermes, with two tapestry panels. Demetrias completed it two weeks ago and gave it to His Eminence, who disposed of it as he saw fit. That is all I know about it."

Eulogios stared at him, the look of savagery yielding slowly to one of bewilderment. "Dyed with kermes?" he said, after a minute. "But . . . but that's a red dye, isn't it?"

Philotimos nodded. "Yes, Your Honor. A very fine scarlet, as expensive as the purple itself."

"You said before that the procurator had commissioned this cloak for the emperor!" exclaimed Eulogios, suddenly going white with rage. He jumped to his feet, his small eyes white rimmed and glaring like an animal's. "An emperor's cloak isn't dyed red, it's dyed purple — what game are you trying to play?"

Philotimos winced. "Y-your Honor, what I said before . . . His Eminence the procurator gave me orders for a red cloak by our finest weaver, I swear it! But what was I to say to you when you came as a visitor? This is the emperor's factory, we're not supposed to waste our time and our finest weavers' skill on private commissions! Was I to accuse His Eminence of misusing public funds to his own gain? Though he did pay for the silk, sir. I have it all in my account books at the factory, and I could show Your Distinction . . ."

Heraklas was staring with delighted astonishment. Eulogios flushed a deep red. "You son of a whore!" he shouted at Philotimos in fury.

There was something artificial about the ferocity of his passion. *He's working himself up deliberately,* Demetrias thought with a shock. *He wants to terrify us — Philotimos, me, and Heraklas as well. And he is terrifying, too.* The agent had leaped round the desk to grab Philotimos' tunic and shout in his face; he was shorter than the old supervisor, and should have been comic, red-faced, reaching upward to shake the old man. But his violence made Demetrias want to scream. "The cloak was purple, you filthy liar!" shouted Eulogios. "It was purple and you know it was purple! Dog! Stinking bastard! Why else was it a secret?"

Philotimos cowered, trying to back away, and Eulogios grabbed the old man's collar with both hands and twisted, shaking and strangling him at the same time. The two guards came closer, watching impassively for signs of resistance.

Demetrias ran forward and caught the agent's arm. "Sir," she cried.

"Sir, please, we're trying to tell you the truth!" She pulled his hand loose.

Eulogios shoved her violently aside without looking at her. "Tell me the truth then," he demanded of Philotimos, releasing him with a jerk. "It was purple, wasn't it?"

"Sir," said Philotimos, trembling, feeling his throat uncertainly, "why would we have kept it secret if it was purple? We're supposed to make purple cloaks for the emperor; we're not supposed to make red ones for the procurator."

Eulogios slapped him. "It was secret because it wasn't for the emperor! God rot you! You are trying to worm your way out of a treason charge, but I'll have the truth if I have to skin you for it! And you too!" He turned on Demetrias. "I'll have the skin flayed off your back and those pretty arms pulled off your shoulders unless you talk!"

Philotimos swallowed several times, staring at the agent in horror. Despite herself, Demetrias began to shake. "Sir," she said, urgently, "we're telling you everything we know. It was a red cloak, and the procurator took it himself."

Eulogios jumped forward and grabbed her shoulders; he shouted into her face, spraying her with spit. "You lying whore! It was purple, wasn't it? It was purple! You know it was purple!"

"It was red!" she shouted back, and he slapped her. She raised her hands to guard her face and he slapped her again. The hood of her cloak fell from her head and she could feel her hair coming down on one side; the slaps themselves were not painful, stinging but forceless and unaimed. The guards moved another step closer; the Goth was grinning. *Two can play at working on their own passions*, she thought suddenly, and allowed herself to burst into the tears she usually suppressed. It was easily done, a relief, even; she went limp under Eulogios' hand, her eyes streaming. "I don't know why you want it to be purple, sir," she cried, "but I promise you it wasn't: it was red!"

"You whore!" he shouted. "What color . . ."

She gave a moan of terror and bent over, shaking and incoherent with sobs. The agent stopped, off balance. He was plainly not going to get any kind of answer from a woman in this condition: he had overdone it. He let her go, distastefully, and she remained stooped, holding her cloak before her face to hide the tears. She was vaguely aware of Philotimos staring at her in astonishment, but she dared not look at him or think of anything beyond the fear of torture: the tears would be less effective if they weren't real. Eulogios shook himself and turned a reduced fury on Heraklas. "Where is it?" he demanded. "What have you done with it?"

"I . . . I gave it to a friend of mine," said Heraklas. "I . . . I gave it to the prefect, to Philippos, as a going-away present." Recovering himself a little, he added, "What are you trying to imply? If you want to charge me with anything, I demand a fair trial."

Eulogios spat at him, then marched back to Philotimos. "I want to see your account books," he stated. "Now. You can take me to the factory this instant. As for you . . ." He gave Heraklas a contemptuous glance. "Don't leave this office or go to see anyone until I return. I'm leaving some of my men here, and if you stir a foot beyond the door, I'll have you for obstructing justice. When you're charged, you can be sure you'll have due process of law — and the full penalty the law allows as well!" He seized Philotimos by the ear and began dragging the old man forcibly from the office: Philotimos was so frightened that he scarcely understood where he was being asked to go, and his ear was twisted until it began to bleed. Demetrias ran after them and again caught the agent's hand.

"Please, sir!" she exclaimed. "We'll come gladly, you don't need . . ."

He turned and slapped her again, this time so hard that she stumbled. "Keep quiet unless I ask you to speak!" he commanded. "And keep your dirty slave's hands to yourself!"

Demetrias allowed herself to fall, and crouched on hands and knees, weeping. Eulogios stamped with rage and let go of Philotimos, then stood at a loss, not wanting to help up the woman he had just knocked down but, equally, impatient to be gone. Demetrias got up just quickly enough to prevent the Goth from dragging her up. She pulled her cloak over her head again with trembling hands. Philotimos leaned against the wall, catching his breath; she succeeded in meeting his eyes. The hood masked her face from everyone else, and she gave the old man a reassuring smile. Philotimos looked startled and bewildered for a moment, then abruptly he understood. It steadied him: he straightened and bowed his head, allowing the agent to precede him out the door. Eulogios set off again for the factory, this time without touching either of them. In the secretary's office he ordered two of his guards in to watch Heraklas — the tall Goth and the Hun accompanied him to the factory.

On arriving at the supervisor's desk, the agent examined the accounts, at first violently and impatiently; then, swearing and more carefully, but he could find nothing amiss. Philotimos had recopied the whole page of his ledger, and matched it to the running tally of silks used by the factory. According to all the accounts, the commission was a special one for the procurator Heraklas, and used silk dyed red with kermes. Eulogios glared at Philotimos and Demetrias. "Summon the rest of your workers," he ordered the supervisor.

Philotimos obligingly rang the bell that signaled breaks, and, when the workers looked up all along the hall, gestured for them to come. Eulogios looked contemptuously at the thirty-nine women and girls and the three boys who assembled by their supervisor's desk. "Are these all?" he demanded.

"We have an annex with twelve spinners," said Philotimos, "and another hundred and three women who spin for us at their homes, on a contract, piece-work basis. I can have them all summoned if Your Distinction requires, but it will take some time . . ."

"Summon the twelve, and let the others be," ordered Eulogios. Philotimos nodded to one of the boys, who went to bring in the silk spinners.

"Now," said Eulogios, when the entire work force was assembled before him. "My patron, the most illustrious Chrysaphios, head chamberlain to His Sacred Majesty, Our Lord and Emperor Theodosius Augustus, has charged me with investigating a suspected conspiracy against our most religious emperor. I have reason to believe that a purple cloak was made here for a usurper — made with the connivance of your supervisor, and executed by this woman here. I will give a pound of gold to whoever tells me the truth about them."

There was a stunned silence. The workers stared at Philotimos and Demetrias in disbelief. They had not seen the cloak — though Demetrias was painfully aware that they had all believed it was intended for the emperor. But the workers had grown up together, and lived all their lives within the sound of each other's voices: it was inconceivable that they should do anything other than protect their own, even when offered a pound of gold. No one replied, and Eulogios' face reddened again. After a long minute, one of the women began to cry. Demetrias at once recognized the loud anguished sobbing as belonging to her mother.

"What is that noise?" demanded Eulogios, angrily. "What are you blubbering about, woman?"

"Oh, sir!" wailed Laodiki. "My Demetrias would never do such a thing! Oh sir, it's all the fault of that procurator!"

"Come here!" ordered Eulogios, viciously, and, when Laodiki stepped out before him, with her fat face red and slobbered with tears, he demanded, "What is the fault of that procurator?"

"You saying this horrible thing, sir!" said Laodiki. "Oh sir, don't believe it! Why, the procurator was never interested in making anything treasonous when he ordered Demetrias to go work on that special commission! All he wanted was to get her in bed, sir, and if he says different, it's because she wouldn't have him, sir: she's a good wife, my daughter is, and respected her husband too much."

Eulogios glared at her, at the other workers, who were all nodding agreement. "Liars!" he shouted, then, "What color was the cloak?"

There was a moment of perplexed silence. "I never saw it, sir!" said Laodiki. "But I'm sure it was whatever color my Demetrias said it was."

"It was red, sir!" Demetrias put in, desperately.

Eulogios turned and hit her again: this time the blow had all the weight of his body behind it, and even careless as it was, aimed blindly, it stunned her. She cut her lip against her teeth and backed away, tasting blood, watching the agent warily. "Will you keep quiet?" Eulogios spat at her — then met her eyes and paused. She had wept and crawled before him earlier; he had expected her to be weeping again. But her eyes were dry, sharp, watching him — assessing him, he felt suddenly, ready to choose whatever course would best undermine him.

She at once bent her head, pulling up her cloak and beginning to weep again, but once again he'd lost the thread of his anger and was off balance. *She did it deliberately*, he thought in astonishment. *Or did she? She's certainly crying now. Where was I? — He paused. — The cloak, the color of the cloak.*

He screamed at the workers again, "What color was it?"

"It would say in the account book, sir," one of the boys suggested helpfully. "We didn't see it, sir. Demetrias wove it at the dyeworks."

"There was a lot of red silk left over," put in a woman. "I remember Demetrias traded it in at the woolen factory. You could check with Daniel the woolen supervisor, sir."

"God rot you all!" Eulogios spat on the account book, glared at the workers once more, then jerked his head to Philotimos to urge him to the woolen factory.

Daniel's accounts, of course, tallied exactly with Philotimos'. The agent swore at the woolen supervisor, then screamed at Philotimos and Demetrias to take him to the dyeworks.

No one at the dyeworks could remember what color the cloak was. Demetrias was certain that Eugenios the supervisor knew, but he protected his old adversary Philotimos without hesitation. "I really didn't see it," he said unblinkingly. "But why would Philotimos lie to Your Honor? Has Your Honor checked the account books?"

"Did you give him a load of silk dyed with kermes?" demanded Eulogios.

"I've given him lots of loads of silk dyed with kermes," replied Eugenios. "We either dye or store silk of every color here."

"Do you have the account for it?"

Eugenios shrugged and brought out his account books. "But you won't find the specific lot there," he warned. "It's spun after it's been dyed, so the measurements Philotimos uses and the ones I use never match exactly."

Eulogios inspected the accounts, swore, inspected the shed, kicked the loom, swore, and shoved Philotimos and Demetrias back to the prefecture.

When Eulogios marched back in the same fury in which he'd left the office, Heraklas looked relieved. Eulogios slammed the door. "You will be charged with misuse of state labor for private gain," he told Heraklas. "And I want to see the cloak."

"I am very sorry to have caused so much trouble," said Heraklas, with some of his old condescension. "I'm sure that if you go to Constantinople and tell my friend Philippos what you want, he'll be pleased to show you the cloak."

"He left for Constantinople when? Why did he go, when he had another four or five months of his office left to serve?"

"His mother was ill, Your Distinction. He went to see her. He left two weeks ago — yes, two weeks exactly."

"Why was the cloak finished four weeks before I was told it would be?"

Heraklas gave a superior smile. "I'd decided to give it to Philippos, Your Distinction," he said pleasantly, "and I wanted him to get it before he left. We had to simplify the design a bit, but we managed. He was very pleased with it — as he should be. It was a lovely cloak, the color of fire."

Eulogios chewed on his lip. "Very well," he said, after a moment, "very well." He sat down heavily on Heraklas' desk. The fury was finished, and the agent suddenly looked simply a rather ridiculous overdressed small man, sitting on a desk with his feet a foot in the air. "I seem to have been mistaken," he said, after a moment. "I will return to Constantinople tomorrow."

*It's over,* thought Demetrias, and leaned against the door frame, weak with relief. *He didn't even mean that about having us tortured; that was said just to frighten us. He's convinced.*

Heraklas smiled, nodding vigorously. "I am sorry to have occasioned the mistake," he said, "and I will of course pay the state back for my . . . misuse of the labor of its slaves."

Eulogios gave him another fierce stare. "You have reason to be sorry — and to thank your luck. Well, I will go home tomorrow . . ." He sat still for another moment, chewing on his lip. When he had first found out about the cloak he had been certain that if he seized it he would have hard evidence of treason to please his master. He had gone posthaste from Tyre to Constantinople, galloping almost a thousand miles in two weeks, to beg Chrysaphios for the authority to deal with the situation himself. And he'd been given authority: an honorary rank equal to that of his superior, the master of the offices — to that of the third highest minister of state. Now he would have to return to the capital with nothing to show for it all but a trivial misdemeanor by a conceited and lustful young procurator. "Yes . . . ," he repeated, and rubbed his face, giving a small shudder as his own rage ebbed away, leaving him with the wrenched, empty sensation he always felt in the aftermath of anger. "I was mistaken," he repeated heavily, then, defensively, "but it's better to make mistakes through an excess of zeal than to endanger the safety of our lord and emperor by complacency."

"Of course," said Heraklas. "Who could doubt it?"

Eulogios shook his head. Chrysaphios wouldn't doubt it — but he wouldn't be grateful, either, wouldn't promote his mistakenly zealous servant. *I will have to show him that I've investigated the matter as thoroughly as I could,* he thought, *that it's not my fault I made a mistake.* "I will want to take something to assure His Illustriousness that the misunderstanding has been cleared up," he told Heraklas. "Some papers . . . perhaps a gift of some kind . . ." His eye fell on the weaver leaning against the door frame. Demetrias stood with the downcast eyes and slightly bowed head proper in the presence of her superiors, but her mouth was curved in a slight smile, and she fingered the patterned border of her cloak contentedly. *The woman is satisfied,* he thought, recovering a flicker of his anger. *She made a fool of me, forced those tears deliberately to make me look ridiculous. Well, I can teach her a lesson, anyway!* "You can sell me the weaver," he said.

"What?" asked Heraklas. Demetrias looked up sharply, not able to understand yet what had just been said.

"You can sell me the weaver!" said Eulogios, angrily. "I said it clearly enough! She's a slave, isn't she? I want to buy her."

Heraklas looked at her: she looked back, her eyes vivid. One cheek was beginning to darken with a bruise from the agent's blows, but it merely gave her a fragile, vulnerable look, though as yet she was not frightened, merely surprised and disbelieving. *And she's not fragile,* thought the procurator, remembering with a stab of resentment how she had treated his advances. *She's a clever little bitch, and it would serve her right if I threw her to this wild beast of an agent. But what would she tell him, if he took her off to Constantinople? No, I don't dare risk it.* "Yes, but she's not mine, she's a state slave," he told Eulogios, smiling politely. "I can't sell a state slave. Why, it would be like . . . like selling a soldier from the legions. If Your Eminence wants a weaver, I know of a private establishment that . . ."

"I don't want *any* weaver, I want this one," snapped Eulogios. "And I will authorize you to sell her. Why not?" He began to warm to his idea. "She's a skilled worker, a suitable present for any person of quality, and my patron can question her himself to be absolutely clear that our suspicions were mistaken. Yes, draw up a bill of sale for her at once."

Demetrias understood, suddenly and finally, what the man meant.

She felt as though some giant had reached down and turned her inside out like a gutted fish. "No!" she shouted in horror. "No! You can't!"

Eulogios frowned at her. "Woman, I've warned you twice to keep quiet!" he said, not even bothered enough to raise his voice. "Once more and I'll have you gagged.

"Draw up a bill of sale for her. I'm giving her as a present to the most illustrious Chrysaphios, chamberlain to His Sacred Majesty. I'll give you the standard price for a skilled worker: sixty *solidi*."

Heraklas let his breath out unsteadily, looked at Eulogios unhappily for a moment, then shrugged. "You can do as you like," he said. "I'll tell my secretary to draw up the deed. We'll have to have your signature authorizing it, though: I'm not allowed to sell the workers."

"But I have a husband and child!" cried Demetrias. "You can't!" She ran to Heraklas. "You can't!" she told him, leaning across the desk. "You can't do that!"

Heraklas leaned away from her with an expression of distaste. Eulogios nodded to his guards.

"Mother of God!" Demetrias shouted. "You have no right!" She threw Heraklas' papers onto the floor. "You have no right to sell me!"

The two guardsmen crossed the room; the Goth grabbed her arms, grinning. "No!" she screamed, and began to struggle.

"Gag this woman," Eulogios ordered his men.

Demetrias screamed again, twisting so that the Goth was jolted against the edge of the desk; his grip loosened for an instant and she tore one arm free. The Goth at once twisted the other arm behind her back, and she gave another scream, this time one of pain. The Hun shoved a cloth into her mouth and began to tie it with one of the leather coils from his belt.

"No," shouted Philotimos, trying to stop him. "No, please, you can't . . ."

"Throw the man out!" ordered Eulogios. "And lock the woman up somewhere till we leave tomorrow. I've had enough of this wild beast show — send the bill of sale to me this evening, Heraklas, and I'll pay the state its money." He started out of the office, then paused in the doorway. "But Berich, Chelchal . . ." The two men stopped tying Demetrias' gag around her neck and looked up. "The woman is a present for His Illustriousness. I don't want her damaged."

He left, leaving his servants to beat Philotimos out of the office, tie

Demetrias' hands, and drag her off, shaking, struggling, and crying into the gag.

When they were all gone, Heraklas sat down at his desk and placed his shaking hands palms down on the polished wood. *A wild beast show indeed,* he thought. *By Apollo, I'm glad that's over! Still, it's come out better than I could have expected. Of course, the slaves were just saving their own skins, fabricating that lie so neatly — and even if they hadn't, I could have got off. They couldn't have tortured me, an Acilius, and I could just dismiss anything the slaves said under torture as being said to please their torturers. Philippos will have a bit of trouble now, but that's his problem — and he should manage to stall it until the emperor's safely overthrown and Nomos installed in his place. Yes, it went better than I could have expected — especially with that Eulogios being such a wild man. A pity about the woman, though. Well, perhaps I'll sort it out when Nomos is wearing the purple. See her restored to Tyre and put back in the factory — returned to her jealous husband, even, if he hasn't found another wife by the time she gets back. Perhaps I could claim a reward from the girl myself. After all, if I fetch her back here, she'll owe me something.*

Trying to stop a nosebleed, Philotimos sat in Heraklas' secretary's office for half an hour after Demetrias was dragged off. Then he went, stained with blood and tears, back to Heraklas' office and tried to persuade the procurator not to sell Demetrias. "Invent some excuse, some reason why the deed of sale can't be written at once," he urged. "The gentleman's in a hurry; anyone can see he's in a hurry. If you can just delay . . ."

But Heraklas dismissed him impatiently. "He has the authority to demand it," he told Philotimos, "and I can't refuse. He'd suspect me if I did."

"But you're responsible!" said Philotimos, forgetting a lifetime's caution. "You and your treacherous schemes are to blame for this; why should she have to pay the price?"

"Are you threatening me?" asked Heraklas indignantly. "You know very well that if you accuse me of anything, you accuse yourself and the woman too. Get out of here before I have you thrown out: you should be ashamed to appear before me in that condition."

"Please, master, be merciful!" cried Philotimos, and desperately, he knelt before Heraklas and seized his knees. "She has a husband and a child, for Christ's sake! You can't sell her to that . . . that devil of an agent!"

"Do you think I want to sell her?" asked Heraklas, softening a little. "At the very least, it's going to make me nervous, thinking what she might say in Constantinople. But there's nothing I can do about it. Eulogios has the power to authorize the sale, and he's used it. And anyway, slaves don't have husbands — as for the child, it's not a baby, is it? Well, then, its father can look after it. Now get out, old man. I need rest after this business — and you look like you do, too."

Philotimos got out. It was dusk outside; the sea wind tore at the date palms in the public square. When he reached the harbor, the waves showed white, dotted far out over the dimness of the rough sea. Philotimos walked slowly along the harbor street. *I called the bastard "master,"* he thought, *and he took it for granted. We don't hold even what we thought was our own. I never thought anyone could sell us. Oh, Demetrias, my sweet girl! God help me now, I've got to tell your husband.*

Symeon was in the apartment when Philotimos knocked. He opened the door looking cheerful — then stared at the old man in shock.

"Christ Eternal!" he exclaimed. "What happened to you?"

Philotimos tried to speak, then shook his head, the tears starting to his eyes.

"Come in," Symeon told him. Meletios had run up to the door and was staring as well, but his father pushed him gently aside and helped Philotimos in. He seated the old man on the couch. "Now, what's the matter? Have you hurt yourself? Shall I call a doctor?"

"He's all covered in blood!" said Meletios in awe.

Philotimos waved the concern aside. "I'm not hurt," he said, "it was just a nosebleed. But Demetrias . . ." He couldn't continue.

"Demetrias?" asked Symeon. "My God. What happened?" Philotimos began to cry. "What happened?" shouted Symeon. "Tell me what happened, for God's sake!"

Philotimos shook his head. "The procurator . . . there was an agent come from Constantinople . . ."

"It's to do with the cloak?"

Meletios did not understand what was happening, but he understood that an adult, a powerful adult, was in tears, and that something had happened to his mother. He began to cry in terror, and clutched his father's leg; his father stooped over Philotimos, ignoring the boy's howls. "An agent came from Constantinople about the cloak," he said, fiercely. "He accused the procurator of treason. What are they doing to Demetrias?"

Philotimos shook his head again, sniffling. "We convinced him that the cloak was red!" he complained. "I had it all straight in the accounts, and nobody could contradict it, and he believed it! But then . . . he wanted to buy her, to show his patron that he'd done everything he could. He didn't want to go back empty handed. And the procurator has sold her."

"He can't! He can't sell a state slave!"

Philotimos began to sob again. "That's what I thought. But the agent had the power to authorize it, and did."

Meletios wailed, still not sure what had happened, but knowing that it was unspeakable. "I want Mama!" he screamed. "What's happened to my Mama? Where is she?" He seized Philotimos' arm. "Where is she?"

"I tried to convince Heraklas not to allow it!" said Philotimos, ignoring the child. "He could have delayed; he could have made problems, and anyone could see that the agent was in a hurry to be gone. But the procurator . . ."

"Damn the procurator," said Symeon, in a level voice. The tone was somehow more frightening than a shout, and Meli stopped screaming and looked at his father in hope. "I can deal with the procurator. Meli, leave Philotimos alone — I'll get your mother back."

"No, don't!" said Philotimos, breathlessly. "No, don't; he'll have you whipped, he won't let you near him, I promise, and if the agent knows that we fooled him and the cloak really was purple, it'll be worse, much worse, for all of us. He's a devil, that agent, a monster."

"I'm not going to the procurator," said Symeon. "But you come with me: you can tell him about the agent. Come on, I can trust you. Meli, love . . ."

"I want to come with you and see Mama!"

"We're not going to Mama; we're going to see a man who can help us get her back. I'll get her back, Meli. You go upstairs now to Granny . . ."

"I want to come!" protested the child tearfully, staring up at his father. "I want to help."

Symeon hesitated, understanding the protest only too well. When his own mother was dying, he had been sent to wait with an aunt. He could still remember how the women had whispered together: "a difficult birth"; "too much blood"; "no, she's too far gone to scream"; "yes, the child's dead now." They had gone in and out of his own home, but he had not been allowed to see her, even to say goodbye. His heart still believed, however many times he pointed out to himself the absurdity of it, that if he had been allowed in, he might have found some way to save her. And he had been twelve then, more than twice as old as Meli.

"Very well!" Symeon took his son's hand. "Come and see for yourself." And he started out the door. Philotimos, bewildered, hurried after him.

The big house in the Old City was quiet, half the men off maintaining their watch of the prefecture, and the other half eating dinner. Two of them, however, were taking their food in the gatehouse, and they directed Symeon to the dining room. Meletios was frightened in the great, dark, creaking house; he held tightly to his father's hand. Symeon picked the boy up and he rested his face against his father's shoulder, completely quiet now, his wide eyes staring into the dimness.

The dining room was as gloomy as Symeon remembered, lit by two lampstands in the far corners. Paulus the secretary was sitting alone at the heavy oak table. His supper plate had just been pushed aside, and the silver goblet was still half full. Paulus glanced suspiciously at Philotimos, then gave Symeon a look of expectant attention. The spies had reported the arrival of an imperial agent, and he had been half expecting some kind of trouble tonight. He had almost hoped for it, wanting some kind of action to justify his long wait in Tyre. Now, it seemed, the waiting was over.

"They've taken my wife," said Symeon bluntly. "I want her back."

Paulus smiled unpleasantly. *At least the fellow comes straight to the point.* "Who are 'they'?" he asked.

"There's an agent from Constantinople — Philotimos was there, he knows what happened. Tell him, Philotimos."

Confused, with no idea who Paulus was except that Symeon expected him to help, Philotimos gave a stammering, abbreviated version of what had happened, pretending throughout that the cloak had been red and for the procurator.

"Eulogios," said Paulus thoughtfully, when Philotimos had finished. "Yes — he's one of Chrysaphios' creatures. Hopes to be master of the offices in Nomos' place, no doubt. Well. We thought he would come back with the authority to interfere — but I must say, I didn't expect this. Acting master of the offices! That's far more than I thought the chamberlain would give him. It complicates matters."

"I want my wife back," said Symeon. "Your master swore by the Holy Spirit to do everything he could to protect her."

"Marcianus is not my *master*," Paulus said sharply. "He's my employer. I have no *master* but the emperor."

"Well, I have no master but the emperor, either," returned Symeon impatiently. "So that makes us equal. What are you going to do about my wife? Your *employer* must have ordered you to protect her."

"Protecting you and your family is the reason I am still in Tyre," Paulus replied coldly. "How long do we have?"

"The agent said he was returning to Constantinople tomorrow," said Philotimos.

"Tomorrow?" asked Paulus, staring. "Are you sure?"

"Tomorrow morning," Philotimos replied. "He was in a hurry."

Paulus nodded to him, and looked back at Symeon, who still appeared simply impatient. *Doesn't he understand what's just been said?* wondered Paulus. *There won't be time for subterfuge before tomorrow morning — and I haven't the men to use force, not against an acting master of the offices.* "That makes it rather difficult," he said grimly.

"What are you going to do?"

Paulus shook his head. *Fool!* "I don't think I can do anything by tomorrow."

Symeon let Meletios slide through his arms to the floor; he stepped forward and leaned across the dinner table. "I've given your *employer* Marcianus some information that is worth lives. He swore by the Holy Spirit and by the emperor's head that he would protect us. I've come here to claim that protection: are you telling me you can't give it? Because if you are . . ." Symeon's voice, which had begun evenly, was rising; Paulus put up his hand to stop it.

"I'm saying nothing of the kind. My employer is an honorable man, and I was specifically charged with seeing that his oath to you was kept. But he never swore to do the impossible, and it is impossible to rescue your wife by tomorrow morning. Think a moment! If we'd had a week or even a day or two, we might have smuggled her out, or brought pressure to bear on the procurator, or bought her from the agent. But as it stands . . . we don't even know where she's being kept! I can find out — but by the time I've done that, it will be midnight. There won't be time to organize a rescue. And Eulogios has authority here; he's brought six of his own retainers, and can request the use of the prefectural guard. I have twenty men. Do you think I can storm the prefecture with them? And if I did, what good would it do you or your wife? She'd still be legally the agent's property."

"You have enough soldiers," said Symeon. "You could break her out if you couldn't buy her out, and you could hide her here safely until you've fixed things in Constantinople. And then you could make sure the sale is canceled."

Paulus shook his head with a look of impatient contempt. "If I tried to take the prefecture by storm, we'd betray ourselves to the enemy and risk ruining all our plans — there'd be no place to hide for any of us. And I don't even think we could succeed. No, it's impossible. I'll try to follow Eulogios when he leaves, if you like, and look for any opportunity to rescue your wife. But I warn you, he can use the posting system and I can't, so he's bound to move far more quickly than we do."

Symeon hit the table. "I want my wife back!" he shouted. "This devil of an agent has her locked up somewhere, and I want her freed, now! Don't tell me it's impossible; you're *bound* to make it possible!"

Paulus looked at him coldly, then turned his attention to Philotimos. "I will not ask you whether your story was completely true," he said, biting off each word. "I merely ask you if Eulogios believed it."

Philotimos stared at him in confusion, then flushed. *Symeon has told him about the cloak*, he realized. *That's the "information worth lives." No wonder someone started investigating here in Tyre: someone Symeon talked to let something slip. Oh, the fool, the thrice-damned fool!* "Eulogios believed it," he replied, with the quietness of despair. "If he hadn't, Demetrias and I would both be on the rack now."

Paulus turned back to Symeon. "If the agent believes that there was no treason, he won't have your wife tortured. If he intends to

112

give her as a gift to his patron Chrysaphios, he won't let his men harm her. She's as safe as she'd be anywhere. The best way to get her back is to allow them to take her to Constantinople and to inform my employer and his patron of what has happened. They will make every effort to get her away from Chrysaphios and restore her to you as soon as possible."

"You want me to let them take her to Constantinople?" shouted Symeon. "Tied up, gagged, locked up in prisons suffering God-knows-what all along the way, and finishing at the mercy of Chrysaphios and his friends? No! Get her back now!"

Meletios began to cry again, clinging to his father's leg; Symeon pushed him impatiently aside. Paulus winced. He disliked children, especially when they cried.

"I risk the lives of twenty men if I attack Eulogios," said Paulus, raising his voice to be heard. "And I risk your wife's life as well! If Eulogios thinks the cloak was red, she's safe; if I act openly to protect her, he'll know her story was false, and he'll try to wring the truth out of her if we fail. Is that what you want?"

"You're not going to do a thing, are you?" said Symeon. "You're going to ride off to Constantinople and forget all about us."

"I will do what I can!" shouted Paulus, now openly angry. "I will tell Marcianus! I will ride after Eulogios myself, for as long as we can keep up! But more than that is impossible!"

"Damn you!" shouted Symeon. "My wife . . ."

He stopped. His wife had said that this would happen, that anyone he turned to would betray him as soon as it was convenient. *And I betrayed her, too*, he thought, involuntarily. *I deceived her and gave away her secrets, and now she is gagged and sold and about to be dragged off a thousand miles in captivity, because of me.* Symeon put a hand to his face. "My wife . . ." he repeated. His shoulders began to shake. "They've taken her . . ." Meletios, pushed aside, lay curled up on the floor, crying in anguish.

"I will do what I can," repeated Paulus coldly. "I suggest you take your child home and try to wait quietly. It will take a few months, but we should get her back for you in the end. But if you are so stupid as to rush about declaring to everyone what has happened, I take no responsibility for the results: God himself can't save a fool."

Symeon said nothing. He blundered unsteadily away from the table and picked up Meletios. The little boy threw his arms about his father's neck, sobbing bitterly. Symeon stumbled blindly out of the room, out of the house, out into the dark streets of the Old City. He walked as far as the causeway that connected the Old City to the rock, then sat down at the roadside, shaking. A waning moon emerged briefly through the tattered clouds, showing the white-flecked sea, the empty street, the huddled bulk of the city of Tyre. *My wife is locked in prison*, thought Symeon, *tomorrow they will take her away, and the men I relied on for protection are rotten wood.*

Philotimos stopped beside him, looking down accusingly. "You told him about the cloak," he said.

Symeon nodded miserably.

"But . . . but who is he?"

"He's the secretary of Aspar's deputy," said Symeon, wearily. "The deputy himself, Marcianus, is traveling to Constantinople a half day's ride behind Philippos. He wants to seize the cloak when Nomos gets it. He promised me his protection."

"You were an idiot!" said Philotimos. "You tell one court schemer and it's not surprising if another finds out. Lord of All! Do you think any of them cares about promises made to us, to slaves?"

The echo of Demetrias was too close: Symeon flinched, going hot with shame. "He swore by the Holy Spirit!" he exclaimed wretchedly. "And he put it in writing."

"So he founds a church dedicated to the Holy Spirit, if he has a queasy conscience — it's still easier than keeping his word. If you'd only let it alone . . ."

"He put it in writing!" said Symeon, recovering some anger. "And he swore by the Holy Spirit — that's the unforgivable blasphemy — and by the emperor's head — that's treason, if he breaks it. He *must* do as he said."

Philotimos shook his head. "We'll never see her again."

Meletios began to cry more loudly.

"I'll make him keep his word!" said Symeon, through his teeth. "I'll go show the paper to his master Aspar; I'll demand justice."

"How? They're in Constantinople."

"I'll go to Constantinople after them," declared Symeon.

"How are you going to do that? It's a thousand miles, so they say. You don't have the money to pay for a journey like that."

"I have a boat," returned Symeon. "And it's a good boat, too. I can sail up the coast during the day, and put in to shore at night or if the weather's bad. We have over forty *solidi* saved up — and I could fish with a line as we sailed, and sell what I caught. There should be enough to get there and back again, that way."

Philotimos was speechless. Meletios picked his head up. "Is Mama in Constantinople?" he asked.

"That's where they're taking her," replied Symeon.

"And we're going there?"

"I'm going there. You're staying with Granny."

Meli's arms locked about his neck. "I am not; I want to go with you."

"You'll be safer with Granny."

Meletios shook his head fiercely. "I don't want to be safe!" he said. "I want to go with you to find Mama and make them give her back. I don't want to be left alone. Don't go away, Daddy. I'll help sail *Prokne*. You know I can help, I can steer while you fish. I promise I'll behave!"

Symeon looked down at his son's face, reduced by the dark night to the gleam on a pair of eyes and the white of teeth. He kissed the boy's forehead. "You're right, Meli. You belong with me. We'll both sail off as soon as the wind's favorable, and go find your mother."

"You're mad," said Philotimos.

"I can sail a boat," said Symeon, "even if it is the winter. And plenty of boats have made the journey — even small ones."

"You can be punished for theft, running off like that!"

"The boat is mine — I finished paying it off years ago."

"And whose are you? You're worth more than the boat, and you're the property of the state. Heraklas could have you whipped as a runaway."

Symeon looked up at him angrily. "I don't like all this constant talk about being a slave," he said. "It may be true in the law, but it's not true in any way that counts. I'm a purple-fisher, and if my supervisor doesn't like me going after my wife, he can tell me so when I get back. I'm not going to cringe to him, or to that cold bastard Paulus, or to Marcianus, and especially not to that whoreson Heraklas, who's going to get caught for high treason and lose his head if I have anything to do with it. I'm sailing to Constantinople to get my wife back, and that's final."

"I'll lend you some money," said Philotimos, with a sudden profound sense of release. It was illusion, it was pure illusion. Symeon was as much a slave as he was himself — but the dogged refusal to admit it shaped a freedom deeper than the laws of servitude. Against his own reason, Philotimos was convinced: Symeon could sail off in his fishing boat all the way to Constantinople, force the great general Aspar to keep his deputy's bargain, release his wife from the all-powerful chamberlain Chrysaphios, and sail back to wreak the state's vengeance upon Acilius Heraklas. Sheer lunacy, thought Philotimos, but his heart was rising. "I have fifty-eight *solidi* saved up," he told Symeon. "You can have it all."

# V

DEMETRIAS SPENT the night in the Old City, locked in a spare bedroom of the posting inn there. She did not sleep; she was too busy struggling to find a way out. She felt certain that if she could escape and hide — somewhere, anywhere — she would be safe: the agent would not wait to look for her for more than a day, and the procurator would be content not to send her on to him. But the shutters on the window were tightly barred, their hinges were new and strong, and the lock on the door could not be forced. Hammering on the door brought only Eulogios' guards to order her to be quiet. She had already seen that they would welcome a chance to beat her — a rape might pass unnoticed in a beating. She gave them no chance and obeyed.

Early in the morning, Eulogios' two favorite retainers — Berich, the tall Goth, and Chelchal, the Hun — came to fetch her. "We go now," said Chelchal, opening the door and grinning his horrible scar-twisted grin. "Come."

Demetrias came quietly, her head bowed. Her mind cast desperately about for an excuse, a trick, a pretext for delay, and could find nothing. In the station courtyard stood a four-wheeled carriage, its horses harnessed and waiting and the driver already in his place. Demetrias stopped, unable to continue toward it. The retainers came up behind her and each caught one of her arms, pushing her forward. There was no hope of escape: she would have to yield, as she had yielded before, and hope that she would have some other opportunity if she went quietly. But she found that she couldn't do it: at the thought of consenting to her own captivity, a sick, hot, violent hatred rose up uncontrollably inside her, and she flung herself backward and screamed, "No!" The word seemed for a moment as solid and real as her own flesh, formed from her own substance, and it brought with it an immense feeling of relief. There was no use in fighting, but she fought anyway, kicking and biting and screaming desperate refusals. The guards had to wrestle her to the ground, tie her up, and gag her again before they got her into the carriage.

Eulogios' valet was already sitting in the vehicle when she was tossed roughly onto the bare planks of the floor; he drew his feet up and glared at her in contempt. The others were all on horseback. The carriage door closed; the driver shouted, and the vehicle lurched forward, onto the road and away from Tyre. She had no last glimpse of the city: twisting her head to look up she could see only the supports of the seat, battered by the feet of a hundred travelers; the padded leather lining of the door; and high up, through the open window, a blue and featureless sky. Demetrias closed her eyes, biting hard on the gag, ashamed to cry in front of the valet.

The carriage was springless and lurched violently as the horses cantered along, each rut and stone of the road individually shaking the miserable passengers. It was worse than a boat in stormy weather; within a mile she had stopped wanting to cry and merely tried not to be sick. Within another mile she had failed. The gag kept most of the vomit in her mouth; it caught in her nose and throat, choking her, and she struggled desperately to breathe.

It was another mile or so before the valet noticed the smell and fastidiously cut loose the gag with his belt knife. By that time she was scarcely conscious, jolting in and out of a gray haze. She didn't feel it the first time he kicked her, though her head was clearing by the third. He shouted out the window to Eulogios, complaining: she had soiled his carriage! It stank to turn his stomach; she must clean it out.

Eulogios apparently agreed to this, for a little while later the carriage drew to a halt, the door was opened, and she was dragged out onto the grass by the wayside. She sat up, still gasping for air. They were at a bridge over a small stream in the countryside, already beyond any landmark she could recognize.

"You can clean out the carriage," Eulogios ordered, standing over her. "And yourself, too. But be quick about it."

The guards untied her and she climbed unsteadily to her feet. The whole party was gathered about watching her with disgust. She had no anger left with which to face them. She picked up a few handfuls of grass and began to clean the floor of the carriage.

When she had wiped it clean and rinsed it with water from the stream, which she fetched by soaking and wringing out her cloak, she went downstream behind a bush to wash her face and try to clean her soiled tunic. Dabbing water on it did no good, and she pulled the woolen overtunic off and knelt on the bank, shivering in her linen undertunic while she rinsed the neck of the garment in the cold water. She was just wringing it out when the Goth Berich came past the bush and stopped, staring at her. "You are trying to escape," he said accusingly.

She glanced upstream to where the rest of the party were gathered on the road, talking among themselves. They were not watching her, but then, they had no need to. They could see the course of the stream easily, and the countryside was open. There had been no chance to slip off unnoticed. "You know I can't," she returned wearily. She stood up and started to pull the tunic over her head.

"You were trying to escape, you liar!" shouted the Goth, suddenly, for some reason, furious. "You've done nothing else since the master bought you!" He pulled the tunic back off her head and slapped her; her foot slipped on the bank of the stream and she fell, landing half in and half out of the water. Berich dragged her out, then slapped her again, so hard that the world went gray again. He pushed her back against the bush, hauled her tunic up and pushed a knee between her thighs, then began unfastening his own belt. For a moment she seemed to stand outside herself, observing calmly: a young woman lying half-stunned under a bush on the bank of a stream, her bare buttocks pressed into the mud, with an armored man preparing to rape her. *Why?* she wondered. It seemed unlikely that he felt any particular desire for the muddy, bruised, soiled creature. Did he want to pay her back for the trouble she'd caused? Or was it that he'd score in some game with his companions, taking the woman they all were guarding? Or was it even simpler: that she was there, not noble, not virgin, a slave — and thus available; nobody's and so anybody's, his. *But I'm not*, she thought, even as he pulled down his trousers and leaned forward, red-faced and grunting. *I'm not anybody's, and I'm certainly not his.* She screamed and drew her knees up hard; one of them jolted Berich full in the groin. He gave a gasp of agony and went white; she rolled out from under him, grabbed her tunic and cloak, and ran back to the road.

The other guards found the incident very funny. Eulogios, however, was merely impatient at the delay, and when Berich reappeared some minutes later, still very pale and walking stiffly, his master swore at him for mishandling a slave he meant to present to Chrysaphios, and promised that the next man who abused his property would be flogged. Berich received the rebuke sullenly and went to attend to his horse; he apparently felt unable to ride, because he tied the animal to the carriage and climbed up to sit beside the driver. The whole party was soon back on the road. Demetrias, soaked, aching, shaken, and exhausted, sat dripping and shivering beside the disgusted valet. *I've died,* she thought wonderingly. *I feel nothing and I can't recognize myself. This isn't me; I died in Tyre, and what Eulogios has taken away is a ghost.*

Beyond the window the miles lurched quickly by.

Symeon had arrived at the posting station shortly after Demetrias left it. He had spent the previous night trying to discover where his wife was being kept — without success. He had persuaded Meletios to rest with his grandmother at home and gone first to the prefecture. The porters and slaves there were already in bed by the time he reached it, however, and the night guards refused to let him in. In the morning he went to the prefecture's stables only to discover that the agent Eulogios had spent the night at the posting station in the Old City. The prefect's grooms remembered Demetrias from the previous day: they'd had to fetch a carriage for her, since she'd struggled with her guards and refused to walk behind the agent's horse. Symeon ran to the Old City, hoping wildly that he'd be in time at least to see Demetrias — to promise her help, if he could, but at any rate, to see her — but by the time he'd reached the posting station, Eulogios and his party were gone.

"Yes, he had a woman with him," one of the grooms said, in reply to Symeon's desperate questions. "A pretty one, a slave he'd just bought. I wouldn't mind buying one like that myself, if you take my meaning! But she wasn't eager to go off with him, and he had her tied up and put inside the carriage. He took a four-wheeler. I don't see why he couldn't have taken one of the two-wheelers; he wasn't using the carriage himself, and he could have fitted the woman and his valet in a two-wheeler and slung the luggage on behind. But no, he had to have a four-wheeler, covered, with four horses to pull it — and he took the best horse in the stable for himself to ride, as well, and another horse for each of his men. Eleven horses, in all! And he set off at the most ruinous canter I ever saw: wear out the horses and the carriage both by the next posting station, I should think. God knows what we'd do if we get another courier coming through this morning; all the other beasts in the stable are worn out."

"The woman — did she seem well?" asked Symeon anxiously.

The groom shrugged. "As I said, she didn't want to go. When they first tried to put her in the carriage she screamed like a harpy, and they had to tie her up and gag her. She didn't look too happy about it, you can imagine. But as for looking well — there was nothing wrong with that one. As I said, I wish I could buy one like that myself. Why?"

Symeon gave him a savage look. "She's my wife," he declared shortly.

"Mother of God!" said the groom, his face falling, "I'm sorry . . . I didn't realize . . ."

Symeon shook his head. "She's a *state* slave," he said angrily. "That bastard of an agent had no *right* to buy her."

"Phew!" said the groom, profoundly shocked. Like all the grooms and veterinarians employed in the state posting system, he was a state slave himself: it had never crossed his mind that he or anyone like him could be sold. He looked at Symeon with the mixture of awe and pity that greets the victims of some spectacular catastrophe. "Well," he said, after a moment, "I don't think they'd . . . hurt her. She was locked up in the posting inn overnight. Look, why don't I see if I can find out how they treated her?"

The groom found out where Demetrias had been kept overnight and relayed the information that the maid was sure that no one had raped her, and that she'd been offered food, drink, and a bath, at the agent's orders, but had refused them. "She'll be all right," he told Symeon. "She's being treated well. But, Lord of All, what a thing to happen! Still, people like us have to yield to the mighty; you can't argue with a *princeps* of the agents. Maybe you'd better go home and have a drink? You'll get over it in the end."

Symeon made no reply and set off back to the Egyptian harbor. The previous day's rough weather had cleared, and the sun smiled on a sea as blue as indigo. There was a light breeze from the southeast. *Perfect weather for sailing*, thought Symeon — *but Prokne's still being painted; I can't set out yet. It'll take a few days to refit — but then, if the weather holds, we'll go. I won't yield to the mighty, not with Demetrias at stake.*

A purple-fisher had to move about a sizable area to check his traps: he needed a boat that was light, fast, maneuverable, and could be tacked against contrary winds. *Prokne* was all of these, and Symeon was proud of her to the point where his colleagues joked that Demetrias should be jealous. She was built of cedarwood, her planks morticed together over her timbers as tightly as the panels in the most expensive cabinets. The paint that was being renewed was blue below and white above, and of a wax encaustic that helped seal the neat joints in the wood; the carved sternpost was pink, black, white, and green. The mainsail was a trapezoid of coarse linen and hemp, dyed blue and white and suspended on a lateen rig across the single mast; it could be supplemented by a foresail tied to the prow in a following wind. The boat was steered with an oar on a pivot by the stern; another steering oar could be used for rowing in a calm. A merchant ship would never have started on a long voyage in December — but a merchant ship needed a deep harbor in bad weather and was not rigged to sail against the wind. *Prokne* could be run up on any convenient beach, and ran almost as fast against the wind as before it. Symeon began preparing her as soon as the new paint was dry.

He told his supervisor and colleagues that he wanted to work quietly by himself for a few weeks, and they fell over themselves to oblige a man they all knew had every reason to grieve. Having obtained privacy, he and Meletios removed the tanks in the middle of the boat, which served to hold the catch, and added a raised bottom and a canopy that could be folded over the top of the boat. "We'll have to sleep in her on the voyage," Symeon told Meletios. "We'll be in strange cities, where no one knows us; they might rob us."

Meletios nodded seriously. "I'll take my knife," he said, "and if anyone tries to rob us, I'll kill him!"

They packed all their warm clothing on the ship, buying a good watertight wooden chest for the purpose. They brought Demetrias' clothes as well. "She'll need them on the way home," Symeon told his son — and he found that the familiar things he had seen his wife wear so often comforted him; it seemed certain that, if they brought them, she would have to be found to wear them. They packed a brazier and some charcoal wrapped in tar cloth. They packed salt fish, journeybread, and cheese, with some dried dates, a three-day food supply for emergencies; they packed extra sailcloth, ropes, an axe, and odds of wood for any critical repairs. They brought a fishing net and some line for the fishing they expected to do on the voyage — and Symeon, rather grimly, brought a vicious harpoon he had never used, and which he hoped he never would use, but which ought to terrify any casual would-be robber. The supply of money — his savings and Philotimos' — he stitched into a canvas belt, which he put on under his tunic. The preparations took, in all, five days — and the weather held.

It was dawn on a cold, bright morning five days before Christmas when Philotimos helped Symeon haul *Prokne* into the water of the Egyptian harbor. The small waves hissed in the gravel of the beach, and the water that foamed around their legs was cold and clear as ice. Laodiki, the only other admitted to the plan, watched anxiously from the shore; Meletios, in the stern, clutched both the readied steering oars and stared at her, pale with excitement. Symeon leaped into the boat, waving Philotimos back out of the water; the old man stumbled up onto the beach, and Symeon took Meletios' place in the stern and pulled the oars to edge the boat out into deeper water. Philotimos and Laodiki were small as dolls when he jumped up and shipped one of the oars, giving the other to Meletios to hold steady while he let out the sail. The wind was blowing almost due east now, and *Prokne* quivered as it caught her. Meli leaned hard on the oar while his father fastened the rigging. Philotimos and Laodiki watched as Symeon again took his son's place at the steering oar, and Meletios stood, holding the mast, and waved to them again and again. The small clear waves rippled up the beach; the air smelled of purple, the charcoal of morning fires, and the sea. The two watched still as *Prokne*, swooping like a bird, rounded the point of Tyre and headed north, her blue sails lost against the dark-blue sea.

*

The dawn when Symeon set sail from Tyre saw Demetrias almost four hundred miles away, waiting while the horses were harnessed for the next stage of the journey.

Eulogios and his party had spent the night in a posting station a few miles east of the city of Tarsus in the province of Cilicia, and the agent was now arguing with the station grooms about the horses and the roads. His entourage stood waiting by the pinewood fire that burned in one corner of the stableyard, its sweet, choking smoke mingling with the smell of dung and horses. It was a cold morning, and the breath of men and animals steamed white; the roofs of the station buildings glinted with frost. Beyond the far wing of the stables Demetrias could see the slopes of the Taurus mountains, white with fresh snow, twenty miles away and clear as the roofs themselves.

Eulogios had lost his temper with the grooms again; he was screaming at them and slapping the man nearest him. "You son of a whore!" he shouted. "I told you to have the carriage ready by the time I'd finished breakfast! And what do I find? You haven't even taken it out of the stable!"

Eulogios' entourage paid no attention. Their master lost his temper at every posting station: either the grooms were too slow, or the horses weren't good enough, or the axle on the carriage creaked. At one station near Antioch they'd arrived to find that all the fresh horses had been taken by another traveler, and Eulogios had the stationmaster flogged because they had to wait. It was nothing to his retainers. Their master was in a hurry, as usual, and other people had better look out.

The local stationmaster came out of the inn, and Eulogios stopped slapping the groom and pounced on him. "What are the conditions in the mountains?" he demanded.

The stationmaster looked at him in surprise, then waved at the whitened peaks. "Your Honor can see that there has been snow," he said, respectfully. "If we see snow like that on the foothills, wc know that it must be three feet deep at the Cilician Gates. No one can use that road until spring, Your Excellency."

Eulogios swore at him. The stationmaster shifted unhappily and suggested that the western pass of the Taurus, by the valley of Isaura, might still be clear.

"You want us to be murdered?" demanded Eulogios. "Sending us through the middle of Isauria? The mountains there are crawling with bandits, as well you know! You filthy dog, get out of my way!" He turned aside and began shouting at the grooms again. The quickest way to Constantinople lay through the Taurus mountains and across the Anatolian plateau. It was the way he had come before — though even then his horses had picked their way along roads slippery with ice. Now the deep snows had come and he had a carriage: he would have to take the road along the coast at least as far as Attaleia, and it would add a hundred miles to the journey. He slapped another groom and went into the inn to abuse the serving maid who'd brushed his clothes.

Demetrias stood quietly beside the fire in the stable yard, watching while the nervous grooms adjusted girths on the riding animals and checked harness and axles on the carriage. She had struggled against leaving Tyre, but it was senseless to struggle now. It had been senseless to struggle then as well, she admitted to herself, bitterly — she had had no hope of escaping, and there had been nothing to gain except a few bruises and the bare consolation that she had not gone without a fight. It had been good to fight, though; much better than to stand, as she did now, in a listless, exhausted despair. But no one could go on fighting forever, not when they were bound to lose.

The first day had been the worst. The sickness, the beatings, and the assault had left her stunned and exhausted. On that last night in Tyre she had resolved that she would try to escape during the first few days, before they had gone too far from the city, but she made no such attempts. She hadn't appreciated the speed of the imperial posts. They changed horses five times in the first day, arriving at night at the posting station at Byblus, seventy miles from Tyre and farther than Demetrias had ever gone in her life. She knew no one in the city; she had no money and no food, and not so much as a change of clothing to trade for them, and she was aware that even if she could escape it would probably take her three or four days to walk back to Tyre. The retainers locked her in the station storeroom and left her, and she was so battered, hopeless, and exhausted that she could do nothing but lie down and go to sleep on the spot. She woke feeling sick and dizzy from the ordeal of the day before, her head aching and her eyes swollen with bruises; she could offer no resistance to the guards when they came to put her into the carriage. And the next night found them twice as far from Tyre. The world was so much vaster than she had ever realized. The road ran along the coastal plain, villages emerged and sank away into the distance as the carriage jolted along. They passed palm groves and olive groves, vineyards and wheat fields, trimmed to the bare branches and stubble of winter. Flocks and herds grazed the thick wet grass; they topped small hills to see the sea brilliantly blue on their left, and fishing towns with the boats drawn up or out dotting the horizon with their sails. There were people working, eating and drinking, loving and hating, bringing up children and growing old: she passed through it like an unquiet ghost, cut off from her own part in life and dragged down an unending ribbon of road.

Now, six days from Tyre, they had rounded the corner of coastline out of Syria and into the great mass of Asia, and the silk factory might have been in another world. *It's like being dead,* Demetrias thought again. *I have left it all behind — home and country, husband and child, the work I was so proud of, everyone I knew and everything I thought I was; I am only a memory, wandering the edge of oblivion.*

The horses were harnessed to the carriage. One of Eulogios' retainers came up to her, grinning. It was Chelchal the Hun. With his deformed head, scarred face, and bowed legs, he was the most hideous creature she had ever seen; his cloak of dirty marmot skins was full of fleas and he stank of sour milk and horse dung. At first she had been more afraid of him than of any of the others, but he was the only member of the party who hadn't hit her, and she now made no effort to avoid him. "You get in carriage now," he told her cheerfully, in his clumsy and heavily accented Greek. "We go quick, reach Seleucia tonight."

She bowed her head and walked slowly toward the carriage; Chelchal helped her into it. Eulogios' valet was already in his place; he gave a sniff and turned his head away. He objected, he said, to sharing a carriage with "a stinking purple-worker." Chelchal patted her hand. "You eat breakfast?" he asked her.

She shook her head; the lurching of the carriage still made her sick, and she wanted no food.

"You must eat!" Chelchal declared in concern. "You get sick if you not eat; die, maybe."

"I want to go home," she told him. "I can't eat here."

He shook his head in regret. "You cannot." He spread his hands and shrugged. "Can*not*. You eat breakfast."

"I have a husband and child in Tyre!" she told him wretchedly — *as though*, she thought bitterly, *it mattered to any of them what or who I was.*

He nodded, slapped his chest. "I have wife, two childs, with my people, the Acatziri. King Attila comes and makes war. He kills many, many warriors and conquers the Acatziri. Then he gives my wife and childs to other man. So. I still eat breakfast. A dead man is no use nothing. I bring bread and you eat." He went off to the inn, and came back a moment later with a warm sesame cake steaming in his callused and dirty hand. "So," he said, grinning at her, "you eat this. Is good."

She took the sesame cake, and Chelchal nodded contentedly and mounted his horse. The carriage began to move, jolting out of the inn gate and onto the road once more.

After that Chelchal seemed to have decided to look after her, and he came up to her at every stop, offering drinks of wine and water, or bread rolls, or a new cheese, and talked to her in a friendly fashion that was desperately sweet after the hostility and contempt she received from all the others. He was a talkative man, and, though Greek was his third language, after Hunnic and Gothic, and he spoke it badly, he also contrived to tell Demetrias about himself. He was a noble of an eastern Hunnish tribe, the Acatziri. The shape of his head — pointed on top and crushed in front — was not natural, but, like his scars, a deliberate piece of deformation practiced on boys of his tribe in infancy. "Doesn't hurt the babies," he told Demetrias cheerfully. "My son has head tied when little baby, doesn't cry at all, oh no! He eats and eats and eats! Becomes big strong child. He is six years old last time I see him; must be nine now. When he is twelve, thirteen, he will go out and kill a wolf, or maybe a boar or a lion: then he will become a warrior and be given his scars." The Hun grinned proudly, then scowled. "Or maybe no. Maybe his master keep him at home for slave."

At a posting station near Aspendus he told her how he had come to be Eulogios' retainer. They had stopped to change horses but the agent was dissatisfied with the animals provided; he spent some time screaming at the stationmaster and demanding different mounts. Demetrias remained in the carriage, but Chelchal came up to lean against the door and talk to her. In Tyre everyone had referred to the Huns as though they were one people, but she learned that, in fact, they formed many different tribes, each with its own customs and its own traditional grazing grounds for the flocks it herded. The famous King Attila had inherited from his father a confederation of several tribes, but he had enlarged his domain by continuous conquests. Chelchal's tribe had been one of the last independent ones. Three years before, the king had invaded their territory, driving off flocks, carrying off women, children, and slaves, and burning huts and wagons until the leaders of the Acatziri had submitted and sworn him obedience. Chelchal's family had been taken in one of the king's raids and been given to one of Attila's warriors as a reward for his service; there had been no hope that they would be returned with the peace. When his people had surrendered, Chelchal had refused to submit with the others. He had instead wandered for a time about the kingdoms of the north, looking for some opponent of the "king of the Huns" whom he could join. But there was no effective resistance anywhere, and Chelchal had finally given up and gone to Constantinople, reasoning that there he would at least remain independent of his enemy. But it was only with difficulty that he had been able to stay in the city.

"King Attila is a very, very big king," he explained to Demetrias. "He conquers the Acatziri, Amilzuri, Itimari — all the brave Hun peoples, they all serve King Attila now. And he conquers all the Goths and the Halani and Gepides and Heruls — all the peoples north of the Danube, as far east as the Ephthalites and as far west as the Franks. It is a very big kingdom, as big as the kingdoms of the Greeks and the Romans put together. And King Attila is a much bigger king than King Theodosius of the Greek Romans or King Valentinian of the West Romans. King Theodosius will not fight him. He pays him very much gold instead. And Attila wants more than gold. He says to King Theodosius, 'Give me all my deserters.' He says I am a deserter, you see, because he rules my people. He says all Huns are his slaves, or else they are deserters and runaways. Then I, and many other Huns like me, enemies of King Attila, we go to King Theodosius and we say, 'Let us stay and we will fight King Attila for you.' But King Theodosius does not want to fight. Most of the men he sends away to King Attila, with much gold besides. Still, Chrysaphios is clever. When many warriors are sent away, he says to Attila, 'All the other deserters are dead; angry Greeks kill them all.' And he gives King

Attila presents so that Attila believes him and makes no wars against Greeks. So I promise to serve Chrysaphios, and Chrysaphios, he says to me, 'For this year you will serve my servant Eulogios; then we will re-con-sider.' " He produced the word with some pleasure, the actual word the great chamberlain had used. "If I serve well, then I stay among the Greeks; otherwise, he will send me to Attila. But he will not send me to Attila. I am a brave warrior, too good to send away."

"What would Attila do to you if he caught you?" asked Demetrias.

Chelchal spat. "King Attila does not kill brave Huns. He wants more men. He must rule over the other peoples of his kingdom — the Goths, Halani, and Gepides. There are many, many Goths and not many Huns. King Attila needs more Hun warriors, and he needs the money from the Greeks to keep the Goths quiet. No, I am not afraid in case Attila kills me. But I do not want to serve Attila. He gives my wife and childs to other man." Chelchal spat again, then resumed his usual grin.

Demetrias sat in silence for a moment. "I once wove a cloak that was sent to King Attila," she told Chelchal. She remembered it vividly: purple and white silk in a pattern of flying birds; two tapestry rondels showing the kings of the Hebrews, David and Solomon, enthroned in majesty. It had taken her seven months to complete. "I suppose that's what started all this trouble," she said bitterly. "The procurator saw it and wanted me to make one for him."

Chelchal nodded, still grinning. "Lord Eulogios buys you to make fine cloaks. That Berich, he says you are a whore, but that Berich, he is a stupid Goth and can't tell whores from nuns." Chelchal laughed. "Stupid Goth wants to rape them all, hah! I tell him you are a good girl, clever at making fine cloaks." He patted his own marmot skin cloak, then put his hand through the carriage window and fingered the edge of Demetrias' cloak, with its pattern of flowers. "You make that?"

Demetrias shrank back — but the Hun seemed more interested in the weaving than in her. "That was simple," she told him. "That's just a pattern done with leashes. For the factory I did tapestry — pictures in the cloth."

"You are clever. I see cloaks like that — rich men own them. The Huns and Goths do not know how to make them. It is the same with swords and knives and cooking pots: the ones the Greeks make are best. If I become a rich man, I will buy all Greek slaves to make things, and all Huns and Goths to fight — just like Chrysaphios. Huns and Goths are brave men, but they are not clever at making things. But are you Greek, all Tyrian Greek? You have eyes like the Goths."

She had been told this before by others, and turned her green Gothic eyes away from him. "My grandmother was a Goth," she said shortly.

"She is a slave too? Or a freeborn woman?"

"She always said she was nobly born, though whether that was true I don't know. She was captured and enslaved by the Romans during the wars when the Goths came into Thrace, and the factory bought her for her spinning."

"Not for weaving cloaks?"

"No." She looked back at him, smiling. It had once been an immense comfort to her that her grandmother hadn't been a good enough weaver to work at the silk looms. "No, she was never allowed near a loom. She couldn't weave anything but checks, and those badly."

Chelchal laughed. "Like all Goths! Your husband is a clever man?"

For the first time since leaving Tyre, she tried to picture Symeon. She had been aware from the first that being taken from the city would leave her gutted; she had cried out again and again against being parted from her husband and child; she had even imagined Meletios weeping, and finding some comfort from Symeon and from her mother. But that part of the void inside her called simply "my husband" she had left vague: a fine net of responsibilities broken, a pattern abandoned, an absence beside her when she slept. And even in Tyre when she had thought of him it had been chiefly as "my husband," a man defined by how he behaved to her, not by what he was in himself. *Is he clever?* she asked herself now — and saw him, deftly repairing a murex trap; scanning the sea to see if the wind was shifting; staring intently into her own face in the moonlight outside the door as he understood that she was trying to lie to him. She was unprepared for the violence of the pain that struck her together with the image; it was as though someone had cut a hole in her heart.

She did not reply to Chelchal. After a moment, he patted her hand, then backed away, looking for his horse. Eulogios had finished with the grooms, the horses were saddled, and the party was ready to ride on.

*I am in love with Symeon,* Demetrias thought in astonishment as the carriage again began to roll. *Mother of God, I want him, him and no other ever: his face, his eyes, his body against mine; his life and mine to remain joined as long as they last. Why? I wasn't in love when I married him. Or was I? I always understood that I liked him better than any other, but I never knew why. I said it was because he would be kind to me and not beat me, that a purple-fisher was a good match, respectable enough to fend off the others, that I wouldn't be poor. But there were other men who were kind and well off and respectable, whom I might have married, and didn't. It was him, it was always him, and never anyone else. And for six years I have been married to him; six years wasted, sitting upon a treasure and living in poverty; six years when I might have been happy and wasn't. All I could want I had in my hands, and I couldn't see it until now, when I've lost it forever. Oh Symeon, my life; my darling Meli, why in the name of God was I so stupid?*

Eulogios' valet sniffed in disapproval and edged primly to the far side of the carriage. His master's new slave was weeping. *Really,* he thought, *what a tedious creature it is, nothing but trouble since he bought her, first screaming and fighting and then being sick and now weeping. I'll be glad when we reach Constantinople and she's put in the quarters with the common slaves. Really, they should have had the decency to make her ride outside.*

Eulogios and his party rolled on along the southern coast of Asia as far as Attaleia, where they turned inland, crossing the mountains at a point where they were scarcely more than hills in the gap between Lycia and Isauria. Even so, the carriage was dragged through deep snow at one point, and the passengers had to get out and walk to lighten the load. Demetrias had never seen snow before. She stared at it in wonder when she first climbed out of the carriage. There was no sound on the mountain slopes; even the wind in the pines was muffled by the snow. Her sandaled feet were cold, and she could feel the ice melting into the edge of her tunic.

"Hurry up!" shouted Eulogios impatiently, reining in his horse. "Help with the carriage, you slut! You, driver, get a move on!"

Demetrias copied the valet and broke pine branches from the laden trees, shoving them under the carriage wheels when the vehicle slipped into a hidden rut in the road. In a little while she was sweating and shivering at the same time and stumbling with exhaustion. She had not eaten much since leaving Tyre, and the water at one of the stations had given her a mild dysentery, much to the valet's disgust.

"Here," said Chelchal, reining up his horse beside her, "you ride with me."

Berich the Goth promptly pulled in as well. "She can ride with me!" he told Chelchal, angrily.

Demetrias had been considering Chelchal's offer — but at this she shook her head. "I'll walk," she told them, and steadied herself against the carriage as she put her battered pine branch again under the rear wheel. Chelchal said something to Berich in a language that she presumed was Gothic; Berich seemed insulted and shouted back; Chelchal laughed at him. Berich kicked his horse and rode angrily to the front of the party. "You ride with me," Chelchal told her.

Demetrias shook her head. She liked Chelchal, but to ride with him now would be to accept something more than kindness — and that something, though still undefined, was unacceptable. "I can walk," she said doggedly. "The snow surely won't be this deep for long."

It was only for three miles that the snow was deep; it wasn't long before they could get back in the carriage and begin the descent toward the city of Colossae. But those miles were long enough for Demetrias. When the labor of climbing and slipping in the snow was done and she was back in the carriage, she found that her limbs were trembling uncontrollably. She pulled her snow-damp cloak closely about her and curled up in her corner; the world seemed to lurch back and forth behind her closed eyes. When the party finally stopped that night the valet had to shout at her to get out of the carriage. She nodded wearily, began to stand up so as to open the door — and then the world spun about her and went black, then gray again. It was as though her shrunken awareness had been chopped free of the sick, cold, exhausted body; she saw herself lying in the corner of the carriage, and the valet slapping her, but she watched it without interest. After a moment, the valet went away and Eulogios himself came and swore at her. She paid no attention: it was easier to sink into the oblivion and drown than to wander anymore.

"You little whore!" Eulogios shouted, leaning toward her from the opposite door of the carriage. "You slut, get out!" She did nothing; he jerked his head for one of his retainers to drag her out. Berich the Goth moved to obey; Chelchal stopped him.

"Is no good, sir," he told Eulogios. "She is a sick girl now." He opened Demetrias' door of the carriage himself, and caught her as she started to fall out.

"Sick?" Eulogios frowned and came to see; Chelchal steadied Demetrias against his shoulder.

"What do you think?" asked the Hun. "She does not eat, she gets sick in the carriage, drinks bad water; then you make her walk in the snow. She is a sick girl now. And if you give her to Berich and he hits her some more, she will get sicker, die maybe."

Demetrias stirred at that and turned her head, looking up in surprise. *I may be exhausted and sick,* she thought, *but I'm not dying — at least, I don't think I am.* Chelchal's marmot skin cloak was warm and stinking against her cheek. Eulogios' face staring at her seemed blurred, as though seen through a panel of glass; she stared back at it. *He'd regret it if I died,* she thought, with an incongruous malicious triumph. *That would teach him — all the money he paid for me, and all this distance he's dragged me, and then I die before we ever each Constantinople. But I don't want to die. I am a fool, I've lost everything — but I don't want to die. The world is too great a thing to leave lightly. I'm not that sick — am I?*

Chelchal met her questioning gaze and winked surreptitiously. She was too exhausted to smile, but felt a wave of relief.

"Well, take her to a warm room," Eulogios ordered Chelchal irritably, "and see that she's looked after. See if they have a doctor here, or at least someone who knows herbs, and have her treated. And don't you harm her, either: she cost me sixty *solidi*, and that was a compulsory price, low for a worker of her skill."

"I will not harm her," said Chelchal, and gently pulled her to her feet. "She is a good girl."

She fainted again on the way into the posting inn, and he half dragged, half carried her to the main room, had the station manager find her a room with a brazier, and sent one of the maids to undress her and put her to bed while he looked for someone who knew herbs. He eventually found a brisk young midwife who diagnosed chilling and exhaustion, and who packed her feet with hot compresses and gave her a decoction against dysentery in a drink of warm barley broth and honey. When they left Colossae next morning, Demetrias had a fever but was able to climb into the carriage on her own. The road was easier that day, Eulogios slowed his headlong hurry, and no one slapped her the whole day: she felt much better by that evening.

"You will be all better in Constantinople," Chelchal told her confidently, the following morning. "We reach Constantinople in five days, maybe; you rest there." He patted her hand, which was holding the carriage window. The carriage was actually moving as he spoke, but only at a walk. Chelchal was riding his horse next to the carriage window. He sat in the saddle with one leg folded up underneath himself, leaning backward, like a man relaxing in a tavern. His saddle was different from those of the other retainers: it was larger, made of wood, and its high front and back were decorated with an inlay of silver scales; he changed it from horse to horse, and she guessed that it was his own and Hunnish. He seemed more comfortable in it than on foot; she had noticed that he could even sleep on horseback. She smiled at him, and he stopped grinning for a minute and looked thoughtful, then said, "What do you think? When we reach Constantinople, Lord Eulogios will give you to Chrysaphios. I ask Chrysaphios if we get married, maybe?"

"What?" asked Demetrias, pulling her hand back.

"You are a good girl, clever, pretty. And brave — you fight off that Berich like a warrior, hah! I want a new wife, new childs, maybe. We get married?" He touched his chest. "I am freeborn, a good warrior, brave. Soon I talk Greek good, and I become a Christian like you. Chrysaphios and Eulogios, they pay me good money. I do not hit you. I make good husband. Yes?"

*Oh God,* she thought, *now I lose the one person I thought was a friend. I should have known better than to expect simple kindness from any man.* "I . . . I have a husband already. I can't," she said, stammering a little.

"Your husband is in Tyre. Is all gone."

Demetrias bit her lip, blinking at the Hun in anguish. It was strange

134

to hear Chelchal stating his qualifications and finding them the same that she had once used to choose Symeon. Of course, Chelchal was hideous and alien and stank — but a soldier in the service of the emperor's chamberlain was potentially a far more glorious match than a purple-fisher in Tyre. She did not doubt it, just as she didn't doubt that Chelchal would be kind to her: it was clear enough that, good warrior or not, he was by nature a kind man. And the idea of marrying him was unendurable.

"I'm sorry," she said, miserably, afraid of offending him, "I . . . my husband . . ."

"Is good, is good!" said Chelchal. "Is too soon, yes? Only two weeks. Is too soon. I will wait, is good!" Grinning, he touched the sides of his horse and trotted ahead to ride behind Eulogios.

Demetrias sat still for a moment, then reached up and touched her earrings. They were the gold ones Symeon had chosen for her in Ptolemais, which no one had taken from her since. She remembered his face as he watched her put them on, the warm glow of pride. She dropped her hands, doubled into fists, back into her lap and bit back tears. *Only two weeks. It seems another life. All gone. But I won't be guilty of such treachery to it as to start another life now with Chelchal.* She looked out the carriage window: the Hun still rode comfortably slouched in his saddle, the silver scales glittering around his dirty fur cloak; ahead of him, the agent sat stiff and impatient on his own mount, leaning forward as though to attack the miles ahead of them. In five days, perhaps, those miles would be gone, and they would be riding into Constantinople to see the emperor's chamberlain. What then?

*I will tell the same lies over again,* Demetrias thought. *And then . . . then who knows? Nomos' plot may succeed — or it may fail, and destroy me in its failure. But I must try to believe that I will live, and while I live I will try to go home. I will serve and flatter humbly; I will save money as I can, and hope that somehow, by obedience or bribery or chance, I can one day earn my way back to Tyre. I must hope for that. Nothing else is worth hoping for, and I don't think I can live this new life without hope.*

The weather north of the Taurus mountains was windy and cold, but Eulogios and his party jolted northward under a sky blue and polished as enamel. South of the Taurus, however, the same fierce wind pushed clouds black with rain, sending them scudding over a heavy sea. Symeon watched them gloomily. *Still firm from the west,* he thought. *Four days now, and no end in sight. God knows how long it will be before we can sail on.*

He and Meletios had made excellent progress during the first few days of the voyage from Tyre, sailing quickly north with a stiff following wind, and rounding the point of Laodicea, a hundred and fifty miles from Tyre, after only three days. But then the weather had broken. The strong breeze from the southeast had faltered, then veered to the west, bringing heavy rain and heavier waves. Symeon had put into shore at the first harbor they came to. This happened to be a tiny fishing village some thirty miles south of the mouth of the Orontes river. The villagers were surprised when the strange and elegant boat slid onto their own muddy beach, and they crowded round with questions and offers of help.

Symeon told them that they were on business up the Orontes to Antioch — he was afraid that if the locals knew he was making a longer journey, and hence had larger funds for it, they would be tempted into robbery and murder. They looked poor enough to be tempted even by the boat and the spare clothing; they themselves had only the most battered of sailing dinghies and wore tattered and threadbare homespun. However, they seemed friendly enough. Strangers from Tyre were a rare wonder and much to be savored: none of the villagers had been farther away from their home than thirty miles. Symeon and Meletios soon found themselves the guests of the chief man of the village, a well-off farmer who made his living selling bread and oil to the fishermen, and who ran a kind of simple tavern in the porch of his home. Symeon greatly increased the custom of this last by sitting in it and telling the villagers the news of the south. They were ignorant as well as poor: none of them could read, and none could even speak Greek, and everything he had to tell them was new. Meletios listened in unhappy silence. Symeon had been raised speaking Syriac as comfortably as Greek, but Meli, though he had heard the language all his life and understood most of what was said in it, didn't feel confident enough in it to say anything. At home they had always spoken Greek.

But as the days wore on and the winds kept *Prokne* on the beach, the villagers' welcoming warmth chilled. The chief man had a daugh-

136

ter, a handsome dark-eyed girl of sixteen. Her father's position and her own good looks made her the most desirable woman in the village — and she was a great deal more attentive to the strangers than she should have been. She abandoned her tasks about the house and hung perpetually at Symeon's elbow, laughing and chattering and running eagerly to fetch things for him. Several of the younger men in the village seemed greatly displeased with this, and the girl's father wasn't happy either. Symeon began to notice stares and mutterings when he appeared, and he caught several of the local men eyeing *Prokne* with something more than idle curiosity. *As if I'd want a dirty, flea-bitten peasant girl nearly half my age!* Symeon thought in disgust. *Even if I were unmarried, and she weren't my host's daughter, I wouldn't touch her. But if we don't get away within the next couple of days there'll be trouble because of the little slut. Christ and Saint Peter, send me a good east wind!*

But the wind blew in obstinately from west, the waves crashed against the open beach, and the rain slanted heavily down. It was now late in the afternoon of his fourth day in the village. From where he sat under the palm thatch of his host's porch he could see the row of boats hauled up on the mud, drabber than ever in the fading, cloud-dimmed light: *Prokne* lay on her side, shrouded in her canopy, her reclining sternpost looking up at the sea like a bored feaster at a sorry banquet. Symeon sighed deeply and scratched at the bite of one of his host's fleas.

Meletios had been playing beside the wood fire that warmed the porch; at the sigh he got up and came over to his father. He pressed himself against Symeon's knee, leaning his head against his father's arm. "When is the wind going to change?" he asked.

"When God wills it," Symeon replied; then, because the boy looked so bored and miserable he added, "Here, why don't we go over your letters?"

Meletios did not look enthusiastic, but he fetched a plank and a piece of charred wood from beside the fire and handed them to his father. Symeon began scrawling letters on the plank and asking the child to identify them. Mariam, their host's daughter, came in while they were engaged in this. She put her hands on her hips and clucked her tongue with surprise.

"What a clever child!" she exclaimed to Symeon. "So little, and he knows all the letters as well as any scribe!"

"Not that well," returned Symeon shortly; the girl made him uncomfortable. He wrote "Prokne" out on the plank and Meletios frowned at it. Mariam came over, squatted beside the boy, and also stared at the letters for a moment before looking up sideways at Symeon and smiling. She was carrying a jug of wine and some earthenware cups — it was about the time the village men arrived for their evening drink.

"Tell me, little prince," she said to Meletios, "what does it say?"

Meletios scowled; he still disliked being spoken to in Syriac. He named the letters one by one, then glared at them. He could occasionally read a syllable, but never a whole word. "Pro . . ." he began. "Progress?"

"No," replied Symeon patiently. "That's a kappa, Meli. Kappa, nu, eta. What does that make?"

Meli sounded them out under his breath; then his face cleared. "Prokne!" he exclaimed. "It says Prokne!"

Two of the villagers came into the porch, a father and his grown son. The son scowled at the sight of Mariam crouched beside the visitor. He sat down heavily at the other table, glaring at her. She paid no attention. "What does that mean?" she asked Symeon, smiling up at him.

He shrugged and dropped the plank. "It's the name of the boat. Hadn't you better . . . ?" He gestured toward the newcomers.

Mariam rose, slowly and with obvious reluctance. She set the jug of wine on Symeon's table and went off to fetch water. The young villager turned his glare on Symeon. His father coughed uncomfortably. "Why's the boat called Prokne?" he asked politely.

"Most of our purple-fishing boats in Tyre were named after weavers," Symeon returned, relieved to find a neutral topic of conversation. "There was a *Penelope*, an *Arachne*, an *Omphale* — all of them famous weavers. My father's first boat was called *Prokne*, so I gave mine that name as well."

Mariam reappeared with the jug of water and more cups. She set one in front of Symeon and half filled it with her father's sticky red wine, though he had not asked for it. The younger fisherman scowled more than ever. Mariam topped up Symeon's cup with water, then, reluctantly, went to serve the customers. Another man appeared, but the girl ignored him and sat down on the bench beside Symeon. She picked up the plank with the writing again and looked at it as though mere staring could turn the smudged charcoal markings into sounds. "What did this Prokne do, then?" she asked.

Symeon glanced helplessly at the new customer. The man scowled back, then crossed the porch and helped himself to a cup and some wine. "She was turned into a swallow," Symeon said resignedly.

"A fast bird, and the most agile one," the older fisher put in quickly. "Good name for a boat like yours."

"That's what I thought."

"It's a horrible story," Meletios said, suddenly and in good Syriac. "I hate it."

Mariam laughed and clapped her hands. "You can talk our language!"

Meli scowled at her. "I like Greek better. My Mama always talks Greek."

At this the young fisherman laughed, though Mariam did not seem put out. "Why is it a horrible story?" she asked. "I think a swallow would be a good thing to be turned into. Much better than a snake or a fish."

Symeon took a sip of his wine. Telling the story would at least keep the girl quiet. "It was what happened to her first that was horrible," he said. "It was like this: there was once a king called Pandion who had two daughters, Prokne and Philomela. Philomela was skilled at music, but Prokne's weaving was the finest in all the land."

Symeon's voice had taken on the distinctive rhythm of the story-teller. The group in the porch fell silent, even the young fisherman listening attentively. A new story was a treasure, and jealousy and resentment could wait until the tale was done.

"This was a very long time ago," Symeon went on, "in the time before King Alexander. I don't know when it happened, except that it was in the days of the old gods, when many strange things were done." He hesitated: most of the villagers were pagans, worshiping Ba'al and Astarte as their ancestors had centuries before. His hosts' family seemed to be the only Christians. But the others accepted the reference: times had indeed changed since the old gods ruled the earth unquestioned. "At that time, there was another king, called Tereus, who ruled in Thrace."

"He was a Hun?" asked the old fisherman.

"I suppose so," replied Symeon. "He was certainly a barbarian. But whatever his nation, he grew powerful and made his neighbors afraid. Pandion, to protect himself, offered Tereus the hand of his daughter Philomela."

"He must have been a Hun," said the younger fisherman. "Our kings are still buying peace with them with gold and marriages to noblewomen. We've had three supplementary taxes in the last three years to pay for it all."

There was a grunt of agreement from the others. "He was going to marry Philo . . . Philomila?" asked Mariam. "Not the other one?"

Symeon nodded. "That's right. Philomela was the elder daughter. Well, Pandion was a powerful king and worth an alliance, so Tereus accepted the offer and sailed south to Athens, where Pandion had his court. But though he'd agreed to marry the elder daughter, his eyes fell on the younger one, Prokne, and he was struck by her grace and her beauty. Secretly he began to lust for her. Still, he said nothing, and married Philomela with great celebrations. He took her away to his own kingdom in Thrace, where for a year they lived quietly. But Tereus could not forget Prokne, and he wanted her still, so that his wife became hateful in his eyes.

"After a year, Philomela became pregnant, and Tereus found her less desirable than ever. So at last, without saying anything to his wife, he took ship again and once more sailed south to Athens.

"His father-in-law and sister were pleased to see him, and asked eagerly for news of his wife; he told them that she was well, but expecting a child; and he told them that she had asked for her sister, Prokne, to be with her in her confinement. The two sisters had always loved one another dearly and Prokne was eager to go: her father suspected no danger in sending her with her brother-in-law to attend the birth of his grandchild, and he happily gave his permission for her to accompany Tereus back to Thrace. So she, poor girl, sailed away to the north — and never saw her home again."

Symeon was silent for a moment, possessed suddenly by the image of Demetrias, carried off to the north and at the mercy of strangers. *But not from lust*, he told himself determinedly, *and I'll get her back.* He shook his head to clear it and went on, "When they got to Thrace, Tereus took Prokne and his attendants and began riding northward to his own city, which lay inland. But when they had gone some way along the road, he sent most of his attendants on, and, telling Prokne that they would rest, brought her to a lonely hut in a forest. As soon as she was inside he locked the door and commanded her to sleep with him.

"She tried to pretend she didn't understand him; she begged him not to dishonor her and his own wife; finally, she refused. Her refusal merely enraged him, and he seized her and forced her, there in the hut, with no one but a few of his own trusted men to hear her screams. When he had finished with her she told him, 'You have dishonored us all, yourself as well as me and my sister. Who will trust a king who has committed a crime like this?' 'No one will know,' he replied. 'I will tell them,' she answered, 'I will tell everyone I meet.' 'You will tell no one,' he said, and, with that, he pulled out his dagger, seized her again and cut out her tongue. Then he left her locked in the hut and rode away. At the next village he appointed an old woman to feed her and look after her, but he told her that the woman in the hut was a Greek slave he'd purchased who'd tried to run away, and that she was to be kept prisoner and set to work. He went back to his own city and his wife, and he told Philomela nothing about what had happened. To Pandion he sent a message that Prokne had fallen ill and died during the voyage. The old king mourned for his daughter, but Philomela knew nothing about it. Shortly after Tereus' return she gave birth to a son, whom his father named Itys, and if she wasn't happy, there among the barbarians, at least as a mother and a queen she had plenty to occupy her.

"Prokne was left in the hut in the forest, and the old woman brought her food but kept her locked in. She could tell no one who she was or what had happened to her. I suppose it was so long ago that no one knew about writing: at any rate, she could write to no one. All she was allowed was her weaving — the old woman had set her to work on that at once, thinking that this would be pleasing to the king. But the king took no more interest in her. So Prokne sat at her loom and wove; she wove a tapestry, and it was the most beautiful piece of work that was ever seen in that country, and the old woman marveled at it more every day. It took more than two years to complete, and when it was done the old woman couldn't bear that it should wait at the hut for the king's attention: she took it into the king's city, and had it hung up in the marketplace, so that everyone could admire it. And after a time the queen looked out of the window of her palace and saw the crowd in the marketplace, and came out herself to see what they were staring at."

Symeon took another sip of wine; his audience waited eagerly in silence. "When Philomela saw the tapestry, she knew at once who had woven it: more, she knew everything that had happened, because it was all pictured in the cloth. There was Athens and her father's palace; there was Tereus and his ship, and Prokne setting foot on the vessel; there was the Thracian forest and the hut in it, and Tereus again, this time with his knife. She understood it all, though no one else in that crowd did. She said nothing, at first, only ran back into her palace — but in a little while, she sent for the old woman and begged her to take her to see the weaver who had made the wonderful tapestry. The old woman saw no harm in this and obeyed, and so the two sisters were reunited and wept in each other's arms.

"But Philomela did not know what to do to rescue her sister and herself. Her husband was still king, and she was only his foreign wife, and powerless. She went home and brooded over what had happened. Perhaps she went mad."

"I hate this part," Meletios declared. He huddled against Symeon's side and put his hands over his ears. Symeon smiled and put an arm around him.

"She certainly acted like a madwoman," he told the villagers. "She waited until there was a great festival among the Thracians, and then she took the son she had borne Tereus, Itys, a little boy of three: she took her husband's dagger, and she cut the child's throat." The villagers gave a gasp of horror. "Then she cut up the body into pieces, and, setting aside the head, she cooked it and set it before her husband that night at the feast. He ate the meat and praised it highly. 'Do you want to know what beast you ate tonight?' she asked him, smiling; and when he said yes, she brought in the head, covered, on a silver plate. 'A savage beast, fiercer than any wolf,' she told him. 'Like its father,' and she uncovered the head.

"Tereus understood what she had done. He turned from the table with a great cry and was sick onto the floor; when he had recovered, he looked for his wife, but she was gone. He drew his sword, summoned his men, and followed after her. Philomela had had horses and provisions ready waiting, and she rode directly to the hut in the forest and fetched her sister, Prokne. The two women rode all through the night, but when the day dawned and they looked back, they saw behind them Tereus and his troops, riding after them with drawn swords. Then Philomela raised her hands to the heavens and prayed to the gods, begging them to keep her and her sister from her husband's hands.

"And the gods heard her. When Tereus rode down upon the two spent horses he found no women there, only two strange birds that fluttered up from the saddles; and when he raised his sword against them it fell from his hand, for his arms became wings, and he was transformed, like them, into a bird. So he became a hoopoe, and Philomela, who loved music, a nightingale. She still remembers the child she murdered, and cries always for Itys, Itys; you can hear her if you listen to her song. But Prokne became a swallow, the swiftest and most agile of all birds, able to fly from any danger, and in the autumn she leaves the cold north where she was kept prisoner and goes winging home.

"There, Meli, I've finished. You can take your hands off your ears now."

Meletios took his hands off his ears. "It's a horrible story," he said, in Greek this time.

Symeon smiled. He remembered thinking the same when his father first told it to him. "Well, I don't think it's true, anyway," he told Meli. "So I wouldn't worry about it."

"If it were true," Mariam said softly, "I would love to see the tapestry."

"Even if it were true," the young fisherman said sharply, "you couldn't see it. If all this happened before King Alexander's days, it would be dust by now."

"My mother makes tapestries," said Meli. "She made one last year that they hung up in a shop on the marketplace for everyone to see before they sent it off."

"Your mother must be very clever," Mariam said humbly. She reached out and touched the edge of Meletios' cloak, where Demetrias had woven a pattern of flying birds, orseille-blue on the soft broom-yellow wool. For Demetrias it had been a simple pattern, done quickly with the cheaper dyes, suitable for a child; the cloak was now small

143

for him, as its replacement with dolphins was long overdue. But Mariam touched it reverently. Her own cloak, like all the villagers', was the plain gray-brown of the cheapest wool, undyed, coarsely woven, and clumsily darned. "What did it look like, that beautiful tapestry?" she asked.

Meletios hesitated. "I don't remember all of it," he confessed, "only the bit my mother did. It was an altarcloth; lots of people worked on it. Mama did the Blessed Virgin going to Ephesus in a ship with Saint John. It was a merchant ship with white sails and a sternpost shaped like a dove, and the Virgin was holding on to the mast. She was very pretty, all in blue with gold around her head. Ephesus was in front of the ship, and it was yellow and white, and had a big church dome rising out of the middle of it. The sea was all blue and green, with fishes in it, and it got darker and darker as it went down, and right at the bottom there was a murex, in purple. Everybody noticed the murex and pointed to it. It was there so that when the tapestry was sent away, the people who got it would know it came from Tyre."

Mariam listened to the description with her eyes half closed, a look of naked hunger on her face. "I wish I could have seen it," she said. "I wish we knew how to make things like that here." She turned to Symeon. "How do you get to be a weaver in Tyre? I suppose you have to learn when you're very little."

"You have to be born into it," returned Symeon.

The girl nodded, unsurprised.

"You have to be born a purple-fisher, too, don't you?" the young fisherman asked bitterly. "We have the murex off our coast as well, you know; I've found their shells on the beach. But the likes of us would be flogged or killed for dealing in purple."

Symeon shrugged. "It's sacred; it belongs to the emperor. I'd be flogged or killed too, if I gave my catch to anyone but the emperor's own factory."

"Does the purple make your guild sacred as well?" the young villager demanded angrily. "Better than us?"

"We're not a guild, we're state slaves," Symeon replied patiently. "We're allowed to deal with the purple because we belong to the emperor as much as it does. That's the difference."

"Slaves?" asked Mariam incredulously, her dark eyes scanning his clothes, so much finer than anything owned by anyone else there.

144

"*State* slaves," he said sharply. "That's different from the ordinary kind."

She shook her head. "Even ordinary slaves are lucky," she said quietly, "compared to us."

Against his will, Symeon found himself imagining what it must be like to live in this village. Tyre was a great city: there were always ships coming into the harbors, and storytellers and ballad singers made a good living in the marketplace. At festivals there was chariot-racing in the hippodrome and vulgar plays in the theaters; there were church processions with music and dancing and civic processions with trumpets and speeches. There would have been none of that here — only the same faces, year after year, and the same unending round of chores that were never fully done. In Tyre there had always been plenty of food: even if the local harvest failed, the city could still import grain, and the ration to the state slaves was kept up no matter what happened in the countryside. If the harvest failed here, even the well-off went hungry. And if there was a surplus, any earnings from it went immediately to pay the crushing burden of the taxes. And Mariam was young, longing for something different, something beautiful — a world out of a story, a tapestry picture. Probably she had never seen a tapestry or a picture. She probably envied Prokne, who, locked up in her hut, had been able at least to make something lovely from her memories. He felt ashamed of his own earlier contempt for her. Of course she had followed him about, wanting to know more about the world away from the village. Perhaps she did hope that he would take her with him when he left. *Probably I could buy her from her father for ten* solidi, he thought, *and if I offered it, they'd both be pleased*. He had a sudden vision of buying the girl, taking her home to Tyre, and presenting her to Demetrias — "I know you said you didn't want a slave, but she was so desperate to get away from the flea pit she was born in that I couldn't leave her." Would Demetrias have understood? Perhaps. She understood people wanting to see tapestries, anyway. But Demetrias wasn't in Tyre; she was being carried off to Constantinople, and Symeon could not buy this strange girl and take her with him on that long voyage.

He sighed and scratched his beard, then glanced out toward *Prokne* and saw that the boat had become merely a black outline against the dark sea; the porch was lit only by the red light of the fire. He stood up. "It's late," he said to the company, avoiding the hostile stare of the young man. "Meli, it's time for you to go to bed." He took Meli's hand and led him off unprotesting into the house. *Safe for another night,* he thought, *and perhaps tomorrow the wind will change. God send it does. Perhaps the girl is only hungry for something different, but she'll set the lot of them at my throat if she keeps this up, and we must get away soon.*

The rain stopped during the night, and the next day dawned blood-red and brilliant, with the southeast wind sweeping away the last black fragments of cloud. Symeon was on the beach before it was fully light, pulling off *Prokne*'s cover, checking the gear, and fetching rollers to slide her into the water. His host came down from the house while he was busy with this.

"You don't mean to go today," said the villager. "This weather won't hold for long: there'll be a storm soon."

Symeon shrugged and glanced at the crimson sunrise, judging the cloud banks. "There may well be a gale this afternoon," he replied, "but we can get at least part way to the Orontes by then, and if it holds off we might even reach the river. It's worth seizing even a morning's sailing weather, after all that rain."

The villager bit his lip. "As you like," he said. Then, after a moment's hesitation, he added, "My house has been honored to host you."

"I am most grateful for your generosity," Symeon returned formally.

The elder nodded, then, after another hesitation, he said, "My daughter . . . ah, I hope you haven't . . ."

"Your daughter is a young girl who's eager to know more about the great world," Symeon said quickly. "Her curiosity doesn't offend me in the least."

His host looked relieved. "I'd hoped that you understood. Yes, that's exactly it. She told me last night that she wanted to go with you when you left, but that's all nonsense, all women's curiosity, and I told her so. She hasn't mentioned it to you? No, she's a good girl; she wouldn't actually do such a wild thing, however much she thinks about it. She's a respectable girl, and will have a good dowry; I've arranged for her to marry the son of a friend, a fine hard-working young man who'll inherit a decent farm a few miles from here. In a few years she'll have settled down there, had some children, and she'll laugh at the silly things she's said."

Symeon was silent for a moment. Mariam would marry a farmer a few miles away — not that hot-tempered young fisherman at the tavern. She would settle down, have children, forget. Age and long denial would break that raw longing in her. She might even be happy then. Why did it seem such a terrible thing?

*I've got to get away*, he thought. *I'm starting to care for the girl. And I don't want her, though she's pretty, though I pity her. I want . . . I want . . .* and his mind filled with his wife's image, her stillness balanced against the sea and her face, calm, half smiling, turned away. The image changed to one of Demetrias bound and gagged and thrown into a carriage, and the moment of pity for Mariam was swallowed up.

"I wish your daughter every happiness," he told his host. "Could you help me move the boat? I want to sail while the weather holds."

The villager helped him push *Prokne* down into the water, and Symeon secured the craft with an anchor at the stern and went to fetch Meletios. Mariam was preparing food for them. Her eyes were swollen, but she said nothing. Symeon thanked her, again thanked his host for the hospitality, gave them some money, and returned to *Prokne*. Meletios bounced up and down joyfully, waving to the shore as his father rowed out into the harbor, then the little boy scrambled to help with the sail. The lateen filled and *Prokne* set off across water blue-violet under the red dawn. *Won't be able to go far today*, Symeon thought, again studying the ominous light, *but, God knows, even an identical village a few miles up the coast will be a relief.*

Eulogios and his entourage arrived in Constantinople on the second of January, having traveled a thousand miles in two and a half weeks. The last stage of the journey was by boat, across the Sea of Marmara — a body of water small enough that even quite large ships could sail it in the winter and rely on finding safe harbor if the weather changed. They reached the Bosphorus from Cyzicus in the evening and, since the wind was rising, put in at the first of Constantinople's ports they came to, a deep double harbor ordinarily reserved for the Egyptian grain ships that supplied the city with wheat. As soon as the ship touched the dock, Eulogios sent his valet running into the city to fetch slaves, horses, and a litter from his city mansion, and by the time the luggage was unloaded and the party respectfully dismissed by the customs officials, Eulogios' men were waiting for their master. Demetrias was bundled into the litter — since her fainting fit she had been judged delicate enough to need such conveyances — and carried by two stout porters through a maze of strange streets. She paid no attention to the city. There had been so many cities on the journey that another one, even the New Rome, the capital of the world, could not move her. The only distinctive thing about Constantinople, it seemed then, was that it was their destination, and the brutal journeying would finally have to stop.

It was fully dark when they arrived at Eulogios' house. The litter swayed through a black passageway beyond a gate barred with iron, and was set down gently in a courtyard brightly lit with torches. Demetrias sat up and put legs still unsteady from the voyage onto the stone pavement, looking about her in a daze. The red torchlight glowed on the dark waters of the central fountain and cast wild shadows through the leaves of the bay tree that grew beside it. The opposite side of the courtyard was full of people — a blur of faces under a house wall studded with windows that shone like jewels in the torchlight. Eulogios had already dismounted from his horse, and was talking to one of the strangers. He finished giving directions for his supper, the stabling of his horse, and his retainers' suppers, then glanced about for Demetrias. He jerked his head for her to come over. She stood, swaying a little; Chelchal appeared at her side and took her arm to help her.

"This is a silk weaver I bought from the factory at Tyre," Eulogios told the strangers, who Demetrias realized must be his household slaves. "She's to be a gift for the most illustrious Chrysaphios. She's been sick on the journey; I want her cleaned up and made presentable by tomorrow morning."

Eulogios' slaves looked at Demetrias. The dazzle of fatigue and torchlight wore off, and she saw them, neat, well-dressed, well-fed, respectable people, staring at her in dismay. She was suddenly aware of how she looked — standing stooped with sickness and weariness on Chelchal's arm, her tunic and cloak filthy and stinking from the journey, her tangled hair loose on her shoulders, her face unwashed and pale. She straightened, let go of Chelchal, and tried to pull up her cloak.

The man Eulogios had been chiefly addressing nodded to an elderly woman, who came over at once and took Demetrias' arm.

"You come this way, dear," she whispered, with a nervous glance at her master. "Lord of All, but you must have had a wretched journey!"

Demetrias found herself hurried off into the back of the house, followed almost at once by Eulogios' other women slaves — there seemed a huge number of them, though Demetrias eventually counted and found there were sixteen. As soon as they were out of their master's presence they began talking and asking her questions about herself, Tyre, and the journey. She found it difficult to answer, but their presence — sympathetic, curious, friendly — was enormously comforting. The bitter journey was over, and here to greet her were women like her fellows from the factory: she had arrived safely.

The old woman brought her to the women's workroom on the ground floor at the back of the house. It was a big room, well lit by a tall lampstand with five lamps burning on it and heated by two braziers. There was a basket of wool and some combs and spindles in one corner, and a loom with some plain homespun on it in the other; some racks of drying clothes stretched between the two. Like the slaves, it was homely and welcoming. The old woman pulled out a large washing tub of the sort generally used for clothes and set it up in the middle of the floor, apologizing as she did so that the bathhouse was reserved for the master. "But the room here is nice and warm, and it's private just to us; the men don't come in here. You can have a good bath, and then we'll fetch you some supper and you can get some rest." Demetrias only nodded. She was longing to be clean and warm again, to feel her skin smooth under clothes that weren't stiff with dirt: she would have been happy to wash in a basin.

Eulogios' slaves fell over themselves to make her comfortable. They admired Demetrias' clothes when she took them off to bathe — she noticed that they were all dressed in colorful but coarse homespun woolens — and lamented that such lovely weaving should have to get so dirty; one of the girls pulled out a smaller washtub and set the tunics and cloak to soak at once. Someone else fetched some scented oil for Demetrias, and another woman warmed a towel ready for her when she came out of the bath; they argued about whose bed she should have that night. Their kindness brought her close to tears.

Clean, warm, and wrapped in the towel, she was eating a meal of lentil soup and cumin bread when Eulogios came into the room, followed by Chelchal.

At once, Eulogios' slaves stood up, their looks of sympathy and curiosity vanishing into one expression of anxiety; they bowed their heads in their master's presence. Eulogios gave Demetrias a critical look. The gray, bedraggled slut was gone, he noted with approval. This woman looked tired but healthily pink, her hair glinting a little in the lamplight where it had dried. She sat very straight on a stool, her bare feet curled about its legs, and her head back with a blank, wary expression on her face. She had wrapped the towel about herself like a cloak, with one corner over her left shoulder, and contrived to wear even that gracefully. *Properly dressed*, he thought, *she'll make a very suitable gift for His Illustriousness.* "Well, it's some improvement," he told the slaves. "What about the clothes?"

"We've washed them, Master," said the eldest woman nervously.

"Good. Hang them by the fire to dry: they're good quality, and I want her to wear them tomorrow when I go to see His Illustriousness." He gave Demetrias another critical look, then jerked his head. "Stand up, you, and put that towel down," he ordered her. "I haven't looked at you properly yet."

Demetrias felt the blood rush to her face. It suddenly seemed that he was asking more than everything he had taken from her already. She was expected to stand quietly naked before him — and Chelchal! — while he studied her and prodded her like a cow or a horse, and decided whether she'd been worth his money. *At least when he had me tied up*, she thought, *I was a woman, not an animal.* She remained squarely where she was and clutched the towel more closely.

Eulogios waited for a moment, then began to flush as well. He remembered how the woman had tried to undermine him at the silk factory. "I ordered you to put the towel down and get up, you slut!" he shouted. "You little bitch, do as I say or you'll get a thrashing! You've been nothing but trouble since I bought you!"

"Why did you buy me, then?" Demetrias shouted back. She was faintly surprised at herself, but suddenly so angry that surprise was only passing. She pulled the towel closer to herself and got to her feet, facing Eulogios across her interrupted supper. "You've got no right to blame me for being a trouble to you!" she shouted at him. "You've had me tied up and beaten, you've cursed me every day since you saw me, you've dragged me a thousand miles from my home and my husband and my little boy — did I ask you to take that 'trouble' over me? Christ Eternal judge it! Whatever the laws say, it is unjust, what you've done to me, and if God is what we call him, Lord of All, you'll suffer for it! Do you think God cares that you're an agent and a friend of the emperor's chamberlain? He sees what you do, and there's no slave or free or male and female with him: he will avenge it, you son of the Devil, as much as if you'd done it to the emperor himself!"

Eulogios was flabbergasted. He went white and stared at her speechlessly. The women looked terrified. Chelchal looked astonished.

"H-how dare you speak to me like that in my own house!" Eulogios said at last, in a strangled voice.

"You can have me whipped for insolence," Demetrias told him, savagely. "You have that right under the law. But you can't have me whipped for lying, because you know perfectly well that what I said was nothing but the truth. I'm sick of your shouting and swearing at me — go give the orders to have me whipped or leave me alone!"

Eulogios opened and shut his mouth several times like a fish, turned deep crimson, stamped his feet with fury — and stalked out of the room. Demetrias sat down slowly, still trembling with rage. One of the women gave a shriek of joy and clapped her hands, and the others all began talking at once.

"Will he have me whipped?" Demetrias asked after a minute, dreading the answer.

The women laughed. "He can't!" One of them explained. "He's giving you to Chrysaphios tomorrow — he can't give him a slave that's just been flogged. He'll have to pretend that you were talking in your sleep or temporarily out of your mind. Oh, that was better than a festival! I wish you were staying with us!"

Chelchal went back to the retainers' quarters of the house grinning and shaking his head. He had gone to Eulogios after his own supper, told the agent that he wanted to marry Demetrias, and asked him to put the matter to their patron the next morning. Eulogios had had no particular objection to this plan, and it had been his suggestion that the Hun join him in inspecting the woman. "No use buying a pig in a poke," he'd said. Chelchal was glad he'd been there. He had no respect for his master's tempers, and had found the scene as enjoyable as the women had.

The other retainers were already lying on their pallets in the long room at the back of the house that they all shared when Chelchal came in. "Well?" asked Berich. He spoke in the Gothic the men used among themselves, and he was familiar with Chelchal's errand: they all knew every piece of each other's business. *Like boys in training,* Chelchal thought sadly, *we follow the master, we push slaves and menials about, and we whore and fight like young warriors w 'i their first scars. I'm too old for this; I want a wife and a house of my own.*

"He'll talk to Chrysaphios about it tomorrow," he told Berich, and took his own sleeping mat from its place by the wall. His Gothic was much better than his Greek.

Berich snorted. "I don't know why you want to marry the little whore. She's pretty, I'll grant you that, and I wouldn't mind a go at her — but marriage? What for?"

Chelchal looked up from untying his pallet and grinned. "She's not a whore, you whore-mongering Goth," he said cheerfully. "You should know that. You had a go at her already and got kicked in the balls for it."

The other retainers laughed; Berich scowled. "She's a little vixen," he said. "She wants to be tied up first."

Chelchal shook his head and unrolled his mat. "You're young, and you've never had anything but whores: you think they're all there is. I tell you, a man gets older, he wants a woman of his own, one that won't belong to every man with the money. This one is loyal, I've seen that. She's pretty and she's brave." He started laughing. "By the sword of heaven, you should have seen her shouting at the master! He told her to take her clothes off and she called him a son of the devil. The old bastard just went red and stammered and backed out of the room. If she has a son with half her spirit, he'll be a warrior to sing songs about!"

The other retainers laughed; Eulogios was unpopular with all his servants. But Berich still scowled, brooding over his abortive attempt at rape. "You had a wife before," he said angrily. "Was she loyal?"

Chelchal stopped grinning. His wife had been loyal enough. Very different from Demetrias: shy, dark, sloe-eyed, Kreka had never said a word to another man, and in public had walked modestly with her eyes dropped. But she had loved him; worked eagerly to keep their huts and wagons fine for him, searched the camps for delicacies to please him, and in bed she had shrieked and giggled and nibbled more wantonly than any whore. She was not brave, though, not a fighter. She would be miserable with her new owner, but she would obey him as quietly as she had obeyed Chelchal; only the eagerness and delight would be gone, ground out of her forever. *Better to be brave*, he thought. *Better to go down fighting. Though have I fought? Gods and spirits, God of the Christians, give me a chance to fight my enemies! Just one chance, before I die!*

"Don't talk about my wife," he told Berich savagely. "She was a good woman, and one day I'll revenge her. And if anyone thinks differently, I'll revenge her now."

Berich was silent. For all his good nature, Chelchal was known to be a dangerous fighter: he was not a man to offend. The Hun waited for a moment, approving the silence, then sighed and lay down on his sleeping mat. They were all tired after the long journey, and he wanted rest.

# ～VI～

EULOGIOS SENT A MESSENGER to the chamberlain's office at the Great Palace when he first awoke next morning; he was just finishing his breakfast when the messenger returned to say that Chrysaphios would see him around ten o'clock, immediately after the morning's consultation with the emperor. It was what Eulogios had expected, but the honey cake he was eating turned to dust in his mouth and he had difficulty swallowing it. He had hurried back so quickly to show the chamberlain his zeal, but now he would have to admit that the zeal had been misplaced — and Chrysaphios didn't like mistakes.

Of course, he was giving Chrysaphios what should have been a handsome present — only he now felt very uneasy about the gift as well. There was no getting round it: the weaver did not behave with the humility proper to a slave and a decent woman. She had deliberately put him off balance in Tyre, and now she had made a fool of him in front of his own slaves. His mind winced away from the memory of the scene the night before. On top of everything, he still hadn't looked at her properly. Suppose she had some huge scar, or a birthmark, or some other defect? Chrysaphios would be insulted to be given a blemished slave. Of course, he could have ordered her stripped the night before — but after what she had said, this had seemed so mild a punishment that he hadn't been able to order it, and he couldn't order a flogging if he intended to give the woman to Chrysaphios. If.

*I'm not keeping her in my house,* he thought angrily, *to make my slaves laugh at me behind my back.*

Below his anger was a deeper uneasiness that her words had stirred in him. The church did claim that all souls were equal before God, and preached, if it did not always practice, charity to all. Remember, it told slave owners, you, too, have a master in Heaven, and "whatever measure you use to measure, you will be measured by yourself." However much Eulogios condemned softness, he had been raised and baptized a Christian, and he knew that he was a bad master. He had no intention of changing and did not want to be reminded of what it could mean. He rather wished that he had left the miserable slave in Tyre.

*Well, if she is insolent to His Illustriousness,* he told himself, *I'll just claim that I couldn't have known, she behaved properly with me. And really, I expect she would have, if she hadn't been out of her mind with weariness and half asleep at the time. No slave in her right mind would call her master a "son of the devil."*

He clapped his hands and sent for his old housekeeper Arete; she came, as they all did, quickly and meekly. "I am seeing His Illustriousness this morning," he told her. "I hope that the weaver has rested and recovered her senses?"

Arete bowed. "Yes, Master. She . . . she remembers little of what happened last night, but she is afraid that she may have spoken improperly to Your Excellent Generosity, and bitterly regrets the insane fatigue that could have caused such wickedness." Demetrias, of course, had no such regrets, but Arete was skilled by long practice in the necessary art of Soothing the Master.

Eulogios did not believe a word of it, but he accepted the account flattering to himself. "She's . . ." He hesitated, not sure how to put it without recalling his humiliation. "She is unblemished, isn't she?" he asked at last, bluntly.

"Oh, Master, she's a lovely creature; anyone would be pleased to own her. We've got her clothes dry, too, as Your Wisdom wanted; she looks like a fine lady. What a treasure she is, to do such beautiful weaving!"

"Good!" said Eulogios, reassured. "Well, find some gold trinket to hang round her neck and have her put in the litter, and tell Stephanos to have my best horse saddled: I'm off to the palace."

Eulogios set off for the Great Palace in style, wearing his gaudiest clothes and riding a magnificent black stallion. Two of his retainers preceded him, mounted on matching bays, and two followed the covered litter that carried Demetrias. He had put Chelchal in front.

To have a Hun in one's service was a mark of the very highest favor and impressed the rabble more than any amount of gold thread — though it was a pity, he thought, that Chelchal could not be converted to the idea of washing. They rode from the house, which was in the city's third region, up to the main, Middle street, and turned right along it.

Demetrias pulled back the curtain of the litter slightly to study the city. The Middle street was flanked with porticoes of white marble, their roofs lined with statues of gilded bronze. The litter bearers paced slowly into a marketplace, a great oval lined with more shining colonnades; in its center was a towering column of porphyry topped by another statue that shone like gold. Bronze lions sprawled about a central fountain; a bronze elephant trumpeted on the right; to the left stood a monumental gilded cross and a row of fabulous beasts. The shops inside the colonnade glittered with silver and there was a smell of perfume. The marketplace was thronged with people, a packed mass of color and sound and movement through which their procession moved slowly; they crossed the marketplace only to go up another wide, colonnaded boulevard even more splendid than the first. Demetrias pulled the curtain back farther to glance ahead: they were about to pass through a monumental archway into another marketplace. To the left rose the tall basilica of a church, and to the right towered the piled-up arches of some stadium or hippodrome. The litter moved slowly beneath the arch into the new marketplace, and on the far side of the square Demetrias saw a forbidding wall, and, in its center, a gatehouse with a door and roof of gilded bronze. Behind that, surely, must be the palace.

She dropped the curtain and sat back in the litter, feeling sick. *What will I do in a palace?* she wondered. *What will I do in a city like this? Oh Mother of God, to be back in Tyre, back in the factory with the people who know me, back in my own home in Symeon's arms!*

But there was no road in that splendid city that would take her home.

*Perhaps it won't take too long to earn my freedom. I'll be set to weaving, surely, and I should be able to do extra work on the side, as I did in Tyre: I could do much more of it than I did before, since I won't have a husband and child to look after. How much would I have to save? Sixty* solidi? *More, probably, unless my new master's inclined to be generous. But a hundred? That ought to be enough to buy my freedom. It will take . . . ten years? Fifteen? More? Oh God. Symeon may have married someone else in the meantime. Meli will be a grown man.*

She set her teeth, trying to calm herself. *Symeon will wait for me if he knows I mean to come back to him*, she told herself. *He loves me. And I'll find some way to get my freedom. And at least Chrysaphios is a eunuch and I don't have to worry about having to sleep with him!*

The litter paused before the Bronze Gate; she heard Eulogios' voice explaining himself to the guards, and then they continued on: step, step, the litter swaying as the porters marched into the palace. They walked on a little distance, and then the litter was set down. Eulogios gave some orders to his retainers; there was a silence, and then his voice very close said, "Come on!" She pulled back the curtain and came out.

The Great Palace of Constantinople was not one building but a sprawling collection of them — palaces, chapels, and barracks, banquet halls and prisons, gardens and terraces — all enclosed within a high wall beside the sea on the southeastern tip of the city's peninsula. The main residence of the emperor, and hence the main offices of state, were in the building called the Magnaura Palace, on the northeastern side of the palace complex. It was there that Eulogios took Demetrias, after leaving the litter, the horses, and the retainers to wait by the barracks of the Scholarian Guards near the Bronze Gate.

Chrysaphios had an office in the center of the palace, between the state offices and the emperor's private apartments. No suitor, no piece of business, no urgent report could reach the emperor — and no imperial edict issue forth to the world — without passing before the eyes of the emperor's chamberlain. And it was plain that Chrysaphios understood his situation perfectly: he had contrived to put a distance between himself and the world. Eulogios and Demetrias walked down a long corridor flanked by the ministries of state and came at last to a small, stuffy waiting room: a dozen men were sitting there, all of them, to judge by their clothing, of the very highest rank. Eulogios walked past them to another small room, an office. Four clerks were working there: two, their backs to the visitors, were industriously copying documents, another was sorting through a box full of files,

157

and the fourth, at a desk squarely facing the waiting room, was writing out a letter. This last looked up at them inquiringly.

"Eulogios, a *princeps* of the *agentes in rebus*," the agent said, in a hushed, reverent tone, like a man in church.

"Ah," said the secretary, in a bored voice. He checked a note in a massive book at the side of his desk. "Yes, His Illustriousness is expecting you. He just got back from consulting with His Sacred Majesty a moment ago — you can go in." He indicated a door behind him with his pen, then resumed his letter.

Eulogios went to the door, gave Demetrias a stern look, then opened it and went in. She followed silently, her head bowed.

The first thing she noticed was the carpet. It was of silk tapestry, woven with exquisite skill, and its subject was the Loves of Zeus. She had not worked on it herself, but she had seen it made, in Tyre, and she knew it had not been made for the man whose office it adorned. She lifted her head and stared in surprise. There was something wrong, something that made her distinctly uneasy as well as afraid, in the notion of the emperor's chamberlain bothering to filch rugs from the empress he had contrived to disgrace.

The rest of the office, and the owner of the office, were of a piece with the carpet: luxurious, tasteful, exquisite. The frescoes of the Iliad painted on the walls alternated with panels of gilded wood decorated with pictures of the saints. Two gold lampstands, intricately cast to resemble trees in bud, stood on each side of another entrance on the far side of the room: their half-opened flowers were made of jewels. The other entrance had no door, but was shrouded with a purple curtain. Although it was day and the room was brightly lit by a tall window on each side of the room, each lampstand held a lighted lamp which burned scented oil that perfumed the air with myrrh. A desk of polished citron wood and enamel stood in the center of the room, and at this sat Chrysaphios, resting his chin on one graceful hand and staring thoughtfully at nothing: he gave no sign of even noticing his subordinate's arrival. He was younger than Demetrias had expected, certainly under forty — though it was hard to tell a eunuch's age. His hair was still a dark gold and looked polished as a helmet, and his narrow, delicately boned face was unlined. He wore the purple-striped white cloak of a patrician over a tunic that seemed made entirely of gold: he was like a statue in a jeweler's window, and he scarcely seemed to breathe. Eulogios closed the door very quietly behind himself and stood humbly still.

"Eulogios," said Chrysaphios after a moment, and took his chin off his hand. He had a mellifluous drawling voice, alto, with the accent of great wealth and culture. "Well." He rested his hands palm down on his desk, inspecting the agent with a cynical expression. His eyes flicked to Demetrias, returned to his subordinate. "I gathered from your messenger that you were disappointed in Tyre. What have you brought me now?"

Eulogios bowed down to the ground before replying. "It is true, Your Illustriousness, that my anxiety over the situation in Tyre was altogether wasted. I expected to find treason; I discovered only a lustful and idle young procurator wasting state labor secretly on a cloak for his own use. I investigated the matter as thoroughly as I could, and I am satisfied that my suspicions were unfounded. While I am disappointed that all my pains went for nothing, of course I cannot help but rejoice that our fears for our sacred and beloved Augustus were groundless." Eulogios paused; Chrysaphios made a slight, weary, speed-it-up gesture. Eulogios took another deep breath and went on. "To assure Your Providence of our sacred emperor's security — which I know is Your Illustriousness' first concern — I have brought you the weaver whose hands wove the cloak about which we had suspicions. Please permit me to make a gift of her to Your Benevolence. She was accounted the finest weaver in Tyre, and it is my hope that, when you have reassured your generous mind by questioning her, you may find her an adornment to your house, as her skill has so long been an adornment to the state."

Chrysaphios closed his eyes for a moment, then opened them and fixed Eulogios with a look of pained irony. Eulogios had thought out this speech on the journey from Tyre, and he was proud of it; Chrysaphios' response was frustrating. The chamberlain then glanced at Demetrias again, and this time lifted one finger to beckon her over. She came, slowly, keeping her head down. She stopped just beside the desk and bowed to the floor, then rose to stand before the chamberlain with downcast eyes. Chrysaphios lifted a strand of the gold necklace the housekeeper had draped about her neck that morning, then took her chin, lifted her head and moved it to each side, studying her face. The dark, disdainful eyes were only a foot from her own.

Demetrias kept her face blank. She felt like a mouse being inspected by a cat.

Chrysaphios let his hand drop as though the effort of keeping it up was too great for him. "Where is the cloak?" he asked Eulogios.

This was the awkward part. "I fear, Illustrious, that I don't have it. The procurator Heraklas gave it as a present to his colleague the prefect Philippos, who left Tyre at the beginning of last month on hearing that his mother was ill. I intend to ask him to show it to me, but I saw the accounts and spoke to slaves at the factory, and all agree that the cloak was, in fact, red and for the procurator."

Chrysaphios smiled very slightly. "Slaves will say anything," he commented, "and most slaves feel bound to protect their fellows."

He stressed the word *most* so slightly that it took a fine ear to distinguish it, but that slight stress, and the faint smile that accompanied it, suddenly spoke to Demetrias more clearly than the words themselves. *Most* slaves feel bound to protect their fellows. Some slaves informed, reporting misdemeanors to their master in order to profit by that master's favor. Chrysaphios had been such a slave, Demetrias knew with an irrational certainty; he had informed to masters, to superiors, to the emperor himself, and so was sitting dressed in gold at the axis of the state, turning the emperor's favor with a languid hand. The sense of unease that had joined her fear at the sight of the carpet quadrupled.

"Did you speak with Flavius Marcianus?" Chrysaphios went on.

Eulogios was taken aback. "No, Illustrious. He had left Tyre by the time I arrived; I believe he went back to his patron's estates in the mountains."

Chrysaphios tapped his desk. "You do not have the cloak," he said, after a long silence. "You have not even seen this famous cloak, and rely on slaves for accounts of it. You have not seen Marcianus, whom I particularly warned you to investigate. You do not seem, my dear Eulogios, to have managed this affair . . . as well as you might have done."

Eulogios shuffled his feet like a naughty child.

Chrysaphios sat up straight, his hands clenching on the desktop. "When did Marcianus leave Tyre?" he demanded. "Why did he stay there so long?"

"He . . . he had business there, I believe. It was coincidence that he was there all that time. His patron has estates nearby — and there was some question about buying some land, I believe . . ."

"I dislike coincidences," Chrysaphios retorted coolly. "And I particularly dislike coincidences involving that particular gentleman. Marcianus is as dangerous as his patron — more dangerous, perhaps. Aspar is a soldier first and foremost, with as much subtlety as a butcher's cleaver; Marcianus is . . . another matter." He slapped his desk. "We hear rumors that Nomos has some business in Tyre, some business that would bear investigation. You proceed to Tyre and discover that a cloak commissioned by Nomos' good friend Acilius Heraklas is being woven in strict secrecy, and Aspar's prize protégé Marcianus is circling the city like a vulture. Instead of acting, you waste four weeks coming here to ask me what to do about it . . ."

"I didn't have the authority to intervene!" protested Eulogios. "The prefect was a friend of Nomos' too: I'd have done nothing but risk my life calling on him to help me! And they told me it wouldn't be done for six weeks."

"They told you!" Chrysaphios sneered. "Who told you? The slaves at the factory told you! The same slaves you believed implicitly when they told you that the cloak was red! And, wonder of wonders, the cloak they told you would be done in six weeks was done in two, and Nomos' friend Philippos has a mother conveniently fallen ill, and just happens to have left Tyre and taken it with him! And, still more wonderful, Marcianus has left Tyre as well — at the same time? Yes, was it the same time?"

"I don't know," replied Eulogios, aghast. "But I checked the accounts . . ."

"A piece of parchment and a little reed pen can do marvelous things, my friend. They can keep accounts honestly . . . or not." Chrysaphios snorted and looked at Eulogios under lowered lids. "Well," he said, after a moment, "at least you have brought me a weaver — to reassure my mind." He turned the gaze onto Demetrias. "And will you reassure me, pretty weaver? What color was the cloak you made for Acilius Heraklas?"

"It was a red cloak, sir," Demetrias replied quietly, "dyed with kermes, sir, with two tapestry panels."

"It was red!" drawled Chrysaphios. "How reassuring!" His hand shot out suddenly and seized her chin again, gripping it with a surprising strength. "Well, perhaps it was. Coincidences happen: procurators do indulge in misdemeanors over pretty silk weavers and fine clothing; mothers do fall ill; Marcianus has perfectly legitimate business in Tyre. But, Eulogios" — and he shook Demetrias' head — "I do not believe all this on the bare word of a few slaves. One must apply a little judicious pressure, and see if their story changes." His fingers applied pressure to her jaw till she gave an involuntary gasp of pain, then released her. Demetrias put her hand to her face, looking away from the chamberlain, down at the polished desk top, and thinking hard. Torture; he meant to have her tortured. Her hands were sweating and she felt dizzy with fear, but her mind lunged about frantically. There must be some way out. Tell him the truth? But he would not believe that she told the whole truth: she would still be tortured, and he would probably have Philotimos tortured too. But there must be some way out!

Eulogios coughed. "Of course, Illustrious, you are entirely right. But the, umm, Hun you lent me wanted to marry the woman, and asked me to put the matter to you this morning. He's a valuable man — we have so few Huns in our service. I wouldn't like to lose him — what should I, um, tell him about the woman?"

Demetrias looked at him in incomprehension. She would be allowed off the rack if she married Chelchal? *Better that than torture!* she thought, eagerly — but another part of her gave a deep silent wail of agony.

"Chelchal wants to marry her!" exclaimed Chrysaphios, in mocking surprise, giving Demetrias another ironic look. "Well, well. He is indeed a useful man — but I think we must put a few questions to the woman first, nonetheless. I will tell the men responsible not to damage her too severely. A man skilled at that art knows ways of questioning that don't cause any . . . disfigurement. You may tell Chelchal that. Well, weaver? What color was the cloak?"

Demetrias screamed.

It was a horrifyingly loud noise, and even as she produced it she was remotely surprised that she could scream so loudly: the sound tore through the palace like a knife through silk. Chrysaphios jumped to his feet, looking alarmed; he took a step backward. Eulogios hurried forward and grabbed Demetrias' arm, jerked her round to face him, and began slapping her. She put her other arm up to shield her face and kept screaming.

"Get her out!" Chrysaphios shouted. He ran to the door of his office and shouted at his secretaries. Demetrias crouched with her arm before her face and screamed as hard as she could. The secretaries rushed into the room; she ducked, wrenched herself away from Eulogios, and clung to the desk. They hesitated, then advanced on her and with a clumsy determination grabbed her and tried to wrestle her out. She fought them, holding on to the desk with all her strength and kicking wildly, screaming all the while.

"Chrysaphios!" came a strange voice. "What on earth is going on?"

The secretaries let go abruptly and fell back, staring in shock at the far side of the room. Demetrias shoved her hand into her own mouth to stop her screams, and looked too.

The man who stood in the doorway, holding the purple curtain aside with one hand, was in his late forties, gray-haired, dark-eyed, and slim, with a gentle, bewildered face. His purple cloak brushed the purple curtain, a color as beautiful as life itself, rich, vibrant, unmatchable. Demetrias remembered that cloak. She had woven the patterned hem for it, and been proud.

She moved before anyone else could. She let go of the desk, dashed past the secretaries, and threw herself at the emperor's feet. "Thrice-august!" she cried. "For God's sake, Master, Emperor, I am an innocent woman: don't let them torture me!"

The emperor Theodosius the Second looked in astonishment at the young woman who had just cast herself before his feet, then looked in confusion at his chamberlain.

Chrysaphios hesitated only an instant before dropping to the ground himself; he rose gracefully and opened his hands in a gesture of surrender. "Master," he said, not drawling at all, his voice very sweet, "the young woman is under a misapprehension. Do not alarm yourself, I beg you: I will explain. I am sorry that Your Piety's prayers have been disturbed."

Theodosius looked relieved. He looked down at the young woman lying at his feet, then bent over. "There you are," he said, gently. "They aren't going to torture you. You can get up, girl."

Demetrias got to her knees, looking up at his face. It remained gentle, bewildered, and concerned. She wiped the tears off her own face and took a deep, shuddering breath. *Safe — for the moment.* Theodosius offered her his hand to help her up — she noticed that the imperial fingers were stained with ink. Hesitantly, she took the hand and rose; found, when she stood, that the emperor was a short man, not much taller than she. It should not have been a surprise — she had known his cloak measurements — but somehow it was. His statues had always towered over her.

"Master," she said, earnestly, before Chrysaphios could speak, as she knew he meant to, "they were going to have me tortured. I am sure they meant to do it out of love for Your Sacred Majesty, but I swear by all that's holy, I am Your Majesty's slave, and never wanted any crime against you." She saw the look of bewilderment grow, and she went on, quickly, "I was a weaver, Master, in your factory in Tyre. Your chamberlain believes that I wove a cloak for some man who means a plot against Your Goodness. Sir, I am only a slave, I weave what your servants the procurators tell me to weave — I don't know anything about any treason. I only know that I have been taken from my home and family, brought here, and threatened with torture unless I confess to crimes I know nothing about. I beg Your Sacred Kindness to believe me."

Theodosius frowned and looked at his chamberlain.

Chrysaphios was looking embarrassed and off balance. "My master and emperor," he said, "we did threaten the woman, it is true. I hope Your Consideration knows me better than to believe I would actually have had her tortured if she was really innocent. It is true, I have reason to suspect that a cloak this woman wove at your factory in Tyre was destined for some evil plot against you, my sacred and beloved master; I threatened her, hoping to learn more. If it offends you, my master, I am desolated — but what I said I said through fear for your own safety."

Theodosius seemed reassured. "Of course I believe you wouldn't have hurt the poor girl," he told Chrysaphios. "You know how I loathe cruelty."

"I hate it myself," said Chrysaphios quickly, "but sometimes, to protect you . . ."

"Oh, you need not protest your devotion to me, my friend; I believe you love me," said the emperor, with a sweet smile. "Still . . . did you have to frighten the poor girl so? Tell me, girl, what's the truth of this story? No one means to hurt you."

She hesitated. To admit that the cloak had been purple would summon up the whole power of the state to investigate it. If she escaped the torture, others would not — particularly since they had lied before. Chrysaphios might say anything he pleased to his master: the emperor would never hear anything the chamberlain chose not to tell him. Philotimos, Eugenios at the dyeworks, many other weavers, probably, including her mother: all would go onto the rack. On the other hand, if the plot were discovered, they might arrest Heraklas, and if they arrested him, they would know the whole.

But Heraklas might escape, and they might not bother with weavers, mere slaves, even if they had the procurator, so long as they had Nomos himself. No, the only safe course was to insist that the cloak had been red.

Still, she could not bring herself to say it, not immediately. The emperor as a statue in the prefecture's porch was one thing; this living man with his sweet smile was another. It was hard to accept complicity in Nomos' scheme to displace him. She knew nothing about Nomos, but Heraklas, his supporter, she hated from the bottom of her heart.

Though Chrysaphios and Eulogios were just as bad. And while this gentle man wore the purple, Chrysaphios would rule.

Demetrias bit her lip. "Master," she said, as the silence grew too heavy, "how can I accuse your chamberlain?"

"Accuse Chrysaphios?" asked the emperor. "Why, you mustn't call it accusing him, if you mean to say he's punished you mistakenly. Anyone can make mistakes, and we are all bound to forgive, and indeed, eager to forgive, when the mistake springs from love. I know that Chrysaphios is the foundation of my reign and my dear subjects' happiness and I value him as dearly as he deserves: don't worry about saying he was misinformed. Though your hesitation makes me like you more, dear girl."

There was no hope. "Master," Demetrias said heavily, blinking at tears, "your most illustrious chamberlain was misled by circumstances. The procurator Heraklas did order me to weave a cloak, illegally and in secrecy, but the cloak was red. The procurator just wished to have a piece of fine weaving for his own use . . . and . . . and he wanted to sleep with me."

"What's that?" asked the emperor, confused again.

"He wanted me to work in a private place, Master, so that he could visit me. I managed to refuse him, but, because I was working privately, none of the others at the factory saw the cloak, and because the procurator took the cloak as his own to dispose of, it wasn't on the record of commissions. That's why your servants thought it must be part of a plot."

Theodosius smiled radiantly. "There!" he told Chrysaphios, triumphantly. "That's all cleared up now, isn't it? I couldn't believe that anyone was plotting against me."

Chrysaphios bowed. "Your Sacred Majesty is good, a living saint — I hope Your Modesty will forgive me for speaking my mind! — but your very goodness sometimes prevents you from seeing clearly. You want to believe all men are as virtuous as you are yourself, and I know only too well how it grieves your noble spirit to see their baseness and ingratitude. But there are wicked men in this world who cannot endure Your Sacred Majesty's goodness, who would not shrink back from laying their violent hands on the sacred purple itself. I have been unable to find the cloak this woman made, and I am afraid. I do not blame the weaver, who is a slave and bound to obey her superiors, but what if she speaks from terror? What if she's been threatened with a dreadful retribution if she dares to give away some depraved secret? I think it is necessary — not to torture her, of course! — but to question her more closely on the matter."

Theodosius gave a worried frown.

"Master, your agent Eulogios went to Tyre," Demetrias put in quickly. "He looked at the factory, and at the dyeworks where I wove the cloak, and at the woolen factory where I traded in the leftover silk, and he checked the accounts at all of them. He was very thorough, and he found nothing that implied that the cloak was purple; nothing at all. The only reason he didn't see the cloak was that the procurator gave it as a going-away present to his friend the prefect: otherwise, he would have found that too. What more can I add to what I have already said? There is no plot, and no treason!"

"I hope it is so," said Chrysaphios, without looking at her, "but I cannot be sure without seeing the cloak."

Theodosius smiled. "You are too fearful, my friend," he told his chamberlain affectionately. "There are wicked men, whom it is our Christian duty to pray for; but if you've never found the cloak, why should you believe evil? Why should we think that all we do not know, is bad? If this agent" — he gave Eulogios a vague glance — "has already been to Tyre and seen everything, what more can you get by frightening an unlucky young woman? She seems to me, too, to be a woman of some character, since she resisted her own procurator when he wanted her to commit a sin: I cannot believe that she would connive at treason. This procurator should have respected his office better than to persecute my workers with his unclean desires. I hope he has been reprimanded for his abuses."

"I reprimanded him severely," Eulogios declared, not allowing this golden opportunity to attract the emperor's attention to slip by, "and I cautioned him to respect Your Sacred Majesty's possessions if he ever wished to hold office again. He was struck with contrition, repaid the state for the labor he had stolen from it, and vowed never to deserve your displeasure again."

"Very good!" the emperor exclaimed happily. "Then all is as it should be; God be praised!"

"If Your Sacred Majesty is pleased, I am pleased," said Chrysaphios, bowing again. "And indeed, my mind is at rest now: I cannot believe, now that I see her before you, that this weaver would have been involved in any treason, and I am sure she would be unable to lie directly to your sacred ears and before the nobility of your countenance." Theodosius beamed. "Permit me, my dear master," the chamberlain continued, smiling, "to make you a gift of her."

"A gift?" asked the emperor, slightly puzzled. "Is she yours? I thought she was a slave of the state."

Chrysaphios smiled again. "My protégé Eulogios used the authority I had given him to purchase the woman from the state; he gave her to me, thinking that, once I had assured myself of your safety by questioning her, I could keep her — I am told her weaving is wonderfully fine, and she is a fitting adornment to the noblest house. But it would please me greatly if Your Sacred Majesty would take her. Then you might rest perfectly assured of her happiness, either keeping her in your palace, or giving her to some other, or even setting her free. I know that otherwise your generous spirit would fret for her security, and your unhappiness in anything cannot but be my unhappiness as well."

The emperor smiled brightly, and gave Demetrias a delighted look. "My friend, you know me so well!" he said. "I would have worried.

And your response is worthy of you, generous and loving. I thank you for your splendid gift." He touched Demetrias' hand. "I am indeed lucky to have such a wise adviser, and one so devoted," he said, to her more than to his chamberlain. "Come, then, girl — what is your name?"

"Demetrias, Master," she stammered, looking at Chrysaphios in confusion. She did not trust his sudden reversal.

"Demetrias! A name blessed by the holy martyr. An excellent name. Come, Demetrias, I will see you into my household, where you can recover from your terror. Chrysaphios — tell whomever it concerns."

"Of course, Master." Chrysaphios bowed, and the emperor ushered Demetrias out past the purple curtain.

The chamberlain waited till they were gone, then clapped his hands and, when the others in the room looked over, gestured them out. The secretaries went at once but Eulogios hesitated, worried. Chrysaphios sat down at his desk, glaring.

"Illustrious," Eulogios said unhappily. "Umm — what happens now? Do you really think that the woman was telling the truth?"

Chrysaphios looked up sharply and scornfully. "She was aware, I should think, that she had nothing to fear if she did because the emperor will never allow her to be tortured. Why shouldn't she tell the truth? And if she was lying, there's nothing to be done about it, now. We can't lay a finger on her. He is susceptible to beauty and she is precisely the sort he finds prettiest. Why couldn't she have been old and fat? He wouldn't have been so eager to listen to her then."

Eulogios shuffled his feet uncomfortably. "I wouldn't have wanted to give Your Illustriousness a slave who was old and fat."

Chrysaphios gave a snort of disgust. "What use do I have for pretty women? I don't like them. They make men do unpredictable things. And a woman who's both clever and pretty ought to be strangled: she's too dangerous to be allowed to live." His eyes glittered as they fixed Eulogios. "Like that one. You should have warned me that she was clever. She had the whole dance step-perfect from the moment she screamed."

"You don't think she was just frightened?" Eulogios asked, wretchedly remembering her words to him the night before. Divine retribution would strike him as if he had offended the emperor himself. Now it seemed that the woman might become an imperial concubine and a favorite, and the emperor himself see to the vengeance.

"Frightened? Of course she was. But she knew what she was doing and did it deliberately. Didn't you see the way she clung to the desk? She was trying to attract attention to herself in here; she knew it would be no use screaming in the prison. She probably hoped that the emperor would come, but she might have contented herself with one of the men waiting in the anteroom — they're all powerful enough to protect her and make trouble for me. And she wept prettily onto the floor and took pains to let the emperor know that she was chaste as well as beautiful, and was very careful to see whether he'd be offended if she attacked me directly — and when she saw he would be, she refrained. Oh yes, you've introduced a dangerous little pet into the palace, and one that would be all too happy to ruin us both, if she could. Fortunately, he'll send her away in a day or so."

"He will?" cried Eulogios, immensely relieved. "But why?"

"Because, probably before this evening, he will examine his conscience in prayer and discover that he wants to sleep with the little vixen. He's pious enough to believe that he's still a married man, though separated form his unfaithful wife — thank God for that, anyway! Eudokia was cleverer than a dozen little weavers and prettier as well. So he will regretfully remove the temptation to adultery, and either set the weaver free or give her as a gift to someone else — probably the second, and preferably a devout and wealthy widow, who'll treat her kindly but see that no one touches her. Pious as he is, he dislikes it if other men get women he wants himself. If I had my way," his voice fell to a whisper, "I would have the creature tortured within an inch of her life, and then send her as a present to King Attila. And you are to repeat none of this or I will make you weep bitterly for it."

Eulogios swallowed. "Of course . . . I am your servant, Illustrious."

"You're a clumsy fool who mismanaged this affair from the start!" Chrysaphios snarled. "Get out! And if I ever want you again — which I doubt! — I'll send for you."

Eulogios got out. Chrysaphios sat alone in his office, looking at the blurred reflection of his face in the fine polish of his desk top. That the emperor was susceptible to beauty had always been to his advantage. It gave an edge of warmth to Theodosius' feelings for him, but did not offend that delicate imperial conscience. And he had danced the dance step-perfect too, setting that other clever and beautiful woman, Eudokia, against the unbeautiful but powerful Pulcheria — and then contriving Eudokia's disgrace, so that he ruled Theodosius and the empire alone. He had what he had dreamed of ever since he was nine years old, when the Persian master he thought had loved him, who had slept with him since he was seven, who had had him castrated "to keep you beautiful," had suddenly sold him to the Romans. He had sworn then that never again would anyone betray him. He would have power and betray them first.

But things had become so complicated now that there was no more power left to scheme for. He was confident of his hold on Theodosius — but even a little silk weaver from a factory was able to slip past his guard and get to the emperor against his will. It irked him, but he also found it profoundly unsettling. Sometimes he thought he genuinely did love his emperor, and he detested love: love was weakness, being a victim, being used; the powerful should not love. But what he felt now was fearfully akin to jealousy.

He sighed and looked up at nothing. *She'll soon be gone,* he told himself. *And I've lost none of my influence because of her. He'll never sleep with her — I don't believe he ever slept with anyone in his life, except Eudokia, and I managed to get rid even of her. And perhaps when he's sent this weaver off I'll have another chance at her. No need to worry about it.*

But he remained depressed and anxious. His mind, whirling away from the distasteful question of love, found no refuge in the gloomy considerations of state. His skill in footwork was no use against the Huns. King Attila kept demanding more and more in return for peace, the people and Senate were restive under the burden of their taxes, and his allies were unreliable, disobeying him or quarreling with him. *It was a mistake to offend Nomos,* he admitted silently, *but I could see the contempt in his eyes, and I know how ambitious he is, and I would not let him betray me, no. But still, it was a mistake. And it was a mistake not to wink at Zeno's insubordination. But I can trust no one, and most of those I do use are inept, like Eulogios.*

Against his will he remembered the fate of one of his predecessors, Eutropios, who had been chamberlain to Theodosius' father, Arcadius. He too had been supreme in his day, had ruled the emperor, governed the state, and been the first and only eunuch ever to hold the consulship of Rome. And he had died wretchedly, betrayed by everyone he had raised to rule with him and beheaded in secrecy after a promise of immunity. Chrysaphios rubbed his own neck, fighting against the vision of it severed, and the image of his face staring with glazed eyes from the top of a common soldier's pike.

*It won't happen,* he told himself. *I'm stronger than Eutropios: I haven't made his mistake and shared my power; no one can rival me. As for Nomos — I'm on my guard. I have him watched, and if he means to act against me I'll know in good time, surely? And the whole empire will fall into line when they see that I've dealt with Attila.*

At that he smiled. He had engaged one of Attila's Gothic subordinates to assassinate the king of the Huns in return for fifty pounds of gold. Attila had no designated successor, and his empire was of diverse origin and dubious loyalty: it was bound to collapse at his death. Then Chrysaphios would be a hero, the savior of the Roman state. What did it matter, compared to that, that he had been outmaneuvered by a clever silk weaver, a slave seen once and never again?

He clapped his hands and ordered his attentive secretary to send in the most distinguished of the noblemen who thronged his waiting room.

Demetrias slept late next morning, and woke at about ten o'clock, muzzy-headed, dry-mouthed, and unrested. She lay still for a few moments, staring at the edge of her pillow. A gray light bathed the fine linen and there was a sound of rain.

She sat up, disoriented. She was in a small, neat room under the eaves of the palace, a fine room with a woolen carpet and a tall window of good-quality glass. She vaguely remembered being shown to it the night before, after climbing endless steps and opening the door to see the red-and-purple bedspread glowing in the lamplight. She had been very tired. The emperor had not said much to her after bringing her into the palace; he had commended her to one of the senior eunuch chamberlains, who had commended her to a junior one, who had introduced her to the keeper of the palace looms, a very junior eunuch not yet twenty years old, who had shown her the whole Magnaura and the looms first and last. The palace had seemed oppressively magnificent, and she had not been able to follow the eunuch's instructions about the complex protocols and rules of precedence that governed the lives of its staff, though she'd tried to be attentive. By the end of the day, the small bedroom, privacy, and silence had come as a profound relief.

She got out of bed and went to the window, opening it to look out. A curtain of rain hung before it like glass beads; beyond this she could see trees, bent in the wind, and the gray water of the Bosphorus, lashed with rain. She closed the window again and dressed, slowly.

The emperor had rescued her from Chrysaphios — for the time being. But she had gathered enough from the keeper of the looms' lectures to be aware that the emperor's chamberlain was the head of all the palace staff and, while she remained in the palace, her own superior. Her escape was no escape unless she could get out of the palace as well. And even if she somehow succeeded in that, if Nomos were caught she might well be recaptured and punished.

*The emperor seems kind*, she thought, belting her tunic. *Perhaps if I have a chance to speak to him I can persuade him to send me home. After all, I was his slave before, and now I'm his slave again: he wouldn't lose anything by it, and I can serve him as well in Tyre as in Constantinople. Better — from what I saw yesterday they don't do much tapestry here in the palace. I will ask him as soon as I have a chance. Oh God, I will beg shamelessly: weep over my poor little boy left motherless, crawl on the floor like a third-rate actress, if it helps. Please God, Mother Mary, let him listen and send me back to Tyre! Even if it all comes out and I have to die, let me at least die at home!*

She was just fastening her sandals when there was a knock at the door and the keeper of the looms came in, flushed and nervous. "The emperor has asked for you," he told her. "You must come at once."

Theodosius was in his private writing room. Copying manuscripts was his favorite form of relaxation, and he was busy on a set of gospels when Demetrias was led in. He smiled and put down his pen, turning from his work; she made the correct bow down to the floor and rose again.

"There you are, Demetrias," said the emperor, giving her a particularly sweet smile. "I hope you have been well treated?"

"Yes, Master," she said humbly, wondering how to begin her plea. "Everyone has been most kind."

"Good, good. However, I've been thinking about you, my dear, and . . . and I've decided that it would not be the best thing to keep you here."

Her heart leaped, and she felt her cheeks go hot; she began to speak, then recollected the extreme respect due to an emperor and stopped herself. If he wasn't going to keep her in the palace, it would be best to learn what he intended to do with her before saying anything.

"No," said Theodosius, gently and regretfully, "I should not keep you. And really, I don't think we do enough weaving here at the Great Palace to keep you occupied. My sister now — she's another matter. She's an excellent weaver herself and always sits at the loom for an hour or two every day; many of her women are skilled as well, and they make wonderful things out at her palace in the Hebdomon. I thought, really, you'd do much better with my sister, so I thought — ah, Chrysaphios, there you are. I was just telling Demetrias that I plan to give her to my sister Pulcheria."

The chamberlain, who had just entered and begun his ritual prostration to the emperor, paused before completing it. "To your sister, Master?" he asked.

"Yes. I thought I could ride out to the Hebdomon today and see her. It's been months since I saw her. I know we have our differences, but I ought to see more of her. She's been very lonely since Marina died."

Chrysaphios hesitated, looking at the weaver with half-lidded eyes and trying not to show his loathing. The woman was to be packed off, as he had hoped; good — but he was not happy about the Augusta Pulcheria. He had forced her into retirement but had never succeeded in disgracing her, and she still held all her titles and wealth, together with the loyalty of most of the finest generals and the affection of the people of Constantinople, on whose poor she had lavished gold. She was as pious as her brother, but as tough and pragmatic as he was gentle and idealistic; she was older than he and had dominated him for years. Chrysaphios calculated that anything that came into Pulcheria's hands was out of his reach forever — and he did not want Theodosius to visit such a dangerous enemy. It was usually a simple matter to suggest reasons why the emperor should not visit his sister; Theodosius was afraid of the strong-willed, harsh-tongued Augusta and readily accepted any excuse for avoiding her. But now he looked charmed with the idea of bestowing his precious new weaver on Pulcheria.

"It is an excellent idea, Master," Chrysaphios told the emperor, smiling, "but could I make a suggestion? It's raining today and it would take you half the day to reach the Hebdomon. Why not just send the weaver and a letter today and ride out yourself some other time when it's sunny? That way you could see how the girl has settled in — and you wouldn't have to worry your most noble sister by arriving unannounced. She's not as young as she was, and has been in deep mourning for Marina: she would undoubtedly prefer some warning to prepare herself and her house to entertain you."

"You're right, of course," said Theodosius, at once chagrined and relieved. "I hadn't thought of that. Well then, Demetrias, I'll send you off to her this morning and arrange some other time for my own visit. Chrysaphios will arrange for your carriage and escort and I'll write a letter for you to give her. Why, what's the matter?"

"I expect she is sorry to leave Your Sacred Majesty," said Chrysaphios, his eyes glittering, before Demetrias could speak.

"It will be better this way," said Theodosius, and hesitantly patted Demetrias' shoulder. "My sister will treat you well."

"I'm glad you've found the girl a good home," Chrysaphios went on quickly, seeing that the weaver still showed signs of wanting to say something. *She's ready to plead with him to keep her,* he thought, with a stab of anger. *She mustn't have the chance.* "I'm sorry to hurry you, Master," he continued smoothly, "but there was some business I thought you should see this morning — could you perhaps . . . ?"

"Of course," said Theodosius reluctantly. He kissed Demetrias gently on the forehead, patted her shoulder again, and went out with his chamberlain.

Half an hour later she was jolting out the Bronze Gate in an inlaid and richly upholstered carriage drawn by four white horses and preceded by an escort of ten of the palace guard. She curled up against the embossed leather of the corner, staring out the window at the rain-sodden streets of Constantinople as they rolled quickly by. Not the journey's end after all, but only another posting station. She leaned her head back and closed her eyes; the lids felt hot and swollen and her throat was tight. She imagined that Symeon was there beside her, looking at her with that intense tender scrutiny peculiar to him, not moving, his hand a few inches from her own. The image was so vivid that she opened her eyes eagerly — but of course the seat beside her was empty and she remained alone.

# =VII=

THE HEBDOMON, a region of the coastal plain just outside Constantinople, seven miles from the Great Palace, was the traditional drilling field of the army. Theodosius the Great had built a small palace and a chapel on the site so that he could be near his men, and his granddaughter Pulcheria had enlarged these when she chose the Hebdomon as a fitting place to live in retirement. The church had been enlarged even more than the palace — the Augusta was famous for her piety. At the age of sixteen she had publicly "devoted her virginity to God," dedicating in the Great Church of Constantinople on behalf of herself and her two sisters a tablet of gold and precious stones engraved with the terms of their oath. None of the princesses had ever married and no men were admitted to the palaces where they were said to lead a life of monastic asceticism, prayer, and, in Pulcheria's case, high politics. Her one recreation had always been reported to be weaving. The two younger princesses, Arcadia and Marina, were both dead, but Pulcheria lived on, out of power, but neither disgraced nor forgotten, a grim pious presence at the boundaries of the turbulent political dance, weaving and praying in the Hebdomon.

It was shortly after noon when Demetrias' carriage drew up in the forecourt of the Palace of the Hebdomon. Demetrias had not seen much of the area as they approached. The morning's rain had turned to snow, heavy flakes that melted when they touched the wet ground, but filled the air with drifts and billows of whiteness, swirling in the strong wind off the sea. She had closed the carriage's glass windows and the world outside had become a pale blur, a muffled beat of hooves and creak of wheels along the road, and occasional shouts or indistinguishable words from the escort. When the carriage stopped and she heard the stamping of hooves and jingle of harness as the escort disposed itself, she opened the enameled door and jumped down. It was snowing hard. The paved courtyard she stood in was white, though the snow had melted on the shrubbery, and the horses steamed in the heavy air. The captain of her escort, who had been charged with delivering her safely, took her arm and hurried her into a gatehouse of stone, dark with melted snow. The inside of the gatehouse was almost black after the whiteness of the outside air: its windows were shuttered against the cold, and the pale light that crept through the chinks was lost among the dark red panels and black hangings that decked the walls. The only sound was the soft hissing of a charcoal brazier. For a moment Demetrias thought the room was empty — and then she noticed an elderly black-cloaked eunuch sitting beside the brazier and watching them with fixed dark eyes.

The guardsman bowed to him, whispered a few words of explanation, and handed him the letter from the emperor. The eunuch nodded and went off without a word, leaving Demetrias and the guardsman alone in the dark entrance room to listen to the drip of the snow as it melted on the roof and the steady hissing of the gatekeeper's brazier.

After some time, the gatekeeper reappeared with a stern old woman, also dressed in black; she cast a disapproving eye over Demetrias' rose-colored cloak and her gold necklace and earrings — then nodded to the guardsman. He bowed to her, grinned at Demetrias, and went back out into the white outer court. Demetrias heard him shouting to his troop of guards, ordering them to turn their mounts and set off back to the city.

"Isn't he going to come in with me?" she asked the old woman in surprise. "I thought he would present me to the Augusta."

"No men are allowed in this palace," the woman returned, severely.

It was what Demetrias had heard, but it still shocked her: a captain of the imperial guards would have to ride seven miles back to the city in the snow rather than pass beyond this gatehouse.

"But . . . but you must have some men here," she found herself stammering, "guards — grooms —"

"For the guards there is a barracks, which you passed on the road, and for the grooms, the stables; for guests there is a guesthouse. But no men are allowed within these walls unless the sacred Augusta herself invites them. I will bring you to the sacred Augusta. I hope you know the correct protocol to use with an empress?"

Demetrias had been told it the day before, and she followed the old woman silently into the palace.

The palace was as dark and quiet as its gatehouse. It contained many of the things the Great Palace had contained — hangings of purple silk, splendid carpets, magnificent mosaic pavements — but the predominant colors were dark purples, blacks, and indigoes, and the only paintings and statues were of saints. The few women they saw as they walked through the maze of corridors wore black, and none said a word to Demetrias and her guide; even among themselves they didn't so much as whisper. Only once, passing a side corridor, she heard singing from somewhere deep in the building. It was a familiar song, a hymn to the Blessed Virgin, with a strong joyous rhythm; in Tyre the workers had sung it at their looms. Demetrias paused a moment, looking down the corridor, which was as dark as all the rest.

"That is the way to the looms," her guide said, in a somewhat gentler tone and with a nod toward the singing. "I heard you were a weaver; we'll go there presently. Now come along."

The old woman at last stopped before a door and knocked twice. The door was opened by another black-cloaked woman, who nodded and stood aside.

The room beyond was fairly large, vaulted, and paved with an abstract mosaic in several shades of blue. A number of braziers set about the walls warmed it, and it was lit by three heavy silver lampstands as well as by the dim light from the snow-fringed windows, but the air remained chill and damp. The walls were hung with purple. Again, it was not the usual bright imperial purple made by mixing the juice of the murex with that of the smaller, crimson-yielding buccina, but the color produced by dyeing with the murex alone, a more valuable dye, but dark and funereal. The gold frame of a large painting of the Blessed Virgin was the only brightness in the room. In the center of the room, three women sat on low chairs, spinning purple wool from a distaff, while a eunuch sitting under one of the lampstands read to them; the book seemed to be a work of theology. All were dressed in black.

Demetrias' guide went up to the group of women, then prostrated herself, slowly, her bones creaking with age. The eunuch stopped reading, marking his place in the book with his middle finger and closing it in his lap. The old woman rose stiffly and said, "This is the slave your sacred brother has sent you, Mistress."

Demetrias came forward and made the prostration, uncertain which woman she was bowing to. The floor was cold and damp against her face. She lay still a moment, waiting.

"You may get up," said a voice, and Demetrias climbed to her feet. The woman who had spoken sat in the center of the group, and, once recognized, her face was familiar from a hundred coins and statues. Time and asceticism had thinned it from the familiar image, left the eyes weary in the fine hollows of bone, drawn down the corners of the mouth — but the square, blunt features were the same. The gray hair was pulled back and tucked simply under a black cap, and the spindle now rested unmoving in the strong, square hands. She looked much older than her brother, though in fact there were only two years between them.

"Your name is Demetrias?" asked Pulcheria. "You are a weaver from Tyre?"

"Yes, Mistress," she replied, in a low, humble voice, dropping her eyes.

Pulcheria sighed. "Well. It seems my brother has made me a present of you." She set the spindle twirling again with a flick of her fingers and began teasing out a thread of fine purple wool as it dropped. "How does it come about that he brought you from Tyre to give to me?"

"It was not he who brought me from Tyre, Mistress. An agent called Eulogios bought me from the factory as a present for his patron Chrysaphios."

The empress looked up again at that. She caught the spindle, stopping it, and tossed it in her hand. "For Chrysaphios," she said, and smiled. It was a grim smile, a smile over some rather unpleasant private joke. "And why did this Eulogios wish to buy you, or Chrysaphios give you to my brother?"

Quietly, choosing her words with care, Demetrias told her what she had told Theodosius. The empress listened in silence — though, after a few moments, she resumed her spinning.

"Girl," said Pulcheria, when Demetrias had finished, "you are altogether a more interesting present than I thought you were." She looked at Demetrias thoughtfully. "What did Chrysaphios say when my brother announced that he was giving you to me?"

"He said that it was an excellent idea, Mistress, but he recommended that the sacred Augustus not visit you to make the presentation himself. He suggested that His Sacred Majesty come some other time, when it's sunny and you've had due warning."

Pulcheria smiled again. "In other words, never. Chrysaphios does not want my brother to see me, and my brother can usually be talked out of any plans to come. I don't flatter him, you see. My voice is like an old harpy's, after the song of that sweet siren Chrysaphios." She pulled up the spindle and set it twirling again. "But there is some nice little game being played that I knew nothing about. Why was Chrysaphios so convinced that your procurator's cloak was purple?"

"It . . . it was done in secret, Mistress. And then the prefect left with it, and so the most illustrious chamberlain never saw it. And he said something, too, about being suspicious of another gentleman who'd prolonged a stay in Tyre about the same time."

"Another gentleman? Who?"

"I think the name he said was Marcianus, and from the way they spoke of him, he was some associate of General Aspar's."

"Flavius Marcianus — yes, Aspar's *domesticus*, a Thracian and, by report, a shrewd man. What was he doing in Tyre?"

"I don't know, Mistress. I know nothing about him. It was all a mistake."

"Though Chrysaphios took it seriously. That is interesting." Pulcheria pursed her lips, then shook her head and twirled her spindle again. "The creature grows nervous. He is aware how badly he has bungled things. Well, Demetrias, so it is thanks to Chrysaphios I have you to weave for me. What do you weave?"

"In Tyre, Mistress, I did mostly tapestry."

"And if you were allotted that task in Tyre, there is no need to question whether you are skilled. Very good. I am content to have another skilled worker. Theonoe" — with a nod at the grim-faced old guide — "I put you in charge of the girl. Show her the palace and the looms, and find her some black clothing." She turned back to Demetrias and explained, "We are all in mourning here for my sister

Marina, who died last July. Theonoe will explain our rule to you and assign you your duties. We live a life of prayer and fasting, but the more onerous burdens of asceticism are voluntary, and you need not take on more than you wish. I trust you are an orthodox Christian?"

"Yes, Mistress."

"Good. You are a virgin?"

Demetrias caught her breath. She knew that the empress asked it with an eye on how Demetrias would fit into this community of dedicated virgins; whether she might, possibly, take vows herself one day. But it struck like a blow to an infected wound. She wanted Symeon, not a servile place in this gloomy palace among these grim old women. "No, Mistress," she said, sharply, "I am a married woman, Mistress. I have a husband and small child in Tyre."

Again the empress stopped her spindle. She looked at Demetrias intently. "I see," she said, after a long silence, and set the spindle twirling again.

The calm, unmoved face suddenly flooded Demetrias with desperation. She dropped to her knees before the empress and reached out to clasp the black-robed knees. "Please, Mistress," she began, almost choking on the urgency of the words, "please, my little boy is only five, and my husband . . ."

"If you're about to ask me to send you home, you don't know what you're saying," Pulcheria interrupted sharply. "As soon as you were well clear of my palace, Chrysaphios would catch you and take you off to question — and this time he'd make certain that my brother never heard of it, and dispose of you afterward. It is not to be thought of — not for several years, at least."

Demetrias let go of the knees and bowed her head. Her eyes stung. *I will not weep*, she told herself angrily. *Bad enough to be passed from hand to hand like a second-hand cloak that nobody likes; bad enough to have begged for a mercy no one wants to give: I will not let them see me weep.* She looked back up at Pulcheria with dry eyes. The empress was watching her with an unexpectedly gentle expression, and her heart caught again as she realized that Pulcheria had not actually said no. "But in a few years?" she whispered, breathlessly, "— if I please Your Sacred Majesty? May I hope?"

Pulcheria looked at her, head tilted slightly to one side, and smiled a different kind of smile, one that resembled her brother's, sweet and gentle, though otherwise she did not look like him at all. Then she shrugged. "But consider what you hope for!" she exclaimed. "Carnal pleasure" — she pronounced it distastefully — "is a high price to pay for the hardships the world assigns to a wife. The condition of a holy virgin is far better, and more pleasing to God as well."

"But I'm married already," Demetrias protested, her hands clenching together convulsively. Still Pulcheria had not said no.

"But chance has freed you. Think what it has freed you from! The pains of childbirth, the daily toil of obedience, of caring for a man and offspring when you've finished the toil you undertake as a slave. And beyond that, as the holy apostle says, the married woman seeks to please her husband, but the single woman to please God. It was for that reason, and not for the fear of carnality, that the saint preferred virginity to marriage. I have understood since I was young that if a woman once submits to a man, she is never any better than a slave; she is below a slave, being the slave of a slave, and her own wishes, her own will, her own abilities, are disregarded by everyone. Yet, free from Man, it was Woman who gave birth to God. Consider this, girl. Your husband will undoubtedly find himself another woman. The church would approve if you used your freedom to choose its discipline, and gave up the pleasures of the flesh, exchanging them for the riches of the Spirit."

Demetrias licked her lips, trembling, trying to think of arguments that the empress would accept. "But I'm married, and the church blessed it, Mistress. How can I take other vows with the vows I made then still valid?" Pulcheria seemed unmoved, and Demetrias went on, stumbling and honestly. "And the pleasures of the flesh never . . . that is, it was no pleasure to me. Only I loved my husband and my little boy. I never realized how much I loved them until I lost them. There was a Hun in the escort on the way from Tyre: he wanted to marry me and I didn't dislike him, but the very idea was a torment; all I wanted was my own Symeon." His name caught in her throat, and she had to pause and struggle with herself before going on. "Please, Mistress. God does not call everyone to the same calling. I admire those who can so love God that they give up all else, but for me, I am contented with less exalted things. If I have work for my hands, and enough to live quietly with my own husband and my children, that is all the blessedness I desire. If Your Grace would restore me to my own home, I would praise Your Goodness next after that of God himself to the end of my life."

The empress sighed. "Oh, child! Goodness, in returning you to a husband? I have never understood why women wish to debase themselves so. But it's clear enough, you were a virtuous wife. Our Savior himself taught that humanity ought not separate what God has joined; He does approve matrimony, though as a lesser estate than celibacy. But I've told you, it's not to be thought of yet. If, after three years, you continue in this resolve you have now, and if your husband shows himself worthy by continuing celibate himself in your absence, I give you my promise that I will return you to your home. Until then, I expect you to live and work in my palace, and to follow our customs humbly. You may find that you like this life more than your old one, and, if you do, I will give you your freedom and you may take vows in our community."

*Three years*, thought Demetrias, stunned. *Only three years. Meli will still be a child — surely Symeon will wait that long for me? Surely he would if I wrote to him! Only three years!*

She bowed her face down to the cold pavement again, burning with happiness. "I thank you, Mistress," she said, "from my heart. I will do my best to please you."

"Very good," said Pulcheria, giving her the gentle smile again. "Now, Theonoe, show Demetrias our palace, and find her some work. Skilled hands should not be idle."

The old guide, Theonoe, found Demetrias a black tunic and cloak in the palace stores, then, after some discussion with another palace official, took her to a long corridor on an upper floor of the palace and assigned her a bedroom. "You should change at once," she whispered, unlocking the door.

"But . . ." Demetrias began.

"Hush!" Theonoe whispered severely. "Talking is not permitted in the corridors or bedrooms."

Demetrias bowed her head and went into the room. It was small, clean, and plain, containing only a bed and a small sandalwood clothes chest; there was a glass window and a woolen carpet and bedspread, both of plain white patterned with the Christian *chi-rho* monogram in blue. She had a sudden suspicion that every room along that corridor would be exactly the same, the same bedspreads, the same windows, the same black-cloaked women dressing at the same time every morning, forbidden to speak. She shivered and undressed very slowly, taking off and folding carefully her rose-colored cloak and the blue woolen tunic with its patterned sleeves and hem. She was glad there was no black undertunic; the thought of the gloomy color next to her skin made her shiver again. She put on the new clothes and set her own things in the clothes chest. When she came back into the corridor, Theonoe was there waiting. The old woman shook her head. "The earrings, girl," she whispered reprovingly. "They're very worldly gear, not suited to a house in mourning."

Demetrias unhooked them without a word, went back into the room, and set them in the chest on top of the tunic and cloak. They were the ones Symeon had chosen that day in Ptolemais. She touched them gently. *Three years*, she promised. *Three years at the most, if I please them here.* She closed the chest and went back outside. This time Theonoe nodded. "Now," she whispered, "have you eaten? Very well, this way!"

They went down several flights of steps, and along another corridor to a set of massive wooden doors; Theonoe shoved them open and showed Demetrias into the palace kitchens. There was a blast of noise, startling after the silence, and a smell of fresh bread and pea soup. The room was full of women, all of them talking and laughing loudly as they worked around the great ovens and cauldrons preparing the evening meal. Theonoe banged on the door to attract attention, and eventually a stout red-faced woman came over, listened to what was wanted, gave a booming laugh, and showed them to a table in a corner. "I'll fetch you some bread and milk, dear," she told Demetrias, beaming at her, "and you can have a proper meal in a couple of hours when the supper's ready. Be right back!"

"Are cooks allowed to talk, then?" Demetrias asked Theonoe, raising her voice to be heard above the din.

Theonoe gave the noisy cooks a disapproving look. "Talking is permitted at work or at meals," she said primly, "though one hopes it is directed to edification and piety, not to frivolity and license." She glared as the red-faced woman came back, carrying a tray with fresh bread and honey, goat's milk, and a handful of dried fruit. The stout cook took no notice, merely beamed at Demetrias again and went back to her work, meanwhile telling one of her companions about an incident in the marketplace that morning: "And I said to him, 'Well, I'm glad I'm not your wife,' and he said . . ."

What he had said was lost in a burst of laughter. Demetrias looked down to hide a smile. It seemed that the Palace of the Hebdomon might not be quite as grim as it had first appeared.

Theonoe cleared her throat, gave Demetrias a severe look, and began to explain the structure of the palace hierarchy and the ordering of its daily life. The organization of the Hebdomon was similar to that of the Great Palace, with the differences that much more of its time was devoted to prayers and religious exercises and that, except for a few senior eunuchs, all the offices were held by women. Theonoe herself was keeper of the looms — though this title seemed more senior and honorable in the Hebdomon than it had been in the Great Palace. "I am familiar, of course, with much of the work that has been done in Tyre," the old woman said, giving her charge another stern glare. "And it is, of course, of a very high standard. But before I assign you a place, I would like to know more exactly what you yourself have worked on."

Demetrias reeled off a list of the tapestry commissions she had worked on and the old woman listened in silence until near the end, when the curtains for the palace were mentioned. Then she gave a start.

"Those were delivered last month," she said, "I was over at the Great Palace, bringing some hangings that our mistress had arranged for the chapel of the blessed martyr Stephen, and I saw them. Did you do the whole of them?"

Demetrias shook her head. "I did Christ giving sight to the man born blind. Then I was interrupted for another commission."

"But that was the best of them!" Theonoe declared with something very like enthusiasm. "I saw the blind eyes glittering with life and I asked the keeper of the looms there to let me study the whole curtain. The whole was well made, but that panel was as good as anything I've seen. Well!" The grim old woman came near to beaming at Demetrias as widely as the cook had. "We shall have to put such talent to work at once."

She showed Demetrias to the palace workroom, an immense long room with windows along its north side: it seemed as they walked along it that it must stretch the whole length of the palace. Looms stood on either side of it, some empty, many occupied. Groups of women sat spinning or weaving in the slanting light; a hundred voices were talking, singing, laughing; braziers sent up a warm, fragrant blue smoke. At the far end of the hall Theonoe stopped before an assembly of silk looms, one of which towered above her head, glowing with jewels. A number of black-cloaked workers looked up from the smaller looms.

"This is Demetrias, a skilled worker in silk tapestry from Tyre, who has been given as a gift from the Augustus to our sacred mistress," Theonoe announced. "She will be working on the altar curtains for Blachernae — the Flight into Egypt, I think. Agatha," she said to a woman who had been sorting silk, "I've given her Sophrosyne's room — next to yours. You can show her around the palace. I must get back to my work."

The rest of the afternoon passed in a blur. Demetrias found a place at one of the small looms and was given the design cartoon for a tapestry rondel showing the Flight into Egypt. Blachernae turned out to be the site of a church: Pulcheria had founded a magnificent edifice there to contain the cloak of the Mother of God, a particularly holy relic that she had acquired. It was apparently a great honor to be permitted to work on the altar curtains; most of the women assigned this task were senior ladies-in-waiting, with only a sprinkling of the more skilled slaves. But, she discovered, skill at weaving was honored throughout the Hebdomon, and even these grand ladies did not resent her presence. Almost everyone in the palace wove, from the oldest lady-in-waiting and most distinguished eunuch down to the youngest kitchen worker, and good workmanship was admired almost as much as piety. The empress herself, the ladies told her, worked for two or three hours every day on her corner of a large altarcloth to adorn the same church at Blachernae. It was this that hung on the large loom at the end of the hall. It was a magnificent piece of work, though, to Demetrias' mind, a bit too gaudy, relying for its effect on lavish use of gold and precious stones rather than any delicacy of craftsmanship. But after examining it more closely, Demetrias decided that the large bold style was well suited to the Augusta, and that fine craftsmanship would merely show up all the defects, which Pulcheria was too impatient to pick out of the weave. Pulcheria, she decided, was a hot-tempered, impatient woman, and, though she could stop it from showing in her face, she was less good at concealing it in her weaving.

As the red-faced cook had said, supper was soon ready; she had little time to take everything in before a bell rang to summon the palace staff to prayers and the evening meal. The silk sorter, Agatha, bustled over and led her off to the servants' hall, explaining that, though everyone worked together at the looms, at mealtimes the senior staff and the common workers separated.

"They go off and have thin soups and long prayers," she told Demetrias cheerfully, "and we get solid meals and a chance to gossip."

A plain but solid meal it was; and gossip the women certainly did. Demetrias found herself warmly welcomed. Somehow the other slaves had heard that she had begun her stay in the Hebdomon by praising marriage to the empress, and they exclaimed shrilly over this and questioned her about it with delighted admiration. Some of the slaves were married women, with husbands among the grooms and guards, and houses and children outside the palace proper; and even some of the single women had doubts about the superiority of virginity. The previous occupant of her own bedroom had apparently been one such doubter, and was now pregnant, married to a guardsman, and living outside the palace. "Theonoe was furious with her," Agatha confided, "and she kept saying she didn't know how Sophrosyne had got out of the palace to meet the man: she never gave her permission." She giggled. "But of course everyone knows she never gives anyone permission to leave the palace, particularly to go anywhere they might meet men. That's why nobody ever asks her!"

One of the others whispered, "But everybody knows there's a way over the wall by the latrines; you just climb onto the roof and let yourself down the other side. Everybody does it."

"I don't think I'll need to," Demetrias replied, thinking of the long miles between Constantinople and Tyre — but then, seeing her companions' faces grow suddenly suspicious, she added, "but thank you for telling me."

When the day was at last over and she was able to return to the small room she'd been given, she lay down on the bed in the dark, fingering the edge of her black cloak. No pattern of flowers on this one, and her fingers ran aimlessly over the smooth tight weave.

*It won't be too bad for just three years*, she told herself, trying to shake off the profound sense of depression. *The weaving will be interesting — A Flight into Egypt: I ought to be able to get the feeling of a journey into that, after traveling so far myself. And the people seem kind and happy. It should be restful, for a time. I'll have nothing but weaving to do — no cooking, no fetching of water or cleaning. No clothes to weave for the family; no lessons for Meli; no Symeon.*

At the thought the darkness seemed to deepen. She lay motionless, aching with longing for Symeon, her body feeling empty. *Three years*, she repeated to herself, in despair; then, determinedly, *only three years — perhaps less, even, if I can please them.*

Unless Nomos' plot failed, and she was discovered to have lied, caught out in the practice and the concealment of treason. She sat up, her fingers clutching tightly at the black cloak. In the events of the past few days she had almost forgotten that danger.

Where was the cloak now? In Constantinople already? Philippos wouldn't have traveled as quickly as Eulogios, but he'd left Tyre two weeks earlier: if he hadn't reached the capital yet, he soon would. What would happen then?

*They won't kill the emperor*, Demetrias told herself again, trying to convince away the terror. *No one would accept Nomos if he'd achieved the purple through blood.*

But what if Nomos had arranged it so that someone else got the blame for a murder, so that no one connected it with him? If he did murder Theodosius, he wouldn't leave Pulcheria alive. There would be another murder, bloody or secret — and Pulcheria's happy, giggling slaves would be handed over to the new emperor or given to one of his supporters, with herself among them. "Three years" would probably become "forever."

*I could tell Pulcheria the truth*, Demetrias thought, with a surge of hope. *She might understand why I had to be silent before — and it's clear enough that she hates Chrysaphios; she wouldn't hand me over to him. She used to be powerful; perhaps she's still powerful enough to defeat Nomos on her own.*

But suppose she wasn't? She would certainly turn to Chrysaphios in preference to seeing her brother murdered. And if the investigation were in Chrysaphios' hands, Demetrias would not be the only one to suffer. Again she found it only too easy to imagine Eulogios returning to Tyre and questioning the factory workers with the aid of the whip and the rack — Philotimos, Daniel, Eugenios, Laodiki, and others could end up crippled or killed because Demetrias had spoken. *I can't betray them!* Demetrias thought in anguish. *I can't!*

But if Nomos' plot failed — and it was clear that the chamberlain suspected him and was on his guard — they would be sure to suffer anyway. Did Pulcheria, after all, offer a greater chance of safety?

Demetrias lay awake most of the night, revolving the possibilities in her mind; she finally fell asleep in the darkness, her head aching and her eyes hot, her exhausted mind spinning endlessly through troubled dreams.

When she woke next morning, it was to the silence. What had been oppressive the day before suddenly seemed wonderfully peaceful. It was possible to float in the calm darkness, drifting without thought into a day's work. She could almost forget that she was involved in a plot against the emperor, and that before very long she would learn if the plot had failed.

She followed the palace routine for the next two days, drifting in the silence and the idle, undemanding chatter. By the third day she found she could fall into the routine almost without thinking: wake; prayers; breakfast; work; prayers; lunch; work; prayers; supper; church. The work was itself a remedy to all misery. Picking the green for the roadside, the pale straw-color for the road beneath the feet of Mary and Joseph, she did not have to remember the cloak she had woven, or wonder where it was now, or whether it had reached the man it was intended for or strayed into some other hands.

*Should I tell Pulcheria?* she wondered again as she sat with bowed head through one of the interminable sessions of prayers. *I feel that she would do something to stop Nomos, and either keep it secret or take the credit for herself; she wouldn't want to share the glory with Chrysaphios. But I know of her only what I saw in one short meeting, what I've seen at the looms, and what her slaves have said. I cannot be sure. And how do I know that she'd spare me even if she could oppose Nomos on her own?*

*And yet, there's a chance she could and would — a good chance. The best chance I have — no, the only chance. I must do it; I must speak to her. Tomorrow.*

On the third morning of her stay in the palace, she told Theonoe that she wished to speak privately with the sacred Augusta. The grim old woman smiled. "Changing your mind, are you?" she asked, with some satisfaction. "You didn't think women could manage without men, did you? And now you've seen we manage better without them than with them, you're having second thoughts about your husband. Well, well, I'll ask her if she wishes to see you, and I expect she will. She likes you, girl: you keep control of yourself."

After morning prayers, Theonoe returned and announced that the empress would see her in the blue reception room during the afternoon work session. After lunch, Demetrias accordingly went to the room where Pulcheria had first received her. But the old doorkeeper had moved her chair outside the room, and when Demetrias came up, shook her head.

"She has visitors from the world," the woman said, disapprovingly. "Men. Wait until they've gone."

Demetrias waited, leaning against the wall. After a time, she could hear voices raised inside the room, male voices, angry. The empress' replies were inaudible but apparently effective: the door flew suddenly open and two men retreated through it, looking angry but afraid. One of them was Eulogios.

Demetrias shrank against the wall and pulled up her cloak. The agent's eyes swept over her without seeing her — one more black-cloaked palace lady hovering in an unlit corridor. The eunuch gate-keeper appeared behind him, dark and implacable, and ushered him out.

"Now we can go back in," said the doorkeeper, and she picked up her chair and marched back through the door. Demetrias hesitated outside a moment, trying to collect herself, then followed.

Pulcheria and her two most favored ladies were sitting in their usual places. The ladies were spinning placidly but the empress sat with her spindle clutched like a dagger in her hands. She looked younger, somehow, and her worn cheeks were flushed, whether with anger or with excitement it was impossible to say. Her eyes brightened when she saw Demetrias.

"So," she said, "I think I can guess what you wanted to speak to me about."

It was the evening of that day, the sixth of January, when Flavius Ardaburius Aspar, ex-master of arms for the East, for Thrace, and the palace; ex-commander-in-chief for Africa and Italy; senator and ex-consul, and six years a private citizen, received a letter from the Augusta Pulcheria.

The messenger, one of Pulcheria's eunuchs, knocked at the general's dining room door while Aspar was reclining at a meal with his deputy Marcianus. Aspar was a large man, bearded, blue-eyed and blond, like his barbarian ancestors, and he lay sprawled on his couch, a wine cup in his hand and a jovial smile on his coarse red face. Marcianus reclined more tidily, but he too was smiling. He had arrived from Tyre not two hours before, and found that Philippos had come that afternoon and was being closely watched.

Pulcheria's eunuch entered when requested, bowed to the floor, then stood and extended to Aspar a letter sealed with the imperial purple. "From the sacred Augusta," he said simply.

Aspar sat up abruptly. He took the letter, stared at the seal a moment, then looked at Marcianus in consternation. Marcianus shook his head and shrugged. Aspar frowned angrily, examined the seal, then ripped open the letter and read it aloud in his deep clear voice. "Aelia Pulcheria Augusta to Ardaburius Aspar wishes health and long life. General, it would please me if you and your *domesticus* Marcianus would present yourselves before me at my palace in the Hebdomon tomorrow at your earliest convenience. There are matters of grave importance to the state which I must discuss with you."

Aspar sat for a moment frowning at the neat black lettering, then looked up at the messenger. "Matters of grave importance?" he demanded. "What matters?"

"That is for my mistress to say," the eunuch replied smoothly. "What answer shall I give Her Serenity?"

Aspar snorted, shook his head in wonder, then carefully folded the letter. He looked at the broken seal for a moment, his anger now mixed with some other emotion; then, deliberately, he bowed his head and touched the seal to his lips. "Tell Her Sacred Majesty that it is my privilege to serve my sovereign and empress. Marcianus and I will be at the Hebdomon tomorrow as soon as we are able."

The eunuch smiled. "My mistress expected no other reply and instructed me to thank you for your loyalty." He again bowed to the floor, then left without another word.

Aspar sat still for a moment, glaring after him, his eyes narrowed in something very like hatred. Then he began to grin. He tossed back his shaggy head and gave a roar of laughter. "Lord of All!" he exclaimed, turning to Marcianus. "How in the world did *she* find out about it?"

"It might be some other grave matter," cautioned Marcianus, frowning.

"It might be — but would she have invited you, you specifically, if it were? No, she's heard something about Nomos' little game and she wants to join in the fun. How she can sit in that nunnery with all those old women, praying and spinning, and still contrive to learn as much about the plots of her brother's ministers as I do, I don't know." He again shook his head in astonishment. "I've known that woman for thirty-five years, since I was a boy trailing after my father, and I still underestimate her. You'd think I'd know her better by now. Lord of All, she's a wonder!"

Marcianus reclined unmoving, one hand fixed and tense on his glass goblet of wine. He knew his employer very well. He had joined Aspar as a lieutenant in Thrace twenty years before, and fought beside him in a dozen wars. He had seen Aspar planning a campaign; had seen him drunk after a battle; had roused him from a brothel, once, with urgent news of a defeat. The general might be grinning now but underneath the grin he was still angry — angry, and something else as well. Uncertain? Suspicious? Afraid? Why? Surely it made no difference if the empress knew what they were about?

"Will the Augusta interfere?" he asked at last.

"Interfere?" asked Aspar. "What do you mean by that?" He waved the question aside with a large hand. "She's the empress, we're her servants: whatever we do it's ultimately on her behalf, and she can order it as she likes. But don't worry. If she does want to change our plan, she'll just improve it."

"I have understood as much from her reputation," Marcianus said, carefully. "In fact, I had thought you might wish to bring her into the plot yourself."

Aspar shrugged, but his eyes fixed his subordinate with a doubtful, assessing look. "I wanted to bring her in when you first wrote to me," he said, after a moment, "but Chrysaphios has had her watched even more closely than he's had me watched. And besides, she's withdrawn, these last years since her sisters died; she hasn't had the taste for the game that she used to."

Marcianus took his hand from the wine glass. "You're watched," he said sharply. "She's watched. If you visit her, will that give the game away?"

There was no movement on Aspar's face, nothing to show Marcianus whether he had hit on the source of the worry or not. He continued, "If it will cause problems, surely we could excuse ourselves, for the present? We don't want trouble now. It's still going to be difficult to catch Nomos and Zeno, particularly since the chamberlain has grown so suspicious. If he thinks Pulcheria will intervene isn't he likely to have Nomos arrested at once, just on the off chance?"

Aspar shook his head, but he was scowling. His voice when he spoke, though, was cheerful. "If Pulcheria thought so, she wouldn't have sent for us," he said. Then, seeing that his deputy was far from satisfied by this, he pushed his cup aside and slapped the table. "Don't worry!" he said. "Pulcheria was born knowing how to manage things like this. Have I ever told you how she got her title?"

Marcianus shook his head, surprised. "She's the eldest child of her father — I thought . . ."

"Nobody makes an eldest daughter an Augusta! Nobody just gives the regency to a girl only two years older than the brother she's regent for! No, when her father died, she was just 'the most noble,' and nobody expected that to change. Her brother was eight, but he was already an Augustus, and had been since his birth. Anthemius was regent — you remember him?"

"He built walls," said Marcianus drily.

"A black mark against him in your book."

"I have nothing against walls," Marcianus replied evenly, "provided they're not used as a replacement for men. The Senate still dotes on the memory of Anthemius, and perhaps he ruled well. We did not approve of him in Thrace."

Aspar snorted. "We didn't think much of him in the army generally. I remember my father damning Anthemius and his policies when I was still a little child. But there was nothing anyone could do. Anthemius had a good tight grip on power and he meant to keep it. Here's something you won't have heard before: he wanted to ally his family to the imperial house. When Pulcheria was sixteen he tried to arrange for her to marry his grandson."

Marcianus stared.

"No," said Aspar, satisfied, "he didn't want to tell anyone after it failed to come off, and of course she suppressed the whole story: doesn't reflect well on a holy virgin. But it looked a certain thing at the time. Anthemius was regent, exercising the power of an emperor: nobody could have expected that a pious little princess would get the better of him. But, as I said, she was born knowing how to do things. When she got wind of Anthemius' plans she didn't weep or refuse or complain to him: she just told him that she needed time to pray and prepare herself. So of course he granted it. She used the time to go to my father and a few other leading ministers who didn't like the regent, and she hinted and half promised and committed herself to nothing, but she left them all convinced that she would marry into their houses, either to them or their son or nephew, and that they could wear the purple one day, if they backed her against the regent." Aspar snorted. "I was twelve at the time, and my father had some stupid idea that she'd eventually marry me. He should have known better. Oh, I don't say that I wouldn't have been willing — there was a time when I'd have been more than willing! — but if she'd married anyone, it wouldn't have been an Arian heretic. Why, she still gives me lectures on the coessentiality of the Holy Trinity and the doctrine of Athanasios of Alexandria every time we meet. And you know how I promised my mother I'd never convert. But Pulcheria let my father think what he liked, and she got his support.

"Then, the next time there were games in the hippodrome, she convinced her brother to stay home and pray, and she turned up in the royal box wearing the purple and her father's diadem. You know the mob — they looked up and saw a princess of the Theodosian house, one already famous for her piety, and they went wild: 'Long live Pulcheria Augusta! The pious, the saintly one! Reign forever!' They gave her the titles freely — it scarcely needed the priming she'd arranged. And she had the title confirmed within the day, by the Senate and by the palace troops. It had all been arranged by her backers, of course. Then she called a meeting of the imperial consistory. She stood up and announced very sweetly that Anthemius was too old for the heavy burden of his office, and that in her prudent and loving care for her father's faithful servant she had decided to let him go to his well-deserved retirement. She was of age now, she said, and could look after her brother's interests herself." Aspar gave a roar of laughter. "Of course, Anthemius hated it, but he soon realized that he had no option but to thank her and back out graciously. Ousted from the regency in favor of a sixteen-year-old girl!"

Aspar took a gulp of his wine, then grinned again. "But that was just the beginning. As soon as she was firmly in control, she went and swore her famous oath promising never to marry anyone, and she convinced her sisters to swear the same, poor girls. Then she called a meeting of her supporters and congratulated them on their loyalty and piety. I wish I could have seen it! I remember my father came home foaming at the mouth, ha!, and went off and slaughtered targets on the practice field until his horse was staggering. Then he called me over to him and said, 'Son, remember this. Never trust a woman.' She'd made it plain that if he wasn't loyal, he was out. She wasn't giving anybody power through a purple-draped bridal bed: she was keeping that color to wear herself. And that was when she was sixteen! She's been at it now for thirty-five years, and what she doesn't know about getting power is a mystery reserved to God. If she's taking an interest in this business of ours I can only be glad."

Marcianus sat silent for a few minutes. *So you say,* he thought, *and yet you weren't glad when you received her letter. You're afraid of what she may say to you, though you won't defy her, and you told me that story as much to console yourself as to reassure me. Is there some other scheme of yours, one I know nothing about, which you fear she'll put a stop to?*

He smiled. He was well aware that Aspar did not tell him everything. Aspar was an Arian Christian and a barbarian by birth; Marcianus, orthodox and Roman: there were limits to trust. But Marcianus had never found the limitations restrictive. If Aspar was working for a new church for his coreligionists or the promotion of one of his countrymen, that was none of his deputy's affair, and nothing to do with the present business, where the Augusta could only strengthen them.

He had been presented to his patron's patroness once or twice, he had respected her reputation — but he had seen only a grim-faced, pious old woman. He thought now of a young girl coolly plotting herself into power; and he thought of the old woman seeing a chink in the golden armor of the enemy who had forced her retirement.

"I think the meeting tomorrow should prove interesting," he said mildly.

Aspar grinned. "I wouldn't miss it for the world."

Aspar and his deputy arrived at the Hebdomon at ten the next morning. When the gatekeeper reported it to her, Theonoe went at once to the palace looms. Demetrias was sitting before her segment of curtain, weaving quickly and competently. If she was pale and hollow-eyed from lack of sleep, at least she kept it from showing in her work. *That's something to be said in her favor*, thought Theonoe. *Something to set against all the trouble she's causing.*

"Demetrias!" the supervisor said sharply. Demetrias jumped, glanced about nervously, then fumbled her tapestry needle into the work and sat attentively with folded hands. The black cloak made her seem pale as mist; her eyes stared huge and vivid from a strained face. Half against her will, Theonoe was softened. After all, the hints of intrigue and deceit, the visits from worldly and corrupt ministers, the upheaval in the routine of the palace, weren't anything Demetrias wanted either.

"The . . . visitors . . . have arrived," Theonoe said, with distaste. "Her Sacred Majesty wishes you to attend her."

Demetrias bowed her head. Pulcheria had told her that her presence would be required at the meeting with the general. On the previous day she had told the empress everything she knew about the cloak; Pulcheria asked no questions about why she had kept silent before, and offered no information about what Eulogios had wanted with her, or what course of action she intended to take, beyond stating that she would summon Aspar. Now Aspar was here, and in a few minutes Demetrias would know if she or her friends would suffer for what she had done and said. She took a deep breath and glanced at her barely begun section of tapestry. Work was so simple. Silk, like choices of action, was slippery, subtle, varied; taking color easily, but easily slipping from the place it was set. But silk could be bound down, tied in, fixed in a pattern freely chosen — or pulled out and redone, if it failed to be what the heart would make of it. The pattern her own actions made seemed to shift and change color with each day that passed, and yet the actions themselves remained unalterable as stone.

She touched the silken warp on the loom very gently, then rose and went with Theonoe.

Pulcheria did not intend to receive her foremost general in her blue reception room, nor did she wear black to greet him. Theonoe escorted Demetrias to a hall known in the palace simply as the "Throne Room." It was a small basilica, lined on each side with columns of porphyry; the walls were decorated with a rich mosaic of the victories of Theodosius the Great. At the far end of the hall, under a painting of Christ Lord of All, stood a throne of gold, its armrests shaped like crouching lions, and on the throne sat the empress. Her purple cloak was decorated with images of the Blessed Virgin, and around her head she wore the imperial diadem, a band of purple silk plated with gold and embroidered with pearls. She sat as still and stern as the figure in the painting behind her. The bright winter sun that lanced through the windows struck angled beams through the clouds of blue smoke, charcoal and incense, that rose from the braziers along the hall. To Demetrias, the slow walk down the hall seemed to last forever, and she could feel her heart pounding in her throat when she at last reached the steps of the throne and made the prostration.

Pulcheria nodded to her, and gestured to a place to the left of the throne. Demetrias went and stood silently where she had been told. Theonoe was silently directed to leave the room. The old woman seemed displeased, but went humbly. Demetrias noticed as she did so that the rest of the hall was empty, apart from Pulcheria's lady secretary Eunomia and one eunuch. Pulcheria nodded to the eunuch, and he bowed and retreated down the long hall to open the door once more for Aspar and Marcianus, and to close it silently behind them.

The general and his deputy strode briskly up the basilica and stopped smartly in front of the empress. Aspar bowed low — ex-consuls were excused the prostration, which Marcianus correctly performed.

Pulcheria smiled. "Aspar," she said, in her ordinary harsh voice, "it's been a long time."

"Longer than I could have wished, Empress," the general returned, grinning at her. "I've tried to interest you in some small matters over the past few years, and received no answer for my pains."

She snorted. "I have neglected my friends; I have not neglected God. I am more bound to Him than to you. And the intrigues you suggested to me were trivial and unworthy of you, General."

"Unlike the present intrigue?" he asked, opening his blue eyes wide.

She snorted again. "You know why I've called you here?"

He scratched his beard, still grinning. "Marcellus Philippos, prefect of Syria Phoenice, arrived from Tyre yesterday afternoon," he stated, "and I think Your Providence knows where he went, and what he brought there."

She smiled and graciously inclined her head. "I am pleased to see that I was not mistaken in your diligence. I am curious, though, as to how you stumbled on this matter."

Aspar laughed. "I might ask the same question of you, Empress!"

"But, being an empress, I am not bound to answer. Proceed, Aspar."

"That tale I should leave to my deputy," Aspar declared cheerfully. "Proceed, Marcianus!"

Marcianus bowed and glanced quickly about the hall. One eunuch at the door, and two women, one old and one young, standing on either side of the throne. His eyes hesitated on the young one: she seemed somehow familiar. But he could not remember where he might have seen her before. At any rate, it was clear that the empress was aware of the danger of gossiping servants, and had trusted only a few of her people to hear his story.

"I was in Tyre on some business connected with one of my eminent employer's estates," he began, "when I was approached by a purple-fisher who said he possessed some information of value which he would give me in exchange for a promise of protection . . ."

There was a gasp on his right, and he looked over to see the young woman clutching the edge of her cloak and staring at him with a mixture of astonishment and pain. He had seen her before; definitely, he had seen her before — but where?

"Proceed," ordered the empress dryly.

Marcianus shrugged, and, reluctantly, looked away from the young woman and resumed his narration. "I questioned the man, and, when I was satisfied that he wished to bind me to nothing dishonorable, I gave him my oath to protect him and his family against their enemies. He then confided to me that his wife, a silk weaver in the imperial factory, had been commissioned by the procurator to weave in secret a purple cloak for the most distinguished Nomos, the former master of the offices. He said that she was, understandably, reluctant to proceed with this work, but, knowing that the prefect of Tyre was also a supporter of Nomos, considered that she had no choice but to complete it as quickly as she could. He was loyal to the emperor as well as concerned for his wife, and had decided instead to bring the matter to me. I judged that the best chance of disgracing Nomos and his allies lay in waiting until the cloak was actually in their hands, but, mindful of my oath, remained in Tyre to make sure of my fisherman's safety. When the cloak was completed and safely delivered, the prefect Philippos gave out that his mother had been taken ill, and himself set out for Constantinople. I followed with some of my retainers, keeping a half day's ride behind the prefect, but determining as I went whom he visited and whether he left anything behind. He came directly to Constantinople, and is presently a guest in the house of his patron Nomos. We believe that Nomos has sent messages to his supporters, but the house is being closely watched by the chamberlain's men as well as our own, and it is difficult to be certain."

Pulcheria tapped one arm of the throne with a restless forefinger, and traced the curve of the gold lion's ear. "And what did you intend to do?" she asked, after a thoughtful silence.

Aspar bobbed his head. "Empress, need you ask? We intended to visit Nomos this very morning, surround his house, and seize as much evidence as we could. Then we could present it to the prefect of the city, and let the traitor pay for his treachery. With your permission, we will follow the same plan this afternoon."

"Nomos is not your enemy," she said evenly. "What do you care about his schemes?"

"I am the servant of your sacred house," Aspar replied. "My father took orders from your ever-victorious grandfather, and from your father, and from you; and I, like him, will do my utmost for the house of Theodosius. And, I confess, I would hope to be appointed master of arms again in Zeno's place, if we can disgrace him along with his friend Nomos."

Pulcheria smiled sourly. "Dream on, my friend. You would be thanked and ignored — if your intention was really what you claim it was."

"If?" asked Aspar, though he seemed more nervous than surprised. "What other intention could I have, Augusta?"

She gave another sour smile. "You could go to Nomos, tell him what you know, and extract promises from him in exchange for your silence — and your assistance. Me you have served well — but we both know how much use you have for my brother."

Aspar went red. Marcianus looked at him quickly, startled, shocked, but, quite suddenly, convinced. *And yet*, he thought, *why should I believe it? He's never shown himself anything but loyal.* He looked at Pulcheria, who sat motionless on her throne, watching them cynically. "He says he wished to invite your aid in this matter earlier," he told her, quietly, "and he answered your summons at once. Have you any cause to question his loyalty?"

"I have cause to question any man's loyalty," replied Pulcheria, just as calmly, "and if my esteemed general were less than perceptive of where his best opportunities lie, I would not value him as highly as I do. Aspar, my friend, I know your loyalty to my house — and I know the limits of that loyalty. I am old, I have been out of power, and my brother and his creature have ignored you and abused the army. Come, tell me: what would you really have done? You meant to see Nomos. And then?"

"I meant to see Nomos," replied Aspar, gruffly, "and have his house searched. And . . . decide what to do afterward."

Pulcheria gave another gracious nod. "I thought as much."

"I wouldn't have betrayed you," Aspar declared, glaring at her. "I would have made that part of the bargain — your brother deposed, but unharmed, you reigning again, with myself as your chief general and Nomos as your colleague."

"As my husband, you mean? That is what you mean by 'colleague,' isn't it? Nomos would have no need to murder anyone if I gave him the prestige of the Theodosian house by contracting a formal marriage with him. And he is a widower — there would be no legal objection to such a match, and he would thank you with all his heart if you promised him your influence with me to achieve it. It would give him a bloodless and safe transfer of power in exchange for a bloody and dangerous one. And you thought that I could be easily convinced to cooperate, if it was a choice between that and seeing my brother lose his life."

Aspar turned even redder and stared at his own feet, then looked up grimly. "Your brother is not fit to rule," he declared. "If you could reign alone, I would try to depose him in your favor. But you know that neither the Senate, nor the people, nor even my own soldiers, would tolerate a woman as sole Augustus: they'd create one rebellion after another. And a woman emperor relying on an Arian barbarian general as a colleague would be just as bad. They want someone like Nomos — a senator, an official, a Roman gentleman, and an orthodox Christian. Yes, I would have helped him depose your brother, and then urged you to accept him — as your colleague at least. I will still urge that same thing. Do as you please, Empress. But I do not apologize for considering a course that still seems to me a wise one."

Pulcheria snorted. "Of course you still urge me to accept this lunatic plan. You wouldn't be here if you didn't think I might consider it! But I tell you flatly, your plan is a very stupid one. Nomos is no emperor. He was a tolerable master of the offices, and has some minor skill as a diplomat — but he'd do a worse job even than Chrysaphios if he came to govern. He's a blind lover of the Senate, the old traditions, the pure and ancient Roman way. Do you think he'd do as you told him to, once he'd put on the purple? You would find, old friend, that it's easier to make than unmake an emperor. He might leave you for a little while, in respect of your bargain, but he'd have a grand purge of barbarian commanders in the army! He'd strip your forces down to a few Armenians and Thracians, and especially pick out anyone loyal to you. And he'd soon find that he had to keep paying the Huns if he wanted to get away with it. He hasn't any idea of finance, either. He'd cut taxes for the Senate and force the rest of the country to starve."

Aspar paled, started to speak, and fell silent. His brow furrowed and he bit his lip. Pulcheria leaned back on her throne and rested her chin on her hand. After a moment, Aspar bowed his head. "Augusta," he said humbly, "I believe you are right."

"Of course I am!" she exclaimed, impatiently. "And, incidentally — I do not like interfering, arrogant men arranging marriages for me behind my back. Any repetition of this, Aspar, and I will forget our old friendship, and you will learn what it's like to have me as an enemy."

He bowed his head again. Pulcheria put her head on one side, then nodded, and said, more gently, "The scheme itself was sound enough — it was the consequences that you didn't consider well enough. Even the idea of marriage, little as I like the prospect, wouldn't be foolish, if we're unable to persuade my brother to adopt a suitable colleague. But if that ever becomes necessary, I will choose the man, Aspar, not you. Do I make myself understood?"

Aspar bowed deeply. "Yes, Empress."

"Good. I will now tell you how I come to know of this matter, and what I intend to do about it. God himself, gentlemen, has placed this affair in my hands. You, Marcianus, learned of it from a purple-fisher, married to a weaver in Tyre; I learned it from the weaver herself, whom All-seeing Providence brought here to my own palace. Demetrias!"

Marcianus remembered where he had seen the young woman even as she stepped forward and made the prostration: she had stuck out her tongue at Nomos' statue and run down the porch of the prefecture in Tyre. He stared at her incredulously. He had left her in Tyre almost a month before, and traveled continuously since; and here she was at home in the empress' palace before him. If Providence had plucked her up and set her down bodily before his eyes, he couldn't have been more astonished.

"Have you anything to add to what you told me before?" Pulcheria asked Demetrias sternly. "You said you knew nothing of this gentleman."

"I told you the truth, Mistress," Demetrias replied evenly. "My husband never told me what he'd done."

"No?" asked Pulcheria, with interest. She glanced at Marcianus, then nodded. "No, he knew he was taking a risk, and didn't want to admit it to you."

Demetrias bowed her head. As soon as Marcianus had spoken, she had seen that of course Symeon had done it; that Symeon had been bound to do it, being what he was. She could not even be angry with him, though he had undoubtedly called attention to her and the protection had been proved worthless. *He has never believed he was a slave*, she thought, warmly, *and he wouldn't believe I was one either*.

"How . . ." Marcianus began, then swallowed and tried again. "Empress, how does this woman . . . how is it that she's here? When I left Tyre . . ."

Pulcheria leaned her head back and smiled down at him. "After you left Tyre, Chrysaphios' agent Eulogios arrived. Finding no evidence of treason, he purchased this woman from the state to reassure his master, and hurried back to Constantinople with all the speed the imperial post could lend him. His master was not reassured — and I will tell you, sir, that one of his chief concerns was your own lengthy presence in Tyre, which seemed to him suspicious enough to call for more investigation. You are known to too many people, and your abilities are respected too widely, for your stay in Tyre to pass unnoticed. Chrysaphios arrogantly threatened the weaver with torture in his own office; she at once cried loudly for help and fetched in my brother. Chrysaphios appeased him by giving him the slave, and my brother gave her to me. Yesterday, Chrysaphios had word that Philippos was at Chalcedon arranging passage to Constantinople and that you were following him closely. At this he was convinced that his suspicions were indeed well founded and sent his agent here to offer to buy back the slave from me. When I refused to sell her, he added threats to promises, and finally confessed the truth of what Chrysaphios fears. The slave had already offered to tell me the whole truth, however, and I commanded the agent to leave my house at once. I am able to protect my brother myself, and need no help from the chamberlain."

Pulcheria rose to her feet, pulling straight the heavy folds of her cloak; she smiled at her generals. "I judge that Chrysaphios is likely to leave Nomos until this afternoon, giving him a good chance to contact his allies before arresting him, in the hope that that way he will discover more evidence of the treason. But I sent my own men to Nomos' house this morning and by now they should have secured it on my authority, which should still be proof against Chrysaphios'. And I have ordered my own carriage and escort to be readied for me. They should be waiting in the courtyard now. If you wish, gentlemen, we can all visit Nomos this noon — and I will strike my own bargain, Aspar. I will allow him to live and to keep his rank, if he assists us in ruining Chrysaphios. Once the chamberlain is out of the way, I will find some good colleague to share the rule with my brother."

Aspar stared at her, then gave a roar of delighted laughter. "Your Sacred Majesty," he said, raising his arm in salute, "you are a true child of your grandfather." He extended the salute to indicate the mosaic picture of Theodosius the Great, armored for battle, arms lifted in prayer, watching as a miraculous wind gave him the advantage over his enemies.

Pulcheria looked at the picture briefly, then gave her sour smile.

"My mother had something to do with it as well," she declared. "Shall we go?"

"One moment!" said Marcianus, earnestly, pulling his eyes away from Demetrias. "Concerning the weaver — I swore the strongest oaths that I would protect her and her family to the limits of my means. I can see well enough that my oaths haven't been fulfilled. I beg Your Charity to allow me to mend them as best as I can. The fisherman will want his wife back; I will pay any price you name to be permitted to restore her to him."

Pulcheria looked at him coolly. "The woman does not belong to her husband, or to you, but to me, and I have made my own arrangements for her. I will not have her sent here and there to please her idiot of a husband or to ease your conscience about your oath. If she is returned to Tyre, I will return her; if she chooses to stay here, she may."

"But I swore by the Holy Spirit, and by your brother's head!" Marcianus exclaimed, alarmed. "Forgive me, Empress, for insisting, but I am afraid to enter such a serious enterprise as this while I'm guilty of blasphemy and treason."

Pulcheria frowned, hesitating, then shook her head. "The danger that threatened the woman is past now and she is safe even without your protection. Even if I made you a present of her it wouldn't restore your oath to you intact. I do not know what provisions you made for her protection in Tyre. But if you swore to protect her to the limits of your means, and what threatened her was beyond those limits, then your oath is not broken.

"My escort will be waiting outside. Do you wish to come or not?"

Marcianus hesitated, then bowed low. "I will come, of course. But I hope Your Sacred Majesty will allow me to return to the subject again. I have always been a man of my word."

Pulcheria gave him another sour smile and proceeded from her throne, calling Demetrias and her secretary in behind her with a quick gesture. Demetrias' eyes met Marcianus' in the instant before she passed him and he fell in behind her. The look was not pleading, but questioning; there was hope and longing there, but also anger. For all his skill at reading faces, he could not read hers, and he followed her soberly, his thoughts tangled. He had sworn a solemn oath, and somehow, for all his honesty in swearing, failed to keep it. Perhaps he should be glad of that, since if the weaver hadn't been snatched from Tyre and miraculously fallen into Pulcheria's hands, he would have been faced with a far worse dilemma. His patron had been seriously contemplating treachery against the emperor, and he had not realized it, though it now seemed glaringly obvious. What course could he have followed then? He had sworn oaths of loyalty to Aspar and to the Theodosian house both.

*I would have chosen the emperor,* he thought, *or at least, this empress, who's shown herself so worthy of her titles. But I thank God I'm spared the choice of whom to betray. Bad enough to have to puzzle at how to keep my oath to the fisherman. The Augusta is right: the danger that threatened the woman is done now — so how am I to protect her? The fisherman will want her back — but does she want to go? What was the question I saw in her eyes? I swore to protect a man and his wife, one family; now they're two, separated, and I don't know what to do. God give me wisdom — and God help us.*

Demetrias followed the empress silently, her head bowed, aware of each step Marcianus took behind her. Symeon had gone to him, and he had promised Symeon safety. *If he swore an oath, he should have taken more trouble to keep it,* she thought, angrily. *Where was he when Eulogios had me thrown into the carriage? All he's done is create more danger!*

*But that makes no difference; the only question that matters is, does he still mean to help us? Does he think that's still inside his oath? Oh God, we are nothing, Symeon and I, here among the rulers of the world. We are stray threads to be pulled out of the weave and tossed aside. Will he even think of us after tomorrow? Will the empress remember her promise? But she's pious — surely she'll want him to keep such a solemn oath; surely, if he asks her again, she'll help him! Mary mother, let him ask her again; let her grant what he asks, and let me go home, safe home to Symeon, and never set foot out of Tyre again!*

# ⁐VIII⁐

NOMOS' HOUSE was on the other side of Constantinople from the Hebdomon, on the third of the city's seven hills overlooking the inlet of the Golden Horn. Because of this, Pulcheria and her escort did not enter the city directly but, instead, jolted from the Hebdomon up along the great land walls for several miles. The January sun shone brightly on the deep snow that covered the plain, and the sharp-edged battlements of the city's massive walls burned here and there with ice. Pulcheria had an escort of some fifty cavalrymen who, uniformed in red and purple, trotted beside her gilded carriage, the light gleaming on their armor and the crests of their helmets tossing with the beat of their horses' hooves. Aspar and Marcianus each had brought twenty of their own retainers to the Hebdomon, so the procession was a long and splendid one. The troops who guarded the city walls thronged the gates and battlements, and the country people coming in to market, the beggars and the shepherds who lived outside the walls, ran to the roadside to cheer for the empress and her general. Some of Aspar's men spurred their horses to make them prance up and down the road; some of Pulcheria's men began to sing a hymn to the Blessed Virgin, their deep voices ringing strong and melodious through the clear winter air. *Everyone seems glad,* Demetrias thought miserably, crouching in the carriage opposite the empress, *and I suppose I should be glad as well. It seems I was right to trust Pulcheria: I and my friends are safe, and she expects to get the better of all the people I was afraid of. But, oh God, I wish it were over with!*

She pulled at her cloak, running fingers over the unadorned black edges, searching for the silken flowers that were gone. Pulcheria's secretary, Eunomia, who was sitting beside her, gave her a stern look;

Demetrias locked her fingers together and tried to keep still. The empress was staring out the carriage window, smiling at the soldiers on the walls. Her face was flushed, and her eyes were bright with pleasure. *She's in her element,* Demetrias decided. *Like a fisherman returning to the sea after a long illness. But why is she bringing me along? What does she mean to do with me when this is finished? Oh God, God, I don't belong here, I wish it were over with!*

Staring blindly at the walls of Constantinople, Demetrias pictured the Egyptian harbor in Tyre, the workers straggling happily back from the factory to their homes, *Prokne* drawn up on the beach at the day's end, Meletios dancing about the prow and Symeon hauling out the day's catch. What would they be doing now? Was it windy in Tyre, or clear weather: would they have the boat out, or would they still be painting and sailmaking? She clenched her hands together in her lap. *Keep still,* she warned herself, *keep still. You are the empress' slave now, and her power is absolute. There is no hope if you displease her. Bow your head and accept what comes, as a good slave should.*

*Symeon would never keep still; Symeon would fight against this force that drives me so quickly, so far away from everything I used to be. Symeon would not let himself be used as evidence of treachery or divine favor; Symeon would stand up for himself. And be destroyed. He's caused trouble enough, fighting fate: why do I wish so desperately that he were here to do more of it? Better to submit, and look for some way out only if the chance offers. That's what I've done all my life, after all.* She felt a surge of self-contempt, and bowed her head to escape Eunomia's sharp eyes. *All my life — except since I left Tyre; I've tried to fight back since then. But that was only because I had to, because if I submitted then I would have lost more than home and husband and child; I would have lost myself somehow as well.*

*Perhaps that's what Symeon felt in Tyre. He always loved me; he couldn't bear to see me used by the procurator, even when I'd forced myself to bear it. Perhaps he loved me more than I loved myself. Why did I never care?*

She remembered, painfully, how he had come into her room after she had given birth to Meletios. She hadn't wanted a child: children were nothing but sickness and backache before they were born and worse afterward. But it was part of her duty as a wife, part of the price she paid for a husband's protection, to produce a son — though when the birth was over with, and the midwife put the red, wet squawking bundle in her arms, she was flooded with an unexpected sense of tenderness. There it was, a new life, just made, totally helpless and utterly dependent. If she failed to care for it, it would die: she was bound to love it. She cradled the baby clumsily, and proudly nodded to the midwife to let Symeon in. He had been at the tavern most of the night, but for hours had been sitting outside the door, and he came in, dirty, exhausted, wild eyes staring from a tangle of hair, smelling of wine and the sea. He sat down on the floor beside her bed and took her hand, looking at her, saying nothing. "You have a son," she'd told him. He had merely glanced at the baby, then looked back at her and, in a choked voice, whispered, "Oh Demetrias!" and buried his face against her leg.

Of course his mother had died in childbirth; he had been terrified. But at the time his anguished relief hadn't meant anything to her. It had seemed mere ingratitude that, after she had gone to great trouble to provide him with a son, and produced such a fine one, he was interested only in her.

*I mustn't think of him,* she told herself now, blinking at tears, *I must keep still. Whatever the uses of fighting, now is not the time.*

When the carriage at last entered the city, the escort shouted and shoved the common traffic aside, and Pulcheria proceeded down the crowded streets to the mansion belonging to Nomos.

Demetrias had never seen the house, but had no trouble realizing which it was. Pulcheria had indeed sent a troop of her guards there early that morning, and she arrived to find an enormous crowd of armed men and casual gawkers backed up from the house as far as the Church of the Holy Apostles a block and a half away. Pulcheria rose a little in her seat, frowning at the uniforms of some of the men, then sat down in her place with a satisfied smile. "Scholarians from the Great Palace," she remarked to no one in particular. "Chrysaphios has heard what I've done and sent his own men. Too late!" She grinned like a cat, then sobered, crossed herself, and sat quietly while her escort forced a way through the crowd.

The carriage stopped at last in a narrow street under a high wall, just before a pair of bronze-worked gates. As it did so, one of the strange guardsmen rode up on a magnificent bay stallion, shouting for attention. Pulcheria's men began to push him aside, but the empress opened the window of her carriage and called out that she would talk to the man. He was allowed to ride up to the side of the carriage; Demetrias saw that he wore a gold captain's collar about his neck. He looked at Pulcheria uncertainly.

"What do you wish?" she demanded coldly.

The strange guard looked taken aback by this blunt question. "You are the Augusta?" he asked, after a moment.

She looked at him wordlessly, her lips compressed in disapproval. "That is a very foolish question," she said at last. "I would have expected better sense from a captain of the Scholarian guard. If I were not the Augusta, whose image you have undoubtedly seen before, why would I be wearing purple and the diadem?"

He went red. "Empress, I must ask you — on what authority have you seized this house?"

She looked him up and down contemptuously. "What authority do you have," she replied evenly, "to question an empress? And are you of consular rank, that you omit to greet me in the customary manner?"

He went redder, hesitated, then jumped from his horse and bowed down, reluctantly and fastidiously, in the street. Despite his caution he got his cloak muddy, and when he stood, found that the empress in her carriage towered above him. His horse sidled off; one of Pulcheria's men caught its bridle, grinning. The Scholarian captain looked unhappier than ever, but steeled himself and declared, "I was sent by the most illustrious Chrysaphios, in the name of the emperor Theodosius Augustus, to investigate the seizure of this house. His Illustriousness has had this house under surveillance and wishes to know why you have ignored all laws and procedures and ordered your men into it. He commanded me to expel your troops and to occupy the house myself with my own men. But your guards have defied me and refused to allow my people in."

"I am glad to hear it," Pulcheria said dryly. "I too have had this house under surveillance, and, now that I have decided to question its owner, I commanded my men to admit no one without my orders. If my brother objects, let him come and tell me so himself, and I will satisfy him that I am acting in his own best interests. But I am under no obligation to take orders from my brother's chamberlain — and you may tell Chrysaphios as much, since he seems to have forgotten it. Moreover, Captain, if your men attempt to enter the house by force, my guards will oppose them with force — and you will have to explain to my brother why you used violence against his sister, a sovereign Augusta. Your best course would be to take your men back to the nearest marketplace and wait for further orders. Driver!" She snapped her fingers and her guards flung Nomos' gate open for her; the carriage lurched forward.

"But, Empress!" wailed Chrysaphios' captain. "I was ordered . . ."

The gate swung shut on his orders. The carriage halted in a small, snow-covered courtyard, already crowded with men and horses. Aspar leaped down from his horse and opened the carriage door for the empress, and Pulcheria pulled up her skirts and stepped calmly down into Nomos' court. She glanced about, and the captain of the troops she had sent earlier stepped forward from the colonnade that bordered the court and began to make the prostration.

"Not in the snow!" she told him briskly. "Save your good cloak, Kallinikos."

The captain, a lean, horse-faced man in his forties, smiled mournfully. "Yes, Empress."

"Have you searched the house?"

"The search is still in progress, Empress. We have taken a great number of letters, which are still being sorted. But we have found no trace of the cloak you mentioned."

"He undoubtedly has a good hiding place for it. I expect the letters you've found so far are completely innocent. He's an experienced man, and must know better than to leave sensitive material lying about where his slaves could look at it. But he's also a trained bureaucrat and has been master of the offices: he'll have all his treasonous correspondence secure somewhere and filed neatly by name and date, and the cloak will be with it. Probably he has a secret room somewhere in the house, somewhere private, which he can reach easily. Try for false walls in his bedroom and study. Where are his staff?"

"We have locked the household slaves in the men's workroom, Empress, with two men guarding the door. The retainers are under guard in the stable. Two of the retainers resisted us, the rest yielded quietly to your authority. Of the two who put up a fight, one was killed, the other injured, and one of my men took a leg wound in the struggle. I have seen that both the injured men are well cared for."

"Good. Leave the slaves and retainers where they are for the moment. Where is the man himself?"

"We are holding him in his dining room, together with his guest, the prefect of Phoenicia. Shall I show Your Serenity there?"

Pulcheria nodded graciously, and her captain escorted her and her followers into the house.

Nomos' dining room faced onto a second, smaller courtyard, where an ornamental tree stood stark and leafless in the trampled snow beside a fountain. The room was a large one, warmed through the floor by a hypocaust, and lavishly decorated with paintings and mosaics. On the central of the three couches that flanked the rosewood dining table sat two men. Demetrias recognized the prefect Philippos, stunned and shrunken under the steady gaze of Pulcheria's guards; that meant that the other man was Nomos.

He did not look worth all the trouble he had caused. A tall, heavy man, with a round face bland as his statue's; blue eyes anxious under thin brows; graying brown hair; the unremarkable dress of a man of great wealth and greater conservatism: the white cloak with its wide horizontal purple stripe, and a long white and purple tunic. He jumped to his feet when Pulcheria entered and he stared at her, his mouth hanging open. She walked toward him several steps, then stopped, allowing her escort to fan out to each side of her. Nomos' eyes fixed a moment on Aspar; Philippos frowned at Marcianus — then he saw Demetrias and his eyes widened.

For a long minute the room was still — still as the hippodrome, Demetrias thought, in the instants before the race begins. Then, slowly and deliberately, Nomos bowed low to the Augusta. Philippos jumped up as his patron began the bow and correctly performed the prostration that Nomos was excused before standing stiffly behind his friend.

"You honor my house, Empress," Nomos said, with a ponderous dignity, "but I do not understand why you found it necessary to secure it first with soldiers. I have always been a loyal servant of the house of Theodosius."

Pulcheria sighed slightly, and gestured for one of her guards to move a couch for her to sit on. She seated herself stiffly facing Nomos, straightened the folds of her purple cloak, then smoothed her brow under the diadem. "Nomos," she said, evenly, "let us understand one another quickly: our time is precious. I know that you plotted treason against my house. You know that my power, which once embraced the whole state, is shrunken now to my own palace and some guardsmen. I have used such shreds of it as remain, and because of this Chrysaphios' men are outside in the street instead of in here questioning you in my place. I am prepared to ignore your treason if you can help me against the chamberlain: otherwise, I will withdraw and let his men in. You would find them far harder to deal with than you will find me."

Nomos blinked owlishly. After a moment, he sniffed and said, in an injured tone, "I am at a loss to understand you, Empress. Can you seriously believe that I would contemplate a crime against you?"

Pulcheria sighed again. "Must we go through this?" — she paused — "Kallinikos, go supervise the search for the false walls. As I said, his bedroom and his study are the most likely places."

The guards' captain bowed and left the room.

Nomos swallowed. Philippos whispered in his ear, and Nomos looked at Demetrias. He paled.

Pulcheria glanced at Demetrias as well. "Yes," she said, turning back to Nomos, "I have the slave who wove the cloak you would have worn as emperor. God has brought it about that your plot was revealed to me: the same God who defended my grandfather, and assured him of victory over his enemies, has defended me, too. Do my men have to knock your walls down, or can we come to an understanding now?"

Philippos stirred. "Slaves will say anything if they hope to gain by it," he declared confidently. "I don't know what this woman is doing here, but I recognize her from Tyre as a troublemaker — a factory worker my colleague Heraklas had to discipline for her lewdness and persistent lying. I hope Your Sacred Majesty would not accuse a gentleman of my patron's standing on the unsupported word of such a creature."

Pulcheria looked at him narrowly. "You are Philippos, I believe," she said, "the son of Anthemius Isidoros. Anthemius the Regent was your grandfather, wasn't he?"

Philippos abruptly lost his confidence and swallowed. "My great-grandfather," he whispered. Marcianus noted inwardly that the story Aspar had told him about the regent was true.

"Your great-grandfather, of course. Being a descendant of Anthemius, you will understand that I have no very great opinion of your family's loyalty."

Philippos straightened. "No one in my family has ever been guilty of treachery!"

"Until you?" Pulcheria suggested mildly. She regarded him wearily for a moment, then shrugged. "My slave kept your secret very well. She told the truth only to me — though her husband was freer of his tongue, and sold the whole story to my general's deputy in exchange for a worthless promise of protection. She even convinced Chrysaphios' agent that the cloak she made was red — pay attention, fellow, the agent will want to see it! You will have to show him a cloak dyed with kermes with two tapestry panels; he's been told to expect this. If you have no cloak that is suitable I will see if I can provide one. And you will have to explain why you have neglected to visit your sick mother, since it was concern for her health that made you leave Tyre before the end of your appointment there. You see, I am willing to help you, if we can come to some arrangement."

The guards' captain Kallinikos came back in and made the prostration to Pulcheria. "There are no false walls, Empress, but, to judge by the shape of the house, there is an extra room above the study to which there is no access."

Pulcheria smiled. "Thank you, Kallinikos. You are most observant, and will be rewarded for it." She turned to Nomos. "Where is the entrance?"

"I don't know what you're talking about!" said Nomos — but his voice was a strangled squeak, and he was sweating.

"Knock a hole in the ceiling of the study," Pulcheria ordered, turning back to Kallinikos.

"No!" Nomos took an anxious half-step toward Kallinikos, then turned back. "No, that's not necessary."

"Where is the entrance?" Pulcheria asked again, settling herself more comfortably on the couch.

Nomos stared at her in anguish for a moment. "It has" — he faltered — "that is . . . there's a . . . a concealed latch." Pulcheria nodded and waited patiently. "It's behind the panel over the desk in the study." Nomos whispered, "The top of the wall panel pulls out, and then the ceiling panel can be swung back; there's a ladder in the room above . . ."

Pulcheria nodded to Kallinikos, and he bowed and went. Nomos swallowed several times, then backed slowly to his couch and sat down heavily. He buried his face in his hands. Philippos hurried to him and clasped his shoulder, then glared at Pulcheria. She smiled sourly.

"Get the man some wine," Aspar ordered a guardsman cheerfully — "if you will permit us, Eminence!"

Nomos looked up at him with bared teeth, then abruptly looked at the guardsman and said, "There's a jug of Lemnian wine in the sideboard."

"Some for me as well!" declared Aspar.

In silence, the guard poured the wine into the gold mixing bowl that stood in the center of the sideboard, added some water, and ladled the drink into the golden cups that had ringed the bowl. He offered the wine first to Pulcheria; when she refused, to Aspar and Marcianus, who accepted, and finally to Nomos and Philippos. Nomos drained his cup at once and held it up for more. Pulcheria nodded to the guard, and he refilled the cup.

"Now," said Pulcheria, as Nomos took another swallow of wine, "to business. I will take with me whatever Kallinikos finds in that room of yours, and I'll keep it secret for as long as you serve me well. Your plot is over, of course: if you need to send messages to any of your allies, canceling arrangements you have made with them, I'll take your messengers out with my own escort and see that they are not interfered with. I presume that may be urgent."

Nomos nodded feebly.

Pulcheria smiled with satisfaction. "Finish your wine, then write the necessary letters. Once I have left this house I will be unable to prevent Chrysaphios' men from entering, so there must be no evidence of your treason. When I leave I will go directly to my brother's palace and explain what I've done here. I will tell my brother — and Chrysaphios, if he asks — that I was troubled by a story Chrysaphios' agent Eulogios told me yesterday, and resolved to investigate it myself. I have had your house searched; I have found nothing. My brother will see to it that your slaves are not tortured for confessions and that your house is allowed some peace."

She paused, then added, to Philippos, "You must have a red silk cloak to show Chrysaphios' agent. Do you have one that would be suitable?"

Philippos shook his head, looking stunned. Nomos licked his lips. "I have a red cloak," he whispered. "I've scarcely worn it and it's in excellent condition. It's a good cloak."

"Good." Pulcheria said, nodding to one of the guards, "Go to the men's workroom, and release His Eminence' valet; tell him that His Eminence wants his good red cloak, the silk one, and have him bring it here."

The guard bowed and left. Pulcheria turned back to Philippos. "You must say that the cloak was given to you by the procurator — what was his name? Heraklas? — as a going-away present when you left Tyre. You must also say that you received news of your mother's recovery from a grave illness while you were still on your journey from Tyre, and so have stopped to see your friend and patron about the possibilities of another governorship." She paused, thoughtfully, and asked Aspar, "Should that cover them?"

Aspar bowed, grinning. "I can't think of anything else Chrysaphios would worry about."

"He was worried about your deputy," Pulcheria said sharply, "and we must contrive to let him know that Marcianus left Tyre after the prefect because he had no further business in the city. And he followed the same route back . . ."

"Because most of the roads were closed with snow." Aspar opened his eyes wide. "What other roads should he have taken? Empress, it's a delight to see you yourself again. I thought you'd lost the taste for the game."

Pulcheria gave him a very sour look. "The game, as you call this treason, is a brutal one and an abomination to God. I can only pray that I will be spared more of it.

"Nomos, in exchange for these favors from me, you will help me to pull that leech Chrysaphios off my brother's palace."

Nomos looked at her, his thick lower lip trembling. "I don't know how to get rid of Chrysaphios," he whispered. "If I'd known, I'd have plotted against him instead of your brother."

She raised her eyebrows. "Perhaps," she said, in a tone that showed how unlikely she thought it. "But you must know something that would be of use against the chamberlain. You were intimate in his counsels until last summer — and I don't believe he's honest."

Kallinikos re-entered the dining room, looking cheerful and carrying a small chest of sandalwood in one arm and a box in the other. He set both down on the table, opened the chest, and pulled out, purple as the sea, the cloak Demetrias had woven. He spread it over the table, and tipped onto it from the box a large pile of letters and a clay seal. "There's another case of letters as well," he told Pulcheria, "all arranged by name and date, as Your Wisdom predicted. But I judge these are copies of his own letters — and the cloak speaks for itself."

"It does indeed," said Aspar. He picked up a corner of the cloak and studied the tapestry panel. It was Victory Crowning Alexander. "That's supposed to be you, is it?" he asked Nomos. "Butchering your lawful emperor? And being crowned by an angel for it! More likely to have been a devil that put such an idea into your head!"

"I didn't commission the patterns," Nomos objected plaintively. "These tapestries were the procurator's idea — and that woman there made them, not me." He gave Demetrias a vicious glance. "I should never have trusted that young idiot Heraklas!"

Pulcheria was examining the Choice of Herakles on the other panel; she ran her thin, heavy-boned finger down the shining silk mountainside, then looked up at Demetrias and gave the rare sweet smile. "It is very fine work, girl," she said, softly. "I pray you'll never again have to do so well in such a bad cause."

"I pray so too, Mistress," Demetrias returned in a low voice, moved, despite herself.

Pulcheria sighed, made a sweeping gesture with her hand. "Take them out," she told Kallinikos, "and put them in my own carriage, together with the other sensitive letters. Nomos, was there anything else that would betray you?"

He shook his head. "It was all in my study — my secret study."

"Good. Kallinikos, check the secret room once more, take everything treasonous to my carriage, then put the room back as it was."

Kallinikos bowed, stashed the letters back in the box and picked up the cloak. He shook it out and began folding it. Nomos' eyes were riveted on it with an expression of bewildered longing.

"That cloak will never be for you," Pulcheria told him, with a quiet ferocity. "Never. Believe it, and forget that you ever thought differently. Serve me well, and you can keep the cloak you're wearing, remarry, if you like, and raise a family to wealth and great honor.

Serve me badly, and you will lose your head, while your relations dress in rags."

Nomos bowed his head. Kallinikos set the folded cloak carefully in the sandalwood chest, bowed again, and left the room. In the doorway he bumped into a middle-aged slave who carried over his arm a cloak of red silk. The slave bobbed his head and apologized, and Kallinikos strode out.

Nomos gestured for the man to come in, and the slave, looking confused, brought the cloak to his master. Nomos glanced at it, then spread it out over the same table that the purple one had decorated a moment before. It was a brilliant scarlet, edged lavishly with gold, and decorated on the shoulders with two small but graphic tapestry rondels showing Eros and an Aphrodite with a Priapus, the fine craftsmanship showing up the crudity of the designs all the more sharply. Pulcheria looked down her nose at the pictures for a moment, then ostentatiously averted her eyes.

Aspar laughed. "If ever I saw a cloak to go whoring in, that's one!" he exclaimed. "I can believe you didn't wear it often."

"It is a very likely gift from a young procurator to a young prefect," Pulcheria said reprovingly. "And it's in good condition. It will do very well."

Nomos nodded and handed the cloak back to his slave. "This belongs to my friend Philippos," he said. "Put it in his room, with his luggage." He turned to Pulcheria, "If that meets with your approval, Empress!"

Pulcheria smiled, and the slave left. "Time is running short," she said to Nomos. "Write your letters, and then tell me quickly everything about the chamberlain that might be of use."

Pulcheria spoke with Nomos for an hour, then, when Kallinikos reported that more imperial troops had arrived outside the house and that Eulogios was with them and demanding an agent's right of entry, the empress ordered Nomos to prepare his messengers and told her guards to fetch her carriage. A few minutes later the gates of the house were again thrown open and Pulcheria's carriage rumbled back into the street. Eulogios and the Scholarian captain were both waiting outside, and Pulcheria ordered her driver to stop so that she could exchange a few words with them. Demetrias sat huddled motionless in the seat opposite the empress, a case of treasonous letters beside her and the sandalwood box containing the cloak under her feet, listening while Pulcheria smilingly gave Eulogios the official version of events in the house and warned him against too much roughness in his own search. Then the empress snapped her fingers, the driver cracked his whip, and the carriage rolled on toward the Great Palace. As soon as they were well clear of the imperial troops, Nomos' messengers galloped off into the city to cancel the revolution.

Pulcheria's arrival at the Great Palace caused a considerable stir. The palace guard milled about the carriage; the palace staff poured in and out of the Magnaura, and finally a senior chamberlain appeared and invited the Augusta in to consult with the Augustus. Pulcheria graciously accepted and descended from her carriage into the glittering throng of her brother's eunuchs. "I'll probably be staying for supper," she told Kallinikos, "but there's no need for all of you to wait. My brother can certainly lend me a carriage to take me home — I'll just want a small escort. Pick thirty men to stay, and take the others home and see that they're rewarded for the day's work."

Kallinikos bowed low, and Pulcheria marched off into the gilded corridors of the Magnaura Palace. Kallinikos picked out the men who would wait to escort her home, then remounted his horse and gave the signal for the rest to regroup. The carriage driver cracked his whip and coaxed his cumbersome vehicle about: Chrysaphios' servants would have no opportunity to inspect its contents.

Demetrias slumped against the side of the carriage as it jolted its way back to the Hebdomon. Outside, the citizens of Constantinople cheered to see the empress' coach in their streets, but Demetrias was too tired to pay any attention; too tired even to feel the strangeness of it, those glad acclamations washing over the dark upholstery where she and the secretary Eunomia sat in silence. *It's as though I've been running all day,* she thought — *or no, not running. Holding something. Holding something as heavy as the world. And all I've done is stand and watch, and been trotted out twice as evidence. Well, it's over now, thank God! And perhaps she will still send me home; perhaps she'll even grant Marcianus' request, and send me home early. Home. If I could just see it, just come up past the grapevine that grows beside the door, and look into the apartment, and see Symeon sitting there, under the lamp, making a murex trap, and*

*Meli whittling with his little knife — if I could even see that, and then die, I'd be content.*

It was dark by the time the carriage reached the Hebdomon, and the household was at prayers. Eunomia took charge of the sandalwood chest and the cases of letters, claiming Demetrias' assistance to deliver them to the empress' private apartments before setting out to join the rest of the household at the chapel. Demetrias followed her slowly through the dark corridors. At the chapel, Eunomia went silently to her own place in the front, and stood listening with bowed head as one of the eunuchs read the Scriptures. Demetrias stayed outside, standing in the dim cold corridor and looking into the place of prayer. The massed oil lamps glowed brilliantly on the gold-framed icons and mosaics that adorned the walls, but the palace staff stood stiffly still, black-clad, somber, only their eyes fixed and bright amid the magnificence. *What have I to do with them?* she wondered. *Oh God, let me get away from this place!*

" 'Who has measured the waters in the hollow of his hand,' " read the eunuch, " 'and spanned the limits of the heavens? . . . Who has directed the spirit of the Lord, or stood his counselor to instruct him? . . . Behold, the nations are as a drop from a bucket, and are counted as the small dust on the balance . . .' "

*Yes, and "Who has directed the spirit of the Empress? or stood her counselor to instruct her?"* Demetrias wondered bitterly. *"Behold, the mighty ones of the earth are like the small dust before her." Even Aspar and Nomos. She is like God — a human god, stern and merciless. I don't want to belong to her; oh God in Heaven, I don't! And yet, am I right to pray to God to go home? To go back to a life centered on worldly things, on work and factory gossip and my family? These people are committed to God and to the empress herself. But I want no such commitment. They are too high for me and they terrify me. God has a universe, and Pulcheria wants to regain her empire — why should either of them trouble with me? I'm no pagan, and I'm as loyal a subject as I'm permitted to be. I've never been very good at loving, I can see that well enough, now; I'd never make a martyr, for either God or empress — but can either of them really expect that? I could never strive for divine favor, for glory, or even for happiness: I've been content if I can scrape by avoiding actual misery. But I do love Symeon. And if my love won't stretch any further than that, surely, Lord God, Lady Empress, it's better used than wasted here in the dark?*

The prayers finished, and the palace staff broke their ranks, nodding and talking happily in low voices as they went out to their suppers. Theonoe saw Demetrias standing at the door and pounced on her eagerly.

"You're back!" the old woman exclaimed. "Where is our dear mistress?"

"She stopped to visit her brother at the Great Palace," Demetrias replied. "I believe she'll return after supper."

Theonoe nodded, but frowned at Demetrias as though she found the answer displeasing. "And you?" she asked. "She no longer needed you?"

"I'd have no place dining with the empress at the Great Palace," Demetrias returned, forcing a smile.

"Yet," Theonoe said bitterly. "Nor would the distinguished Eunomia — yet. I would hope that none of us ever has a place there. But I suppose you are not permitted to say what happened today?"

Demetrias hesitated. *More than that,* she thought wretchedly, *I am so deep in secrets now, and the secrets are so critical and dangerous, that I should probably pretend that they don't exist at all. I'm not even permitted to say that I'm permitted to say nothing.* "It would be improper for me to gossip about our mistress' affairs," she told Theonoe, temporizing.

The supervisor snorted. "I am rebuked for asking," she snapped, "but I am sure your reserve on the matter is correct, and required by our sacred mistress. Well, go on to your supper." She turned her back and marched off to the supervisor's dining room, her black cloak swishing angrily with each short, sharp stride.

"Don't mind her," said the silk sorter Agatha, coming up behind Demetrias and smiling at her gaily. "She believes that public affairs are evil and corrupting, and doesn't want the Mistress to have anything to do with them. She thinks our Augusta should've become a deaconess. Come to supper with me, please, and tell me whatever you're allowed to! I'd love it if our mistress could get her power back; there's nothing I'd like more than to see her reigning from the Great Palace again as she deserves."

"I don't know what you mean," Demetrias replied miserably. But she let the woman carry her off to the slaves' dining hall, where the kitchen staff had set out a meal of coarse bread and barley soup. She found herself at once the center of a small crowd, all eager for information, all regarding her with keen and respectful attention. *How do they even know that a scheme exists?* she wondered. *They've been told nothing; they know only that the carriage drove into the city today and that guards were sent to Nomos' house. And yet, they expect me to tell them when their mistress will move back into the Great Palace and take control of the offices of state.*

She answered the questions the other slaves tossed at her with short, barren phrases: Yes, they had been to Nomos' house. Yes, the Augusta had had it searched. No, she didn't think the search had been successful. She didn't know what the guards were looking for; she thought that it was all a false alarm. No, Nomos had not been arrested. No, she didn't know why she'd been brought along.

The other slaves looked at each other disbelievingly, but did not contradict her. Ashamed, feeling desperately alone, she pushed her bread aside and looked directly at Agatha, wishing that she could make her understand. The silk sorter was an experienced worker some ten years older than herself, a cheerful and enthusiastic woman, much given to gossip and giggling. But her eyes dropped under Demetrias' and her head bowed; there was a sudden profound silence around the table. Demetrias might be a fellow slave and a foreigner, new to the Hebdomon, but she was favored by the mistress, privileged, entrusted with secrets that she would not share: ordinary slaves must treat her with respect.

*Oh no*, thought Demetrias, desperately, understanding the gesture only too well, *not that. Not that, please. I'm of your own kind, not the empress': if I belong anywhere in this palace, I belong here. I can't bear it if I'm to be left entirely alone.*

One of the other weavers stirred. "I'd love to go back to the Great Palace," she said wistfully.

Another disagreed. "I like it out here. It's peaceful and comfortable and orderly. You can get on with your work and nobody bothers you. I'd be sorry if we all had to move back."

"Oh, but it's so dull!" exclaimed Agatha. "Nothing ever happens. At the Great Palace there was always something going on — if there wasn't an ambassador to be received there was a general."

"You never knew where you were," complained the woman who liked the Hebdomon. "We were always being turned out of our own rooms to make space for some visitor's slaves. And you never got a chance to finish a commission: they kept changing their minds about what was urgent. And everything was always so complicated. I could never keep the orders of precedence straight."

"Yes — but it was so exciting! Meeting all those people! And we were right in the middle of the city. We could get to the races at the hippodrome on holidays, and all the shops . . ."

"And you could flirt with the emperor's staff?"

"Well, why not?" demanded Agatha, laughing a little. "Talking does no harm. I would love to go back." She looked back at Demetrias, and this time her eyes were pleading. "If the mistress does go back, she'll take you with her, at least," she began, hesitantly, "even if she keeps most of the rest of us here. Do you think that you could . . ."

"I don't know anything about it!" Demetrias interrupted miserably, before the other could finish. "How could I possibly ask the empress for anything? And all I want is to go home to Tyre."

"Of course," said Agatha, and dropped her eyes again humbly. Again there was silence.

Demetrias swallowed and looked down at her cold, half-eaten soup, sickened with a sudden sense of shame. Agatha had been helpful and friendly, and she had refused the request without even waiting to hear it. "Why does Theonoe think the Augusta should become a deaconess?" she asked, desperately trying to start a conversation, any conversation, to fill the silence about her.

"Oh, that!" said the silk sorter, with a forced gaiety that was almost worse than her silence. "Why, as I said, she thinks secular power is corrupt, and our mistress is best out of it. And the order of deaconess is what the Empress Eudokia suggested she take up. Though they say it was Chrysaphios' suggestion, really."

"The Mistress and Eudokia had quarreled," supplied another woman, when she saw that Demetrias looked blank.

"Eudokia adopted the Monophysite heresy," said the Hebdomon's champion, with relish, "which denies Christ's full and distinct human nature."

Demetrias blinked. "I have heard of this," she said cautiously. She was aware of the furious theological controversy that raged over the nature of Christ's humanity — a bishop of Tyre had recently been exiled for taking a view neither of the other parties agreed with — but she had made no effort to follow it. It had seemed too abstract and academic, too remote from life in the factory. How could anyone determine what the divine nature was, or the human nature, for that matter, to say how the two could and could not be related? But she did know that Pulcheria had accepted one of the two competing theories, and Eudokia the other.

"Eudokia wasn't even a Christian until her marriage," Agatha explained. "I don't believe she cared a fig for theology, really, she was just looking for something to quarrel about. Chrysaphios is a Monophysite, of course, and he'd already made an alliance with her: they say that he kept reminding Eudokia that our mistress outranked her — our mistress had control of her own offices, and had her own head chamberlain to manage them for her, and Eudokia didn't. Finally, Eudokia publicly declared that our mistress ought to take holy orders, as these would be more consistent with her piety than running the state. Our mistress decided that she couldn't oppose Eudokia and Chrysaphios both, and she sent Eudokia her chamberlain and retired out here. And, of course, Chrysaphios managed to get rid of Eudokia within two years, and now he has the Great Palace all to himself."

*But Pulcheria did not accept ordination as a deaconess,* Demetrias noted bitterly. *Of course. It would be forbidden for anyone in holy orders to hold secular power — and the empress always, always intended to take her power up again, in time. I wonder what scheme she had against Eudokia originally, and how it went awry?*

"But perhaps not for much longer?" asked one of the other women, giving Demetrias another look of bright, pleading inquiry.

Demetrias looked away. "Who knows?" she said, wretchedly.

She was relieved to be saved from further lies by the bell ringing for church. The slaves swallowed the last of their suppers hastily, crossed themselves, and dashed out of the dining hall for the evening service.

Supper, church: the pattern of the day resumed itself around her. But the quietness of the Hebdomon again seemed oppressive, and she felt bitterly, desperately, alone. *It will be better in the morning,* she told herself wearily, as she undressed for bed that night in her tiny, unheated sleeping cubicle. *Tomorrow I can go back to work and try to forget the mighty ones of the world, for a little while, at least.* She pulled off her tunic and snuffed out the lamp.

She was just falling asleep when there came a knock at the door of her cubicle, and Theonoe's voice called, "Demetrias! Her Sacred Majesty wishes you to attend her!"

"What?" asked Demetrias stupidly, sitting up in the darkness and staring at the crack of light that shone under the door. "Now?"

"Now!" returned Theonoe, impatiently. "Hurry up, girl, get your clothes back on and come with me!"

Pulcheria was in her own bedroom, leaning back on the purple-draped couch beside the purple-draped bed and soaking her feet in a gold basin of hot water while one of her ladies released the thin gray hair from its elaborate braids. The diadem lay discarded on her ivory dressing table, but her purple cloak was still draped loosely about her shoulders. When Demetrias came in and made the prostration, the empress smiled.

"There you are, girl," she observed. "I wanted to talk to you. Theonoe, you may go off to bed; it's late."

Theonoe bowed, radiating disapproval, and left. Demetrias stood before the empress, her head bowed and her hands folded before her. Pulcheria pulled one angular, bony foot out of the basin and rubbed the side of it thoughtfully. She glanced at the golden sandals she had worn during the day and sighed. "I have been out of power for so long," she remarked, "that my good shoes give me blisters. Well, girl, and what did you make of what you saw today?"

"Mistress?" said Demetrias, confused by the question.

Pulcheria looked at her cynically. "I asked what you thought of what you saw today. Come, girl, you have a mind of your own, for all that you spend your time pretending to be the ideal slave, with not a thought in her pretty head but respect for her owner's orders. You fooled Eulogios, you nearly fooled Chrysaphios, you fooled my brother, and you fooled me with your lies about that cloak. It takes some degree of ability to trick liars as skilled as we are. You have an opinion; I want to hear it."

Demetrias bit her lip. "Mistress," she said, slowly, "my opinion is of no relevance."

"In other words, you're afraid it may offend me. Of course your opinion is irrelevant and will change nothing: I want to hear it nevertheless."

Demetrias looked down at the red-rubbed foot in the basin. It might have belonged to any old woman, tired and impatient after a day's work weaving or cooking or working in the marketplace. "Mistress," she said, "today I saw you humble the foremost general and the foremost minister in the empire. They were both men of great power and authority, and you pushed them into the dust as easily as twirling a spindle. You made me afraid."

"Ahh," Pulcheria said, in a kind of satisfaction. She put her foot back in the water and wriggled her toes. "And why does that frighten you?"

"Because I am without power, Mistress, and because I am your slave and must be less to you than the water in that basin."

"To be used and thrown out?" asked Pulcheria, looking up at her again, smiling a little. "What makes you think you're powerless, girl? After today, you'll find yourself sought after for your influence. Perhaps you've found it so already. Ah, I see you have! That frightens you too, does it? And I also refused to give you to Marcianus, didn't I? To return you to your fool of a husband and let you settle yourself back into the dim little existence you had before. That made you even more afraid, ·didn't it?" She stretched with a creaking of stiff joints and ran her fingers through her hair. Her impassive lady picked up a hairbrush and resumed work on the crumpled tresses. "To tell the truth, I think Marcianus was the most interesting element in today's affairs. It was quite evident that Aspar had not told him a word of his own plans, and he was not pleased about it. Interesting that he was not pleased; more interesting that Aspar had known he would be displeased and had not trusted his own authority to override that displeasure. And I found the fellow's concern for his oath surprising. A man to watch, Marcianus, if ever Aspar needs bringing into line again. Which he will. No, my dear, I didn't humble him; that is beyond even me. I pointed out to him that he hadn't planned far enough ahead, and he was relieved to see that his old patroness hadn't lost her political instincts, and yielded gracefully. He's a loyal man, Aspar, in his way — but he likes to have his way, and he fancies himself as a kingmaker. Chrysaphios, now," Pulcheria leaned her head toward the brush, "Chrysaphios thinks of Aspar as a crude, uneducated barbarian who only understands war — which is what Aspar likes people to think. The biggest problem with Chrysaphios is that he is unskilled with people and bad at judging them. He doesn't know whom to trust or how far, and ends up trusting no one, and you have to trust someone if you are to govern efficiently. I can trust Aspar a long way, provided he remembers which of us is in charge. And I can trust Nomos from now on — because now I can destroy him with a few words. So you find me terrifying, girl? Ruthless, cynical, and starved for power? Well, perhaps you're right."

Demetrias clenched her hands together. "I didn't say that, Mistress."

"You don't need to." Pulcheria sighed and leaned her head back. Her attendant brushed her hair steadily, her face stern but unmoving. "I made a vow a long time ago," Pulcheria said, very softly, and more to herself than to Demetrias " — a very long time ago now. I thought when I made it that I did it for the love of God. It took me nearly twenty years to see that I'd done it for the love of power. But I saw it in the end. I had to. God must have been listening, and took me at my word: power seems worthless now — after I've used it, at least. What is the point of tyrannizing over slaves and scaring stupid old senators like Nomos? And yet, I rejoiced to see him afraid of me, and I still prate about the sacred majesty of the house of Theodosius. Sacred majesty! The only woman who had any real claim to that quality was a carpenter's wife in Palestine. 'He has cast down the powerful from their thrones, and he has exalted the humble; he has filled the hungry with good things, and the rich he has sent empty away.' " Pulcheria sat up abruptly and the lady put down the hairbrush. The empress unfastened the emerald clasp of her cloak and lifted herself so that it could be slipped out from under her. The attendant shook the garment and began to brush it down. "The sacred purple, too." Pulcheria remarked, eyeing it sourly. "I was given the cloak that belonged to the Mother of God. We've enshrined it in a cask of gold and jewels, and you're helping us to deck out the church I built to honor it in purple — but the cloak, her cloak, is plain blue wool. Blue and powerless as Heaven. Aspar is right: I'm tired of the game. And yet, I can't give it up."

There was a long silence. The attendant folded the cloak and put it away, then busied herself straightening the bedspread.

"Why are you telling me this, Mistress?" Demetrias asked.

Pulcheria shrugged. "Because you're young and innocent and looked so wretched this morning. And I wished, too, to discuss your own position here, in the light of what has happened. Do you want to take vows as a consecrated virgin?"

"I'm already married," Demetrias reminded her quickly.

Pulcheria raised her eyebrows. "Yes — and your foolish husband called down this trail of calamities on you by meddling where he should have left alone."

"He told Marcianus the truth. I thought Your Wisdom was angry because I lied to you."

"You made a reasonable assessment of your chances of being believed and your likely fate if you were, and acted accordingly. When you saw that you were safe with me, you were willing enough to speak. Why should I be angry at that? You, I should think, have a right to be angry with your husband. Or do you yield to him as the duty of a Christian wife?"

Demetrias stared at the floor for a moment, then looked up. "I admire him. He was wrong, perhaps, but at least he didn't give up without a fight. And I think you take risks if you love well. You don't think only of your own security and calculate each step."

"Tch! A wise man knows when to fight and when to give way. Girl, I like the discretion you've shown, I like your good sense, and I think highly of your skill. You deserve better than a narrow life as a state slave, married to a man without the wit to know when to keep his mouth shut."

Demetrias took a deep, unsteady breath. "Mistress, there's no shame in a narrow life. You yourself said just now that our Lord's mother was a carpenter's wife."

Pulcheria chuckled. "Well answered! Yet I think we have a duty to conduct ourselves wisely and to use as well as we can the powers God has given us. Look at my poor brother. He is a good man, and far from stupid, but because he is afraid to act he's caused more trouble for this empire than if he'd been genuinely wicked. It shouldn't be the case that a bad man makes a good ruler — but the devil has as much to do in the world as God, and it often is so. I would even tolerate Chrysaphios' government, if he weren't such a lover of heretics, and if he could only use power with half the skill he employed to acquire it. But there, the fellow thinks only of himself and stumbles from crisis to crisis. Well, soon we'll see an end of him."

Demetrias bowed her head, afraid again. Pulcheria's voice went on above her, gentler now. "But you weren't born to inherit any great authority, let alone an empire. You own only yourself — and that in trust from the state. Still, I would be sorry to see you waste yourself. I will tell you plainly: you could expect my favor if you decided to remain and take vows here. Do you still want to go home?"

She looked up. Pulcheria's expression was gentle, even affectionate. "Yes, Mistress," she said evenly, "I am sorry if I am unworthy of your favor."

The empress sighed. "I expected that answer. Well, loyalty is a virtue, too. Leave affairs as they were: you have three years to think it over."

Demetrias bowed. "And Marcianus, Mistress? He wished . . ."

"The time for Marcianus to keep his oath was before you left Tyre. Let him busy himself providing for your husband, if he wishes: my household is my concern. Go to your bed now, girl, and get some sleep. Your part in these affairs is done with, and you can rest quietly tonight."

Demetrias made the prostration and left. The empress was right: she did rest quietly. Only in her dreams she was sailing — sailing with Symeon and Meletios, across a sea blue as the Virgin's cloak, following a dolphin that leaped joyfully from the shining water. Even when she woke alone in the cold cubicle to the sound of the palace bells tolling for prayers, the dolphin's joy clung to her, and, improbably, she was happy.

# ≈IX≈

IT WAS THE AFTERNOON of the second of April when Symeon and Meletios arrived in Constantinople.

The voyage had taken more than three months. The red sunrise the morning they left the village south of Antioch had indeed prefigured a gale, and when they tried to put in to shore around noon of that day, the steering oar had snapped. Symeon knew he would remember that moment to the end of his life: the heaving sea, green-black and laced with foam; the savage copper-colored sky and the dark shore; *Prokne* heeled over on her side, sails flapping like clothes on a line — and the oar breaking, the sea crashing over the side, and Meletios falling with a scream under the boat. Luckily, the boy had had the sense to dive and Symeon had been able to turn the craft with the other oar and fish his son out of the water. But they hadn't dared to fight the wind and waves to try to beach again, and had run all that day and night before the storm. The next land they saw was the island of Cyprus, where they had remained for several days repairing the damage to gear and sails. Then they had been kept by bad weather for two weeks in a tiny fishing village near Syedra, and for ten days each at Rhodes and Chios, and they had been forced to refit again at Ephesus. The other steering oar had been broken in a quarrel in the harbor of Rhodes; they had split a plank not far from Patara, and bailed frantically all night in a howling gale; in Ephesus they had had to buy new sails. In Mytilene they had been awakened by robbers and forced to fight for their lives; near Alexandria Troas they had come across a small boat packed with survivors from a shipwreck, whom they had towed to safety. And now, at last, *Prokne*, patched and worn but running as sweetly as ever, tacked widely against contrary winds to pass the tip of the city's peninsula — past the deep double harbor of the fleet, past the grain ships, past the marble-paved harbors of the Great Palace — and slipped easily into the Golden Horn.

The waters of the inlet were choppy, crowded with merchant ships as well as ferryboats and other small craft; Symeon brailed up the mainsail until the lateen had only enough speed to keep her steerage way, then he sat holding both steering oars and scowling at the busy harbor. In the prow, Meletios bounced up and down excitedly, calling out directions.

"There's a big buoy to starboard, Daddy! There — there, we'll miss it. Oh, look at the statue of the lion! It's all made of gold! Watch out, there's another boat to port — no, he's seen us, he's veered! Do you see the bridge? It goes right across the harbor! The middle arch is clear — no, it's not. Steer to starboard, Daddy, we can go through behind that barge. Oh, look, there's more city the other side of the bridge! It's even bigger than Ephesus! Where do you suppose the other fishing boats are?"

"The man at Heraklea said there was a beach near the end of this inlet," Symeon replied, veering sharply to avoid a ferryboat, then letting out a fraction more sail to recover steerage. "Can't you see it yet?"

"No — look, there's another bridge! Oh, look at the sea horses on it, and the gold dolphins!"

"Is it clear?" demanded Symeon, impatiently, disregarding the dolphins.

"The starboard arch is — no, it isn't — yes, it is! Do you think we'll have trouble with the customs people, Daddy?"

"The man at Heraklea said they don't worry about fishing boats. If they bother us, Meli, just remember that we've come here to sell the mullets. They might make trouble if we told them we've come for your mother. Remember that they will think we should have stayed in Tyre."

"Yes, 'cause we're slaves — sort of," agreed Meli, still squirming with excitement. "Look! There's a beach! There to port! There are lots of fishing boats on it, look! All with spritsails. I think spritsails look stupid. And I bet they're all made of that soft pinewood, too, not good cedar. I bet they couldn't sail as far as *Prokne* has."

"Shh," warned Symeon, brailing up the sail again and steering the craft toward the beach. "Don't tell them we've sailed so far. *Prokne* will attract enough attention as it is. Remember, Meli, we must say that we've come just from Troas, and that we want to sell our fish and see the big city. Don't mention your mother to anyone. We're in unknown waters here, and we have to go carefully until we know how things stand."

Meletios nodded obediently, and Symeon grounded the lateen on a vacant patch in the muddy beach, then jumped out and shoved her farther out of the water. Meletios ran aft to ship the oars, then jumped out to help his father secure the boat. The other fishermen stopped their work and regarded them in motionless suspicion.

"Greetings," said Symeon, turning to them with a smile. "Any objections to us beaching here?"

One of the fishermen spat. "That's Black John's place there."

"Black John's away this week," another said mildly. "Won't hurt him for a stranger to beach there. Going to be here long, stranger?"

"Oh, I think not," said Symeon. "My son and I had a mind to see the great city, which we've heard so much about, and we have some fish to sell. If we can sell it this evening we'll spend a day or two seeing the sights, and then be off."

The sympathetic fisherman nodded. Constantinople attracted many visitors. "You from down the coast?" he asked. "You talk foreign — and that's a strange boat there. What is she, island built?"

"South of the islands," Symeon returned easily. "My father was a Syrian, and came north in her. My name's Symeon."

"Simon?" the unsympathetic fisher said suspiciously. "That's a strange name."

"No, Symeon," the other said, cautiously, "like that holy man — you know, the fellow who lives up on a column. Well. I'm Matthaios. What're they like to sail, those lateen-rigs?"

Symeon discussed the relative merits of lateens, spritsails, and square rigging for a few minutes, and was advised where to sell his fish, how much to ask for them, and what to see in Constantinople once he'd sold them. Meletios waited impatiently, shifting from one foot to the other and interrupting his elders with the statement that spritsails looked stupid. At last they unloaded the wicker box of mullets that they'd caught that morning, and took them up to the market by

231

the city's sea wall. Symeon spread out the fish on top of the box lid and sat down on the ground beside them.

"When are we going to look for Mama?" demanded Meletios.

"We have to find out where things are, first," Symeon told him. "We might as well sell the fish — we'll attract too much attention if we let them rot. And it's late now. We'll sleep here tonight, and tomorrow we'll go into the city and see if we can find Aspar's house."

"Will it be all right to leave *Prokne?*"

"I think so. Those men know who we are now. I'll buy a good big jug of wine to go with our supper, and give some to our neighbors: that ought to keep them sweet. And there are guards over there." Symeon indicated the bored guardsmen who kept nominal watch over the Fishmarket gate in the city wall.

Meletios scowled and sat down beside his father. It had been a much longer voyage than he had dreamed possible: in Tyre he hadn't thought you could sail so far without sailing right out of the world. But he had worked on the boat, helped as well as he could with sails and steering and fishing lines, and tried to be good, always knowing that, in the end, they would reach Constantinople and find his mother. Each day, for the whole of the past week, he had expected to see Constantinople before the evening. Now they were here — and still he must be good and cautious and wait. He fidgeted with his sandal strap. The leather was worn and salt stained; it would probably break if he pulled at it, and then his father would be cross. He let go of it and twisted his hands together. If he closed his eyes he could see his mother, warm and solid, rose-colored, with arms open to hold him. She had not always been happy or welcoming, but she had been there, steady, loving, and providing, and necessary as food. The world now was broken; she had been taken away, and he and his father had sailed out of the familiar fragments that were left to fetch her back and restore it. And she was here, somewhere in this city, locked in one of the houses behind this grim overhanging wall, waiting for them. So why were they sitting here selling a handful of undersized fish to strangers?

Meletios looked up fiercely and declared, "I want to find Mama right now. You know the name of the man who took her away. Why do we need to see Aspar? Where does Eulogios live?"

Symeon sighed and patiently repeated an explanation already given many times during the voyage. "We can't do much without Marcianus' help; we have to talk to him and his master Aspar before we see her. Eulogios has a deed of sale, Meli, which says he owns your Mama, and somebody has to buy her back or get the deed annulled before we can go home safely. We can look for Eulogios' house, but the person we have to see is Aspar. If we have time, we can ask directions to his house this evening once we've sold the fish — yes, sir, fresh red mullet, caught this morning, only twenty *drachmae* each!"

Constantinopolitans liked fish, and Symeon had no difficulty in selling the handful of mullet, undersized as they were. There was time for a foray into the city and a few discreet inquiries before an evening meal and the night's rest in the boat.

The following morning they secured everything aboard the boat and set off into the city. Symeon brought his good cloak, but was nervous of putting it on before the local fishermen and thus giving them an idea that he might be worth robbing. He packed it carefully in one of the wicker baskets and gave it to Meletios to carry. The signed parchment attesting to Marcianus' oath he put, folded, in the purse in his belt.

From the Fishmarket the city rose in a steep hill. A major road ran along the harbor, just inside the sea wall, but only small alleyways struck off from it. The previous evening Symeon had been instructed to go up the hill to the Middle street and ask directions from there, so father and son took the first alleyway they came to and started up the hill. The cobblestoned path twisted and forked, narrow and dark under the overhanging balconies of the houses. Occasionally it emerged into the brief sunlight of a tiny public square, with a fountain, a few plane trees, and the stone staircase from which the public bread dole was distributed, each square exactly like every other. Within a few minutes they had lost their bearings, but by going steadily upward they at last reached a larger street. This was a very wide, fine thoroughfare, paved with large flagstones, flanked by a marble colonnade along one side and shadowed by a massive aqueduct on the other; it was bustling with buyers and sellers in the mild spring morning. After determining that this was, indeed, the Middle street, Symeon asked for the house of General Aspar, and was directed left into the Taurus market. He went slowly, trying to read the busy,

233

closed faces around him. Meletios trotted behind, gaping delightedly at the shops that sold swords or spices or toys, and occasionally exclaiming over a statue of a hero or some mythical beast.

The Taurus marketplace was a huge public square and they had come on the day that it was used as a sheep market. The whole space was crowded with woolly beasts and their owners, and resounded with the bleats of the animals and the cries and bargaining of the dealers. Urgent inquiries by Symeon led to the discovery that the first man he'd asked had misunderstood: there was a statue of Aspar in the marketplace — but the general's house was another four miles to the west, near the Golden Gate. Aspar's image, bronze, armored, mounted on a warhorse, stared defiantly westward over the milling flocks of sheep, threatening them with a drawn sword. Meletios was unused to long walks. He put down his basket at the foot of the statue and sat on it disconsolately. Symeon squatted beside the child and patted his shoulder.

"I want to see my Mama," Meletios said miserably. "You said she was in Constantinople, and I thought we would see her. But it's still a long, long way."

"We'll see her soon, Meli. Only a few days now, only a few miles. It's hard for people like us to fight the rulers of the world; it takes time."

Meli shook his head and wiped his nose with the back of his hand. "Maybe we could see if Eulogios' house is near here?" he asked. "And then go see Aspar? I do want to see my Mama."

Symeon sighed. "We don't even know that Eulogios still has her. They said he was going to give her as a present to his patron."

"We could find out!" said Meletios. "Please, Daddy?"

Symeon hesitated, looking at his son: the boy's eyes fixed his, pleading. *It wouldn't hurt to find the house,* he thought. *It wouldn't hurt if we could strike up a conversation with the slaves, and find out where she is and how she is. We'd have more to say to Aspar — and it would cheer us both up.*

"We'll see if Eulogios' house is nearby," he told Meletios, "and if it is, we'll see if anyone there knows what happened to her. But remember, we mustn't tell anyone who we really are. If we find Eulogios' house, and if we can get in easily, we'll pretend . . . we'll pretend that we're selling dyestuffs for an importer at the harbor. We can say my cloak is a sample of cloth dyed with them. That ought to let us talk to the household slaves about weavers without anyone guessing who we really are."

Meletios' face lit up like a beacon and he scrambled to his feet, looking eagerly about the marketplace. Symeon smiled and began asking directions to the house of the agent Eulogios.

The first two people he asked had no idea: a *princeps* of the *agentes in rebus* was not a sufficiently public figure that his house was a city landmark. However, as it happened, the house was not far away, and the third person Symeon questioned, a woman who kept a flower stall, knew of the agent.

"He's a proud bastard," she told Symeon. "Rides through here with his barbarians, dressed like a tetrarch, and woe to anyone who gets in his way! One of his savages hit my little daughter once with a riding whip because she stopped to pick up her doll. Bad luck to him! Why do you want to see *him*?"

"I heard he might be interested in buying some dyestuffs," Symeon said mildly. "Where's the house, then?"

The woman told him, and Symeon thanked her, took the basket from Meletios, caught the little boy's hand, and set off southward.

The house, when they reached it, was a forbidding one. A high, windowless wall frowned down on the street, and the iron-barred oak gates were close shut. The single window in the gatekeeper's lodge was shuttered tightly, like a blind eye fixed menacingly on the quiet street. Symeon stood before the window for a moment, looking at it, not moving. He had pictured a sprawling mansion with a back door where he could enter casually, presenting his supposed sample to the housekeeper and engaging the slaves in gossip. This secretive building with its blank, eyeless glare unnerved him. As he looked at the shuttered window he felt suddenly that it would be dangerous to make it open. It was as though some lethal animal were penned inside. If those iron-barred gates ever closed behind him, he would never get out again.

He shook himself and took a step away from the lodge. He could knock, he could pretend some legitimate business — but not casually. The gatekeeper would take his name, and his going and coming would be noted. What if someone guessed the truth? The husband of Eulogios' new slave would likely be arrested as a runaway and returned to Tyre. *I would risk everything,* he thought, *just to see her a few days early. We can't. It isn't worth the risk.*

"Isn't this the house?" asked Meletios expectantly.

"Meli, I don't think we can go in," returned Symeon. "It's not safe, and they might be able to guess who we really are."

Meli stared at his father for a moment. Then his face crumpled and he burst into tears. "But I thought . . ." he began.

"Hush!" Symeon exclaimed urgently, and seized his son's hand.

A bolt on the inside of the window creaked; the gatekeeper inside was opening it. Meletios swallowed a sob, and Symeon turned and started back toward the marketplace. Meletios followed, half-running, half-dragged behind his father, still swallowing tears. A grizzled head poked out of the window and looked after them, but Symeon merely quickened his pace. He didn't stop until they were safely back in sight of the market.

"I *did* want to see my Mama!" complained Meletios through his tears when they paused by the corner. "You *said* we would see her in Constantinople, and it's been a long, long time, and we've been sailing and sailing across the whole world, and now . . ."

"Hush!" said Symeon again. "I just don't think it's wise to go into Eulogios' house. He's a bad man, Meli. I promise you, I want to see her as much as you do, and I'm doing my best to find her. Look — we'll see Aspar this afternoon, and he'll help us get her away. We'll stop in a tavern now, and I'll get you something to drink and a cake."

Meletios sniffed, wiped his eyes, and followed his father quietly.

They found a small wineshop on the corner of the marketplace. The front was set about with benches, crowded with wool-cloaked sheep dealers and a small knot of armed men, the private retainers of some local gentleman. Symeon picked his son up and elbowed his way into the shop. He bought a flagon of well-watered wine and a honey cake for Meletios, then went back outside into the sunlight and found a corner of a bench to sit down on, taking his son onto his lap. Meletios took the honey cake, but was still too unhappy to eat it. He sniffed and wiped his eyes again. One of the other customers noticed it and grinned at the little boy. Meletios gaped back in astonishment: the other customer was a barbarian with a horribly scarred face and deformed head, dressed in a cloak of dirty fur.

The Hun grinned more widely, showing a missing tooth. "Phew!"

he exclaimed, shaking his head at Meletios. "Why don't you eat that good cake, little boy? You don't like? You want to give it to me?"

Meletios closed his mouth and clutched the cake. He looked up at his father nervously.

The Hun laughed, rose, and came over. His fur cloak, which he'd loosened in the warm spring weather, swished softly against the hilt of the dagger at his side. But his face under the scars was friendly, with the expression of a fond father indulging in a little gentle teasing of someone else's children. His companions, all armored barbarians, looked annoyed with him, as though they considered this beneath his dignity. "You don't like cake?" he asked Meletios, squatting down before him.

Meletios looked at his father again. The Hun grinned at Symeon, and Symeon smiled back. "He's disappointed," Symeon told the other man, with the parent's resigned acceptance of the vagaries of children.

The Hun nodded. "It is a big disappoint?" he asked. "We–ell. You are a good big boy. Sit here with your father, eat your cake, be brave."

"But I wanted to see my Mama!" Meletios burst out, forgetting everything in the urgency of his need. "And we can't!"

"Your mama?" asked the Hun, surprised. "Why can't?"

"Because that Eulogios is a bad man," Meletios said bitterly. "He won't let us see her."

The other retainers suddenly looked up, their irritation with their companion giving way to something sharper, more focused. They were Eulogios' retainers, Symeon realized suddenly. Of course. Off duty and having a morning drink at the local tavern. He gripped Meletios' arm hard, and the little boy looked up in surprise.

"Eulogios?" said the Hun. "He is my master. He is not so very bad — your mama, does she work in his house?"

Perplexed and anxious now, the boy looked up at his father questioningly.

"She works in his house as a hired maid," Symeon told the Hun quietly, "doing odd jobs when his slaves are busy. We had the morning off and we hoped she might be able to join us, that's all. We didn't mean to be offensive about your master."

But the Hun was frowning now, and one of the other retainers had come over, a harsh-faced man in a gold collar, very tall and blond. "What is her name?" asked the Hun. "I get her permission to come with you, maybe? It is not so busy at the house now; is good if she joins you."

Symeon clutched Meletios hard. "Her name's Maria," he said, after a moment. It was almost certain that there'd be some woman called Maria at Eulogios' house; there must be some woman called Maria in every large household. He could only pray to the Mother of God that there was one of the right age, and that the retainers didn't know her well. They might not. A nobleman's retainers wouldn't know the history of every hired maid their master brought in.

"Is black-eyed Maria married?" asked the other retainer in surprise. "I thought she was too young to have a man, let alone a boy-child."

"She's older than she looks," Symeon said hastily, silently thanking the Blessed Virgin.

But the Hun was still frowning. "We can go to the house now," he said. "I will ask for you and they will send your wife out. Is good. I can do. Come."

"Thank you — but they've already said she's busy. Don't trouble yourself, friend."

"Is no trouble," said the Hun, getting to his feet and putting a hand on his belt. "Come."

Symeon sat still for a moment, clutching the child. *It's a public tavern*, he thought. *They can't attack me here.* "No," he said, slowly, "I don't want to disturb her this morning." He took a drink of the wine, trying to look unconcerned. The watery fluid was bitter on his tongue, and he had difficulty swallowing it; even down, it sat in a knot on his contracted stomach.

"He's a spy," the other retainer said softly. "He went to the house to spy on the master. The child is just a blind." There was a rasp of metal, and Symeon looked up from the drink to see the drawn sword, the other retainers on their feet and closing in, the rest of the crowd in the tavern frozen to watch.

Wide eyed, Meletios clutched his father tightly. "I'm not a spy," Symeon told the retainers. Carefully, he detached his son's arms from his neck and set the boy down on the ground beside him.

"Come with us," said the harsh-faced retainer. Though he was blond, shaggy, and clearly barbarian, his Greek was much better than that of the Hun, who had backed off, frowning unhappily. "If you're no spy you have nothing to fear."

238

Symeon shook his head. "I don't see that your master has any right to interrogate me. Who runs this city, a *princeps* of the agents or the magistrates? If you have any complaint against me, you can complain to them, and I'll come with you." He did not dare glance sideways to see if the sheep dealers heard this and approved; he did not dare take his eyes off the retainers.

"You'll come with us, spy, and answer to our master, not the damned magistrates!" exclaimed the retainer. "To your feet!"

Symeon bowed his head. He put his hands on the bench as though to help himself to his feet — then jumped backward over it, hauled it up, and hurled it at the retainers. He grabbed Meletios and swept him frantically into the gaping crowd of sheep sellers. Behind him came furious shouts of rage and a scream of terror. He thrust his way into the crowd, heading into the marketplace: behind him he could feel the press clearing as the retainers came after him. Meletios was crying. There was a sudden whistling sound, and then his feet tangled in something and he fell bruisingly onto the stones of the marketplace, instinctively turning as he fell to avoid landing on Meletios. Feet thudded up beside him; he struggled to his knees to find himself surrounded by a ring of swords. He knelt motionless, still holding the child, breathing in ragged sobs. Meletios clutched his neck, crying.

"Get up and come with us," said the blond retainer.

Symeon didn't move. One of the swords shifted up and slashed down, striking him with a half-turned edge, bruising more than it cut. But it still drew blood. Meletios gave a scream and burrowed into his father's neck. Symeon gasped and looked around at the ring of angry faces above the swords. Six of them. Only six. And yet, the crowd beyond them did nothing, accepted it without a murmur. "I'm not a spy, and your master has no right to arrest me!" he declared angrily.

One of the men kicked him viciously in the side; the blow was cushioned by the money-belt he still wore under his clothes, and he managed to keep his balance. He tried to stand to face them, but his legs wouldn't work properly; something still gripped them.

"Is no good," said the Hun, ducking under the swords. "He has the bola still about his legs, he cannot get up. Here, spy, sit: I will take it off."

Symeon leaned back, then, between the strange pressure round his legs and the weight of the child round his neck, toppled over on his side. One of the retainers laughed. The Hun paid no attention, but methodically began unwrapping a tangle of leather from about Symeon's ankles. The tangle resolved itself into a leather cord weighted at either end. The Hun coiled it up and fastened it to his belt.

"A nice weapon, Chelchal," said the tall retainer. "And your cast was as pretty as a Syrian whore."

Chelchal grinned. "It is a good weapon. Among the Acatziri we use it to catch sheep and horses."

Symeon climbed to his feet, Meletios still clinging to him, face hidden in his father's shoulder. The boy was trembling. *So am I,* thought Symeon: his legs were unsteady and he felt sick. As soon as they reached the house, the retainers would know he'd lied; the gatekeeper would remember him and tell them that he had stood outside, but had asked for no one. And if they were afraid of spies, they would question him.

The Hun nodded again, grinning at Symeon. "Is good. You come with us now, spy."

"I'm not a spy," Symeon said again, savagely. "I went to your master's house to see my wife — but I thought better of it because I knew your master for a bastard and a bandit. I demand to see the magistrates. You've got no *right* to do this to me!"

The Hun raised his squashed-down eyebrows and grinned more widely. "You say that to the master," he suggested. Then his eyes fell on Meletios and the grin vanished. "What do we do with the child?" he asked his fellows.

The tall retainer shrugged. "His Eminence won't want a screaming child. You like children — you look after it. I'll take the man into the house for questioning."

Chelchal nodded, and without another word seized Meletios and pulled him off his father. The child screamed and kicked desperately but the Hun paid no attention, slung him over his shoulder, and carried him off toward his master's house. The retainers hauled Symeon about, and with three swords pricking his back, marched him after Chelchal. The Constantinopolitan crowd watched in unresisting anger. A powerful man's retainers might do what they pleased; God would revenge it, but a citizen would be a fool to interfere. And besides, there were still sheep to sell.

The iron-barred gates were closed behind the party and bolted tight. Symeon's hands were tied and he was led off into the house to be questioned by the master; Chelchal carried Meletios into the stable and dropped him on a bale of straw.

Meli jumped to his feet, still sobbing, but now with rage as much as terror. He pulled out the little horn-handled knife which he had so proudly fastened to his belt in Tyre. He had remembered it while the Hun was carrying him to the house, but it had been, most unfairly, stuck against Chelchal's shoulder and he had been unable to get it out. Now he waved it wildly in the air and shouted, "You let my Daddy go! You let him go right now or I'll kill you!"

Chelchal took a step backward and drew out the leather bola again. He swung it about slowly, eyeing Meletios with approval. "You are a brave boy," he said gently, "but this is not good. I will not hurt you. Put the knife away."

Meletios had lost both parents and was a thousand miles from home: he knew as thoroughly as he knew his own name that these men had hurt him already and that if he didn't defend himself they'd hurt him further. He made a frantic, clumsy lunge at his antagonist. Chelchal swung the bola neatly about the child's arm and gave a jerk, and the knife fell to the floor. Chelchal picked it up. Meletios burst into tears again and lay down on the straw to wait for death.

"Tch," said Chelchal, sympathetically. He had first begun the conversation at the tavern because he liked children; he liked this boy the better for his eagerness to defend his father. He squatted beside Meletios and patted his shoulder. Meletios angrily struck his hand away, then covered his head against the anticipated blow, sobbing. Chelchal sat back on his heels. "Be brave," he said, after a moment. "It is no good crying. It helps nothing."

Meletios paid no attention.

"Tell me the truth," Chelchal went on, raising his voice to be heard above the sobs. "Is your Daddy a spy?"

Meletios picked up his head and glared. "My Daddy never spied on anyone!" he screamed, almost incoherent with tears.

"So why he does he lie to me? Why does he try to visit here, and then not come in?"

"Because you're bad men here! He said you were bad, and we shouldn't go in! You're bad, bad, bad! You stole away my Mama, and now you've stolen my Daddy too!" The thought was unbearable. He had lost everything and everyone, there was terror and danger everywhere, and he couldn't even fight it. Meli folded himself up on the floor, hugging himself and screaming with anguish.

Chelchal looked at him thoughtfully. He waited until the violence of the screams had eased, then asked, "Who stole your Mama?"

"Eulogios!" Meletios replied at once. Between fear and the blind need to defy his enemies, caution and obedient silence were lost. "He came to Tyre and took her away. It was all because of that cloak. I hate that cloak. I hate it, I hate that procurator, and I hate you too, all of you!"

"You are from Tyre?" asked Chelchal in astonishment. "You are Demetrias' child? How do you come here?"

The sound of his mother's name penetrated even through the boy's hysterical grief. He looked at the Hun with a slobbered face. The sobs became irregular, half gulped down. It was hard to stop crying, with the terror and loss so raw and unendurable, but he tried. "Do you know my Mama?" he asked at last. "Is she here?"

Chelchal shook his head. "She is not here. But I go with my master to Tyre, this winter, and we come back with her. I talk to her much on the journey; she is a fine woman. How do you come from Tyre? It is a long, long way — a thousand miles. And it is winter. How do you come?"

Meletios looked at him suspiciously, belatedly remembering his father's instructions.

"Is good to tell me," urged Chelchal. "I am your mother's friend. I will help, if I can. You tell me how you come here."

Meletios blinked at him for a minute. This misshapen monster was a friend of his mother's? He didn't believe it. But he wanted to; he must have help, and here help was offered. And everything had been lost already; to tell the truth could hardly make things worse. "We came in *Prokne*," he said at last. "She can sail even in winter. She's a very good boat, much better than the ones they have here."

Chelchal whistled. "You stole a boat?"

242

"My Daddy owns *Prokne!*" Meletios said scornfully. "We didn't steal anything. You stole. You stole my Mama. You didn't have any right to do that: we're state slaves, and nobody is allowed to sell us."

Chelchal regarded him for a moment with open admiration. He was a horseman, born into a land of scrub grass, dry plain, and hills: he had never even seen the sea until he had arrived in Constantinople. To commit oneself to the frail protection of an inch of planking and traverse the deep water at the mercy of the winds seemed to him to require courage verging on lunacy. Whenever he had been forced to do so for short voyages, following his master, he had only been able to step up the gangplank after fortifying himself with drink. And he was aware that even experienced sailors were afraid to sail the Middle Sea in winter. Yet this child and his father had sailed all the way from Tyre, to fetch back a woman. *I wouldn't have done it*, Chelchal thought to himself, in his own language. *Indeed, I'm not even willing to ride to Attila and demand my wife back. But I should have guessed that a brave woman would have a brave husband — he's a fighter too, and he very nearly got away even this morning. And the child has all the spirit I would have expected in Demetrias' son. Still, they won't get her back any more than I'd get Kreka — even if Eulogios still owned her, he wouldn't give her away. And what will become of the man now? Is he a slave as well?* "What does your Daddy do?" he asked.

"My Daddy is a purple-fisher," Meletios said proudly. "I'm going to be a purple-fisher too, when I grow up."

"Maybe," said the Hun, and shrugged. The customs of the Romans still puzzled him, and he didn't know what a purple-fisher did, let alone whether he would be slave or free: the whole concept of state slavery was meaningless to him. But he suspected that a slave's husband would also be a slave. If a slave among his own people had shown such courage, he would have been rewarded with freedom and a warrior's rank. *But the Romans don't like courage in their slaves*, Chelchal thought, resignedly. *They prefer obedience. If the man is a slave, he's likely to be returned to his owner. Well, at least he'll take the child with him; the boy won't be orphaned.*

"He is a brave man, your Daddy, to come so far to fetch his wife home," he told Meletios — then, still puzzling over the events of the morning, he added, "But you come such a long way, you come to this house — and then you do not go in. Why not?"

"My Daddy said we would be sent straight back to Tyre if we went in," the boy said dolefully. "He said we should see . . . no, I won't tell you anything about it. My Daddy had a plan, and he was going to rescue Mama and take her home. But now . . ." He stopped, thinking over how dreadful that "now" was. They would not rescue his mother. They would lose her forever. And even his father was not safe, was tied up and at the mercy of the bad men. "What will they do to my Daddy?" he asked Chelchal desperately. "Will they . . . kill him?"

Chelchal shrugged. "They will ask him many, many questions about what he does here. Then . . . we see. I think he says right: they will send you both home."

Meletios wiped his face. His eyes felt swollen and his face was hot, and something inside him kept shaking, threatening to tear open his throat in the screams again. But at least it seemed that no one was going to kill him or his father. He tried to steel himself, to be ready to help his father if the chance offered — *And it was my fault*, he thought wretchedly, *it was all my fault that this happened. Daddy told me we should see Aspar first. I won't do it again, please, Daddy, I'll be good now.*

But of course, his father wasn't there to receive the unspoken plea. Nor his mother. There was only this terrifying half-human monster — who seemed, nonetheless, to be genuinely friendly. "Where is my Mama?" he asked nervously. "You said she wasn't here."

Chelchal's interest in Demetrias had been respected: he had been told what had happened to her. "She is safe," he told Meletios gently. "She is the slave of the old she-king, Pulcheria Augusta, in the Palace of Hebdomon, outside the city."

"Oh," said Meli. This didn't sound too awful, but it was puzzling. "Why is she there?" he asked, doubtfully.

Chelchal laughed. "My master gives her to his master, Chrysaphios; Chrysaphios gives her to King Theodosius, King Theodosius gives her to his sister, the old she-king Pulcheria. There is big, big trouble over it here afterward, much shouting, my master and his master very, very angry. They want the Augusta to give your mother back so that they can ask her more questions. But it is no good for them: the she-king is a very big king, and never gives anything back."

Meletios sat in silence for a few minutes, considering this. He had seen Pulcheria's statue in Tyre and in the other cities they had stopped in on the voyage; her image was familiar to him, and he knew vaguely that she was supposed to be very holy. If this monster was telling the truth, then Mama really was safe. And a holy empress would certainly return her to her own family if she knew they wanted her. Meletios felt much better. "When will I see my Daddy again?" he asked Chelchal.

"I will go ask, in a little while. Can you be a good, brave boy, and wait quietly? If you promise to be good and not run away, I will take you to the kitchens now and leave you with the housekeeper. Then I can go find out about your Daddy."

"I'll wait quietly until you come back, if you'll tell me what's happening to my Daddy," Meletios promised seriously. "I swear it by St. Tyrannion."

Chelchal agreed to this oath and solemnly escorted Meletios to the kitchens, then went quickly to see his master.

Eulogios had a reception room off the courtyard of his house, a large room decorated with the ostentatious luxury he was fond of. The decoration was not a success. The painted panels of the walls clashed in color with the pictures hung there; the fine greens of the mosaic landscape on the floor were obscured and made hideous by the equally fine rusts and oranges of the silk carpet. The elaborate furniture was richly made, but ugly and uncomfortable, and the good glass windows merely poured an unforgiving light over the worst shortcomings. Eulogios nonetheless liked the room, and he was sitting at the gold side table going over the accounts from one of the posting stations in his charge when his retainers brought in their prisoner.

The agent was in a bad mood. He had been in a bad mood for nearly three months now. When Philippos first arrived in Constantinople, Chrysaphios had sent for Eulogios and offered him "one last chance" to redeem his previous failure. Eulogios had gone eagerly to the Hebdomon, and had been furious at his frustration there; the job of searching Nomos' house had been undertaken with passion. The agent had stormed and threatened and beaten the slaves, and found nothing. When he reported it to Chrysaphios, the chamberlain had been convinced that Pulcheria had removed the evidence of Nomos' treason and was using it to blackmail the official into informing against himself. He had dismissed Eulogios furiously, and the agent had sulked at home, making the lives of his slaves a torment; even his retainers had not been immune from his rages. And yet, three months had gone by and nothing had happened. Eulogios was beginning to feel vindicated: he had found nothing because there was nothing to find, and Marcianus' presence in Tyre, like his arrival close behind Philippos, had been nothing more than coincidence. The cloak had certainly been red: he had seen it. *Perhaps,* he had taken to telling himself as the weather grew slowly warmer, *perhaps Chrysaphios will call for me today, and admit that I wasn't at fault, and give me some other job. He can't have meant to dismiss me forever. He hasn't recalled that Hun he lent me last year. Perhaps I can hope for promotion again soon?*

But perhaps he couldn't. The Sacred Offices were full of ambitious men, and Eulogios was uncomfortably aware how easily he could be replaced. As for Chelchal, his year's engagement would end in a few months, and unless he was specifically ordered otherwise, he would then go back to the Great Palace and reattach himself to the chamberlain's forces. Eulogios would be left to live on his own salary, guarded by his own retainers, and be unable to hope for any further promotion. *It wasn't my fault!* he would tell himself angrily — and then, irritable and impatient, look for a fault in his slaves so he could order them whipped. He was pleased when his retainers brought in a man they said they had caught spying.

"He came up to the house and waited about in a suspicious fashion," Berich, their leader, informed him. "The gatekeeper noticed him. Then he went down to the tavern on the marketplace. Chelchal got into conversation with his child, and he and the child both spoke insultingly of Your Eminence, not realizing who we were. When he understood, he attempted to cover himself by lying, and said that he was the husband of a hired maid here, which he isn't. When we accused him of being a spy and insisted that he come back here to explain himself, he tried to run, and would have escaped, if Chelchal hadn't caught him with the bola. He refuses to explain himself or what he really wanted here."

Eulogios looked at Symeon with satisfaction. *So, somebody thinks I'm still worth spying on. Who? One of my rivals? One of Chrysaphios' rivals? Chrysaphios himself — Oh God, not that! If the man is Chrysaphios', I'll already be in trouble for interfering with him. But why would Chrysaphios bother?*

*If it is Chrysaphios, he'll have some reason. Better go easy with this fellow until I'm sure who pays him.*

Symeon stood with his legs braced and his hands tied behind his back, his head bowed. He felt desperately, sickly, afraid. The fear was not so much to do with the retainers, and certainly nothing to do with this overdressed, mean little man before him — Eulogios seemed almost too ridiculous to merit the hate Symeon had felt for him in Tyre. No, in some peculiar way he was afraid of the house itself, the shuttered windows that had stared at him like blind eyes, and the iron-bound doors that had snapped shut like a shark's teeth behind him. He could do nothing to fight back. From the moment Chelchal's bola had twisted about his legs, he'd been like a sheep trussed for the market.

He had had just enough time to think on the walk from the marketplace to the house: just enough time to decide that his only hope of safety lay in lying. He did not like lying and he was bad at it, but every other course led to disaster. He must find some convincing story to explain away all the circumstances that accused him. *Lord of All*, he prayed, desperately, *give me quick wits and a ready tongue; let him believe me! And protect my little Meli! And, oh God, if I can't save Demetrias, at least don't let my presence here harm her!*

He cleared his throat uncertainly and, heart pounding, launched into the ingratiating whine of a Sidonian merchant who'd once illegally tried to buy murex from him. "Your Eminence," he said, "I'm sorry to trouble a gentleman like you, but your men have made a mistake. I'm not a spy."

One of the retainers shoved an elbow into his stomach, and Symeon folded over, then pulled himself unsteadily straight again.

Eulogios smiled and made a restraining gesture to the retainers. "If you're not a spy, you'll come to no harm here," he said, appeasingly. "What did you want?"

Symeon struggled to produce a sickly smile. "I wanted to do some business, Your Excellency. I'd meant to talk to Your Kindness' slaves about some dyestuffs — I sell dyestuffs, sir, from a supplier at the harbor — but when I saw how shuttered the house was, I decided I might not be welcomed. There's no crime in that, is there, Eminence?"

The agent's eyes narrowed. "You're not Constantinopolitan, are you?" he asked, after a moment. "Your accent is Syrian. Why would you come so far just to sell dyestuffs? And why lie about it?"

"His child said they came to see a woman," supplied Berich. "I imagine that's why he didn't spin this story before."

"So, Syrian, what did you come here for?" Eulogios asked.

"To sell dyestuffs," Symeon said. "There are plenty of my nation engaged in trading in every city in the empire, sir: we make our homes where we can make a living. And I admit, my son had a fancy that his mother might be here. She . . . she ran off a year ago, with another man. She used to work for a Eulogios sometimes — perhaps it was a different gentleman. She never told me much of what she did, sir — I suppose because most of it was bad. At any rate, my little boy wanted to look for her. I didn't say as much to your men because I don't boast about being cuckolded, and there's nothing odd in that." *Oh God, I sound like a slave, I tell lies like one. Let him believe me!*

"You're a very fluent liar," Eulogios told him, the first note of anger creeping into his voice, "but I'll have the truth. If you were selling dyestuffs, you'd have some samples."

"I do," Symeon said at once, eagerly. "Not the stuffs themselves, of course, they're too messy to carry about. But I had a cloak in a basket, dyed with the stuffs I sell. One of your men has it, I think."

Eulogios glared in irritation, then looked at the retainers. One of them produced the wicker basket, which he had picked up from the tavern. Eulogios opened it and took out the cloak. *Red*, he thought, bitterly, *and dyed with — yes, I think it is kermes. Mother of God, how it haunts me, that color!* He glared at Symeon. "That's a sample?"

"Yes, Eminence," Symeon said, almost cheerfully. Any worker from the factories of Tyre knew dyestuffs and could give a convincing imitation of a dyeseller. "The blue is indigo; I have a supplier who can get you some, best quality, already prepared, very cheap, sir. And the red is kermes — a beautiful color, isn't . . . "

"A loathsome color, an abomination!" shouted Eulogios. He bunched up the cloak and hurled it back in the basket.

"I'm sorry to offend Your Eminence," Symeon said humbly.

Eulogios glared at him. "Why didn't you say this to my retainers?"

"As I said, Eminence, I don't boast of being cuckolded. And I'm a man with a temper, sir, which I lose when I shouldn't. I don't like taking orders from barbarians. Well, they've made me pay for it."

248

*And they can make you pay some more*, thought Eulogios, *for wasting my time*. "Search him," he ordered his men shortly.

Berich caught the anger in his master's eye and grinned. He felt humiliated by the turn events had taken, and was eager to get back at this Syrian, dyeseller or spy or whatever he was. He kicked Symeon in the shin so that he fell heavily onto his knees, then slapped him. One of the other retainers grabbed Symeon's hair to hold him upright, and Berich unfastened the belt and pulled the purse off it. He paused an instant, then, deliberately, kicked Symeon in the stomach before tipping the contents of the purse onto the gold side table before his master. A handful of change and a letter. Eulogios picked up the letter and read it aloud, expecting nothing.

" 'I, Flavius Marcianus of Thrace . . .' " he began, and stopped.

The harsh voice was like the recording angel's, reading out at the Last Judgment some secret and long-concealed sin. Kneeling in pain on the silk carpet, trying not to vomit, Symeon heard the sentence of his damnation passed. He raised to Eulogios a face gray under its tan and said nothing.

"Flavius Marcianus of Thrace," repeated Eulogios, savagely, horribly, triumphant. "Marcianus. 'I, Flavius Marcianus of Thrace, did swear the strongest oaths to protect Symeon and Demetrias . . .' " He stopped again. "And Demetrias! I know a little slut by that name, and Marcianus appeared very interested in some business connected with her." He jumped up and stood before Symeon, grinning at him with bared teeth. "You'll give me the truth now, fellow," he said. "You'll tell me everything. Why did Marcianus promise you and this Demetrias his protection? Eh?" He caught Symeon's tunic and twisted it, pulled his head forward to glare into his eyes. "You may as well tell me quickly and freely now, because otherwise you'll tell it on the rack," he hissed. He let go of the tunic; when Symeon said nothing he slapped him hard, twice. "Tell me the truth! No more lies now — Symeon, is it? Your name, isn't it? — Don't hope for help from your patron. Marcianus has no influence here."

Symeon bit his lip. His mind was numb with terror, and the only image it held was Demetrias'. *I've brought ruin on her*, he thought, despairingly. *I must say nothing. Anything I said might incriminate her. The least I can do is try to shield her now. Oh heavenly God, what have I done? They'll put us both on the rack, and it's all because*

*of my obstinacy, my refusal to admit that there were people I couldn't
get the better of. My arrogance. O God forgive me, and give me the
power to keep silent now!*

Chelchal arrived at the room a few minutes later. About to knock, he
heard the sound of a blow, followed by the unmistakable sound of
retching. He hesitated, surprised. He recognized the sounds instantly,
but could not understand why his master thought it necessary to have
Demetrias' husband beaten.

He rapped on the door sharply and went in. The silk carpet had
been rolled out of the way, and Symeon was lying doubled up on the
mosaic in a puddle of vomit, his hands still bound, gasping for breath.
His nose was bleeding. Berich and the others stood round him; Eulogios was sitting on the couch waiting until his victim was able to
speak.

"What is this, sir?" Chelchal asked, taking advantage of his favored
position in the household to question his master.

"Ah, Chelchal!" Eulogios grinned like a cat. "I gather you were
responsible for capturing our spy: you'll be rewarded. Our spy is
reluctant to talk — but you work for Marcianus, don't you, Symeon?"

Symeon only gasped for air. His nose was full of blood and vomit,
and he could barely take in what Eulogios was saying.

"Him?" said Chelchal. "He is the husband of Demetrias from Tyre.
He sails up here with their little son to fetch back his wife. He's no
spy. There's no need to beat him."

Eulogios gaped at him for a moment, then demanded, angrily,
"What do you know about it?"

"I talk to the little boy. He says they come to fetch back his mama
and have a plan to rescue her and go back to Tyre."

"A plan!" Eulogios exclaimed hotly. "He has a document signed
by Flavius Marcianus of Thrace, promising him and his wife protection! They were both in the service of Aspar all along!"

Chelchal shook his head doubtfully. "Maybe he goes to Marcianus
for help when he gets here to the city, and promises to spy later.
Maybe he forges the letter, or steals it. He comes here to fetch back
his wife. The little boy doesn't know how to tell big lies; he's too
small."

Berich had mentioned that there was a child, but Eulogios had forgotten this. He disliked the tone of authority with which Chelchal pronounced on the child's honesty, and glared at his retainer; Chelchal responded with his usual grin. *The barbarian has no respect for his betters,* Eulogios thought angrily.

And yet, perhaps the Hun had a point. A young child wouldn't have the skill to lie as his father had, and wouldn't be as obstinate — Symeon had not uttered a word since the letter was first discovered. Perhaps the child could be useful.

"The child seems to be more talkative than its father," Eulogios said sourly. "How old is it?"

"Five, six maybe. A fine brave boy. I come to ask you if Your Excellency will send the boy back to Tyre with his father. Not good now, maybe."

"Bring him in here," Eulogios said. "I'll talk to him myself."

Symeon groaned and tried to sit up. Chelchal's grin vanished. He looked at the helpless figure on the floor, then looked back at his master. He recognized that white-lipped, impatient look. Eulogios would accept no argument; any attempt to cross him would simply throw him into one of his rages. Chelchal shrugged and went off to fetch Meletios.

The little boy was sitting quietly on the floor in the corner of the kitchen where Chelchal had left him, hugging his knees. The slaves were preparing lunch for the household. Someone had tried to give Meletios a piece of fresh bread, but he was not interested in food, and the bread steamed untouched on the counter above his head. When Chelchal appeared he jumped up and watched the Hun approaching with a look of almost desperate hope. Chelchal flinched. He would not have wanted his own son to see him beaten by enemies; he felt that a boy should believe in his father's strength and courage. But there was nothing to be done about it. He had vowed to serve Chrysaphios, who kept him from the service of Attila, and Chrysaphios had directed him to obey Eulogios.

"Hush," Chelchal said softly, taking the child's hand. "You must be a brave boy now. My master still thinks your Daddy is a spy; he orders that stupid Berich to hit him. Your Daddy is a brave man and says nothing. Now my master wants to ask you about spies too. You must tell him the truth. Is good?"

Meletios blinked. "Will that help my Daddy?"

"I think so. Come now, and remember, you must be brave."

Symeon had managed to get to his knees by the time Meletios was led in. But he could not stand. He had been kicked in the stomach three times now, and he knelt doubled over, his nose dripping blood onto the green leaves of the mosaic. When the door creaked open he had to fight an urge to scream. This was no place for Meletios. *Oh God, what have I done?* he thought again. *I should pay for my own stupidity, pay alone. But I've dragged in my wife and my son, and anything I do will only make it worse for them.*

Meletios saw his father, kneeling, covered in blood and vomit, and gave a convulsive jerk away from him. He tried to back out of the room, white with horror; Chelchal held his arm and bent down to whisper to him. "It is not so bad as it looks," the Hun told him softly. "He has a nosebleed. Nothing broken."

Meletios started to cry; he wiped his nose with the back of his hand, his eyes fixed miserably on his father. Symeon looked back in silence.

"Well, boy," said Eulogios. "You see what can happen to spies."

"My Daddy never spied on anyone!" Meletios shouted back, flushing abruptly and furiously red. "You — you evil devil! You let him go!"

"I'll let him go if you tell me what you came here for," Eulogios replied savagely.

"We came to fetch my Mama home," Meletios said. "You stole her, you did! You didn't have any *right* to buy her, but you took her away. My Daddy was going to fetch her home."

Eulogios nodded to Berich; the Goth turned and gave Symeon a straight punch in the jaw that knocked him flat again, then kicked him. Meletios screamed and tried to run at the Goth. Chelchal caught his shoulders and held him.

"Tell me what your father's plan was, boy," Eulogios said, angrily, "or I'll have him killed."

Meletios screamed hysterically, struggling with Chelchal; the Hun picked him up. "Do what he says!" he whispered in the boy's ear. "He thinks worse things. What you say may help."

Meletios stopped screaming, but sobbed wildly, his eyes white-rimmed. Chelchal put him down. "Tell him," he urged.

"My Daddy had a bit of parchment with a promise on it." Meletios faltered. "He got it from a man called Marcianus, who has a big scary house in the Old City, and is very powerful. He promised to help my Daddy if there was any trouble about that cloak, but he didn't. My Daddy was going to show the parchment to Aspar, who has a big statue in the marketplace here, with a sword. Aspar is Marcianus' master, and my Daddy said he'd make Marcianus keep his promise, and they'd get the . . . the deed of sale . . . for my Mama annulled, and my Mama could come home with us."

Symeon groaned, trying to get up again. Meletios looked at him in misery. "I'm sorry, Daddy!" he said, wretchedly.

"Meli," said Symeon wretchedly, and spat blood. "Meli . . . I'm sorry. Your mother . . . tell him your mother didn't know anything about it. She didn't!" He looked up at Eulogios. "I went to Marcianus, but I never told her. She didn't know anything about it. Don't . . . don't touch her, please . . ." He felt the tears spring to his eyes and blinked them back. He had never begged before. And he could see that begging now would do no good, but he could feel the pleas trembling at the back of his throat. Don't hurt my son. Don't hurt my wife. It wasn't their fault.

But Eulogios didn't care whose fault it was, and whether Demetrias had known about Marcianus or not was irrelevant to him. He cared only to discover if there was a real conspiracy or not, to find evidence to please Chrysaphios.

"But Daddy," Meletios said, "Mama isn't here. She's . . ."

"Silence!" Eulogios shouted. "You miserable slave! You little bastard! I'll teach you to talk before you're asked to! Chelchal!"

The Hun shrugged, one hand on Meletios' shoulder. "What does he say wrong, sir? He answers your question."

Eulogios made a noise of disgust. "He answered nothing. Boy, why did Marcianus promise your father protection? Tell me quickly."

Meletios looked distraught and uncertain. "He . . . it was about that cloak, I think. Was it, Daddy?"

Symeon set his teeth and said nothing.

"What cloak?"

"The cloak my Mama wove at the dyeworks. The procurator ordered her to weave it, and my Daddy wasn't happy, because the procurator is a bad man. And she worked and worked on it, all day till it was dark, for a long, long time. And . . . and I think my Daddy told Marcianus how bad the procurator was, and Marcianus promised to help him. But you came, and you were angry about that horrible cloak, too, and you took my Mama . . ."

"What color was the cloak?" demanded Eulogios, eagerly.

"I don't know," returned the child. "She wove it at the dyeworks. Please, sir, my Daddy . . ."

Eulogios nodded to Berich; Berich kicked Symeon in the groin. Symeon gave a jerk and a strangled scream of agony, and Meletios screamed again. "I don't know!" he told Eulogios, his face contorted with tears. "I don't know! Daddy!"

Eulogios nodded again; this time the blow was to Symeon's face.

"Daddy!" Meletios screamed again, and struggled against Chelchal's restraining arms. Chelchal held him firmly.

"He does not know," Chelchal said, angrily. "Sir, this is bad, it is very bad. It is not good to beat a man in front of his child. I will take the child out."

"In a moment," replied Eulogios. "If the child doesn't know, I think the man does. What color was the cloak your wife wove at the dyeworks? Eh? No common color, for Marcianus to promise you protection for news of it. Tell me."

Symeon lay on the floor, dizzy with pain. *Tell the truth,* he thought, *and someone will make Demetrias suffer for it.* He shook his head, his teeth set. "I never . . . saw it," he gasped. "I only guessed . . . you must . . . have seen it. You tell me."

Eulogios stared at him a moment, then looked at his retainers. "Berich," he said slowly, "take the child."

"No!" screamed Symeon, struggling to get back on his knees. "For the love of God!" He was crying and couldn't see the Goth, couldn't even see Meletios.

Berich took a step toward Meletios. Chelchal took one hand from the boy's shoulder and dropped it to the bola at his belt. He had fought and killed many other men; in raids he had shot old men and women; once, after burning an enemy village, he had been forced to kill an orphaned three-year-old girl. But that was in war; the child had been too small to take captive and would have starved if left behind. He would not assist in the deliberate torture of a child for some improbable and abstract political advantage — and he wouldn't tolerate anyone else's doing it, either. His eyes met Berich's, and he shook his head. The Goth stopped. Chelchal turned to his master.

"No," he said. "Sir, this is very bad. It is bad luck, sir. No good to torture childs, sir, no good. God hates it. I know men, sir, Huns, who beat childs before killing them. They all die soon after. Very, very bad thing, sir. You must not."

Eulogios hesitated. He felt sure that Symeon would confess everything if they tortured the child — but Symeon would probably confess everything anyway. It might be better to wait, and let Chrysaphios extract the whole truth from him: that would gratify Chrysaphios. Yes, it was probably a necessary piece of tact to allow the chamberlain to discover the truth himself. And perhaps it was bad luck to torture children, an arrogance that invited divine vengeance. Better to avoid it, particularly since it was unnecessary.

"Very well," he told Chelchal, irritably, "you keep the boy, then. Sell him, if you want and you can find a buyer: that can be your reward for capturing his father. Berich, I want you to go to the Great Palace and inform His Illustriousness about this spy — I'll give you a letter for him. The rest of you take the fellow out and lock him up in a storeroom. Untie his hands and give him food and drink: we'll want him in good shape for the questioning he'll get tomorrow. And send in the women to clean the floor — the place stinks."

Chelchal picked Meletios up and carried him out; the other retainers dragged out Symeon. Eulogios sat down to write the letter to Chrysaphios while his women slaves came in to wash the floor. *What a piece of luck!* he thought, trimming his pen. *His Illustriousness will be delighted. I'll be promoted this time for certain!*

He dipped the pen happily in the ink and began to write.

Meletios was hysterical. Chelchal carried him grimly back to the stable and set him down gently in the straw. He went over to the stalls at the side of the low building and set about saddling his horse. When he had the animal ready to ride, he led it up to Meletios and squatted down beside the boy, the reins over his arm. "We go now," he said.

"My Daddy!" said Meletios, in anguish.

"It is very bad, yes, I know. But he does not kill your Daddy. Is good now, he will leave your Daddy today. He will wait for tomorrow and let Chrysaphios say what to do. We go now."

Meletios looked up at the Hun. His face was swollen and red with weeping and his nose was running. He looked a completely different child from the one who had sat on his father's lap in the market tavern. "Where are we going?" he asked, after a moment. "Are you going to sell me?"

"No," Chelchal said firmly. "I have a little boy. He is your age, last time I see him. He is a slave now. I do not like that and I do not want to sell you, either. It is not good, to sell little boys to strange men in big cities. I am your mother's friend, and I will not do it. I will take you . . . I will tell you soon. You come."

Meletios got to his feet, and Chelchal hoisted him up and set him in the front of the tall wooden saddle, then jumped up behind him, gathered the reins, and the horse trotted out into the yard. Meletios had always wanted to ride a horse, but now he scarcely noticed it, wrapped in an intense and hopeless misery.

Chelchal shouted for the gatekeeper. "I go into the city and take care of the little boy," he declared. "I will be back late, after dark maybe, is good? Good."

Grumbling, the gatekeeper opened the gates. Chelchal trotted through them, out into the open street and back to the Taurus marketplace. Meletios began to cry again, quietly and hopelessly. "My Daddy," he repeated.

"It is very bad," Chelchal agreed readily.

"Eulogios is a devil," said Meletios, with a flicker of his old fierceness. "He's bad, bad, bad. My Daddy!"

"Your Daddy is a brave man," returned Chelchal. "He will not say what my master wants him to say. Better you are away from him; then he can be stronger, not afraid for you."

"It was my fault," Meli sobbed. "I wanted to see my Mama. I made him go to the house. He knew it was dangerous, but I made him go!"

"He does not go into the house," Chelchal pointed out. "Is bad luck that I start talking to you, is all. Don't worry." He turned his horse westward, skirting the sheep dealers who were departing after the morning's business, jolting quickly through the city.

"Where are we going?" Meletios asked, after a long silence punctuated only by choked sobs.

Chelchal's grin reappeared. "We go to the Hebdomon. Is good for childs to be with their Mamas and Daddys. You cannot be with Daddy, so I take you to Mama. Is good."

256

"To my Mama?" asked Meli, not daring to believe it.

"You will see," Chelchal replied easily. "You sit safe there? Is long way, still, we hurry."

He tightened his securing grip on the boy and touched his horse to a canter, weaving through the crowds on Middle street and heading toward the Golden Gate. Meletios clung to the saddle, gasping. Going to see his mother. Perhaps the world was not quite as vicious and terrible as it appeared. Perhaps someone could free his father and destroy the horrible devils who held power, and they could go home to Tyre, and everything would be as it was.

But his six-year-old confidence was broken at its roots, and he already knew, certainly and beyond question, that nothing would ever be the same again.

# ~X~

IT WAS THE MIDDLE of the afternoon work session when Theonoe came to Demetrias and told her that she was wanted at the gatehouse.

Demetrias set the tapestry needle carefully in the recently begun picture of The Wedding at Cana and crossed herself before rising to her feet. The gesture was used by everyone at the Hebdomon — whenever one task was finished, before another was started, before eating, after eating, and at every casual mention of Christ or His Mother, Pulcheria's people crossed themselves. Demetrias had picked up the habit almost without noticing it — it was simply one more tiny adjustment to life in the Hebdomon, a life that no longer felt alien to her. She was used to the black clothes now, the silence and stately walks of the palace. The routine of work and prayer was calming, the stillness restful after the terrors that had preceded it. Her favored and influential status was generally recognized, and though she still disliked it, she was resigned to it. The other weavers were, at least, still friendly. And the work, as ever, was absorbing. Her tapestry of the Flight into Egypt had been admired by everyone in the palace — "It makes my bones ache from traveling just to look at it," Agatha had commented. The Wedding at Cana, she thought, would burst from the curtain with joy. Once again she felt that life as Pulcheria's slave would be bearable — until her real life began again. But she felt more certain than ever that Pulcheria's palace, even if she died in it, would never be home.

"Who wants me?" she asked Theonoe in surprise.

The old woman frowned disapprovingly. "There's some man, a barbarian, I was told, who has come to the gate and asked urgently to see you. I will escort you there, girl, and supervise his conversation. I hope you have done nothing improper?"

"Of course not," Demetrias returned. "I have never willingly done anything improper, and I like this place all the more because there has been no one to ask me to." She crossed herself again. Theonoe softened and gave an approving nod, and they set off together through the quiet corridors toward the gate.

*What I said was true enough, I suppose,* Demetrias thought, uneasily, *even though I did say it to please Theonoe. But I wonder what barbarian would come here to see me? Not Chelchal, I hope. He was kind to me and I've no wish to offend him — which I'll have to do if he still wants anything from me. Well, I'll know soon enough.*

Chelchal was not actually waiting in the gatehouse but in the courtyard before it. The peach tree was budding, and crocus flowered, purple and gold, in the flowerbeds below the warm brick of the walls. The Hun was watering his horse at the fountain, his back to the gatehouse, but Demetrias recognized the filthy marmot skin cloak instantly. She looked at Theonoe; the old woman raised her eyebrows in question. Demetrias sighed, pulled her black cloak up, and stepped out into the afternoon sun. "Chelchal?" she called, inquiringly.

He turned — and a child dashed across from the other side of the horse and ran toward her. He slowed for a moment, seeing the unfamiliar black cloak; then his eyes fixed on her face and he sprinted foward again. "Mama!" he shouted, an instant before hurling himself into her arms.

Demetrias dropped to her knees to hold his weight, her arms going round him. She looked down at the tight bronze curls in astonished disbelief. The small hard body shook against hers, and the arms were locked tightly about her neck. She had given birth to that body, nursed it, rocked it to sleep, washed it, and fed it, and watched it grow. Every inch was familiar to her — and already half unfamiliar again, changed in the short months, half forgotten. She felt as though a spell had been broken, and that the calm resigned woman who had walked out of the palace a moment before was all at once transformed, Prokne changed from a bird back into a woman. "Meli," she gasped, "Meli, darling, my little love — how did you get here?"

"What is this?" demanded Theonoe in an icy voice.

Demetrias answered the old woman without shifting. "This is my son," she declared. "This is Meletios. He was left in Tyre."

"Are you sure of this?" asked Theonoe, still coldly.

"I know my own son!" snapped Demetrias. She pulled back from the child a fraction and held the side of his face with one hand. "Meli, darling, how did you get here?"

"Chelchal brought me," Meletios told her. "Eulogios said he should sell me, but he didn't because he has a little boy of his own who's a slave and he thinks it's a bad thing."

Demetrias looked up at Chelchal, who had sauntered over, grinning. The Hun nodded at this description of his opinion. "Childs should be with their mothers and fathers," he declared authoritatively.

"But how . . . did you bring him here, to Constantinople?"

Meletios answered before the Hun could. "No! Daddy and I came in *Prokne*. But I wanted to go to Eulogios' house to see if you were still there, and Daddy wouldn't go in, but he stopped at a tavern to buy me a honey cake, and some bad men were there, and they caught us, and they took us back to Eulogios' house, and they said that we were spies, and . . . and . . ." Meletios remembered his father screaming, and began to cry again. It was safe to cry now, in his mother's arms. He pushed himself into her lap and wept, quietly now, no longer fighting the sobs.

"Your husband will have big trouble," Chelchal told her. He looked down at her regretfully where she knelt on the pavement before the flowers, the afternoon sun picking out the gold in her hair and in the hair of the child in her arms, her green eyes raised to him in doubt and astonishment. *A fine woman,* he thought once more. *What a fool she made of my master! Yes, she would have been worth marrying — and I suppose her husband knew that. Well, she's not for me, not now: she's for God or that man they've locked in the storeroom.*

Chelchal believed firmly that all women should marry, should look after their men, and bear children. It was what they were for, after all. The Roman admiration for virginity bewildered him completely. What use did God have for a woman? True, if the Romans were right about their God, he'd once had a son by a virgin — but they all insisted that this was a unique event, and unlikely to happen again. Why did everyone applaud when a pretty woman shut herself up and vowed never to sleep with a man? Demetrias would be much better married, even to somebody else, than locked up in the Hebdomon Palace. *But I doubt that Demetrias' man will ever go free now*, he thought, sadly. *My master and Chrysaphios will question him until he's a heap of torn skin and broken bones, and then kill him. They'll have to kill him. It must be against their own laws, what they're doing, so they won't be able to set him free. And Pulcheria will stop Demetrias from marrying again: she will live out her years here at the Hebdomon, with only God and old women for company — apart from the child. And he may end up a priest or a monk, raised in such company. What a waste!*

"When my master searches your husband," he told her, the regret adding sharpness to his tone, "he finds a parchment which says that Marcianus promises to protect you and your husband. Because of this, he has your man beaten and asks many questions of your child. Then he sends for his master Chrysaphios. Why Marcianus signs this parchment, you know. Your husband, he says nothing, and I think he will say nothing, even to Chrysaphios."

"My husband is in Eulogios' house?" asked Demetrias, flushing. "A prisoner? He's been hurt?"

Chelchal nodded curtly and tossed the reins back over his horse's neck. "Eulogios tells me to sell your son. Instead, I bring him here. Now I go back to my master's." He set one foot in the stirrup.

"Wait!" Demetrias jumped to her feet, though she still clutched Meletios. "I . . . I must thank you. But my husband . . . how . . . "

*Loyal to the man*, observed Chelchal, without resentment, *I might as well not exist.* He grinned at her, but mounted into the saddle. "Is no trouble. I will go back now. I tell your husband you are safe here, yes? He must not fear for you?"

"Yes . . . yes. Say I'll find some way to help him. Oh, thank you! What can I do to thank you?"

"You make me a cloak someday, maybe? A better cloak than the one you made for King Attila, ha! Is good. Much health! Meli, you be a brave boy!" Grinning, Chelchal turned his horse and cantered back past the gatehouse and away, the sun glittering from the silver scale-work on his horse's harness.

"Well!" exclaimed Theonoe, stiff with anger and outrage. "What piece of intrigue is this? What has that barbarian to do with you, girl?"

"He's one of the agent Eulogios' retainers," Demetrias replied evenly. "He was in the party that brought me from Tyre — the only one who treated me with any kindness. And he's just shown himself twice as kind." She hugged Meletios, who had stopped crying and put his head against her shoulder, a limp and exhausted dead weight in her arms. *My son*, she thought, triumphantly. *Mine. And Symeon is here, in Constantinople; he came to find me. Eulogios has captured and injured him — but I have a place with a stronger patron than Eulogios, and everyone believes I have influence. Very well, if I have any power, I'll use it, and Eulogios will regret what he's done.* "Theonoe, you heard what he said. My husband came here and has been captured by Chrysaphios' people. That's not just my concern, that could affect . . . that is, the Augusta will want to know about it. We must tell her at once."

Theonoe stared at her bitterly. "And what do you intend to do with that child?"

"He's my son; he stays with me."

"He's a boy. He's not allowed in the palace."

"Don't be absurd!" Demetrias exclaimed impatiently. "He's barely six years old! And he won't be the only child at the Hebdomon."

Theonoe glared. Three months had passed since the events that had followed Demetrias' arrival at the Hebdomon, and she had begun to hope that her fears were groundless; that there were no plans being laid to regain for her mistress a power that Theonoe herself regarded as inevitably corrupt. But here was a clear sign that she had not been wrong: the barbarian's news could "affect" something that concerned the empress. Within the year, perhaps, she would have to leave the contemplative silence of the Hebdomon and move back into the tangled and despicable world of the Great Palace. Moreover, Theonoe had grown fond of Demetrias, and had hopes for her: now the girl showed herself more set than ever on the affairs of ordinary women, and was even proposing to bring a squawling brat into the sacred corridors of the Hebdomon itself! "The maids who are married all live outside the palace," she sniffed, "with their precious guardsmen or stable-groom husbands. That would hardly be a fit place for you, girl."

"Then someone will have to find a fit place for me to keep my son! Theonoe, please! He's very young and frightened. Surely no one is going to separate us? Just go to the Mistress and tell her what's happened: I'm sure she'll arrange everything."

Theonoe sniffed again, then, reluctantly, bowed her head. Whatever she thought of the empress' plans, her own first duty was obedience to them. "But stay here," she ordered, "and don't take the boy into the palace before I come back." She swept off, her black-robed back rigid.

"I don't like that woman," said Meletios, watching her go.

"Hush, darling," returned his mother, "you mustn't say that. She's a supervisor and a lady-in-waiting upon the empress Pulcheria. And she's quite kind, really; she just doesn't like men or children." She sat down on the pavement, still holding tightly to Meletios. "Oh Meli, darling! Listen; in a little while the empress will send for us, I hope. She's an old woman, and a bit frightening, but she likes us. She's very, very powerful. Procurators and prefects to her are like you and me to procurators. If you're brought in, you must lie down on the ground before her, and then get up again, and be very quiet unless she asks you a question, and if she asks you a question, you must answer it honestly and at once. We want her to help your Daddy, darling, so you must be very, very good in front of her. Do you understand?"

Meletios nodded, wide eyed. "She's more powerful than Eulogios?" he asked.

"Much more powerful."

"Eulogios is very bad!" the little boy burst out. He began to tremble again. "He had them hit Daddy — and he was all covered in blood, and he was crying, and they kept asking me and asking me about that cloak, and they said they would kill Daddy if I didn't tell them what color it was, but I didn't know, Mama, I didn't!"

"Hush," Demetrias told him, and began to rock back and forth to calm the child. But the image of Symeon, covered in blood and crying, took a horrible life in her mind, and even as she rocked she felt the sick fear seize her. Symeon, crying? Symeon! Dear God, what had they done to him? What would they do?

The image of her husband in pain was an anguish in itself, filling her with a helpless rage so great that she realized with a shock that she would prefer to endure the torture herself rather than to picture him enduring it. *Oh, Symeon, you idiot!* she thought. *Why did you go anywhere near Eulogios? Oh my poor darling. Please God, let Pulcheria help him!*

She rocked Meletios until he was calm, then cleaned his dirty, tear-streaked face in the fountain, sat him down on the rim, and managed to get from him a coherent account of the day's events. He was just finishing this when Theonoe returned with the expected summons to attend the empress.

Pulcheria was in the blue reception room again, and back in her black cloak. She was dictating a letter to one of her lady secretaries when Demetrias was admitted, but she stopped at once and dismissed the secretary with a nod and a wave of her hand. Demetrias paused while the secretary closed her tablets, bowed, and left, then came forward and made the prostration. She was more aware of Meletios behind her than she was of the empress; the child lay down as she'd told him, then jumped up and stared about himself with keen interest. Demetrias rose more slowly, just in time to catch the slight twist of a smile on Pulcheria's lips at the sight of the little boy gaping at her palace.

"So this is your son," said Pulcheria dryly. "I am not quite clear on how he came here. Tell me."

Demetrias took a deep breath and told the empress what Meletios had just told her. Pulcheria sat impassively through the narration, her eyes hooded and her strong thin hands hooked clawlike on the arms of her throne. When Demetrias had finished, the empress gave a long sigh. "Your husband is a fool," she told Demetrias shortly.

Demetrias bowed her head. "He was a fool, to go near Eulogios' house. But, Mistress, he wanted to see me; my son wanted to see me, and urged him on. He had some plan to gather information from the slaves without revealing who he really was — and in the end, he didn't go in at all. Please, Mistress, don't hold it against him."

"It was my fault!" Meletios volunteered, in a painful whisper, forgetting his mother's instruction to remain silent. "I wanted to see my Mama, and I thought she was there."

"He was a fool even to leave Tyre!" declared Pulcheria impatiently. "Marcianus had left a man there to take charge of your affairs. This fellow was quite willing to be of assistance, but was unable to act in time: he apparently promised your husband to follow Eulogios here and see what could be done for you. He arrived six weeks ago — oh yes, Marcianus has written to me about you, telling me all this and offering to buy you back. His oath worries him, it seems — What did your husband think he could accomplish that Marcianus could not?"

*Perhaps Symeon was a fool*, thought Demetrias, *but what right has anyone to reproach him with it now, now when he's suffering torture for it?* "Why should he have believed Marcianus?" she demanded sharply, looking up and meeting Pulcheria's eyes. "Marcianus was gone, and if he left anyone in Tyre, that man was no help to us when he was needed. Symeon believed what every slave has to believe: that he can put no reliance on any master, and must trust to his own strength for safety." Then she bit her tongue, trying to revoke the bitterness of the words. But Pulcheria seemed pleased by this plain speaking.

"It seems to me your husband trusted his own strength rather more than it warranted," she observed, "but I suppose he had no option, if he wished to see you again. And it would appear that he was as devoted to you as you to him, since he was willing to sail so far and risk so much to fetch you home. I suppose that, if he had gone directly to Marcianus, I would have been impressed enough by your mutual devotion to give you back."

Demetrias gazed at the empress eagerly, her heart pounding. Meletios took a step forward and caught his mother's hand. He waited impatiently for his mother to say something, to ask for his father's freedom. But Demetrias said nothing, merely watched her mistress' face in an agony of hope. Pleading was pointless. Pulcheria's use of her power could never be forced.

The weary eyes blinked at her in their hollows of bone; the mouth twisted slightly, a fleeting expression that was neither a smile nor a scowl. "You expect me to intervene to free your husband," said Pulcheria.

Demetrias bowed down to the ground and knelt there, still watching Pulcheria. "Mistress, I only pray for your kindness to save us. Prayer is all I have to sway you, and all I can offer in grateful thanks."

Pulcheria sighed. She began to shake her head, then made an angry, impatient movement of one hand. "Girl, I can't," she said. "I would like to, but I can't."

Demetrias stared up at her in anguished disbelief. Meletios took another step forward, then stopped, looking at his mother, not yet understanding that they had been refused.

"You are not stupid, and you have some knowledge of what business we have been conducting here," said Pulcheria deliberately. "Think for a moment. My intention is to get rid of my brother's chamberlain. My brother is weak-willed and merciful. Chrysaphios has a stranglehold on him: no one can come near him, not even me, without passing through the chamberlain's office. If I went to my brother with the evidence Nomos has given me of the chamberlain's crimes Chrysaphios could not stop me — but he would know. Much of what Nomos told me is hearsay, unsubstantiated: the convicting evidence is in the hands of Chrysaphios alone. If he knew what I was doing he would destroy it at once. Then he would stage some elaborate repentance for the crimes of which he was indisputably guilty, shedding tears and pleading, and my poor brother would forgive him and reinstate him. And after that, you can imagine what would happen to those of us who had plotted against him.

"However, there should be one opportunity to catch him. Nomos was master of the offices until last spring: he made many contacts among the barbarians, and many of his agents among the Huns have remained loyal to him and not to his successor. From these agents, Nomos has learned that our bold chamberlain has bribed a man to assassinate King Attila. I find nothing objectionable in that, except that Chrysaphios apparently exercised his usual bad judgment, and picked the wrong man for the job: Attila has been told everything. He should be sending an envoy to the court very soon, certainly within this next month. There will be a scene, of course, and accusations, and Chrysaphios will no doubt be relieved of his duties while the envoy is actually at the palace, and, again no doubt, will be back in his office as soon as the envoy is pacified with money and sent home. But while he is out of office, I can act. Then I must prove my case so certainly that even my brother will have to have Chrysaphios deposed and exiled as a danger to the state. Do you see? We must wait until then, and we can do nothing to disturb things before that moment comes. Chrysaphios suspects what I've done about Nomos, but he doesn't know, and he certainly has nothing to accuse me with, nothing he could use to forestall me. For the success of our plan I must not change that."

"But Symeon knows about the cloak!" Demetrias exclaimed, angrily. "I told him — he knows everything about it. Surely . . ."

"Of course he knows! I understood that from Marcianus. But what he knows isn't evidence. One slave from Tyre says under torture that there was a purple cloak sent to Nomos — what use is that? Nomos' house has been searched, and no such cloak was found. No one will look twice at the slave's evidence. However, if the slave says under torture that a purple cloak was made, and if that same slave is then seized by the Augusta who conducted the first search of Nomos' house — that puts a very different complexion on the matter. Chrysaphios could demand that my palace be searched, and, if I refused, could petition my brother to strip me of my titles and rank under suspicion of treason."

"You're telling me to accept that my husband must die by torture," said Demetrias in a choked voice. "Mistress, surely something . . ."

"Girl, I have an empire to worry about! I can't jeopardize the government of hundreds of thousands of people for a silk weaver's husband! I'm sorry, but he must be left to his fate."

Meletios had cried so much that day that he had no tears left. He stood motionless, looking silently at the empress. Demetrias cried: the sobs she could stop, but the hot tears fell against her will. She wiped them away angrily. *I knew as well as Symeon did that I could place no reliance on any mistress*, she thought. *Slaves are all expendable. But I will not abandon Symeon, not while he's still alive. If Pulcheria can do nothing, I will see what I can do, with my own strength alone. It surely won't spoil her plan if a Tyrian silk-weaver sets out privately to free her husband.*

"You have your son, at least," Pulcheria said, more gently. "I give you permission to keep him here, for the time being. When he is older you'll have to move out of the palace with him, but for now he may share your own cubicle and receive rations with the other slaves. No doubt we can find some suitable work for him. Now go and tend to him. You may have the rest of the day off."

Demetrias made the prostration in silence and left, leading Meletios. Pulcheria watched her go regretfully. *I told the girl too much*, she thought. *Carried away by sentiment, and at my age, too. But I did want to help her. Poor thing — abused and disregarded by everyone, myself included. And yet, she's able and intelligent, and is capable of much more than she's ever been allowed. I wanted her to understand why I answered as I did. They must have been a pair, she and her husband — but what a fool the man was, to walk straight into Eulogios' hands! Holy Mary, Mother of God, support him in his time of trial, and bring him at last to your joy.*

Pulcheria crossed herself, then clapped her hands to summon back her secretary with her interrupted letter.

It was late in the afternoon when Demetrias left the audience with Pulcheria, but most of the palace staff were still at work, though a few were already gathering for prayers. She took Meletios to the kitchen and begged some bread for him, then took the little boy back to her own room and told him to sit down on her bed. He looked up at her in anguish. "Is Daddy going to die?" he asked.

She kissed him. "My darling," she said, gently, "I don't want him to. But if he's going to live, we'll have to be the ones to save him, because the empress can't."

"I didn't understand why," he whispered.

"Never mind. Don't think about it, and don't tell anyone else what she said, because it's very, very secret. But she can't save your Daddy. And because she can't, I have to try. Meli, I want you to stay here for a little while without me. Can you still be brave?"

He stared at her in fear. "Don't go away!" he whispered. "Don't leave me alone; don't go to Eulogios' house, please, Mama, please don't!"

"I want to see Marcianus," she told him. "Not Eulogios, darling, Marcianus. Daddy asked him to help before, and from what the Augusta said, he really wanted to. Maybe he can help us now. I . . . I have an idea, Meli. It's the only chance we have of saving your father."

His face crumpled, and he hugged her fiercely. "I don't want to be left alone!" he wailed.

"Hush, darling." She stroked his hair. "I promise you, I'll just go to Marcianus' house. It's only a couple of miles away, and it's nowhere near where Eulogios is. I'll tell Marcianus my idea, and maybe . . . maybe when you wake up tomorrow morning we can all be together again, as though all of this were just a bad dream. Try to think it was just a bad dream, my love. Have something to eat, go to sleep, and I'll be right here in the morning."

He was a thousand miles from home, and his father was being killed somewhere. It was not a bad dream, it was true: the world was a fearful and horrible place and could not be trusted with love, and the people he had thought were strong and wise had been proved helpless to protect themselves, let alone him. To part from his mother even for an instant was terrifying. But somehow, he could not hold her. It was his father's life at stake and he recognized, without understanding how or why, that she was inexorably bound to do everything she could to save it. He raised his face to hers earnestly. "Promise you'll come back?" he asked.

"I promise you. Now you be a good boy and lie down. There's a chamberpot under the bed if you need it, and if you're very frightened tonight you can knock on the next cubicle. The woman who sleeps there is called Agatha, and she's a silk sorter. She's a nice woman; she doesn't have any children of her own, and she'd like to look after you for a little while. Nobody in the palace will hurt you, so you'll be quite safe, darling. I'm going to leave now, while the staff are all at prayers. I'll put out the lamp and if anyone knocks, you pretend to be asleep."

"What if someone asks me where you are?"

"Then you must tell them the truth. No one will hurt us, darling, you don't need to be afraid. But if they knew I was going they'd try to stop me, and it's better if you don't talk to anyone before morning. Can you be very brave now?"

Meletios nodded uncertainly. Demetrias picked him up and kissed him, almost angrily, then set him back down, stroked his hair, and silently, resolutely, left the room.

Marcianus had a house near that of his employer, Aspar, in the region of Constantinople called the Psamathia, the Sands, near the great fortress of the Golden Gate. Aspar's mansion took up the whole of the opposite block; Marcianus' house was a far more modest establishment, one of a row of large townhouses belonging mainly to army officers whose troops were stationed in the region. He had lands elsewhere, and was away from Constantinople more than he was in it, but he still considered this house his proper home. His sixteen-year-old daughter, his youngest and only living child, lived there, and she and the housekeeper managed it and the ten slaves in his frequent absences. His wife had managed it before her death: she had chosen the pictures that hung about the walls, picked the cheerful red-and-blue carpet for the reception room, and planned the small formal garden at the back, planting the low hedges of rosemary and sweet lavender with her own hands. Marcianus liked to sit in that garden in the evenings when the day's work was over, listening to the crickets sing above the raucous sounds of the city beyond, in the scent of the herbs and the charcoal from the evening fires. Despite the cold of the early spring evening, he was sitting there, wrapped in his cloak, when one of his slaves appeared to tell him that a young woman had knocked on the door and urgently demanded to see him.

Marcianus sighed, reluctant to leave the peace of the garden. "What does she want?" he asked.

"She says it concerns the purple-fisher Symeon, Master," the slave said apologetically. "She said you would want to see her."

Marcianus started. "And she's right. Where is she? The reception room?"

At the slave's nod, he went directly there.

Demetrias stood quietly on the center of the blue-and-red carpet, looking at the pictures on the wall, which showed warm and vivid by the light of the rack of lamps. Marcianus recognized her instantly and paused in the doorway; she looked away from the pictures and met his eyes. Her face was still and determined — *like a soldier's*, he thought, surprised at it, *before a battle.*

"Your name is Demetrias," he said, going on into the room. "I am pleased to see you here. Does your mistress know that you've come?" He indicated one of the cherrywood couches to her and seated himself on another.

She shook her head, ignoring the invitation to sit. "If my mistress knew that I was coming, she would have stopped me," she told him evenly. "But I learned from her that you're still trying to fulfill the oath you swore to my husband. I've come to ask you to do just that."

He hesitated, his heart sinking. So, she did want to rejoin her husband, after all. But she belonged to the empress he had sworn to serve. "I cannot steal you from her, if that's what you want," he said, unhappily.

"It isn't," she replied sharply, then paused before saying, slowly, "I learned this afternoon that my husband has come here to Constantinople by himself, after sailing from Tyre in his fishing boat with just our little son. He meant to go to you and force you to keep your oath."

Marcianus stared at her in astonishment; Demetrias nodded, and went on steadily. "But he went first to the house of the agent Eulogios, intending to discover my own whereabouts, and he has been captured."

"Dear God," he whispered — then, as the implications struck him, he added urgently, "has he . . . told them anything?"

The woman's face remained calm, but her voice took on an edge of anger. "He would have said nothing — nothing but lies to mislead them. But when Eulogios questioned him, he found a piece of parchment, signed by you, promising your protection. They know now that you're involved, and they know that it concerns the cloak. They're having Symeon tortured as a spy, trying to make him tell them everything."

Marcianus winced and sat still for a moment, rapidly assessing the situation. How much could Symeon tell, if he told "everything"? He knew that the cloak had been purple, and that Marcianus and Aspar had been waiting for it to arrive in Constantinople before moving against Nomos. He knew nothing about Pulcheria's intervention, or what Nomos had told her, or any detail of the plan. After learning "everything" from Symeon, Chrysaphios would have to assume either that Symeon had lied and was still lying about the cloak's color, or that what Nomos had told Pulcheria was not enough for her to act upon: he would worry and suspect, but almost certainly do nothing to threaten the plan's success.

But that success now depended on leaving Symeon — and his own oath — to die miserably.

"I am very sorry," he said, quietly and helplessly.

"Your protection has caused us nothing but suffering," Demetrias said bitterly. "But I have come to ask you to change that." Her eyes, meeting his, were merciless, Justice weighing his oath and watching silently as the balance tipped.

Marcianus abruptly turned his own eyes away. "I am surprised you did not first appeal to your mistress," he said.

"I did appeal to her," Demetrias replied instantly, "and she refused to help me. You probably understand why without my telling you; she's undoubtedly told you what her plans are."

Marcianus winced again, then forced himself to meet the accusing eyes. "I have an oath to her house as well," he told Demetrias quietly. "I cannot betray, even for the sake of my own honor, the safety of our plan and the security of the empire."

"You don't need to!" She took a step toward him, her stillness suddenly transformed into a blaze of passion. "I have an idea — all I'm asking is that you listen to it! I think Symeon is still at Eulogios' house, that he hasn't been sent to Chrysaphios yet. If he's gone tomorrow morning, and if it looks as though he managed to bribe his guards into helping him, won't that keep both him and the plan safe? Won't Chrysaphios simply punish Eulogios for his inefficiency, and not look any further?"

Marcianus stared at her a moment. The fair, pretty face was flushed above the black cloak, the eyes brilliant and hard. It was the face of a young soldier about to lead troops into his first skirmish — or of a volunteer for a suicide mission. *Intelligence*, thought Marcianus, judging her suddenly as he would that soldier, *yes — and strength of purpose, and courage. But not rashness: she's the deliberating kind, slow to fix on something but thorough and unyielding once decided. She's weighed the probabilities and the costs and she's not preparing to strike blindly. If she were a man she'd be officer material. I misjudged her. I should have realized that any woman Pulcheria valued could hardly be a silly girl. And did I really doubt that she wanted her man back at all?*

*But is this plan sensible? She may have weighed the costs, but the price she'd be prepared to pay is a high one — her life, certainly, and mine as well. Yet the basic idea seems sound enough. Are any of the guards susceptible to bribery? She must have reason to think at least one of them is — and she would have come to know some of Eulogios' retainers on the way from Tyre. Perhaps —* he felt his own hope rise fiercely at the prospect: escape from this tangle of conflicting loyalties with all his oaths intact and obligations fulfilled — *perhaps there is a chance.* "What is this plan?" he asked. "Tell me the whole of it, and what it will require: if there's any chance of its working, I'll do all I can to help."

Chelchal was not, in fact, late in returning from his expedition to the Hebdomon; although he stopped on the way back to watch a bear-baiting and a cockfight near the gate, he still arrived at Eulogios' house before dark, only a few minutes late for supper. All but two of the other retainers had taken their places on the bench in the servants' hall, but the food had only just been served. The other retainers were in a jubilant mood. "That spy was rich!" Berich told Chelchal, in Gothic, when he sat down at his place on the bench at table. "He had sixty-two *solidi* stitched into a belt under his tunic! And it's all ours!"

Chelchal looked at him in surprise. "That's a lot of money!" he exclaimed. "When did you find it? I thought he was being left in the storeroom for the whole afternoon."

Berich snorted. "When we told the master's master about the fellow he was out of his mind with joy, and couldn't wait to get to work on him. He sent over one of his experts in questioning right away, though he wants us to keep the spy here, for the time being. Nervous about someone telling the Augustus what's happening if the fellow goes to the palace, I suppose, not wanting to be caught twice in the same trap. We've got to guard the spy, by the way — that'll be shift work, damn the man. Maximus and Athalaric are watching him now; you and I have the second shift, midnight to dawn. Anyhow, the expert set up a rack and gave the spy just a taste of it this afternoon. It was when we stripped him for the rack that we found the money."

Chelchal grunted and pushed his food aside. *Poor miserable fisherman*, he thought, *come so far with his life's savings and ready to take that sweet Demetrias home, and instead he's stripped and racked and waiting for more. And if I share the shift with Berich I won't even be able to tell the fellow his wife's safe without being punished for it: he'd sneak on me to the master. Maximus or Athalaric would've been more tolerant. Why am I always paired with this stupid brute of a Goth?* "Did he say anything on the rack?" he asked Berich.

The Goth shrugged. "Not a word. Screamed a bit, that's all. The expert didn't keep him on it long, though: he just wanted to get him ready for tomorrow. He says it works very well if you soften them up first and they spend the night wondering what happens next. Did you sell the child?"

Chelchal grunted again. He had no intention of discussing what he had done with Meletios, knowing full well that, despite the favor he enjoyed, he would be punished for it.

273

"Get much for it?" asked another of the retainers. "You were away a long time."

Chelchal shrugged and shook his head. "When I'd seen the boy safe, I went and ordered a new cloak made." He grinned, remembering how this was true.

"A new cloak? What do you want with a new cloak?"

Chelchal glanced at his bedraggled marmot skins. "This one is old," he said, seriously.

The statement was so self-evidently true that the other retainers sniggered. "Can you get fur cloaks here?" one of them asked.

"I'll get a good woven one," Chelchal responded easily. "A very fine one, with tapestry. That will mean the same here as marmot skins do among my own people."

"If you earned enough from selling the child to buy a cloak with tapestry, you don't need a share of the father's money," said Berich, eyes glinting greedily.

Chelchal only grinned. "The child was a reward. I captured the spy, not you. Anyway, I wasn't looking to get much for him; I wanted to be sure he'd be well treated. I get my share. It should be . . . ten *solidi* one *tremissis*."

Berich and the other retainers all scowled and shook their heads. "No. It's only seven," one said gloomily. "The expert claimed the biggest share for himself. Still, at least the master didn't take the lot."

Chelchal stared. "That torturer took twenty *solidi*? Just for racking a man who was tied up and couldn't fight back?"

The others nodded gloomily. *Sometimes I think King Attila would be better than Eulogios,* Chelchal thought bitterly. *Twenty* solidi *for torturing a slave, on top of whatever salary the man gets already! These Greeks!* He spat. "They don't know how to value warriors, here," he said aloud. "We ought to get more than the expert; we caught the fellow."

The others nodded again, even more gloomily.

But the Greeks were at least neutral, and Attila was an enemy: anything was better than serving him, even taking second place to a torturer. Chelchal shrugged the matter off and picked up a piece of the roast goat that formed the main course of the retainers' supper — an extravagance of meat unusual among the Romans, but granted as a special concession to barbarian tastes. He ate it without really tasting it, his mind again on Symeon. "That was a lot of money, for a slave," he said, after a moment.

"He probably got it from Marcianus," said Berich. "I wonder if he has any more?"

Chelchal shook his head. "More is too much for any slave."

"But he came on a boat," said Berich obstinately. "He may have left some other things of value on the boat. Some of those state slaves earn a fortune, and spying for a man as rich as Aspar should've been even better."

Chelchal snorted. "You go look at the boat, then, ha! You go sail it!" Berich was no more a seaman than he was himself.

The Goth glared. "You've no right scoffing at me, Hun!" he snapped. "You were soft as an old woman about that child, mooning over it like a granny."

Chelchal just grinned back. "My old granny wasn't soft, Goth, whatever yours was like. The women of the Acatziri are breeders of warriors. Your own people know all about that now. Ha! Why shouldn't I like children? I'm a proper man and I like making them well enough!"

Berich put his hand on his sword, then took it away again. "I've got bastards of my own," he declared angrily. "I don't go soft over them, let alone some brat made by a Tyrian whore and a stinking fisherman."

Chelchal laughed and clicked his tongue. "By my grandfather's head you're a fine one! Nobody would guess that the whore had kicked you in the balls and the fisherman knocked you over with a tavern bench."

"He knocked you over too," returned Berich.

Chelchal shrugged. "So he did. But I brought him down, him and the child both. I got the whole story out of the child. All you did was beat the father, and only after he'd been safely tied up. Which of us is soft?"

Berich's face set. "Are you saying I'd be afraid to meet the man — a stinking slave — in a fair fight?"

"No, you wouldn't be afraid," said Chelchal contemptuously. "That fisherman would be a soft target even with his hands untied; he's probably never held a sword in his life. Though I'd put money on it that he'd mark you first; he was fast enough on his feet. Sometimes,

Berich, sometimes I wish for a good fair fight, myself against . . . another warrior." He met the Goth's eyes and held them for a moment; Berich's hand slipped again to the hilt of his sword and, this time, stayed there.

"I'm sick of hitting slaves," Chelchal went on, very quietly. "I'd like to see battle again. Sometimes I even think I'd like to see how the bola and the bow manage against a sword. That's how soft I am, Goth." Berich remained leaning back in his seat, waiting, but he was beginning to sweat. He had seen the Hun shoot, and he had a deep respect for the bola. Chelchal grinned, his scars twisting, pleased to see it.

"But," he finished briskly, "I'm either the faithful servant of the master and the master's master, or the servant of King Attila. All due honor and profit to torturers: I don't want to oppose them, and I don't fight any of my comrades." He tossed his goat's thighbone back onto the platter and stood up. "I'm going to see to my horse's harness; I'll see you at midnight, Berich, for the shift."

Symeon lay on his side on the floor of the storeroom, staring at the crack of light that came under the door and trying not to move. The joints of his hips and shoulders flared with agony every time he shifted — that was the worst pain, the legacy of the rack. His stomach and groin ached savagely, too, and his face, especially the left side of it where a blow had loosened his teeth, and his knees hurt where he had fallen on them. *Still*, he thought, bitterly, *there's nothing much wrong with me — yet. Tomorrow . . .*

He pressed his forehead to the bricks of the floor, trying not to think about tomorrow. The floor was ordinary, comforting; like the room it smelled of dust, lamp oil, beeswax, and tallow soap, the ordinary contents of the room when it wasn't used for prisoners. Cleaning rags and lampwicks still hung about the walls, and there was a pile of twig brooms in one corner. It seemed impossible that he would really be tortured in such an ordinary place. But Chrysaphios' expert, the pale, hairless creature who had set up the rack so quickly, had whispered possibilities to him as he fastened the lead weights to Symeon's arms and legs that afternoon: the whip and the irons and the fire, boiling oils, castration and mutilation and blinding. *Oh God*, he thought, remembering against his will every whisper, *I won't be able to hold* out. *I'll tell them, and then they'll torture Demetrias, too. Wherever she is. Meli was going to tell me, but they stopped him. My poor Meli. I hope that Hun sold him to someone kind, someone who'll treat him well. Bless the man for stopping his master from turning that brute loose on my son! Anywhere would be better for him than here!*

He closed his eyes. He was exhausted with pain and grief, but fear and the twinges of agony prevented sleep. *What can I tell them tomorrow?* he asked himself again. *I mustn't tell them the truth, and I'll have to say something. They have to believe that Demetrias is innocent: they have to leave her alone.* His mind filled with images — the way the light caught in her hair, the dreaming happiness of her eyes when she was working, the softness of her skin under his hand, and the warm curves of her body against his. Evenings in their apartment, and the scent of fish cooking in a sauce of wine and spices; walking out to the beach with her in the morning, the wind making the waves white and pulling at the cloaks she had woven. *I wanted her back,* he thought wearily. *I risked everything to get her back, and now I've lost it all — and not just for myself, but for her and Meli as well. And probably she wouldn't even have wanted to come home! Whatever happened to her on her journey, she's been safe for months now. She must be Chrysaphios' slave, with a good place in his house. She's sure to be valued there — anyone would value her, if only for her skill. Probably she's been happy. She never loved me. I could never give her anything she wanted, and I took what she hated to give. I came to fetch her for my sake, not hers; because she was mine — only she was never mine, never in any way that counted. I married her, slept with her, lived with her, had a son with her, but it never counted, it never reached her: I could never really say even that I knew her. And now I've arrived to destroy everything for her again. Oh God, I mustn't. What can I tell them instead?*

*Lord of All, Eternal Christ, I don't ask for my freedom or even my life — only the strength to find a good lie and hold on to it, and keep my wife safe.*

There was a tramp of feet outside the door, and a few words exchanged in Gothic: his guards were being changed. The new guards settled themselves with grunts before the door; one of them rapped on it. "You there?" he asked. It was the Hun's voice. Symeon pulled himself painfully up onto his elbows.

277

"I'm here," he replied. "It's you, is it, Chelchal? For the love of God, man, can you tell me what you did with my son?"

"He is safe," came the voice, cheerful and unconcerned. "I make sure he is well cared for. Is good?"

"But where is he?"

"What does that matter? He is in the city, he is safe and well cared for. Is good, you rest."

Symeon lay down again, staring at the door. The Hun began to talk with his companion in Gothic, and the conversation went on for some time.

*I can tell them that I never saw the cloak,* Symeon thought, closing his eyes again. *That's perfectly true; I never did. Then I can tell them that I don't know what color it was, that Demetrias never told me; I can say I was suspicious about it because I was jealous of the procurator, that I wanted to make trouble for him — there's even some truth in that. I can say I exaggerated my suspicions to Marcianus to get his help against Heraklas. Will that work? Where's the flaw in it?* He lay quietly, half-asleep without realizing it, inventing complicated flaws in his own story and looking for ever more improbable alternatives; on the other side of the door the voices of the two guards rumbled on and on.

Symeon came fully awake again when, through their voices, he heard footsteps approaching. The two retainers abruptly stopped talking. The light changed as the retainers rose to their feet — and Symeon noticed a piece of parchment that lay on the floor beside him, in the corner of the door. He stared at it blankly. Had it been there before?

"Chelchal," said another voice — Constantinopolitan Greek, upper class and sour, Eulogios' voice — "I've been thinking about what you said just now . . ."

"Oh, yes?" said the Hun, suspiciously.

"I suppose I could arrange a small extra payment, seeing that you got so little for the boy . . . say perhaps ten gold pieces . . ."

"Is not good!" said Chelchal. "I capture the spy with my bola, I by myself. Without me, he gets away. Is good. You give me child to sell. You know I like childs and I will not sell him to any bad men. I sell him cheap, two *solidi* only, for good home. Where's my reward for the capture? The spy has money, much money. That expert, he takes double shares — triple shares, almost! For what? For torturing a man who I catch, who is tied up and cannot fight back! It is a coward's job, a bad man's, a slave's. I am a warrior. You give me the expert's share."

"But he's *Chrysaphios'* expert!" objected Eulogios. "I can't take the money away from him. If I give you eleven *solidi* you'll have earned as much as he has . . ."

"As much, as much! I am worth more! Ha! As much as a cowardly torturer. Is not good. I am a brave warrior of the Acatziri, I capture the spy myself, I am worth more!"

"Worth more to Attila!" snapped Eulogios, losing his temper. "Don't forget, you can be sent back to Thrace if you think you're undervalued here — and King Attila would be delighted with you, though I doubt he'd pay as well as I do."

Chelchal was silent.

"I'll give you a bonus of ten *solidi* as a reward for capturing the spy," said Eulogios. "And no more. Good night."

His footsteps retreated again; the light dimmed as the retainers sat down. Symeon reached out slowly and picked up the parchment. There was writing on it. He angled it so the light fell on it and the words jumped out, black and sharp: "Pretend that you have a great treasure on your boat, and you will direct to it the man who helps you escape. Destroy this."

Symeon read it twice, slowly and mumbling, then stared at it. *It wasn't here before*, he thought, still numb with surprise. *It wasn't here when the expert left. One of the guards must have slipped it under the door. Who? When? The writing . . . the writing looks familiar. Marcianus!* The realization, the memory of the other letter, brought a surge of hope so violent he thought for a moment he would be sick. He shoved the parchment into his mouth and chewed at it, clumsily because of his sore jaw; the bitter taste of lye and ink almost overpowered him. Chelchal and his companion were talking in Gothic again, more excitedly than ever. Their voices rose and fell like waves, Eulogios' name tossed occasionally between them in the sea of unintelligible words. Symeon swallowed the lump of sodden leather. The voices rose, and then the light changed again. A shadow swung about; the other guard got to his feet. With a flare of agony, Symeon sat up just as the door opened.

He recognized the other guard as the brute Berich, who had taken such pleasure in beating him; the man was grinning now. Chelchal was grinning too, and he had out the weighted leather bola and was swinging it idly back and forth. "We have some questions for you, spy," said Berich. The lantern in the corridor outside cast his shadow, black and threatening, into the dark recesses of the storeroom.

Symeon groaned, sitting back stiffly on his heels. "You all have questions," he said bitterly.

"We have some private questions," Berich told him, "which you may want to answer. Where did you get all that money you had?"

Symeon hesitated, unable to decide whether to lie or tell the truth. "What does it matter?" he asked, playing for time.

"Was it all the money you had?" demanded Berich, crouching in front of him. The Goth pulled out a dagger and began trimming his nails with it, a very ugly grin on his face.

Symeon licked his lips. "No," he said, "there was more. What's it to you?"

"We want the rest," Berich told him, and brought the dagger up to his chin. The blue eyes were glasslike, depthless, a few inches from his own. "You could tell us and not the others — and we might be prepared to help you."

Symeon licked his lips again, ran his tongue over the aching teeth. "I kept most of the money on my boat," he whispered. "It should still be there. Three times what I was carrying. More than that."

The Goth's mouth opened, damp and red, the teeth uneven and very white. "A hundred and fifty *solidi*? Two hundred? Marcianus must have been generous."

"Never mind where I got it!" Symeon exclaimed, suddenly sick with fear that this would prove to be a trap. "You can have it if you help me escape."

"Where's the boat?"

"Get me out of the house and I'll show you."

"You can tell us," whispered Berich, his eyes gleaming.

"No. You'd go take the money and leave me here. I'm not stupid."

Berich slapped him on the bruised jaw; the pain launched redly inward. Symeon held his face, blinking; his left eye saw black, then stabs of white light, blinding. "Just tell us where the boat is," the Goth whispered, "or you'll regret it."

"What could you do to me worse than what's going to be done tomorrow?" Symeon demanded angrily. "And Chrysaphios' man won't be pleased if you use that knife on me; he has plans of his own."

Berich sat back on his heels, considering, then grinned again. "Tell me," he said, "and I'll give you this." He held up the dagger.

*Painless death*, thought Symeon, staring at the metal that glowed golden in the lamplight. *Yes, that could be worth two hundred* solidi. *I'd make that bargain — if I hadn't been led to hope for more.*

"The boat's in the Fishmarket harbor," he whispered. "Take me there and I'll point her out to you."

"What does it look like?" Berich leaned forward again, eagerly. "Just tell me, and you can . . ."

There was a swish and a blur of movement, followed at once by a thud of body hitting body. Then Berich was on the floor and Chelchal was sitting on top of him, holding the dagger at his throat.

"Do not shout," said the Hun, grinning. "I don't want to kill a comrade, Berich — but I never like you."

Berich lay half-stunned, staring at Chelchal in disbelief. Symeon saw that the Goth's hands were tangled in the bola. Painfully, he shifted his own weight back and stood. Chelchal glanced up at him, grinning. "You take me to the boat," he said. "Me only. I help you, I get all the money. Yes?"

"Yes," agreed Symeon, bewildered. So had it been Chelchal who pushed the parchment under the door? But if so, why this mime?

"Get some rope," Chelchal ordered, "and cloth for a gag."

Hastily, Symeon looked about the storeroom. He picked up a coil of lampwick — not strong enough to hold a man, he decided, though it might do for the gag. There were plenty of cloths among the cleaning rags, and he grabbed a good one. There was a yard or so of thick rope around a soap vat behind the rags, and he untwisted it and pulled it loose. He brought his haul to Chelchal. The Hun jerked his head at Berich. "The gag first," he said.

"Chelchal," whispered Berich, furiously, "you can't . . ."

"I never like you, Berich. And I never like Eulogios. Worth as much as a cowardly torturer, ha! He doesn't know how to value a warrior. You keep quiet or I make you quiet for good. Open your mouth."

Berich glared wildly; Chelchal grinned back. In the long shadows cast by the lamp he looked monstrous, his misshapen head and scarred face like an ape's stuck upon a human body. Berich opened his mouth and Symeon shoved the cloth in. Chelchal whipped off the Goth's helmet and Symeon tied the gag on firmly with the lampwick. Chelchal at once took the rope and bound Berich's ankles, then unfastened the Goth's sword belt, drew the sword and put his foot on it, and loosened the bola that still held Berich's arms. He tied the Goth's hands with the belt, drawing it so tightly that it cut into the flesh, then sat back on his heels and looked speculatively at Symeon.

"Take his helmet," he ordered, and began coiling up his bola. "Also the cloak. We will go out the front gate in the darkness, and nobody will know who you are."

Symeon picked up the discarded helmet and fitted it over his own head; it was a shade large, but not so it mattered. He pulled off Berich's cloak and swung it about his own shoulders. It was a riding cloak, and stopped short of the knees; Symeon's legs, bare below his tunic, and his Tyrian sandals showed ludicrously beneath it. Chelchal looked at him critically and shook his head. He picked up Berich's sword and laid it significantly across the Goth's groin, then untied the rope around his ankles; Berich did not stir. Chelchal pulled his comrade's boots off, picked up the sword and pulled off the trousers. He handed them to Symeon, then tied the rope again. Symeon put them on, and Chelchal nodded. "You will take me to the boat," he ordered. "Can you ride a horse?"

"I've never ridden a horse in my life and I can barely walk," replied Symeon bitterly.

"We must walk then. Take too much time, anyway, to fetch the horses, maybe we meet people. Come."

Chelchal strode from the room; still not daring to believe it, Symeon followed. The Hun closed the door and fastened the bolt, grinning. "I never like that stupid Berich," he confided. "Come, come quickly."

Symeon came, though "quickly" was difficult: his hips felt as though they were joined with red-hot rivets, twisting at each step. The household was asleep. Along the corridor, out a door, and into a courtyard; the night air was frosty, the stars white in a clear sky. Symeon took a deep breath, fighting tears: this was no time to cry. "Quickly!" urged Chelchal, taking his arm.

They were at the lodge by the iron-bound gates; the Hun rapped at the window; knocked again. After a moment it opened, and the grizzled doorkeeper stared out, bleary-eyed and angry. "What is it at this time of night?" he demanded.

"Berich and I go whoring," replied Chelchal calmly. "Open up!"

The gatekeeper had no idea of the retainers' guard shifts, and he was used to midnight expeditions, though not usually as late as this. He swore under his breath but stumbled out and unlocked the gate. Chelchal and the other strode through; drowsy, eager to get out of the cold, the gatekeeper did not notice that Berich was not as tall as usual, or that he walked stiffly, like an old man trying not to stumble on an icy street. He closed the gates, locked them, and went back to bed.

They walked a block in silence, Symeon setting one foot blindly before the other, drunk on the cold, clear air, and the sight of the free stars above him. Words tumbled through his mind, a jumble of phrases from the psalms sung in the church of Tyre: "Then the waters had overwhelmed us, the stream had gone over our head; blessed be the Lord, who has not given us as a prey to their teeth." *Oh, Demetrias, I'm alive, I'll get you out too, somehow!* "Our soul is escaped as a bird out of the snare of the fowlers; the snare is broken, and we are escaped." *Escaped out of death, out of sure death, into this night, this air, this freedom.*

His hip gave way with a twist of exquisite agony and he staggered; Chelchal caught his arm. The Hun laughed. "It is very good, yes?" he said, beaming at Symeon.

"I don't have a copper *drachma* on the boat," Symeon told him stupidly, smiling back, confusedly — then wished that he'd torn his tongue out. "That is . . ." he began hastily, trying to make amends.

But Chelchal only laughed again. "I know. Is good. Come quickly, now, there is not much time."

More bewildered than ever, Symeon started forward quickly, then staggered again and almost fell. Chelchal pulled Symeon's arm over his shoulder and helped him the remaining blocks down the street and into the marketplace.

It was quiet in the marketplace. All the shops were tightly shuttered, and even the late night revelers were in their beds. The torches by the great mansions burned guttering and low. Chelchal helped Symeon across the square toward a grand mansion; as they stumbled into the pool of light before it, the gate opened and a figure in a black cloak ran out toward them, followed like a shadow by another. Symeon stopped; the black shape paused, looking for the face under his helmet, then hurried forward again and caught his free arm.

"Symeon," it whispered, breathlessly. "Come on, we must hurry. This way; we have a cart."

It was Demetrias — her voice, her face in the shadows of the hood, her body now urging him forward — but how could it be her? He stopped again. "Demetrias," he whispered, bewildered. He pulled his arm away from Chelchal, caught her shoulders and stared into her face. He had come over a thousand miles and through the depths of pain and despair to find her, and now that she stood before him he did not know what to do.

She reached up, linked her hands behind his head, kissed him hungrily, then remained for a moment looking into his face. Her mouth was set in determination and anger, but her eyes were wide and dark, fixed on his own with an intense stillness. His strength suddenly dissolved and he stumbled against her, unable to stand; the tears he had fought off before burned his eyes. "Demetrias!" he whispered again, in disbelief.

"Hurry!" she returned, taking his arm again. "There's no telling when someone may find out that you're gone, and we still have work to do before morning."

The figure that had followed her from the gateway gestured to someone unseen behind him, and a cart rumbled out from the mansion. He recognized Marcianus when his arm was taken, and he allowed them to bundle him into the waiting cart.

# ⚓XI⚓

PULCHERIA WAS EATING her frugal breakfast after her early prayers the next morning when Theonoe appeared at the door in great agitation.

"Mistress!" exclaimed the old woman, hurrying forward and lying down beside the breakfast table, saying, "Mistress," pulling herself up onto her knees again, "your slave Demetrias is gone!"

"Gone?" asked Pulcheria in alarm. She put down her slice of coarse bread. It was early, still, and she was wearing only her black tunic and a pair of black stockings; her gray hair hung thin and limp on her gaunt shoulders. "Are you sure?"

"Yes, Mistress. Her neighbor Agatha was awakened by her son, who is hysterical. The child says she left last night and said she was going to see Aspar's man, Marcianus, but she hasn't come back. The child thinks she's dead."

"Oh, stupidity!" cried Pulcheria, passionately. She struck the table. "Blessed Mary, give me patience! Oh, the fool girl! Oh, how could I have been so stupid — of course she went after her idiot husband, of course she did, anyone could have seen she meant to! Theonoe, fetch Eunomia, and Marius from the corps of messengers, at once! Where's some parchment? I must send to Marcianus and see if this can be stopped — thank God the girl had the sense not to go straight to Eulogios like her imbecile of a husband!"

She had written a brief, imperious message to Marcianus and was handing it to her fastest messenger, when the lady-in-waiting who was acting as chamberlain that morning appeared. "Mistress," she said, after making the prostration, "I have just been informed that Flavius Marcianus is at the gate, with one of your slaves; he begs admission to your Serene Presence."

285

Pulcheria closed her eyes for a moment and gave a less-than-serene snort of relief. "Holy Mary, Mother of God; Holy Lord Jesus Christ, thank you," she said fervently. She crossed herself, opened her eyes, then glanced down at the parchment she held. "You won't be needed after all, Marius," she told the messenger. "You may go back to your quarters and await my orders." He bowed, and she turned to her lady. "Admit Marcianus at once. I will see him in the blue room as soon as I've finished dressing."

Marcianus and Demetrias had been standing in the blue room for barely a minute when the sovereign Augusta swept in, black-cloaked and bareheaded, her thin hair pulled behind her head and fastened quickly; she was followed by her lady chamberlain, Theonoe, and her secretary. The two suppliants made the prostration at once. Pulcheria frowned at them and took her seat in icy silence.

"So," she said, settling herself firmly on the throne, "you are here. Demetrias, you have merited a whipping even if running off is all you achieved — though I fear it may be the least of your offenses. May I know what damage has been done to our cause, Marcianus?"

He bowed. "Our cause has suffered no damage, Empress."

She snorted. "I am profoundly relieved. I hoped that you had too much sense to rush into any unsanctioned enterprises, but I did not dare to trust it. My slave did go to you and ask your help in freeing her idiot of a husband?"

"She did, Empress. She also told me that you had refused to help her in the matter, and indicated why. She then told me a plan she had conceived to release her husband without implicating Your Sacred Majesty, and, as it seemed a good plan and workable, I adopted it, modified it slightly in the interests of security, and we have carried it out."

Pulcheria stared at him, frozen. She looked quickly at Demetrias. "Where is the man?" she demanded, after a silence.

"He is at my house, in concealment," returned Marcianus evenly. "Let me again assure Your Sacred Majesty that I am fully confident that nothing we did last night threatens the security of our plan. Chrysaphios will believe that Eulogios' prisoner bribed his guards and escaped by himself, and will punish only Eulogios. As for the man Symeon, I swore him an oath, and I have done my best to keep it. But I am returning your slave to Your Providence, as I may not steal from those I profess to serve."

Pulcheria gave Demetrias a withering glare, then fixed her eyes on Marcianus. "Tell me precisely what happened," she ordered, "and let me judge the security of it for myself."

Marcianus stood motionless for a moment, collecting his thoughts, then looked up, met the empress' eyes, and began his account.

"Your slave Demetrias told me that most of Eulogios' retainers were susceptible to bribery, but that one, a Hun, was not only well disposed toward herself, but also gravely dissatisfied with his position serving the agent. She suggested that he would be willing to help us if he was sure that he would not be returned to King Attila as a deserter if he did; she said further that he hated the king of the Huns, and was eager to serve in a war against him. It was this same man who brought her child to your palace and told her what had happened in the first place. She said that, at that time, he had asked her to make him a cloak finer than the one she had woven for the king of the Huns, and she suggested that we send a message to him at Eulogios' house, pretending to come from a member of the weavers' guild, and asking for advice on the pattern for the new cloak he'd ordered — a message he'd understand at once, but which would seem innocent to the rest of the household. She intended to take this message herself, but I instead sent one of my own household slaves, judging that I could not risk a woman you had honored with your confidence." Marcianus gave Pulcheria a polite bow of the head.

The empress snorted. "Honored mistakenly, it seems," she observed sourly.

"I think not, Empress," Marcianus replied quietly. "The ruse was entirely successful. Apparently the Hun had already mentioned to his comrades that he'd ordered a new cloak, and certainly he came at once on receiving the message."

"Came where?" demanded Pulcheria. "Were you observed?"

"Your most noble sister Marina had a house on the Taurus market that has stood empty since her lamented death: we met the Hun in the courtyard, and closed the gate. Before we spoke I made certain that the Hun was not followed from his master's house. We were unobserved."

"Marina's house?" Pulcheria asked in surprise. "How did you get in?"

Marcianus coughed behind his hand. "I picked the lock — I learned the trick from a petty thief in a Vandal prison in Africa; it's proved useful on occasion."

Pulcheria looked at him with an expressionless face. "I see," she said at last. "Very well, and you succeeded in convincing this Hun to help you?"

"Indeed, Empress. I convinced him that no enemy of Attila ought to serve Chrysaphios, whose policies support the king of the Huns, and I offered him a reward and a position as my own retainer if he abandoned Eulogios — in fact, he's a valuable man and I'm pleased to get him. I had not entirely trusted his good will, however, and I'd posted one of my archers on the roof of your sister's house, in case the Hun proved unreliable. I was pleased that the precaution was unnecessary."

Demetrias, who had been watching her ally, looked away. She remembered the long nightmare in that courtyard, waiting silently in the bright moonlight beside the dry fountain while Marcianus and Chelchal argued, horribly aware of the concealed man waiting to kill the Hun if he declined to help. Marcianus had insisted on the archer. "I may have to let your friend know that we expect to get rid of the chamberlain," he'd said. "I cannot let him go back and report as much to his master." And she had accepted it. *Power makes you callous,* she thought now, looking at the impassive face of the empress. *You don't just agree to pay for what you want; you're willing to have other people pay, too. I wouldn't have done it for anyone but Symeon — but that would have been no consolation to Chelchal. Well, he agreed to help — thank God! Could I have lived with myself if he hadn't?*

"We learned from the Hun," Marcianus was continuing, "that Chrysaphios had already sent an expert torturer to question the purple-fisher Symeon, but apparently had no intention of moving him to the Great Palace, afraid that someone would detect the illegality of the proceedings if he did. Eulogios' own retainers were to guard the prisoner in pairs; the Hun and a Goth had been allotted the second shift, midnight till dawn. Your slave urged the Hun to pick a quarrel with his master over money, so as to establish prior cause for his desertion, and to suggest to his comrade that they ask their charge whether he had any funds. This task was apparently made easier by the fact that the prisoner had already been discovered to have a considerable amount concealed on his person, and the Goth was greedy. I wrote the prisoner a note which the Hun secretly passed on to him, telling him to pretend that he had an immense treasure

288

concealed on his boat with which he could reward the man who freed him, and this he accordingly did. The Hun then assaulted the Goth, tied him up, gagged him, and left him in Symeon's place, ready to tell his master that the Hun had deserted in exchange for some money that had been left on a boat in the Fishmarket harbor. Symeon himself left the house in the Goth's cloak and helmet and walked as far as the Taurus marketplace, where we had a cart for him. We'd thought he might be unable to walk, and indeed he couldn't have gone much farther."

*He had been used appallingly,* Demetrias thought, with a flicker of the anger she had felt then. She remembered him stumbling across the marketplace, leaning on Chelchal like an old man leaning on a grandson; remembered his face staring into hers for that long moment in the moonlight. It was swollen with blows, and his beard was matted with blood; he stank of vomit and filth. When she had helped him into the cart he had lain very still on the straw that filled it, shivering with pain at each bump. Between anger at the way he'd been made to suffer and anxiety about the rest of the plan, she hadn't known what to say to him. It was not the triumphant joyful meeting she had dreamed of.

"This was all your idea?" Pulcheria asked Demetrias.

"Yes, mistress," she replied quietly.

The empress watched her a moment with narrowed eyes, one finger tracing the spiral carving on the arm of her chair. "And does your husband have a boat in the Fishmarket harbor?" she asked.

"He did, mistress. There was no treasure on it, of course: the money the retainers found was simply the savings he'd brought with him to pay for our journey back to Tyre. But I thought it would help the appearance of the thing if Eulogios knew the boat had been there, and was gone."

"And is it gone?"

"Yes, mistress. We went straight to the Fishmarket harbor, and one of his honor Marcianus' slaves helped Symeon take it out into the Horn."

Marcianus smiled. "Symeon left our cart half a block away first," he put in, "and went down to the harbor with just the Hun: the guards at the Fishmarket gate will remember them. Then the two made a great show of searching the boat, which many of the people

289

in the neighboring houses will have noticed; and they left the super-structure of the boat littering the beach, together with some oddments belonging to it. When the fisherman took the boat out to sea, the Hun returned to the cart through the gate, carrying a large box, which contained, in fact, merely clothing from the boat."

Demetrias remembered that moment well; Chelchal's reappearance, cheerful as ever, to hand her a selection of her own clothing from Tyre. "But it is a very *small* boat!" he exclaimed to her as they jolted back across the city. "Small, small! I do not want to sail up the Horn in that. He sails all the way from Tyre?"

"Symeon sailed about the city to the Harbor of the Psamathia on the other side," Marcianus continued. "This harbor, as Your Wisdom is no doubt aware, has been little used since your sacred brother's improvements to the Eleutherian harbor nearby; it is also near my own house. My slaves were waiting not far from it in a larger fishing vessel they had borrowed from my patron earlier in the evening, on the pretense of doing some overnight fishing. Symeon and his assistant transferred into this, and his own boat was filled with stones, holed, and allowed to sink in the deep water."

And Demetrias remembered that, too, though she had not seen it. Vivid in imagination, *Prokne* slipped silently beneath the black water, only a rush of white on the surface of the sea marking her descent. Symeon had wept; he was still in tears when the others brought him ashore and put him back in the waiting cart. "She was a good boat," he said angrily. He did not say that he had loved her; he was ashamed to confess love for sixteen feet of cedarwood, rope, and paint. But Demetrias remembered how he had painted her, his hand tenderly touching up the decoration on the sternpost, how he had sailed her, taking pride in turning her across the wind and sending her skipping over the waves. She had touched his hand in the gray half-light of dawn, silently begging him to understand. It had been important that Symeon and his boat disappear without trace, so that Chrysaphios, unable to find them, would have to assume that they had sailed beyond his reach.

"We then returned to my house," Marcianus said, as he finished. "I had the fisherman made comfortable and rewarded the Hun for his assistance, then at once set out for your palace to return your slave to you and to set before your sacred judgment all that I have done."

Pulcheria sat in silence for a moment, frowning. "How long was this purple-fisher in the city before Eulogios captured him?" she asked.

"He had arrived only the night before," Marcianus replied, with satisfaction. "Chrysaphios will be able to establish quite clearly that he had spent the night at the Fishmarket harbor, and had had no time to contact anyone in the city. The Hun told no one of his own visit here the following afternoon. There will be no evidence whatsoever connecting him to any of us."

Pulcheria grunted and sat silent for another minute. "It was well planned and well executed," she said at last. "I believe you are right to be confident, Marcianus. It will deceive Chrysaphios."

He bowed.

"It still seems to me, however, that it was an unwarrantable risk."

"There was no risk to the state, Empress. My name had already been mentioned in connection with the purple-fisher, and, had we been caught at any stage, the plan would have rested on my authority alone. I did not involve any of my employer's people, let alone any of Your Sacred Majesty's."

"Except Demetrias. Who knows more than she ought to."

"She would not have been captured, Empress," Marcianus said quietly. "If that had been imminent, I would have killed her."

Demetrias stared at him a moment in shock, remembering suddenly how he had kept within easy reach of her every moment of the long night, how companionably he had waited next to her at the dry fountain. She shivered.

Pulcheria blinked, studying Marcianus. "And how would you have settled *that* with your oath?" she asked.

He bowed his head and made a gesture of surrender, opening both hands. "Empress, it could not have been settled with my oath; it would have left me guilty of perjury and murder. And not to do it would have contradicted my oath of loyalty to your sacred house, and left me a traitor, and, again, a perjurer. My oaths and loyalties have contradicted each other often, of late. Seeing this, I resolved that I would guard my private honor as well as I could, but that, where it conflicted with the public good, I must sacrifice it. The monks are right when they claim that in public life no one can keep free of sin. The world is corrupt, and no one who tries to keep himself sinless can hold power in it. And yet, how can anyone who cares for justice

291

leave all power to those he knows are wicked, who rule corruptly and inflict ruin and death upon the innocent? I thought I was bound to do as well as I could, and trust God to look to my heart's intention and judge me fairly."

"Well said," she replied softly. She sat for another moment watching him with narrowed, assessing eyes, then said, briskly, "Your house may be searched. As you observed, your name was already mentioned in connection with your fisherman, and having lost him, Chrysaphios may try what he can learn from you. You will need to move the fisherman and the Hun elsewhere."

"I wished to ask your august assistance on that very matter, Empress."

She smiled sourly. "I have a house in the city, near the Horn, which I use sometimes when I visit my churches. I will send a letter to its steward at once, and you must make arrangements to transfer your people there immediately and in secret. If you wish, I can arrange for a wagon with a load of hangings for the church at Blachernae to stop near your house and then to stop at mine. It would be a discreet way to move . . . anything that requires moving."

He bowed. "That would be most suitable, Empress. Thank you."

She paused another moment, then said, deliberately, "You said that you convinced the Hun that, as an enemy of Attila, he ought not serve Chrysaphios, whose policies support the king of the Huns. I would like you to expand on that."

Marcianus was taken aback. "I am a Thracian, Empress," he said, after a moment's pause. "I have seen my home destroyed. I hate the king of the Huns and his empire, and I detest the policy of subsidies, which strengthens our enemies. The chamberlain Chrysaphios has given more with less struggle than any ruler of the Romans before him, and I pointed this out to Chelchal. He was easily convinced: the Huns all know how essential Roman money is to Attila's government."

"But to stop paying the subsidies would lead at once to a war with King Attila." Pulcheria objected. "We fought, in the days before Chrysaphios. We lost battles, sir, and thousands of men, and were forced to pay more to keep our provinces safe. If you were emperor, could you really stop the subsidies, and see your own provinces, your home, delivered to the sword yet again?"

"We lost battles by a hair," returned Marcianus impatiently, "and paid the money through laziness, unwillingness to raise more men and continue the struggle. As for delivering Thrace to the sword — the sword has gone right through it. The north of the diocese belongs entirely to Attila, and the middle is waste; if the present policy is continued it won't be long before the south goes, too. Yes, if I were emperor I would stop the subsidies. I would do more: I would close all the markets where the Huns buy our good weapons with our good money, and punish with death any merchant who dealt with them. They can't so much as forge a sword blade for themselves! I would offer good terms, though, to the Huns' subjects if they allied themselves with us. Their toleration for the Huns would soon end when the Huns ran out of money, and they themselves were barred from dealing with us because of Attila. I would recruit a new army, and use the Huns' money to pay it. And we would see how eager Attila was to fight us then! If he could be held even for a few months without a decisive victory or a city sacked, I think he would have a large rebellion on his hands."

Pulcheria regarded him for a moment with a smile. "A very interesting strategy," she said finally. "I would like to discuss it with you further, sir, at another time. But your affairs are urgent now. Theonoe" — with a snap of the fingers — "run and have a cart prepared for the hangings for the church at Blachernae, such of them as are ready; order the driver to start for the city at once, and to call at the most excellent Marcianus' house for some goods to be left at my house at the Horn. Eunomia, I will dictate a letter to you in a moment, and Marius can take it to my house in the city. Marcianus, will you need a fresh horse to take you home?"

"I thank you, no, Empress," he said, bowing. "Might I ask if Demetrias will be staying here? My eagerness to purchase her from you is unchanged."

"For the time being she will stay here," Pulcheria replied firmly. "I will decide what to do with her in due course — but I will change nothing until I have deposed Chrysaphios. You may go."

He made the prostration and went. Demetrias, still not dismissed, stood silently and with folded hands before the empress. She wondered where Meletios was, and if he knew she was safe.

Pulcheria stretched, smiling contentedly; yawned and closed her jaws with a snap. She looked at Demetrias tolerantly. "Well, girl," she said, almost affectionately, "running off was indeed the least of your offenses, and, as I said, you'd deserve a whipping for that alone — but no harm has been done, so I'll overlook the matter. So, you've rescued your precious husband. What am I to do with you now?"

Demetrias looked at the floor, trying to gather her thoughts, which were shapeless with exhaustion and the spent passions of the previous night. "Mistress," she began, very slowly, raising her eyes to the sharp, cynical face of the woman on the throne, "you were once generous enough to confess to me that you took your vow of virginity mostly for the wrong reasons, and only partly for the love of God. But God took you at your word, you said, so that the other reasons now seem pointless, and only the love still matters. Mistress, my marriage was much the same. When I entered it, there was a part of love in it, but much fear, a craving for safety and protection, a helpless obedience to the world's expectations. I suppose then I could as easily have vowed virginity, and taken up a life like the one Your Kindness has offered me. Probably I would have been happy in it; I might have learned strength. But I have been married for over six years; my life shaped itself with Symeon's. I know now that we can offer each other no protection, and that obedience won't help me. But the love has grown. It has shaped me, Mistress, and become the best of me; while my husband lives I cannot abandon him. If I make a cloak on the loom with a plain border, and halfway through someone comes to me and says 'That should have a patterned border,' what can I do? I can't start the border halfway up the cloak. I would have to unpick the whole thing and start again from the bottom. I can't unpick my life: the plain border's there now, and the patterned one can't be put in. I am a wife, and can never take vows as a virgin. And I beg you, Mistress, to restore me to what I am and always will be, and send me and my husband home."

"You can't go home, my girl," Pulcheria said gently. "Your home isn't there anymore. Your husband left Tyre for you, and I think if you went back you would both find that the life you left is gone forever. But I can and will restore you to your husband: God forbid that I should separate what His will has clearly joined. As for strength, I think you've learned it. You must wait until I have deposed Chrysaphios, to avoid raising his suspicions, but then you may leave the palace with your child, remain with your Symeon, and finish your plain cloak in peace. Now go. Your son has missed you."

Demetrias made the prostration and went. In the doorway she paused. "I thank you, Mistress," she said, and the pious and terrible empress smiled at her sweetly as a young girl.

Three days later, Eulogios, sick with fear, went to visit his patron at the Great Palace to report on the outcome of his search for Symeon.

He was admitted to the chamberlain's office immediately, but for once he was not certain that this was a good sign. The eunuch was at his desk, reading a report in an undertone. He did not so much as glance up when his agent closed the door, and Eulogios stood waiting nervously for fifteen minutes while his superior finished reading.

Chrysaphios finally flipped the pages of the report together and looked up coldly. "Well?" he demanded. "You have news?"

Eulogios cleared his throat uncomfortably. "There is no trace of either of them, Illustrious. I've . . . I've offered a reward . . ."

"There is no trace!" repeated Chrysaphios, mimicking him bitterly. "And you've offered a reward! Is that all?"

Eulogios shuffled his feet. "Illustrious, I've done my best. I found where the boat was; I found that they went there, and that the Hun took the treasure from it and went back into the city, while the fisherman sailed off. I've sent messengers to all the nearby cities, asking if either of them has been seen, I've been personally to all the city gates, and asked after the Hun. He at least should have been noticed; people always remarked on him. And the fisherman couldn't have gone far; he could barely walk."

"He didn't need to walk," returned Chrysaphios. "He had a boat. You should have secured the boat the day you secured the man! As for the Hun, what use was it asking at the gates? He was no fool; he knew more than one way to get into or out of a city. He must be halfway to Sardica by now. They travel fast, these Huns, when they put their minds to it, and he could buy any number of horses with the amount your Goth says he was to get from the fisherman."

"I didn't know the boat mattered!" protested Eulogios. "How was I to know he had a boat?" Chrysaphios looked at him unblinkingly, expressionless. Eulogios grew more vehement. "But Illustrious, how *could* I have known he had a treasure hidden on that boat? The fellow told me a pack of lies when I first spoke to him, and then, after we found the paper, nothing! Even your expert couldn't get a word from him! All the information I got, I got from the child — and I only spared the child to please the Hun. And as for the Hun, he was your man; you lent him to me."

"Not for you to ruin, though!" Chrysaphios replied. "You incompetent idiot, you miserly, arrogant brute, I know what your subordinates think of you! You grudge them a bit of money and you lose your ugly slavish temper and threaten them, and it's not surprising that they end up disloyal. He was a valuable man, that Hun, and you'd deserve to be punished if losing him was the only mistake you'd made — and it's not even the least of them! I had evidence to catch the Augusta almost in my hand" — shaking the graceful, fine-boned hand before his agent — "and you let it slip away!"

Eulogios stood still, his shoulders hunched with fear, not looking at the chamberlain. *You left the man in my house,* he thought; *you could have kept him in the palace, where you have thousands of guards instead of just my six, but you left him in my house because you didn't trust your own servants, you thought they might be loyal to the Augusta or tell the emperor. And say what you like, but it was still your man, and not one of my own retainers, who let him escape. Besides, even if the fisherman had admitted that the cloak his wife made was purple, and we were absolutely certain that the empress had suppressed the fact, what good would it do us? It doesn't prove anything. He didn't know anything about Pulcheria. If he'd known anything about Pulcheria he would never have come near my house. Nobody would call the word of a slave under torture enough evidence to catch an Augusta, and Pulcheria wouldn't let us have the woman back.*

But it would not help him to say any of this, so he said nothing.

"You searched Marcianus' house rather thoroughly," Chrysaphios declared after a moment.

"Yes, Illustrious," Eulogios replied eagerly, brightening. "We tore it to bits, as the saying goes, and we shook the slaves up enough to give them a good scare. I'm sorry it wasn't any use. The man himself . . . he gave you no satisfaction?" Eulogios had searched the house the previous day, and had sent Marcianus himself under guard to the palace to be questioned by Chrysaphios.

Chrysaphios snarled. It was against the law to torture a man of senatorial rank, but he had had Marcianus put into the guards' prison and kept him there until the middle of the afternoon without food or drink, before appearing, showing him the parchment Eulogios had taken from Symeon, and threatening him with death unless he told the truth about it. Marcianus, however, had seemed not at all discomposed. "He said he'd given the parchment to a tenant on one of his employer's Syrian estates," the chamberlain told Eulogios bitterly. "He said he had no idea how it came to be here. I said that it was taken from a criminal and a spy. He asked how I knew that the man I took it from was a criminal and spy. Had he been convicted? he asked. Had he even been charged before the magistrates? Who was he, anyway? And why didn't we ask him why he had the paper! He knew perfectly well that I could prove nothing, and he gave nothing away. And it grew worse. Was he himself charged with anything? Then why had he been arrested? He could not be responsible for every sneak thief who had a bit of paper with his name on it. He is a senator, our friend Marcianus, a gentleman, as he reminded me with every third word. My conduct in questioning him, he said, was improper, illegal, and unworthy of the dignity and office that I hold, and he would make a speech about it to the Senate." He slapped the report on his desk. "And he has made the speech, too! He made it this morning."

Angrily, he flipped the report open in the middle and read out, " 'But let that pass. I was released, at last, late at night, and sent home on foot, unattended, like a common beggar. I arrived at my house to find it looted — I use that word as one who has seen war, Conscript Fathers, I use it advisedly. They dug up the bushes in the garden and tore the panels out of the wall, and you may be sure that everything small and valuable was missing. All my slaves, from the kitchen maid to my valet, had been beaten; the gardener's arm was broken. My young daughter had been threatened and subjected to abuse which a girl of rank ought not to hear even by report. And why? Because some unknown fellow who is believed to have been a spy, on what evidence I know not, had a piece of parchment signed by me! Is that now become a crime for which the slaves of a gentleman, a senator of Constantinople, the New Rome, may be tortured? What is to become of us all, if such horrors may be done to us on such impertinent and trivial grounds? Is the chamberlain ignorant of the law? Has he gone mad? Or has he always been mad — mad with the unbridled and insatiable lust for absolute power? Oh yes, I see you are of my opinion on the matter, fellow senators. He should remember that power belongs first to God, and second to the emperor God has chosen, and that he himelf is the slave of that emperor and the servant of the Senate; he has forgotten this. He believes that we are his lackeys, and all the empire his slaves.' "

Chrysaphios set down the report of the speech and looked bleakly at Eulogios. "This speech caused a great sensation," he said bitterly. "The Senate is in an uproar." He slapped the desk with a sudden, passionate violence. "I told you that we didn't have sufficient evidence to charge Marcianus with treason!" he shouted. "You know perfectly well we can't torture evidence out of a man's slaves to use against him unless he's charged! You can pull it off with the common rabble, but never with a senator. You dog, what did you think you were doing?"

"We didn't torture them," protested Eulogios. "We just beat them a bit. The gardener broke his arm accidentally in a scuffle. And you said that I should push the law to its limits, Illustrious; you wanted results. You did say it; I remember it. Anyway, what does it matter what Marcianus said to the Senate? They've hated Your Illustriousness for years, but it hasn't mattered. They're a pack of old fools, and they don't have any authority in the government."

The eunuch glared, his dark eyes glittering with hatred. "That 'pack of old fools' without any authority still comprises all the wealthiest and most powerful men in the empire! It can be dangerous to offend them too deeply — particularly now, with the empress plotting something." He caught a deep breath: the fingers of one hand tensed and loosened on the polished desk top, then pressed hard for a moment against the wood, the tendons showing white. He stared down at the report, then looked up quickly, his face calmer. When he spoke again, he had resumed his usual polished, insinuating manner. "And Nomos made a very similar speech a few months ago. The Senate has voted to send a deputation to the emperor to complain at the treatment of its members, and to demand compensation for them. It is very difficult, even for me, to redirect a whole deputation of senators; and it will be more difficult to explain the situation to His Sacred Majesty if the deputation does speak to him."

"I'm . . . I'm sorry," said Eulogios, horribly aware that the words were meaningless, to Chrysaphios. *I'm finished*, he thought. *I'll be demoted; I'll be thrown out of the agents.*

Chrysaphios nodded. "I'll only be able to manage it by yielding to the demand for compensation at once, apologizing, and . . . telling them that the man responsible for the outrages has been dismissed and punished."

"And that's me," said Eulogios despairingly.

At this, Chrysaphios smiled. The smile frightened the agent more than the anger, more than the glitter of hatred: there was something so unnatural about it that he felt sick at the sight of it. "So it would seem," said the chamberlain softly, "and it would also seem" — he picked up another report, which had lain hidden under the first one — "that you have been guilty of taking bribes."

Eulogios looked at him blankly. He was far from the worst of the agents when it came to accepting bribes. "Not from your enemies, Illustrious," he said, at last, half angry and half terrified. "If anyone has told you that, he lied, sir, he lied shamefully. I have always regarded you as my patron, and worked to please you alone; I would never betray you in the hope of gain from anyone else."

The chamberlain's smile became a catlike baring of teeth. He opened the report. "Yet you have betrayed your responsibilities," he said in a tone of injured surprise, his voice particularly smooth and mellifluous. "You have betrayed the duties entrusted to you by the state. I have here a statement" — glancing down — "from an inspector of the posts for Cappadocia, who says that the stationmaster of the postal station at a place called Naze, twelve miles from Caesarea, had been buying top-quality horse fodder in the name of the state, reselling it at a profit, and feeding the public beasts an inferior diet; he says further that you accepted a bribe of eight *solidi* to overlook this malpractice."

Eulogios looked at him in bewilderment, trying to remember the post station in question. He succeeded and was even more bewildered. The incident had occurred — but it had occurred exactly as the chamberlain had said; there had been no unpleasant double meanings. Eight *solidi*! The amount, the whole affair, was trivial and irrelevant. If Chrysaphios was going to dismiss and fine him anyway, he could not see why it had been brought up.

"Do you dispute it?" asked Chrysaphios, still smiling.

"Well . . . Illustrious, surely . . ."

"I cannot countenance outrages against the houses and slaves of senators, Eulogios, and I cannot permit bribery. I am going to have to ensure that you lose your position and rank — and suffer the penalty proscribed by the law for officials who accept bribes."

Eulogios went white. "But . . . but, Illustrious, that's amputation of a hand! That's never done . . . I've never seen it done to any agent, let alone a *princeps*, you can't mean . . ."

"It's the penalty set down in the law code, Eulogios," returned the eunuch, the smile now one of open and delighted malice. He got to his feet and moved quickly round the desk; he opened the door of his office.

"But Illustrious!" Eulogios hurried toward him. "Please, sir, please, you can't . . ."

Chrysaphios turned and slapped him across the face. He snapped his fingers and his secretaries appeared, quick and attentive as ever.

"No!" Eulogios screamed. He flung himself on his knees. "Please, Illustrious, not my hand, please: dismiss me and fine me, very well, I've deserved it, but oh God, not that!"

The chamberlain reached forward and lifted from round the agent's neck the gold chain on which hung the official onyx stamp of his rank. He swung it about in a circle and then brought it smashing down against the mosaic tiles of the floor. The seal broke in two, and he kicked it contemptuously aside. "I won't be spared if I fail," he told Eulogios in a hissing whisper, "and I won't spare you. I'll at least have the satisfaction of seeing you weep for what you've done, and weep bitterly." Turning to the secretaries, he snarled, "Take him out!"

Eulogios was weeping already as the secretaries carried him out, not loudly, not fighting, but limp — except for his hands, which clutched each other frantically, as if to shield each other from the descending knife.

Chrysaphios sat down at his desk again. *At least I'm rid of that bungler,* he thought. *I should never have trusted him to hold on to anything of value.*

But the thought was comfortless. He was afraid.

*There is still my plan to kill Attila,* he thought. *No one will be able to touch me when that has succeeded. And perhaps there was no cloak, and nothing to compel Nomos to give evidence. Or perhaps Nomos had no usable evidence to give. If there was and he did, why has the empress waited so long to use it? I must be safe. I have the emperor's favor, so I must be safe.*

He settled to work again, but when his eye fell on the broken seal in the doorway he felt sick. The image of Eulogios with his hand strapped to the block suddenly transformed itself to his own image kneeling, head outstretched; to the head dancing bloodily on a soldier's pike. He closed his eyes, but that only made the image clearer.

*It won't happen!* he told himself desperately. *The emperor would never permit it. I won't panic. I can guard myself. No one can reach the emperor except through me, and I won't allow anyone in who could hurt me. I'm safe.*

He clapped his hands to call in someone to clean the floor and got back to work.

# ~XII~

A WEEK LATER, Aspar and Marcianus were at the Hebdomon with the Augusta Pulcheria.

The luncheon was simple, but prolonged. They had discussed Marcianus' theories about the best way to conduct a war with the Huns; the fiscal reforms, now lapsed, of the praetorian prefect Antiochos; and theology. It was now the middle of the afternoon and Aspar sat nursing his cup of wine, looking rather glazed after a lecture on the stupidity of denying the coessentiality of the Father and the Son, while Pulcheria and Marcianus warmly denounced the resolutions of the Second Council of Ephesus, which Chrysaphios had called, and agreed on the absolute necessity of another general council as soon as Chrysaphios and his religious advisers had been deposed. The empress had discovered that Marcianus' views on the relation of the humanity and the divinity of Jesus Christ were, as she put it, pious and godly — they coincided exactly with her own.

"Have you got your house into any kind of shape again?" Aspar asked his deputy, when there was finally a pause in the discussion he could use to change the subject.

Marcianus looked at him, the eager animation slipping from his features and leaving them grim. "No," he said shortly. His house was still a stripped-down ruin inside; in the garden, the torn-up bushes of rosemary and lavender lay on their sides, their hacked roots whitening in the sun. He had moved his family across the road to stay as guests of Aspar.

"I am sorry about your house," said Pulcheria, after a moment's silence. "Chrysaphios must be more desperate than we thought, to be willing to offend the Senate so deeply. But I believe he has given you compensation?"

Marcianus nodded. "But I have yet to use it. That was my wife's house. It would be better for me to buy an entirely new one than to have it redecorated."

"I see. Tell me, sir, was the price you've paid for keeping your oath worth it?"

He smiled. "Well worth it, Empress. The information I bought from the fisherman has already proved its value — to me and my employer at any rate; God himself put the matter in your hands. And if the cost was more than I expected, I cannot complain that it is beyond my means."

She nodded approvingly.

"There remains the question of the woman . . ." Marcianus went on, meeting Pulcheria's eyes questioningly.

Pulcheria laughed. "The woman has been told that she may go to her husband as soon as we have disposed of Chrysaphios. She is waiting impatiently — but at least she waits quietly, which is more than can be said for her child. Are you contented now?"

Marcianus bowed his head. "Thank you, Empress. I know that you value the woman, and I am grateful for your generosity."

Pulcheria snorted. She glanced down at the table, and fingered the stem of her empty wine goblet. "So, now we must all wait for Attila's envoys," she declared, "and then our path will be clear."

"Unless the chamberlain has been frightened enough to destroy evidence," warned Marcianus.

"He hasn't destroyed it yet," replied Pulcheria. She smiled sourly at Marcianus. "I have sources in the Palace."

Marcianus inclined his head in admiring acceptance.

"However, gentlemen," the empress went on, "there remains one question we have not yet resolved — the matter of a colleague for my brother."

Aspar shrugged. "Does he need one, Empress? If we have him to keep the Senate and the army happy, I'm content to take orders from Your Serenity."

"I'm an old woman," she snapped. "My health is bad — and, come to that, my brother was always a delicate, sickly thing. Besides these considerations, I have no desire to risk the appointment of another Chrysaphios. My brother would love to choose some cultured man of letters for his colleague, some impractical philosopher who doesn't know one end of a sword from the other and whose idea of finance is to ensure a ready supply of parchment for the Palace libraries. We need to pick our own candidate for the purple, and the sooner the better."

Aspar grinned. "We, Empress? I believe I was recently ordered to leave such matters to your own august decision. You can tell me whom you've picked, and I'll complain if I don't like it."

"Would your brother accept a colleague chosen by you?" asked Marcianus.

She shrugged. "I don't know. Once I could have told you, sir — once I could have said, yes, my brother will be guided by me. And once I could have said, no, my brother listens to no one but his wife or his chamberlain. How he will receive me after I've destroyed his opinion of his beloved chamberlain, and with the memory of my quarrels with his wife still rankling, I cannot say. However, we must choose our candidate — and if my brother cannot be persuaded to accept him, then I will have to confer the purple on him myself. As you observed, General, there is a way I can do that — though I'd prefer to persuade my brother."

Aspar grinned. "So, to what wealthy senator does Your Sacred Majesty propose to offer her hand in marriage?"

Pulcheria looked at him sternly. "That is the last resort, General! I have no wish to change my way of life, and I would demand that any husband I picked respect my oath. But as for a colleague for my brother, I've picked a man: Marcianus."

Marcianus jumped, sat up straight, and stared at her. Aspar gave him a look of surprise that became thoughtful, assessing.

"Your Serenity chooses well," the general commented, after a moment's silence. "I can hardly object to my own deputy." Turning to Marcianus, he said, "You're in good standing with the Senate after that speech, Marcianus, and the army knows you. The people could be persuaded — you could found a hospital or something. The Augusta is right, and shrewd: it would be easy to do, and profitable to us all."

Marcianus flushed red. "Are you serious in this suggestion, Augusta?"

"Of course I am," she returned impatiently. "Does the idea horrify you?"

His face set. "Empress, when I first came to this city I had to borrow money from a brother officer to buy an apartment. My family is not undistinguished, but our lands were ravaged even then, and they're destroyed now. I've bought more lands since on the strength of my service with your general — but I am not wealthy, and I am still only another man's deputy."

"Quibbles, sir," Pulcheria replied. "You know that the Senate and the army would accept you, and with my help the people could easily be persuaded. It lacks only your consent before I can order the cloak and the diadem."

He said nothing.

"Refuse, if you wish!" she said, brushing the offer toward him with an elaborate wave of the hand. "I can choose another man, if it genuinely offends your conscience, or if you are afraid. But spare me false protestations of modesty and mock refusals: save those for the mob. You have shown yourself a man of principle, but one who is practical and prepared for flexibility; you have demonstrated shrewdness, intelligence, and certain . . . unexpected resources." She gave him a tight smile, her eyes glinting, and he realized that it had amused her that he'd picked the lock on her sister's gate. "I think you would be capable of ruling well, and I believe that I could work with you. I can give you the diadem and the sacred purple, the inheritance of my house, which are in my power to bestow. Will you receive them?"

He stared at her grimly. "The power to direct the state, and the war, as I wish?"

"Once you wear the purple, sir, it is very difficult for anyone to take it from you. Once you have put it on, even I will be unable to check your direction of the war."

He was silent for a moment. Then, resolutely, he crossed himself. "I accept."

One evening two weeks later, Symeon was playing dice with Chelchal. He had played dice with Chelchal a great deal since his escape: there was very little else to do except look out the window. The two of them were shut into three rooms of Pulcheria's mansion overlooking the Golden Horn, waited on by one dour old serving maid, and visited occasionally by the house steward, who was a plump and oppressively jolly old eunuch. The steward knew where they had escaped from, however, and, being an enthusiastic gossip, did at least bring them all the news.

At first there had been quite a bit of news for him to relate: Eulogios' futile search, Marcianus' arrest and release and speech to the Senate, Eulogios' public dismissal and punishment. The Senate, rallying behind one of its own, voted Marcianus the rank of consul, though, as the office itself was full for that year, he would have to wait some time to take it up. And, the steward told Chelchal and Symeon importantly, Marcianus appeared in high favor with his mistress, Pulcheria, and was summoned almost every day to the Hebdomon to consult with her. "She has seen his courage and resolution tested," said the steward approvingly, "and she rewards it — my sacred mistress knows how to reward merit. What's more, she's learned that Marcianus holds the correct and pious view concerning the nature of our Lord and Savior Jesus Christ, and she is a lover of orthodoxy and piety."

"Well, nobody thought he was an Arian," said Symeon irritably. "That's Aspar."

The eunuch gave him a forgiving look. "Of course he isn't an Arian, but he's not an Alexandrian, either, nor yet a Nestorian: he holds the correct faith concerning the relation of the human and divine natures in our Lord's person, and abominates that Robbers' Council at Ephesus which foisted a single-nature heresy upon our holy churches."

"Oh," said Symeon, weakly. He had followed the theological battle even less closely than his wife. The steward, like his mistress, was extremely devout, and, seeing that Symeon was not clear on the theological issues at stake, delivered a long lecture on them. Symeon understood very little of it. Chelchal listened with a wide grin, understanding nothing at all, though he nodded obligingly whenever the eunuch paused. His own people worshiped the spirits of the dead or of the earth, and just occasionally the war god, giver of victory; he had considerable difficulty understanding the difference between ghosts, gods, and demons, let alone the complex distinctions drawn about the incarnation and the Trinity. He found Greek theology admirably unintelligible and often thought of converting, if he could ever make head or tail of it. But this talk convinced him that that day was still a long way off. Still, it was clear that Marcianus must understand it, and that it had raised him considerably in Pulcheria's esteem, and that, thought Chelchal, was all to the good.

But all this had happened in the first week after the escape, when Symeon was still recovering from the rack. Then the house steward had appeared two or three times a day, giggling delightedly over the latest tidbit of news and offering it to the invalid along with a series of vile-tasting potions intended to ease his strained joints. Now there was no news, Symeon was well again, and even a theological lecture was beginning to seem an interesting diversion. But the steward appeared less often and there was nothing to do but pace from one end of the day room to the other, look out the window at the harbor, and play dice with Chelchal.

"Three," said Symeon, calling out his score gloomily.

Chelchal took the dice and rolled them about his hand, then tipped them out. He grinned. "Six," he said with satisfaction.

That was the other irritating thing about playing dice: Chelchal usually won. Symeon got up impatiently and went over to the window; if he held his head at the right angle he could see the Fishmarket harbor. It was a bright, breezy evening; only one or two boats were drawn up on the beach, but the waters of the Horn were dotted with returning sails. A barge was moving down the Horn toward one of the merchant harbors, laden with charcoal; its oars beat slowly against the wind, and it crawled across the gleaming water like a large black beetle. Symeon sighed.

"The wind is good?" asked Chelchal, cheerful despite the abandoned game, calling for the comment that he knew Symeon would make. *The damned Hun is always cheerful*, Symeon thought gloomily. *I don't believe he's ever lost his temper in his life.*

"Set firm from the east," he replied. "They'll have hard work getting the big ships out of the harbor tomorrow if it holds." He turned away from the window: the wind was irrelevant. He didn't even have a boat, anymore. "I wonder how Meli is," he said, even more irrelevantly.

Chelchal shrugged. "He is with his mother at the Hebdomon. I say — *say-yéd* — so already." He had asked Symeon to correct his Greek, and was struggling with the past tense.

"But will he stay there? Will he come to me? A palace full of old women is no place for a boy."

"Of course he will come to you. Your wife will come, too. Marcianus say-yéd so."

"Marcianus also said that the empress thinks highly of her," Symeon told him unhappily. "Will she want to leave the Hebdomon?"

Chelchal could see no point to these continuous and fruitless forays into the future. "Why wouldn't she come?" he asked. "She is your wife."

Symeon leaned gloomily against the window frame. "She was never happy with me in Tyre. Out at the Hebdomon she's got all the work she could want and the favor of an empress besides, with everything that means in honor and power. Why should she want to come back to me?"

"I was surprised when you first said this, that she was not happy in Tyre," Chelchal said impatiently. "All the way to Constantinople she said, 'I want to go home to my husband in Tyre.' That Berich, he tried to use her like a whore; she kicked him and runnéd off. I offered to marry her. 'No,' she said, not even stopping to think of it, 'I have a husband.' And when I telléd her you were a prisoner, she thinkéd of a plan to get you free at once, and carried it out, too. So. How can you say she doesn't want to come back to you?"

"I don't know her at all, anymore." Symeon replied miserably. "I don't think I ever understood the first thing about her."

"Nobody understands women," Chelchal told him firmly. "Nobody ever understandéd women. Don't try."

"*Understood*. Perhaps. But don't you see, on top of everything else I've now made a fool of myself? I set out to rescue her, and she ended up rescuing me. How can she even respect me after that — let alone love me?" Bitterly ashamed, he remembered how the cart had picked him up in the gray predawn at the Psamathia harbor. He had been exhausted, weeping for *Prokne* and for the pain, unable, after the agonizing voyage about the city, even to walk; Marcianus' men had carried him from their boat and tucked him into the cart like an infant. Demetrias had helped them, then sat next to him in the cart. She'd been pale under the black cloak, but self-possessed — and underneath, he sensed clearly, very angry. Except for brief whispers to Marcianus about their plan, she'd said nothing all that night. True, she had kissed him again before she left for the Hebdomon, but what could that mean? And true, there had been a moment when they first met when he had thought — believed — that she'd looked at him the way she never had before, the way he had always dreamed she might — but it had been only a moment, and his head had been dazed with pain and immense relief, and he could easily have imagined anything. "I don't know what to do anymore," he told Chelchal, despairingly. "I've lost my boat and all my money, I'm in debt to one of her friends, I have no way of getting her home or even of supporting her here, and I can't begin to guess what she must think of me."

Chelchal tossed the dice idly in the air and caught them again, frowning. "Do you want her back or not?"

"I want her, of course! Why else would I be battering the question to death like this?"

"So? It is good sense to want her back. She seemed to want you back. Marcianus said she will come. And Marcianus sweared you an oath; he will buy you new a boat, repay all the debt, and see you well settled. So, we play dice?"

Symeon sat down heavily and picked up the dice. There was a knock on the door and he set them down again. The steward bustled in.

"And how are you both?" he asked, in his sweet high voice, beaming at them. "My dear friends, I have such news! Chrysaphios has been suspended from office!"

Chelchal's grin widened to reveal his missing back tooth. "Is good! You tell us everything."

The steward sat down on the floor beside the Hun, quivering with delight. "It's all over the city!" he exclaimed gleefully. "Some envoys from King Attila arrived in Constantinople last night, and were granted an audience with the emperor this morning. His Sacred Majesty received them in the Grand Throne Room in the Magnaura Palace, sitting on the new mechanical throne that Chrysaphios gave him as a present — you know, the one that goes up in the air?"

"I have not see-éd it," said Chelchal, regretfully. "I have hearéd. It is very fine, yes?"

"Oh, King Solomon himself couldn't have had one so splendid! It has gold lions about the base, which growl and lash their tails when the throne ascends into the air; and the gold birds on the lampstands sing. Chrysaphios could have endowed a dozen churches with what it cost. But it is very impressive to the barbarians — begging your pardon, of course. However, Attila's envoys were not impressed. What do you think they'd come about?"

Chelchal and Symeon shood their heads. Like the steward, they'd heard nothing of the complexities of Pulcheria's plan.

"It seems," said the steward, breathless with excitement, "that Chrysaphios tried to bribe one of the envoys who came last year to assassinate the king of the Huns!"

There was a moment of silence; Chelchal fingered his dagger enviously. "But it didn't work," he said, letting go the dagger in disappointment.

"No. He chose the wrong man as the assassin; the envoy told Attila everything, and gave him the money that Chrysaphios had bribed him with. When the new envoys were admitted to the audience room this morning, one of them whipped out the bag that had held the bribe, threw it down right before the chamberlain, and asked him if he recognized it!"

"Immortal God!" whispered Symeon.

The steward beamed. "He had no chance to make excuses, either. The envoy turned at once to the Sacred Augustus and revealed the whole scheme. And then" — the smile disappeared — "he made a vile, vulgar, and sacrilegious speech to the Augustus himself, reviling him and saying he was a wicked slave, to conspire secretly against his master! His master! Attila! As though the Most Religious Augustus were not lord of the world, and God's chosen! Our sacred emperor retired in great distress of mind, telling the envoys that he would speak to them after he ascertained the truth of their accusations. But he has suspended Chrysaphios from office while his conduct is investigated." The smile reappeared, and as quickly disappeared. "Though they say in the city that Chrysaphios will have no difficulty in convincing even the Augustus that assassinating Attila was a good and virtuous plan, and the only pity is that it failed."

Chelchal was showing his missing tooth again. "But your mistress, she goes — has gone — to the King Theodosius, yes? She will say to him all the evil Chrysaphios has done, yes?"

"My mistress has, indeed, been in consultation with the sacred Augustus all afternoon," replied the steward, surprised. "But I didn't think there was evidence . . . that is . . ." He stopped. "You know something about this?"

Chelchal shrugged, still grinning. "Marcianus knows, I think. He knows from Nomos, whose house he helped to search. Is good." He turned the grin on Symeon. "Is very good. I think we will see Marcianus tomorrow, maybe, and" — a pause — "we *will be allowed* back into the city." He grinned so that his scars tied themselves in knots, and, so it seemed to the irritable Symeon, was as pleased with his future passive of the verb *allow* as with the prospect of restored freedom.

However, Chelchal's prediction was correct: Marcianus arrived at the house the following evening.

He did not much resemble the plain and businesslike soldier Symeon had first met in Tyre. He was wearing a long tunic, white and gold, and a white cloak with the narrow vertical purple stripe of the senatorial order; he looked like a Roman noble from an earlier and more austere age. The first thing he did on entering the room was sit down on the couch by the window and put his feet up with an air of exhaustion that was, for him, also uncharacteristic.

"You talked to King Theodosius today, sir?" asked Chelchal, grinning at him confidently.

Marcianus looked at him sharply. "I was present at an audience, yes," he said, with an odd hint of suspicion in his tone. He looked at Chelchal for another moment, then seemed reassured. "Chrysaphios has been relieved of his office," he said matter-of-factly. "The Augustus has permitted him to retire to his house in the city and has given the title of chamberlain to Irenaios, formerly treasurer of the privy purse. The Augusta Pulcheria selected him as the one eunuch on her brother's staff most likely to . . . discharge his duties correctly."

"You mean, he was the least likely to allow Chrysaphios access to the emperor?" asked Symeon sourly.

Marcianus shook his head. "No, actually, just the least arrogant. None of the other chamberlains liked Chrysaphios. As soon as they saw that his power was gone, they all jumped in to reveal some new petty misdemeanor he'd involved them in. I pitied the wretched creature. If I'd had charge of his punishment, I'd have ordered him beheaded at once — the fellow can't be trusted until he's dead — but I pitied him. He wept like a girl, and begged the Augustus not to send him away."

311

"But the Augustus did?" asked Chelchal eagerly.

Marcianus nodded. "He did. He could hardly do otherwise. We gave him evidence yesterday, and it was all corroborated today from Chrysaphios' own files. Embezzlement; acceptance of bribes; extortion of bribes with menaces; sale of offices — that hardly counts of course, though most of it wasn't legal; conspiracy to pervert justice — multiple occasions of that, both to let off the guilty and to punish the innocent who'd offended him; simony; abuse of the Sacred Offices, particularly the *agentes in rebus*; and suppression of information intended for his master. That, I think, was the most damaging of all. He had a file of letters to the emperor from the former empress Eudokia. The Augustus had never seen them. They won't help the poor woman now, but her husband was in tears over them. No, even Theodosius won't keep Chrysaphios now. He's lost his office for good, and his finances will be under investigation for a long time. It's over now, more or less."

"And now we go fight Attila, sir?" Chelchal asked, happily.

Marcianus smiled, but shook his head. "It won't be as soon as I'd hoped. I'd overestimated how quickly the army could be readied: the troops are in a deplorable condition. We'll need a few months to recruit and train some more men before we can risk a war. But, my friend, I could certainly use your help with the training. I'll want you to tell the recruits how your people fight.

"Attila's envoys are still waiting to hear what answer the emperor will give to their complaint. They're demanding Chrysaphios' head, a thousand pounds of gold in addition to the yearly subsidy, and the return of all Hunnish deserters. We're sending some of our own envoys to talk to Attila. We're offering to pay the usual subsidy and not close the markets if he withdraws all his people to north of the Danube and forgets about the deserters and Chrysaphios. We'll see what he says to that! And, at the very least, the diplomats can gain us some time. We're sending Nomos as the chief negotiator, by the way; the Augusta feels that he can conduct intrigues capably." He smiled again.

"Is good!" exclaimed Chelchal. "It is very good. The war will start this year, yes?"

"This year or next," said Marcianus. "I hope next, as by then we'll have more chance of winning.

"However, I did not come here to discuss wars with the Huns; I stopped to tell you that Chrysaphios is out of power, together with all his agents and followers, and there's no further reason for you two to remain in concealment. You probably heard that there was a reward offered for news of either of you, but I've had that withdrawn. Chelchal, if you still wish to serve me, I'm willing to give you the rank of standard-bearer in my troop of retainers; the pay is thirty-five *solidi* a year, plus donatives. Is that acceptable?"

"Is good, sir," said Chelchàl, with his usual grin. "Better than Eulogios."

"I choose my men more carefully than he did," replied Marcianus mildly, "and when I find merit, I think I know better how to esteem and reward it. I am pleased to have you, Chelchal. Well, then, I'll send my second-in-command, Dalmatius, round to fetch you tomorrow morning." He took a deep breath and looked at Symeon. Symeon looked back at him, bleakly and in silence.

"Your position is more complicated," Marcianus told him, after a moment. "Technically you are a slave of the state, and ought to be returned to the factory in Tyre as a runaway. I take the view that my oath to you requires that I ensure that you are, at the very least, no worse off than you were when I met you. Given time, I could arrange it that your procurator took a lenient view of your absence — and I could replace the boat and the money you lost by coming to Constantinople. The Augusta has promised to release your wife and child: you could go home as soon as you've made arrangements for the voyage. However, there is another possibility that I hope you will consider. I feel that your abilities are wasted in a purple-fisher."

"Why?" Symeon asked bluntly. "There are plenty of men to envy me; it's a good job. And I like the work."

"You do not make a very good slave," Marcianus retorted, just as bluntly. "You have, however, shown a degree of courage, resourcefulness, strength of will, and independence that would be of considerable value in a soldier — or, though I know little of the navy, in a sailor. I would far prefer to see those qualities used to defend the state than wasted on a search for shellfish. I could get you manumitted and procure you the captaincy of a small naval vessel. I have influence now, in the new government, and . . . and I have been given to understand that my influence will shortly be established in a high office. The Augusta, you see, feels that she could work with me. I will want men in all the services whom I can rely upon, and I would, of course, promote and reward them as they showed merit."

Symeon was silent for a minute. "I want to go home," he said, at last, wearily. "What do I know about the navy, or people in high offices? You were too high and mighty for me as Aspar's deputy; what would I want with favors from a master of arms — or whatever your promised new title is? I'm sick of intrigues and plots and wars; I don't want anything more to do with the rulers of the world! I want to go home; I want everything to be as it was — and already that's impossible. You said you could replace my boat. Another boat wouldn't replace *Prokne*; I've spent half my life on that craft, and she lies on the bottom of the Psamathia harbor. My wife and child will be released — but I scarcely know what to say to my wife, and as for my child, I was tied up and beaten before his eyes, and whatever he thinks of me now, it won't be what he thought a month ago. And if I go back to Tyre now . . . my God, what could I say to people? There I'd be with my new boat, my wife the property of an empress, a purseful of your gold, and a writ direct from the Augusti commanding the procurator not to beat me! I don't belong there anymore. I'd be a foreigner with my own kind; all my old friends would look at me sideways and not speak until spoken to!"

Marcianus sighed. "You are angry," he observed. "You relied upon me, and I failed you. I am sorry; I am trying to make amends as best I can."

"Oh, I believe you — and I'm sorry about your house, and for the trouble I caused your slaves. But your man Paulus didn't even try to help. He had men and money, but he did nothing at all. He thought a couple of state slaves were beneath him, not worth risking a *drachma* for, let alone any trouble between himself and the authorities!"

"He did not have much time," Marcianus objected quietly. "He did inform me of what had happened to your wife — though his letter traveled more slowly than she did — and he did try to follow Eulogios and ascertain that she was unharmed. I agree that he could have received you with more attention, explained the position more carefully, and done more to help you, and I have reproved him for it — but there was little anyone could have done for your wife in the time available. Will you consider my offer?"

Symeon scowled. Ships of the imperial navy — lean, hungry-looking triremes with their rows of oars flashing in the sun, their sails decorated with dragons and eagles, and their bronze-sheathed prows burnished like gold — had occasionally visited Tyre, and when he was a boy he had admired them enormously. As he grew older, he had learned to scoff at any vessel that couldn't sail against the wind, and sneer at the triremes' shallow decks, so easily swamped in a storm. But at heart he still loved them. They had speed and beauty; they came from another world, more vivid and glorious than his own. As a purple-fisher, the most he could hope for was a seat on the city council — unless he was thrown off as a slave — and a modest degree of comfort at home and respect from his fellow citizens at large. A successful naval captain could expect much more. Yes, but what sort of life was the navy? Months, years, posted away from home; loneliness and long voyages; danger not just from storms and contrary winds, but from enemies — ramming, burning, shooting. He did not want more danger; he wanted peace. And yet, the thought of a captaincy . . . "What sort of naval vessel?" he asked.

"I know very little about boats. There was a type we used to use on the Danube that had a crew of about a dozen, working both sails and oars, very maneuverable: the men used to call them frog-catchers. They were very valuable to a general for scouting or message bearing, because they could travel almost anywhere in almost any weather. There's a kind of boat they use on the Middle Sea, a little larger but looking a bit like them; I think it's called a 'runner.' I was thinking of one of those."

Symeon ran a hand through his hair. He had noticed the runners on the voyage from Tyre — he had admired them. They were a kind of cross between a trireme and a square-rigged fishing boat. *You could easily rig a lateen on the foremast,* he thought, *and sail against the wind; the keel is deep enough to take the strain. Pretty craft, too, with those high prows.* Against his will, he began to imagine owning one, seeing how it sailed, learning the use of the oars: he forced himself to stop. "I don't want to reject your offer," he said at last, "but I can't accept it. I need time to think."

Marcianus spread his hands in the gesture of surrender. "You may have time, of course. There is no hurry. Remain here for tonight — I believe the empress indicated you could stay here with your wife as long as you wanted. The Augusta is sending Demetrias here tomorrow morning, with your child. Talk it over with her, and tell me your decision when you're ready."

It was, in fact, a long and magnificent procession that arrived at the house the next morning: the empress Pulcheria had decided to visit the church she had founded for the Blessed Virgin at Blachernae, and stopped at her city mansion to rest on the way. Symeon, released from the three rooms overlooking the Horn, watched from an upper window as the carriage pulled up in the courtyard, followed and preceded by the glittering ranks of the imperial guard. Chelchal was already gone, collected earlier that morning by Marcianus' chief retainer. Symeon had found himself parting from the barbarian as warmly, and as reluctantly, as from an intimate and long-standing friend.

"You will take that ship from Marcianus, yes?" the Hun had said, shaking Symeon's hand warmly and showing the missing tooth. "Join the navy? You are a brave man, to have sailed such a long way in that small, small boat; it is no good, for you to stay a slave and hunt fishes. I will see you in the city, still; I will come to dinner and teach your son to use the bola. He will grow up a fine brave warrior, yes? Is good?"

"Perhaps," Symeon had replied, grinning back. "We'll see. Good luck!"

*Perhaps*, he thought now, as imperial guards dismounted and stood to attention, and the steward rushed to the gilded carriage door and opened it. *But I don't want that ship in the navy. I want to live peacefully with my family. I wish I believed that we could go home — but I don't.*

The steward prostrated himself on the paving stones as the empress, a strong gaunt figure outrageously splendid in purple and gold, descended with dignity from her carrriage. Symeon remained at the window, watching. After a moment, another old woman climbed out of the carriage, this one dressed in black: the empress' lady chamberlain. The steward rose and began to usher his mistress into the house. Only when the important people had moved off was there another movement at the carriage door: another woman descended, a young woman in a cloak of rose-colored wool. She paused, then lifted down a young child. They looked about themselves uncertainly, then the woman took the child's hand and followed the empress into the house.

Symeon found his throat constricted painfully. It was difficult to move; his knees were unsteady. He turned from the window and went blindly down the stairs toward the magnificent reception hall on the ground floor. *What will I say to her?* he wondered. *Will she have gone into the reception room, with the empress — or will she be looking for me? Does she want this, want me, or does she despise me and has come only from a sense of duty?*

316

She had not gone into the reception room; she was waiting outside it, talking earnestly with one of the household slaves. He stopped at the bottom of the stairs, watching her: the hair, brown and dark in the still light of the interior, the face half turned from him, thinner than he remembered; the body held just so, quietly graceful under the rose-colored cloak, the border of woven flowers draped over one shoulder. Meletios was looking up at the slave, solemn, anxious, and far more familiar. He glanced about the entrance hall and saw his father. The child's face was blank for a moment, registering only a man standing at the foot of the stairs — and then recognition struck and it lit like a torch.

"Daddy!" he shrieked, and tore away from his mother, pelting across the mosaic floor of the anteroom and embracing his father like a storm wave, half hugging, half beating him.

"Meli!" replied Symeon, kneeling to catch him, and standing up with the boy in his arms.

"They didn't kill you!" said Meletios, hugging his father. "Mama *said* they didn't. They cut off that bad Eulogios' hand! He's gone away forever, and Mama said we were all going to be together again! And it's true!" He crowed it like a cockerel at the dawn. "It's true! We are all together, aren't we?"

"We are," replied Symeon. Demetrias had crossed the floor toward him, and he looked at her over the child's head. She looked back, solemnly and unsmiling.

*I've waited for this so long,* she thought. *I've imagined, so many times, what it would be like — and now I don't know what to say. I hadn't realized how much had changed. Am I still the same person as that woman he loved in Tyre? Is he angry with me? I've cost him so much — months of the voyage, all our money, silence under torture,* Prokne, *and I think his pride as well. And the future is still a blank mystery. But here we are together, I and the man who loved me. What should I say?*

"You look better," she told him. "How are you, though? Have your joints recovered?"

"Yes — almost completely," he responded, eagerly seizing on any words that would bridge the gulf between them. "I still get the odd twinge, though."

They stared at each other for another moment. Meletios gave his father a kiss. "You're all better, though, aren't you?" he said happily.

"Yes, Meli, I'm better," Symeon replied patiently, and stroked the boy's hair without taking his eyes from Demetrias.

"I've been manumitted," she told him abruptly. "I'm a freedwoman now — the Augusta had the deed drawn up. She's my patroness now, not my mistress."

"Oh." *The empress' freedwoman,* he thought, his heart sinking. *That's almost a title in itself. The empress' freedwoman — what would a woman like that do in a factory in Tyre?* "What does that mean?" he asked, uncertainly. "If I stayed a slave, would your condition revert to mine?"

"I don't know. I didn't ask." She hesitated. "The empress said that if we stayed in Constantinople she would establish me as a member of the weavers' guild, and I could do contract work for money. She said she could promise me commissions at once."

"Is that what you want?" he asked.

She looked down. She had tried to imagine it. A silk weaver favored by the empress would own a large apartment or small house in the city, together with three or four slaves to look after it; she would take commissions only from the wealthiest and most fashionable of Constantinople's glittering nobility; she would ride in a sedan chair to buy silk from the importers, discussing the prices and supplies with them and the other members of the guild in bored, superior tones. It seemed a way of life so unutterably foreign, so totally different from everything she had been and known, that in all her imaginings she was unable to picture such a weaver with her own face. And yet the thought of being free, slave to nothing and no one, without a supervisor to appease, let alone a procurator, able to accept or reject a commission and design it herself — that was almost irresistibly attractive. "I don't know," she repeated. "It . . . it is hard to imagine being back in Tyre, after so much. I don't know that I could belong in the factory, anymore — though I miss it."

"Marcianus offered me my freedom," he said, plunging in, "and the captaincy of a small ship in the navy. I can choose between that and going back to Tyre."

"Oh," she said, echoing him, watching his face as he watched hers, hungrily and uncertainly. "What will you do?"

"I haven't decided. I wanted to see you, first. Demetrias, did you want to come here? To come back to me, I mean?"

"Yes, of course!" Her eyes widened, vividly green in her pale face. *Surprised?* he thought, not quite accepting it. *Can it be so certain that she's really surprised that I even ask it?*

"Of course?" he asked, testing it, afraid.

"I've been begging the Augusta to send me back to you since I was first given to her. I've wanted nothing else. What did you think I wanted?"

"I don't know . . . to stay with her, to take vows, maybe. Demetrias, I know you never really wanted to marry; you only took me to get away from the others. If I had any right to you I must have lost it by now; I've done everything wrong since you were first ordered to make that damned cloak. You don't need to lie to me. I'm a man; if you don't want to stay with me, I can bear it."

She shook her head; her eyes stung with tears. Symeon's face was set, watching her own in the intense, unsmiling regard she had remembered so often. *Why should he believe I love him?* she asked herself. *I never did before. Why should he trust me, want me, love me, when all I can have given him in the past is frustration and pain? But he does want me — even if it only meant more pain for him, still he'd want me. He's made a generous offer of the last thing on earth I want, but he's terrified I'll accept. He's a fool still, as Pulcheria said — and thank God for it!* "I know I'm bad at loving," she told him, struggling to keep her voice steady, "I know that . . . but I have learned, I could go on learning . . . to love you."

The eyes that met his did not have the look he had always imagined, the calm, smiling stillness. The intensity of the gaze was the same, but the expression was one he had never seen on her face before — and yet it was unmistakably love. He put Meletios down, put his arms about her, and kissed her. There was no coldness, no dutiful resignation; her arms were around him and she kissed back. He pulled away and blinked down at her in wonder. *Why?* he thought. *Why now, when I've done everything wrong? Why am I given for nothing what I tried so long and hard to earn? Chelchal was right: it's no use even trying to understand women. Glory to God and all the angels of heaven!*

Meletios grabbed an arm of each parent and tugged. "I want a kiss, too!" he declared.

319

They laughed, relieved to fend off the tears and the too-strong passion of reunion; and both bent to pick him up and kiss him, so that he beamed at them in proud self-satisfaction: the world was set right again, with two parents and himself in the center. Then there was a sharp clap of hands, and they turned to see Pulcheria's lady waiting disapprovingly in the doorway of the reception room.

"The Sacred Augusta wishes to speak with you," she declared. "Both of you."

Pulcheria was reclining on the gold couch in the reception hall, flanked by her secretary and another of her ladies; the steward stood in proud attendance behind her, and a table laden with fine wine and untouched delicacies was at her elbow. Her mouth twisted in the suppressed smile when they entered together, the child bouncing gleefully between his parents and making the ritual prostration look like part of a game.

"So," said Pulcheria, when they were on their feet again. She looked at Symeon critically. "You're the man who caused so much trouble."

Symeon bowed. "Augusta, I did what I thought was right," he replied, happily because of the immense new happiness. "If I'd had the knowledge then that I have now, I would have kept what I knew to myself — but I didn't, and that I didn't was no disadvantage to Marcianus, Aspar, and the state."

"Meaning me," she finished dryly. "I suppose that's true enough. Well, you have a loyal and clever wife; if you use her badly, you deserve worse than you've suffered already. I believe Marcianus made you a most generous offer for your future employment; I trust you have accepted it?"

"He hasn't decided, Mistress," Demetrias said quickly. "For my part, I can only accept your kind offer if he accepts Marcianus'."

Pulcheria frowned. "And why hasn't he decided? You are offered a choice between slavery and freedom, fellow: do you seriously want to choose slavery, and drag your wife back with you? If she remains in the city, I have employment for her, employment proper to her skill. Do you obstinately intend to go back to your factory, and take her with you?"

Symeon swallowed and looked at Demetrias. "We had a home in Tyre — friends, family . . ." He looked back at the Augusta. *Here I am, arguing with an empress,* he thought incredulously. *And she knows my wife, and my name, and has wishes concerning me.*

More than any of the words she had said, it bore down on him: there was no going back. There could be no slipping into a vacant place in Tyre. He would be unable to bear struggling with the sidelong looks of the other fishers, the distrust of the supervisors, the cautious favoritism of the procurators. Too much had changed, around them and within them, to live the life they had before. They would have to try to make a new life together.

"I suppose we could write to them," he finished weakly.

The empress leaned back, satisfied. "Excellent. You have made the correct decision. Demetrias, I wish to commission a cloak from you at once. Begin on it as soon as you can: it is urgent. You will have about six months to complete it, I should think — perhaps less. It is to be for the man I have chosen as my brother's colleague."

"Yes, Mistress." Demetrias bowed her head humbly. "May I ask if this is to be done with your brother's approval?"

She smiled dryly. "Have no fear, this will be entirely legal, and done on my authority, which is sufficient to guarantee you even against my brother. But no, my brother does not know yet that I've chosen him a colleague. I may have to give the man the title myself without my brother's agreement; if it is necessary to do so, I can and will. Yes. The cloak is to be purple, a *paludamentum*, with two tapestry panels, one to represent King David defeating the Philistines, and the other, King Solomon enthroned in majesty. Keep it secret, girl, until it's done."

Demetrias looked up and met the shrewd, cynical eyes. Pulcheria was amused, fully aware of the irony of what she was doing, commissioning a cloak, another cloak, to be woven in secrecy. Beside her, Symeon was looking obstinate and fidgeting angrily. Demetrias found herself smiling.

"And the measurements, Mistress?" she asked. "How long should it be?"

"You will have to consult Marcianus," replied Pulcheria with satisfaction.

"Marcianus!" exclaimed Symeon.

"He is eminently suitable," replied the Augusta. "Orthodox and capable, and presently much respected by the Senate and the army. I have discussed the matter with him, and he has accepted my proposal." She gathered up her purple robes and rose to her feet, glanced about at her secretary. "Eunomia, find Demetrias and her family an apartment in the city, a good-sized place suitable for a skilled worker and able to contain a loom. Get the loom and the silk she'll need from the palace. I want her to start on this as soon as possible. Demetrias, Symeon, you may remain here in my own house until Eunomia has found you accommodation of your own. Now, I will go to my church at Blachernae and thank the Holy Mother of God for listening to my prayers and casting down the enemy of good government and true religion; but you may remain here, as I have no doubt that you have much to say to one another."

The empress swept from the room, followed by her train of attendants and guards, and left the three of them alone. Demetrias turned to Symeon.

"Marcianus to be emperor!" repeated Symeon, incredulously. "My own patron . . ." He stopped himself. "Patron," he repeated slowly. "I'm using the language now: patron and protégé. The transference of power. I never wanted any of this!"

"I never wanted to touch another purple cloak. But it seems that I will."

"It won't be a bad cloak though, this time, will it?" Meletios asked anxiously.

"No, Meli, it will be a good one," Demetrias told him. But her face was sad. There would be no repetition of the circle of intrigue and violence — but that was no guarantee of safety. Other things might happen: other plots, other wars.

*But I suppose things could happen in Tyre as well,* she thought. *After all, it began there. And even if there were no more intrigues, there would still be the usual risks: lustful procurators; storms at sea to smash boats and drown men; disease; death in childbirth. There is never any guarantee of safety anywhere: we are simply more or less aware of the risks that surround us each moment that we live.*

She took Symeon's hand and he clasped hers, turning to study her uncertainly. "We can get used to it," she told him, "given time."

"I suppose so," he returned. And, looking at each other, equally hesitant, they began to smile.

# WHAT REALLY HAPPENED

## *(and why it isn't in the history books)*

There is a wealth of historical sources for the fourth century A.D.; there is a reasonable number for the sixth. The fifth century is far more obscure: none of the political and military histories written at the time has survived intact, and scholars pick their way through a tangle of poetry, legend, and church history, helped sometimes by a handful of historical fragments as fascinating as they are frustrating. To complicate matters further, much of what the existing sources say is probably wrong, the result of gossip, political malice, or real misunderstanding. The extent of our ignorance may be illustrated by the fact that the Huns — one of the major powers of the century — are variously conjectured to originate in Mongolia, Korea, Afghanistan, and Central Asia, and are claimed as ancestors by both the Turks and the Hungarians; nobody is sure how big their empire was or who was included in it, how they lived, or what became of them after their empire's demise; of their language, only one word survives, and that is probably corrupt. The ground is somewhat firmer in the two halves of the Roman empire — the Greek East and the Latin West. But even where we have an account of events it's often clear that what we know doesn't explain what happened — in other words, that there was something funny going on behind the scenes that we've been told nothing about. A good example of this is Pulcheria's appointment as regent for her brother Theodosius II. I have given what seemed to me a likely explanation for a surprising fact, but it is, necessarily, pure conjecture.

A similar fog of doubt and mystery clings to the last years of Theodosius II. Chrysaphios and Nomos were historical figures, both said to be highly influential after the empress Eudokia's exile; Chrysaphios seems to have fallen from grace in the spring of A.D. 450, but Nomos' name continues to appear in the annals of the years that follow. Theodosius II broke his back in a riding accident in July 450; on his death a few days later, his sister Pulcheria bestowed the imperial diadem on Flavius Marcianus, later confirming the gift by a formal contract of marriage, which gave the new emperor the immense hereditary prestige of the Theodosian house. One of Marcianus' first acts was to order the execution of Chrysaphios.

That Nomos quarreled with Chrysaphios and plotted a coup d'état, is, like most of the intrigues in this book, entirely my own invention. (The plot to assassinate Attila is an exception; that happened, and is recorded in a fragment of Priscus.) The most I can say in defense of this liberty is that nobody knows what really happened, and that what we do know hints at factions and intrigues that are buried forever in oblivion. I have tried not to contradict any historical fact and to keep within the bounds of possibility, but where so much is doubtful all historical accounts are mainly conjecture — and my first concern as a novelist must be to tell a story.

Marcianus was an immensely popular ruler; half a century later, new emperors were still being greeted with cries of "Reign like Marcian!" He stopped the tribute to the Huns, a clear invitation to war with them, but the war itself never came. King Attila was distracted by new opportunities in the Western empire that kept him occupied until his death in 453; the East was thus spared further invasion. Thrace recovered somewhat, and continued as a Roman diocese for another hundred years, though it remained a very depressed and impoverished region until its eventual resettlement by the Bulgars. However, Marcianus' reputation, good as it was, was exceeded by his wife's. Pulcheria died in the same year as Attila, four years before her husband: she was canonized almost at once, and is considered a saint by both the Eastern and the Western churches. She would undoubtedly have been delighted.